Praise for
The Pirates of Sufiro

"When I first 'met' Ellison Firebrandt in *Firebrandt's Legacy*, the last thing I even imagined was a future where our hero and his devoted crew did not immerse themselves in swashbuckling space battles and clever intrigues played out against challenging opponents within the dark reaches of outer space. Firebrandt's creator, author David Lee Summers, was far more ambitious in the future he envisioned for his hero.

"In *The Pirates of Sufiro*, Firebrandt faces challenges that press even his courageous heart and clever mind to the limit, as well as testing the loyalty of those he loves and trusts most deeply. This dynamic generational saga provides enough twists and turns to satisfy the most devoted space opera fan." Jane Lindskold, author of the Firekeeper Saga.

"Not unlike his other works, David Lee Summers' novel, *The Pirates of Sufiro* offers extraordinary storytelling, diversity, and battles combined with fine writing, tight plots, and rich, memorable characters. This is definitely one author I'd read again and again." Nicole Givens Kurtz, author of *Sisters of the Wild Sage*

"Along with fine storytelling, David Lee Summers shows a fine wit for cultures." Uncle River, author of *The Mogollon News* and *King Freedom*

"*The Pirates of Sufiro* is a fast-paced adventure filled with vivid characters including rebels, pirates, interplanetary pioneers and the mysterious Clusters—the children of the old stars. [This novel] starts the tale in rip-roaring, page-flipping action against a backdrop reminiscent of Asimov's Foundation series." Gary Every, Pushcart and Rhysling-nominated poet and author of *Inca Butterflies*

Other Books by David Lee Summers

The Solar Sea
The Astronomer's Crypt

The Space Pirates' Legacy Series
Firebrandt's Legacy
The Pirates of Sufiro
Children of the Old Stars
Heirs of the New Earth

The Clockwork Legion Series
Owl Dance
Lightning Wolves
The Brazen Shark
Owl Riders

The Scarlet Order Vampires Series
Dragon's Fall: Rise of the Scarlet Order Vampires
Vampires of the Scarlet Order

The Pirates of Sufiro

David Lee Summers

Hadrosaur Productions, Mesilla Park, NM

The Pirates of Sufiro
Hadrosaur Productions
Fourth Edition: July 2020.

First date of publication: December 1996
Copyright © 2020 David Lee Summers
Cover Art Copyright © 2020 Laura Givens
Map of Sufiro Copyright © 2020 Laura Givens & David Lee Summers

ISBN-10: 1-885093-93-4
ISBN-13: 978-1-885093-93-6

This is a work of fiction. Names, characters, places, and incidents are
either the product of the author's imagination or are used fictitiously,
and any resemblance to any person or persons, living or dead, events
or locales is entirely coincidental.

To
Kumie Wise
and
William Grother

… and everyone else with the courage to
chase thirty-foot-long unicorns.

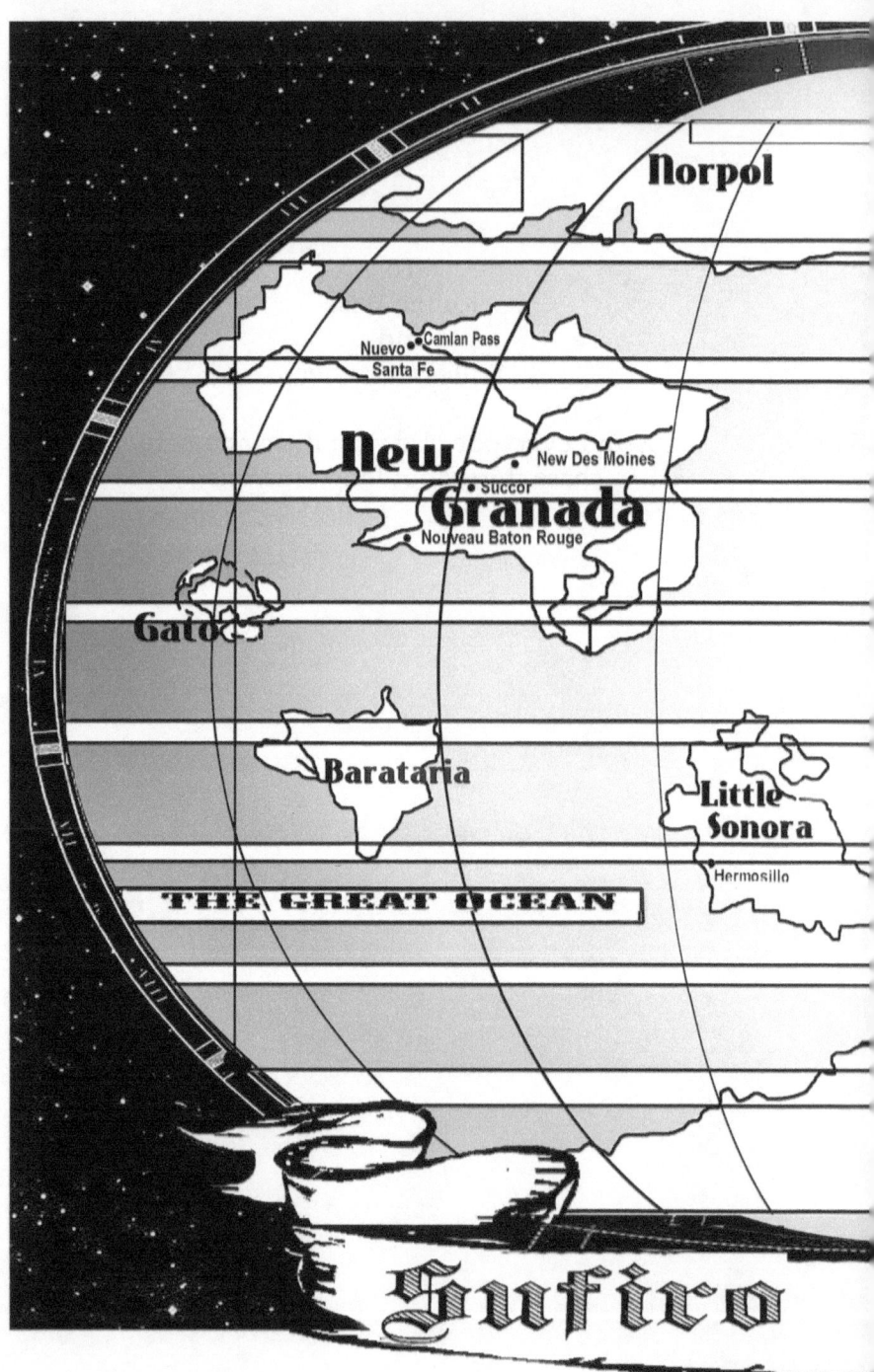

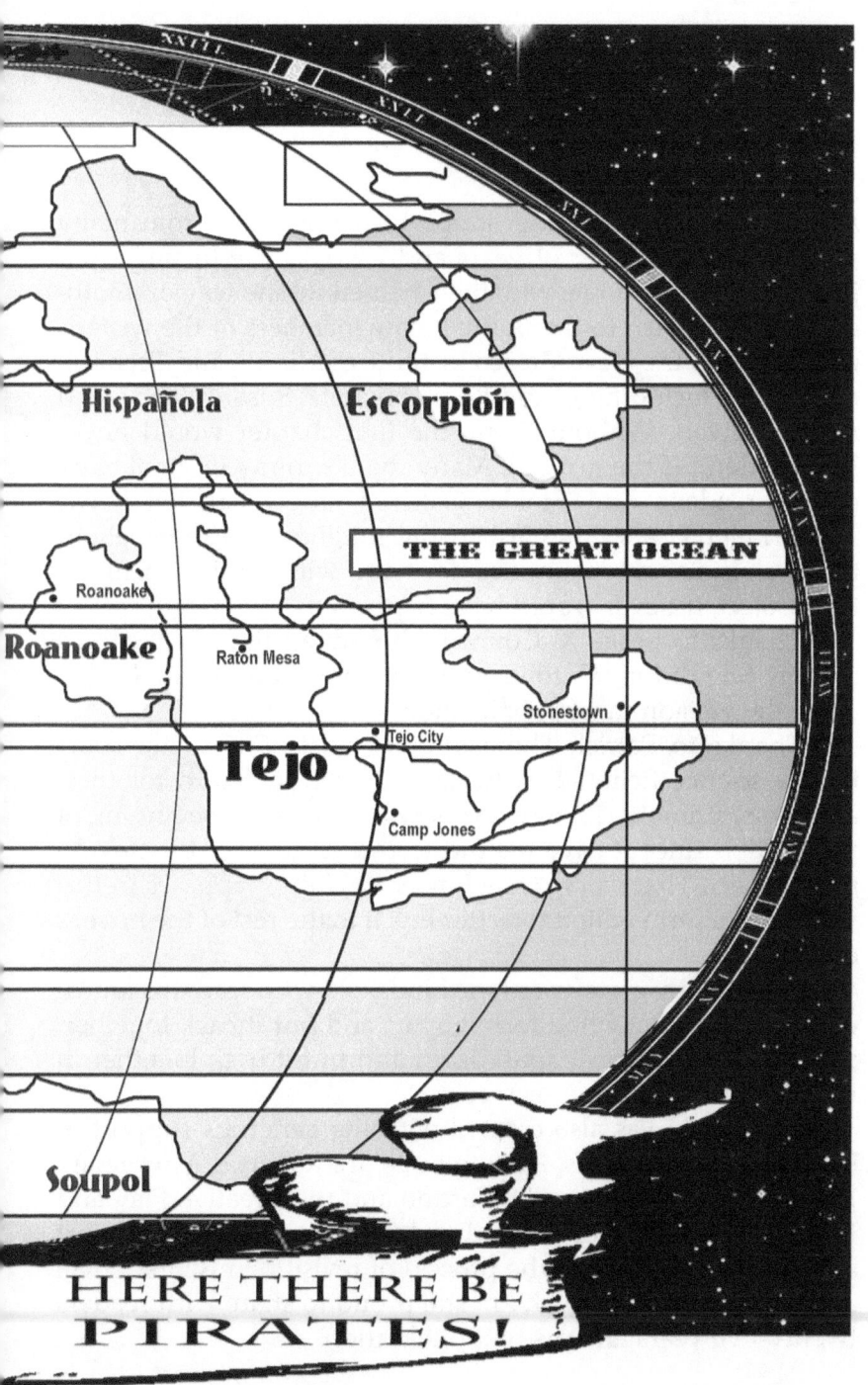

Hispañola

Escorpión

THE GREAT OCEAN

Roanoake

Roanoake

Raton Mesa

Stonestown

Tejo City

Tejo

Camp Jones

Soupol

HERE THERE BE
PIRATES!

Acknowledgments

I have received input and support on this work from many people over a number of years and I would like to single out just a few of the people who have helped in one way or another. First off, I wish to thank the fellow members of the writer's group held at the New Mexico Institute of Mining and Technology in 1988 including Jo and Ross Lomanitz, Susan Woods, and Anne Sullivan. Without them, the first chapter would never have gotten off the ground. Many thanks to my original team of beta readers, Amy Stoklas-Oakes, Paul Avellar, Jeff Lewis and Bridget Watts. They asked the toughest questions about the book in its various incarnations and without their belief in this project, it never would have happened.

Thanks to Leslie X. Council who edited the novel's third edition. She did much to improve the novel and helped it become the version most people know.

Thanks to Patrick Thomas and John L. French for soliciting a science fictional Arthurian tale set on Sufiro for their anthology Camelot 13. In many ways this was the beginning of this edition since it gave me the correct ending for the novel's second part. That story, "The Power in Unity," appears in this volume in a form edited to better link it to the rest of the novel's events.

I am deeply grateful to Jane Lindskold who read this fourth edition twice after I had torn it apart and put it back together. She suggested I tear it apart again and put it back together in ways that made even more sense.

This book was also created with the generous support of my Patreon supporters. Among them are Robert E. Vardeman, John D. Payne, Anthony D. Cardno and the Creative Play and Podcast Network. I'm pleased to have received their support and comments through the process of revisiting my first novel and turning it into a book I'm still proud to share with readers twenty-five years after its first publication.

The Pirates of Sufiro

Part I: New Granada

The Years 2925-2928 Earth Standard Calendar

"Many historians and romantics view the founding of New Granada as a renaissance. They see it as a place where people came to make a new life. The reality of New Granada represented a lot of hard work. We only did what we did in order to survive."

—Suki Firebrandt Ellis from *Sufiro, A History*

Chapter One

THE SMOLDERING EMBER

Bright, almost fluorescent, orange blood together with darkening red blood was splattered along the alien freighter's walls and deck. Humans made their way through the triangular corridor toward the battered airlock of their own ship, the *Legacy*. They hefted crates containing hominid/computer interface cards over flaccid, tentacled Alpha Centauran corpses.

One man stood to the side. Sweat-matted, long, red hair clung to his forehead. He stroked his mustache, pleased to note few casualties among his crew. Captain Ellison Firebrandt began to relax. As he did, he realized he still gripped his high-energy pulsed ray pistol. The captain holstered the hepler, but allowed his fingers to rest on the grip.

Juan de Largo slipped on an orange blood puddle and dropped onto a soft, gray corpse while interface cards clattered across the deck. Out of reflex, Firebrandt yanked the hepler from its holster and aimed at the sound. When he realized the sound was not an enemy ambush, he holstered the pistol and helped the cursing de Largo to his feet.

Firebrandt's lieutenant, Carter Roberts, ran forward and gathered the cards back into the box. "Give me a hand."

Firebrandt nodded to de Largo. "Let's get to work. We don't have much time."

"You are correct, Firebrandt," growled a voice at the other end of the deck. "In fact, you have no time at all." Firebrandt stood, then whirled to face a nine-foot, tentacled Alpha Centauran who'd appeared in the doorway. Firebrandt's hand returned to the hepler grip as he identified the creature to be the ship's captain. The Alpha Centauran leveled a weapon at Roberts and de Largo. "This weapon fires a projectile. Once

3

it's in the body, it blossoms, ripping and tearing its way through your internal organs." The Alpha Centauran grinned at Firebrandt. "It's no less than you and your crew of pirates deserve."

"Allow me a last request." Firebrandt lifted his hand from the hepler and pulled back his coat. With care, he retrieved a pipe and match from his trousers pocket. The Alpha Centauran captain narrowed his gaze at the wooden contrivances as though deciding whether or not they could be harmful.

The Alpha Centauran looked from Firebrandt to Roberts. "Do I kill you Firebrandt, or shall I let you watch as your friends writhe in unspeakable agony?" The Alpha Centauran stood silent for a moment. Firebrandt betrayed no concern for either his crewmembers or himself.

He raised the pipe to his mouth as the Alpha Centauran pointed his weapon at the captain. Roberts recognized the signal and hurried de Largo through the airlock.

"Ever since wooden ships sailed Earth's seas, sailors have taken care to minimize the risks associated with fire. After all, fire can be deadly, especially in enclosed spaces." The captain struck the match on his boot sole and raised it to the pipe. The Alpha Centauran stared in wonder as Firebrandt exhaled smoke. "Too bad Alpha Centauran blood is so combustible." The captain tossed the flaming match into a pool of orange blood, then turned and sprinted for the airlock as flame erupted all through the corridor. Automatic fire suppression kicked in, filling the corridor with chemical rain.

Blind shots pierced the veil behind Firebrandt as he leapt through the airlock. Roberts slammed his fist on the control, shutting the heavy doors.

☠

Later in the afternoon, Captain Firebrandt entered his quarters. He eased into a large, soft chair and raised a familiar, battered pipe to his lips. He watched as smoke swirled upward. Fire on a ship could be deadly. He grinned to himself. If not for the drug, Dairtox, the fire burning in the pipe could well represent an early death. The smoke comforted him and he melted into the chair's contours.

Fine wood paneling covered the cabin walls. Stained glass overlaid the windows. A brass lantern hung from a chain over the table. The captain sighed contentment. He'd never had a better home and he couldn't imagine a place he'd rather be.

A voice sounded on the intercom. "Sorry to interrupt, sir. This is Roberts, at the helm."

The captain stood, hating the creaking of his bones. He placed the pipe on the table next to the chair, walked to the far wall, and touched a glowing sensor pad. "This is the captain, go ahead."

"Computer's picked up a ship at long range," said Roberts. "She's large. A freighter I'd say, sir."

A knock sounded at the door. Firebrandt didn't answer, but the door opened anyway. Suki Mori peered in.

The captain gestured her inside. "A freighter," he said to the intercom. "Are you sure? What's Computer say?"

Roberts hesitated. "She's still a long way off, sir. If you want, we can take a closer look."

Firebrandt thought for a moment. "Don't approach any closer than you have to. If she's a warship, I want time to put some distance between us."

The captain chewed his lower lip for a moment before he hit the touch pad and turned off the intercom.

"Trouble?" Suki sat on the cabin's couch, then narrowed her gaze.

"Maybe." Firebrandt sat down beside the woman he was growing to love. He brushed a strand of black hair from her cheek, then kissed her full, red lips.

She inched closer to him. "Is it a warship?"

The captain shook his head. "Probably a freighter."

"Another raid? So soon?" She looked down at her hands.

"I do it for us. I do it for the crew. They need me."

She stood and ran her hands along the cabin's wood paneling. She grabbed a book from the bookshelf and thumbed through it. "Do you really need all this? Or do you just love the power that comes with being a captain of a pirate ship." She closed the book.

Firebrandt stood, collected the book, and put it back on

the shelf. He reached out and gently turned her face toward his. "Easy, Suki. This is no pirate ship. This is a legally licensed privateer. I fight for Earth. You know that."

"I know, but it doesn't make much difference if you get caught." She turned away from him and crossed to the desk.

Firebrandt looked down at the floor then shook his head. "It's all I know how to do."

"You could get a smaller ship … just you and me…"

The captain shrugged. "I ran the numbers. Private trade on a small ship just doesn't pay well. At that rate, I would do as well returning to the home system to be a miner, like my father."

She nodded. "We need to keep investigating choices." She turned, walked back to him, and embraced him. Her warmth radiated through his shirt. "I just want you to think about us. I want you to consider the good you've done and maybe you've earned a real rest. It may be time for us to settle down." She shook her head. "Sometimes I wonder why you're so driven."

"It's a passion, like a smoldering ember. This ship is the only place I know in the galaxy where I can be free." The captain looked into Suki's eyes. "We're both free here."

She looked away as a tear ran down her cheek. "What would you do if you were captured?"

He looked back to the chair and table. The embers in the pipe faded. "I'll burn the bastards. Fire is deadly, you know."

She smiled back at him. "Fire can also be very warm." She ran fingers through his long, red hair.

He stroked her hair and smiled, happy to be free. Firebrandt embraced Suki as her long, delicate fingers explored his back.

☠

The captain dreamed a near-memory from childhood. He ran away from home, through an asteroid mine's dark tunnels. He hid behind a robotic cart. His mother—tall, broad and imposing—reached around and grabbed him. If his dream had followed his memories, he would have remembered her pulling him close, telling him his father waited and worried with dinner. She might have even said she loved him, but he couldn't remember that part for certain.

In the dream, she shoved him back under an overhead lamp's sharp glare. She drew her hepler and aimed. Just as she squeezed the trigger he gasped and sprang awake, the image so vivid, it seemed more real than faded memories.

He shook his head and rubbed sleep from his eyes. He stood, wavered a moment, then padded over to a wall unit where a coffee carafe waited. He poured some in a cup, sipped it, and sighed.

His thoughts returned to his mother. He knew little about her other than his father's stories. She left them when he was quite young. He did remember she carried a hepler pistol, but he never understood why. The recollection made him shudder.

His mother—Barbara was her name—had left Earth to join the navy of Alpha Coma Berenices. Alpha Coma and Earth had long been rivals, but this personal connection enhanced his desire to give the Alpha Comans trouble by raiding their ships.

In space, battles played out like chess tournaments. All moves were made with calculated precision. Firebrandt could never decide whether he was a pawn or a knight. All he knew for certain was that Earth's admiralty controlled the moves.

The intercom chimed. The captain continued to sip his coffee as he padded over to the wall. He pushed the touch pad. "This is the captain."

"Computer's got a positive identification on that ship as well as distance and bearing." Roberts sounded annoyed, as though he'd been trying to raise the captain for some time. The captain glanced over to Suki among his bed's rumpled sheets. Had it been the dream or the intercom chime that had awakened him?

"Well, since we aren't running, I presume it's not a warship."

"She's a large freighter. Computer says she's from Alpha Coma Berenices."

"Really?" The captain shuddered. It wasn't completely unexpected news given the region of the galaxy they were in, but it unnerved him given his dream. Still, a large freighter from Alpha Coma could mean a big payoff in cash as well as giving him personal satisfaction. "Alert the crew. I'll come up."

Firebrandt bent over Suki's sleeping form and kissed her gently. She snuggled further into the sheets. He reached over the bed and retrieved a clean, white tunic. From his chair, he grabbed a pair of crisp black trousers. The captain fastened a wide belt around his tunic, pulled on a pair of boots and strode from the cabin.

He arrived on the *Legacy's* command deck a moment later. Sloping metallic walls bordered the deck. Wooden handrails ran the length of the walls. Two gunner's consoles stood near the door at the stern. Nicole Lowry and Edwin Neal worked through the weapons' checklist.

Instead of a forward wall, the deck continued into a breathtaking hologram of space. The captain's footsteps resounded on the metal grating. Lights blinked as the ship's network relayed data about fuel consumption, speed, course, and other information throughout the vessel. The helmsman, Kheir el-Din, stood at the deck's center in front of the ship's "wheel"—in fact, a console with controls to steer the ship. A pale man, with hair grown long to cover a scar in the middle of his forehead where a computer chip had been implanted, sat against the starboard wall, ice-blue eyes roving the deck. The man called Computer was the anti-embodiment of the crystalline matrix pulsing with light beneath the captain's feet. The ship's network was a massive thing, interacting intimately with all the ship's systems. Computer was a frail thing, passing along the captain's orders and repeating answers from the ship's network.

The captain looked around el-Din at the glowing status indicators on the wheel console. Pleased with the ship's condition, he turned his attention to the hologram and tried, in vain, to find the freighter among the stars.

"Computer," said the captain, "show me the freighter." A three-dimensional grid appeared within the hologram. A red dot sprang to life in the center. A few words typed out in space above the ship detailing the freighter's size, crew complement and armaments. Roberts leaned against the starboard wall just ahead of Computer and nodded.

Firebrandt folded his arms. "I think the Alliance would be most pleased to see Alpha Coma lose some riches. What do you think, Roberts?"

Bald with gaunt features, Roberts grinned, making him resemble a death's-head. "I think they would be most pleased indeed, sir." Roberts approached the captain.

"Now, for the problem," mused Firebrandt. "Getting to her. How far away is she?"

"Twenty light-hours," responded Computer in a monotone.

"On her course, how far is the nearest jump point for Alpha Coma?" asked the captain.

"Three light-hours," responded Computer.

"That's it, then," grumbled Roberts. "She has all the time in the world to fire up her EQ engines and jump out of range before we even get close."

Firebrandt sighed. *Legacy* had a way to deal with this situation, but he'd used it more than he had wanted over the last several months. It had already brought him undue attention and it was expensive to use.

In the late twenty-first century, a scientist named Thomas Quinn had discovered time-traveling particles that could inject three-dimensional vessels into fourth dimensional reality, which had made apparent faster-than-light travel possible. Ships had to jump between gravitational nodal points. For most ships, only stars possessed sufficiently strong gravitational fields to be the focus of those nodal points. However, Firebrandt had acquired a generator that created nodal points anywhere in space. Suki had adapted it to the ship's systems.

The captain concluded they needed to use the nodal point generator. "Have Ms. Mori get to her post. We need to jump to a position one kilometer off the Coma ship's stern." Firebrandt sighed as he grabbed a handrail along the wall.

Two minutes later, Suki arrived on the command deck, shirt untucked and several strands of hair trying to escape a hastily formed ponytail.

"Intrasystem jump is calculated and coordinates are sent to Miss Mori's station," reported Computer.

Suki sat down at the engineering console and activated the nodal point generator. She adjusted the settings and confirmed Computer's calculations. After a moment, she nodded to the captain. "We're ready."

"Jump!" ordered the captain as he closed his eyes. Within a few seconds, he felt as though someone struck him repeatedly in the face. In a dream-like state he imagined the tentacles of an Alpha Centauran encircling his neck to strangle him. As he fought to hold onto the railing, he realized the ship had already jumped. He struggled to look at the hologram image. A hepler pulse fired from the Coma ship's stern.

A moment later, *Legacy* shuddered. Firebrandt lost his grip and dropped to the deck.

Roberts ran to the stern. "Return fire!"

Neal and Lowry entered firing sequences and unleashed hepler beams from the turret guns.

The two cylindrical ships careened through space, EQ generators glowing blue at the stern. The nearby star bathed the black, erdonium hulls in orange light. *Legacy* unleashed a second hepler salvo which tore into the Coma vessel's thruster pack. One shot ripped through the hull plating near the Coma ship's bow where its bridge would be. Roberts whirled on Lowry. "Careful! Engines only!"

"Damn you, I know that," she responded.

Roberts looked as though he would fire back a retort, but a glance from Firebrandt stopped him. This was not the time to argue.

The Coma ship returned fire. This time the captain maintained his grip on the handrail.

"Our starboard thrusters are destroyed and we've taken damage to the starboard gangway port," reported Computer.

The *Legacy* fired again. This time they scored a hit on the EQ generator and its glow diminished. The bulky freighter fired several more shots, clipping the privateer's hull.

Sparks sputtered from Neal's station. The gunner screamed when the panel burst into flames. Roberts grabbed him and pulled him to safety.

"Get the extinguisher," snarled Lowry, giving the panicked man something to focus on.

The captain ordered fire crews onto the command deck while Lowry maintained the barrage on the enemy vessel.

"Computer," called Firebrandt. "Assume control of starboard weapons and maintain assault!" Computer's brow creased as he took control of the guns. Computer might not be as good a shot as Neal, but the captain preferred it to losing half of *Legacy's* fire power.

A firefighting team stormed onto the command deck and helped Neal extinguish the flames at his station. Acrid smoke issued from the console.

"Second direct hit on enemy's EQ generator, sir!" shouted Computer over the firefighters' din.

"Another shot should do it," observed the captain.

The freighter started to turn. Firebrandt gulped. He suspected their adversary brought a large bow gun to bear. "Evasive!" shouted the captain. Behind him, the fire crew gaped at the holo-viewer.

"Clear the bridge!" called Roberts. The fire crew scurried off the deck and Neal dropped back into the foam-covered seat and secured his harness.

"We're hardly moving, Captain," reported el-Din.

"Ship's performance down twenty percent," reported Computer.

Roberts pounded the wall. He looked at the captain as a thought came to him. "The starboard gangway port!"

The captain turned to Computer. "Seal off deck two, section two. Open the starboard port!"

"Inadvisable, Captain. Opening the port will damage it further."

"I know. Open the port," ordered the captain as he waved smoke out of his face.

Computer nodded. When the port opened, air rushed out and swung the ship out of the hepler gun's range. Roberts pointed to the holo and Lowry fired, destroying the gun.

The freighter shuddered as it resumed course. "Let's shut the rest of those thrusters down." Firebrandt nodded to Lowry.

Roberts coughed. "Get those fans on in here!" he called to the helmsman. Fans buzzed to life and the acrid electrical smoke began to lift. Two red energy pulses struck the freighter's thruster pack. It exploded in a silent shower of sparks and shrapnel. Inertia carried the freighter forward on an altered trajectory at lower speed.

"Catch up with the Coma ship," ordered the captain. He lit his pipe and studied the enemy vessel. "We knocked out her main gun," he mused. "She'll have others to fend off an approaching ship." He sucked the pipe stem. "Computer, using other Coma ships on record as a norm, what would be the range of the guns we have not destroyed?"

"Standard range for close proximity weapons is one kilometer." Computer considered for a moment. "I should also point out, sir, that the large gun we destroyed is not standard for Coma merchant ships."

"That was military hardware," said Roberts as he walked up to the captain.

Firebrandt turned to the helmsman. "Bring us out to five kilometers distance. Fly us in a spiral pattern until we're two kilometers away from the Coma ship." He turned to face Lowry. "I want all of her short-range armaments knocked out. Keep an eye out for surprises."

"Aye aye, sir," said the gunner.

Stars moved in the hologram. The captain turned his attention to the other gunner, sitting dazed in dried foam. "Mr. Neal, you panicked while at your station."

"Yes, sir." He lowered his head.

"Have you settled down enough to perform your duty?"

"Yes, sir," responded Neal, hope glimmering in his eyes.

"Then get your station back on line as soon as possible." The captain contemplated the pipe for a moment. "Do you understand, Mr. Neal?"

"Yes sir, I understand, sir."

Firebrandt walked over to Suki. "Get a toolkit and give him a hand. Let me know if he needs a break from duty."

She nodded. "Shouldn't you give him one anyway?"

The captain considered that. "I want his confidence restored. If he takes a break now, he'll be questioning himself."

Suki gave him a curt nod and strode over to a storage locker.

The captain watched the holographic viewer. Lowry picked off the remaining guns on the freighter's hull. *Legacy* maneuvered far too sluggishly with the starboard thrusters out of action. Even so, by the time el-Din reported that they'd reached the target position, two kilometers from the ship, all armaments had been disabled.

"Helmsman, you may proceed with docking," ordered the captain.

"Aye aye, sir." Kheir el-Din entered the maneuver, then stroked the beads weaved into his beard.

"Preparing bow grappling ring," reported Computer.

"Mr. Roberts, assemble the boarding crew and meet me at the airlock." The captain tamped out his pipe and strode off the command deck.

Twenty crewmembers raring for a fight waited with Roberts near the bow airlock when the captain arrived. He looked them over. They had all been on raids with him before and had proven themselves to be brave, sturdy souls. Wordless, the captain strode to the airlock. He turned and faced the crew with a confident grin. His confidence was a ruse, but their eyes and chins lifted, alert and ready just as he wanted. Alpha Coma was a human colony. There would be no terrible aliens on the other side of the airlock. Firebrandt needed a crew who would fight without doubting themselves.

The captain drew his sword and held it high. The crew let out a fierce battle yell. Firebrandt nodded, satisfied. The boarding party fell silent as they waited. Firebrandt drew a hepler pistol. At this signal, the crew drew their own weapons. *Legacy* bumped into the freighter. Hands tensed.

Roberts moved to the captain's side. Air whooshed as the airlock doors opened. The captain and Roberts blasted through the freighter's airlock. Armored defenders waited on the other side. The boarding party charged headlong into the pulsed high-energy weapon's fire.

Swords cut into armor designed to defend against pulsed rays. Bladed weapons may be anachronistic, but they still served a purpose and inspired a terror that no other weapon could. Heplers fired, flesh burned, and screams came from all sides. Blood splattered the freighter's deck.

The captain stood, breathless, and took in the battle's

aftermath. His white tunic had been torn and stained red. Sweat dripped from his forehead as he looked around. All the defenders had fallen. Firebrandt counted himself, Roberts, and two of *Legacy's* crew still standing—Lowry and de Largo.

"These were professional soldiers," noted Lowry.

The captain turned to give instructions to Roberts. Just then, a hepler pulse crackled through the air. The first mate crumpled to the deck and stared in horror at the cauterized stump where his right hand once had been. Firebrandt and his people dropped to their knees, scanning the passageways to see where the shot had come from. Lowry and de Largo covered the corridor while the captain moved to Roberts' side. Firebrandt helped Roberts to sit up against a wall, then stood, hepler drawn, to face his new adversary.

A gray-haired woman wearing a Lord High Admiral's uniform emerged from the shadows at the far end of the deck. A scar ran from the edge of her mouth to her chin. In one hand, she held a sword. In the other, she held a hepler pistol. Behind her stood a young man and a young woman, both in Alpha Coma military regalia—the admiral's flag lieutenants. "Order your people to drop their weapons!" shouted the admiral, her voice hoarse as though she had been shouting orders for the past hour.

"Looks like a stand-off to me," noted Firebrandt.

The male flag lieutenant fired his hepler. Juan de Largo fell to the deck with a gaping hole in his chest. "Not anymore," said the admiral.

Firebrandt put his hand on Lowry's shoulder. Her hepler clattered to the deck.

"Now, why do I find pirates attacking a military vessel?" demanded the admiral, stepping to Firebrandt.

He sneered. "Transponder records indicated this was a freighter. Disguising a military vessel as a civilian vessel is entrapment and a treaty violation."

"Piracy brings the death penalty on Alpha Coma Berenices," the admiral answered.

"We are privateers operating under a letter of marque. We are not subject to Coma's jurisdiction," growled Firebrandt.

The admiral looked into his eyes. "No?" She looked to the

deck and the walls. "Look's like you're in Coma's jurisdiction to me."

Firebrandt raised the hepler. Something pierced his arm. Pain seared through every nerve in his body and he crumpled to the deck. The female flag lieutenant holstered a mini dart gun. The admiral and her lieutenants stepped into *Legacy* as he blacked out.

☠

A sick pain throbbed throughout Firebrandt's body and he groaned. He managed to look around. Roberts and Lowry had vanished, but bodies still littered the deck. The captain decided he could not have been unconscious for long. He tried to stand, his head still swimming from the Alpha Coman dart. He staggered on the slippery metal deck. After a second try, he managed to cross back to the *Legacy*.

The privateer vessel appeared undamaged. Firebrandt stumbled through the corridors to the command deck. Roberts sat at his station, weak and pale, his arm bandaged. No one else occupied the command deck. Even Computer was gone.

"What's happened?" asked Firebrandt. "Where is everyone? Where's Computer?"

"Those who didn't fall in action are my prisoners," came a gruff voice from the stern door.

Firebrandt looked around to see the admiral. As he moved toward her, the female flag lieutenant led Suki onto the command deck. He stopped. "If you've harmed her..." The captain aimed his finger at the admiral.

"Harming her is the last thing on my mind." The admiral flashed a queer smile. "For some reason, she seems to love you."

"That's none of your business," Suki said.

"Humph," muttered the admiral. "What do you say, Firebrandt?"

"How do you know my name?" demanded the captain, even as he realized she seemed strangely familiar.

The admiral narrowed her gaze. "Don't play those games with me." She looked at Suki, then to Roberts. The captain began to fume. "And don't blame them. They're loyal to you. Damn it, everyone on this ship was loyal to you." The admiral snorted. "They're all misguided fools!" She walked up to Firebrandt and looked him up and down. "I don't understand why, but both Suki and Roberts are especially loyal to you."

"So, what are you going to do with us?" asked Firebrandt.

"Ellison Firebrandt is known throughout this sector of the galaxy. I'm within my rights to have you executed." The admiral pursed her lips as she studied the captain. He was defeated and she knew it. "However, I have no desire to destroy you. I will let you go."

"What about my crew?" Firebrandt asked, numb.

"They are good fighters. I may have use for some of them."

"And for those you can't … use?"

"Fair trial. If your letter of marque is genuine, they'll be returned to Earth."

Firebrandt looked at his feet. "What about us?"

"Well, I've stripped your ship of parts necessary to get mine operating again, which is allowed by treaty. *Legacy* will still fly. I've disarmed your weapons. I want you out of this sector. With Roberts and Suki, you'll be able to manage the ship."

"That's far from certain," complained Roberts, looking down at his bandaged arm, now missing a hand.

"I think you'll manage," said the admiral. "I want you to find a world—a world to make your own. I do this under one condition—that I never hear about new raids by the dread pirate Firebrandt." She took a couple steps away and turned. "If I see you in my jurisdiction again, I will not hesitate to execute you as war criminals."

Firebrandt nodded. "I understand."

The admiral turned to leave. Firebrandt rushed forward and grabbed her arm. "Wait a moment," he said. "Who exactly are you?"

"I'm sad to say, it's been far too long and the years have no doubt changed me." She laughed at his perplexed expression. "I'm pleased to meet you." She held out her hand. "I'm Lord Admiral Barbara Firebrandt."

Chapter Two

MAROONED

A s soon as the admiral left the *Legacy's* command deck, Suki ran forward to Roberts. "How are you doing? Should we get you down to the medical bay?"

Roberts shook his head and closed his eyes. A moment later, he opened them again. "They shot me with enough pain killers, I'm in decent shape … for now."

Suki turned her attention to the captain. He paced the command deck like a caged tiger, glancing at blank computer screens. Even the command deck's main hologram tank was an empty, gray void. Aside from the lights and the graviton generator, it seemed most systems were powered down.

A series of short, sharp shocks rumbled through the deck and walls. Firebrandt stopped in his path. "They're blasting themselves free of our grappling clamps." He shook his head. "We need to get some power on in here." He sat down at the engineering station and Suki walked up behind him to see what he did. He activated a series of bypasses. The whole ship lurched.

Roberts groaned and punched a command into his console. His personal holographic display sprang to life. A launch boat flew away from *Legacy* to join the admiral's ship, which drifted away from the stranded privateer. "She's only leaving us one boat to disembark. At least they didn't breach the hull when they fired those charges," said Roberts.

Firebrandt tapped several indicators on the engineering console. "I don't have engine control. We'll have to go down and see if we can restore main power. We won't last long stranded in space, running on batteries."

"What do you need me to do?" asked Roberts.

The captain frowned. "You should lie down and rest."

Roberts shook his head. "I can work now. If they raided our medical supplies, I may be out of luck later." Sickly pale, the first mate's face looked more skull-like than ever.

"I'll check the engine room," volunteered Suki. "If they just powered down the engines, I should be able to engage the restart cycle on my own. Otherwise, I'll need your help."

Firebrandt nodded. "You might check the hold before going to the engine room. It'll tell us what we have to work with."

Suki struggled to give the captain a brave smile. He stood up from the engineering console and gathered her in his arms. He took a shuddering breath and sniffed. After a long moment, he took a deep breath and stepped back. Firebrandt's eyes glowed with moisture and his Adam's apple bobbed, but he didn't say anything. She had never seen him fight so hard to hold himself together.

She left the command deck before she burst into tears herself.

Suki's footsteps made an eerie clanging as she strode down the deck. The ship seemed all too quiet with so few people aboard. She reached the ladder and climbed down two decks and entered the ship's hold.

She discovered most of the cargo carriers and bins were in good order. She checked the spare parts cabinets. The ship's mechanic would have remembered the inventory better, but Suki found a few duplicate parts missing. Most critical spares remained. The person who had raided their spares had cherry-picked just the ones they had needed.

As she closed the last cabinet, she glanced over to the rear bulkhead. Plans for *Legacy's* vessel class showed circulation pumps and junction boxes behind the bulkhead. However, Firebrandt had installed newer pumps and had rearranged the space to serve as a secret compartment for his most valuable items. A hole had been blasted into the wall.

Suki's heart sank. She ran forward and peered into the space. Admiral Barbara Firebrandt had removed the captain's most valued possessions, including paintings by Van Gogh, da Vinci, and Rembrandt. The paintings had been declared lost when the Louvre had been destroyed in the Lunar uprising, but Firebrandt had found them on a ship he'd raided. He had wanted to return them to Earth. Now that would never happen.

If the captain was struggling to hold it together now, what would he do when he learned this? She swallowed down her own sob and stepped away from the jagged hole. She had more work to do.

Suki climbed up one deck and continued back to the engine room. Air blew through louvers reminding Suki of holovids depicting tumbleweeds blowing through old, abandoned western towns from the American continent. She smiled when she saw the nodal point generator still connected into the engine. The admiral's staff must not have recognized it, or perhaps they hadn't known about it. She continued on to the main engine control console and pulled out a book covered in greasy fingerprints—the engine manual. She opened to the restart instructions and pressed the buttons indicated. Once all the indicators showed green, she grabbed a lever and pulled it toward her, then pulled another lever.

Soon, a rhythmic throbbing like a giant heartbeat started. Suki sighed, pleased to hear the engines running. She still missed Sanaa Golan yelling at the other mechanics and Roberts' strong voice over the intercom calling for power to be diverted from one system to another.

She checked the Quinnium reserves and frowned. It seemed the admiral had raided their supply. There was no way they could use the nodal point generator to make an intrasystem jump. She reached over and activated the intercom. "Engine restart completed, Captain. Our Quinnium reserves are nearly depleted."

"I see that here," grumbled the captain. "Looks like we only have enough for one or two jumps. Not enough to try to pursue the admiral."

"Do you want me to wait here, or should I come back to the command deck?"

"Come back to the command deck," said Firebrandt.

Before she left the engine room, Suki checked the ship's thrusters. Three units no longer functioned. From the readings on the main engineering console, she could tell they'd been stripped for spare parts. One thruster pack was still functional. The admiral had left them with limited maneuverability.

By the time Suki returned to the command deck, Firebrandt and Roberts had restored the main holographic display. They'd activated thrusters and had managed to get the ship to hold position.

"I hate losing Computer," said Roberts. "The ship'll be a bear to operate without his help."

"We'll do our best." The captain patted Roberts on his good shoulder. "Right now, I think we need to eat and maintain our strength. We can look at our options in more detail in the morning."

Roberts put the ship's sensors on automatic and programmed them to alert them if any danger approached. With that, they went down to the mess. Firebrandt found some spaghetti and sauce in the refrigerator and heated it up. All three were so exhausted and hungry, they ate as though it was the best meal they'd ever had.

"How has work on the command deck been going?" asked Suki.

"I think we're far enough along to attempt to plot a course," said Roberts. "Maybe we can get somewhere, find a crew, set out again."

Firebrandt stared off into space for a time. Suki tried to discern his thoughts. After a moment, he blinked and looked at Roberts. "Sounds like a good plan for tomorrow. For now, I think we all need some rest."

Roberts nodded. "I'll check de Largo's stock in the medbay and see if there's something there to keep the pain under control and let me sleep."

After taking her dishes to the autocleaner, Suki followed the captain to his cabin. The room had been ransacked, but little seemed to be missing. One key item that had vanished was Firebrandt's letter of marque and reprisal. It had hung in a frame on the wall. He sat on the bunk and put his head in his hands. Suki sat down next to him and put her arm around his shoulders. "Are you okay?" she asked.

Firebrandt nodded, his head still in his hands. They sat in silence for some time before he looked into Suki's eyes. "A boy is supposed to love his mother, isn't he?"

"You barely knew your mother," said Suki.

Firebrandt sighed. "I buried my love for her because she abandoned my father and me. Now that she's turned up after all these years…" His eyes glazed over. "I'm all twisted up inside. Soldiers have to follow orders. I became a privateer because I could support Earth, yet chart my own course. I crave that freedom, and yet she's found a way to limit my choices." He shook his head.

"We don't know how much she's limited your freedom. We won't know until we find out where we can go." Suki reached out and took Firebrandt's chin, making him look into her eyes. "Once we know the choices, you'll make the best one. You always do."

"I feel like the universe has closed in on me, limiting what I can do."

"Those limitations were imposed by your responsibility to the crew, to the Earth Alliance." She shrugged. "Maybe your mother's given you the best gift of all, an opportunity to start all over again." She stroked his long, red hair until he relaxed.

"It could be quite an adventure," he said.

"I can't wait to see where it takes us." She looked into his gray eyes. They kissed. Her lips parted and their tongues intertwined. She helped him pull off his tunic and pants. His hands caressed her body. She let him control, allowing his mind and heart to work together. He took his time as he removed her clothes. She gave herself to him, let him enter her. She sighed, then moaned as his thrusts became more urgent. Soon he grew tense as he reached his climax. She pulled him close and held him as she reached her own peak. At last, she let her hands trail down his back.

"I love you," she whispered.

He trembled and nodded. "I look forward to seeing where our adventures lead us."

They held each other until they fell into a deep sleep.

☠

The next day, Suki and Firebrandt found Roberts in the mess.

He looked better despite a few red spots on his face where he had burned himself using the sonic razor with only his left hand. His mouth was set into a determined scowl. He had made coffee and now attempted to break eggs into a skillet using his one hand. Suki offered to help.

"No." Roberts nudged her away with his elbow. He apologized when her face crumpled into a frown. The egg he held crushed into little fragments and egg yolk oozed over his fingers. Roberts growled, his skull-like head lending him an especially fierce expression.

Suki took a deep breath and stepped closer. "Won't you please let me help?"

Roberts sighed. "It's just that whatever comes next, I need to be able to do things for myself. I can't rely on your help."

She nodded, but took an egg. "Then let me help you to help yourself." She broke it on the bowl's edge one-handed. Roberts watched, then nodded. He grabbed his own egg and broke it into the skillet. It wasn't perfect, but he picked out the shell fragments and could use the egg this time. He scrambled the eggs and fried some ham.

Suki sat down next to Firebrandt and they watched as Roberts set out plates, then divided the meal.

"Looks like a good high protein breakfast," remarked the captain.

Roberts nodded. "We have a lot to do today. I wanted us to be in top form." He brought the plates over one at a time. "You two slept late enough."

"As you say," said Suki with a wink, "we have a lot to do today. We needed our rest."

The three finished breakfast in silence. After eating, they stacked the plates next to the dinner dishes in the autocleaner. Roberts tried to activate the unit. "Really?" he asked when nothing happened.

"What's the matter?" asked Firebrandt.

"They took the autocleaner motor." Roberts sneered. "The ships in the Alpha Coma fleet must be in pretty bad shape."

"Leave the dishes," said Firebrandt. "I'll get them later."

The three walked forward to the command deck. Firebrandt half-expected Computer to report the ship's status, or Kheir el-

Din to nod and wink. He even missed Nicole Lowry greeting him with a clipboard and a report of items they needed at their next port.

The three gathered around Roberts' console. The first mate turned it on and both the hologram over the console's dais and at the front of the command deck flickered to life. "Captain on deck," he said. As Roberts spoke the words, a ship's status report appeared in the main holoviewer.

Firebrandt nodded his appreciation.

"The important question is, can we make it anywhere?" Suki brushed black hair from her face.

Roberts typed a command. A list of stars appeared in the hologram. "We have fuel to take us to the jump points for twenty-seven G-type stars," he reported. He scanned the list and nodded. "We could even go home, to Earth, if we really wanted to."

The captain shook his head. "No, not to Earth." He stopped himself, thinking he should ask what they wanted. However, he had been captain for a long time. He would have to learn to ask for opinions.

"I agree," said Roberts. "Things could go very wrong if we turned up in this wreck of a ship."

"Why *not* go to Earth?" Suki's brow creased. "Couldn't we sell the ship, maybe get something smaller that the three of us could manage?"

"And we'd face a bloody board of inquiry," said Firebrandt. "They'd want to know how I let this happen. What's more, they'd take the intraship jump engine, which is about the only thing of value I have left." Suki had broken the news about the paintings before they had left bed that morning. "We'd never have a chance to help the rest of the crew. No, Earth is not the place we want to go." He stepped over beside Roberts. "You say we can make it to the jump points for twenty-seven stars, but how many of them have planets worth going to?"

"Good point." Roberts entered the new constraint. They had to be able to travel from the receiving jump point to a planet habitable by humans. That left six star names.

"Now," said Firebrandt, "which ones are inhabited?"

Roberts entered the constraint, cutting the list in half.

Firebrandt shook his head. "I don't like the looks of those." The list included Epsilon Indi 2 and New Georgia. The latter world was a penal colony. Firebrandt had rescued Suki from a crime lord on the former. He saw little or no chance to repair the ship or acquire another on those worlds. "I don't recognize that last one."

"It's a Zahari water world," said Roberts. "According to the records they'd welcome human colonists on some of the islands, but the gravity's about three times higher than that of Earth."

"What about the uninhabited worlds?" asked Suki.

Roberts displayed the other three names.

Firebrandt spat a curse. "They're all charted by Rd'dyggian ships."

"So?" asked Suki. "Who cares who charted them? After all, the Earth Alliance and Rd'dyggia are both members of the Confederation of Homeworlds."

"The Rd'dyggians are quite possessive," explained Firebrandt. "At least Rd'dyggians can live in the same planetary environment we can."

Roberts looked at the list again. He pursed his lips and sat back. "Rd'dyggia has only taken possession of two of the worlds."

"What's wrong with the other one?" Firebrandt's bushy, red eyebrows knitted.

"Don't know." Roberts rubbed his head, then requested more details. "All it says is that the Rd'dyggians left the planet open to general colonization."

"Meaning?" Suki's eyebrows rose.

"Meaning the Rd'dyggians didn't find anything they wanted there." The captain looked at the description and the system's galactic coordinates. "It's way out on the galactic far side."

"No doubt about it," said Roberts. "It's a frontier world."

"Sounds like a good place to regroup and get our bearings." Suki nodded. "At least we wouldn't have to worry about the air, or power dying while we figured out what to do next."

Roberts shook his head. "Don't be hasty. If we went there, there's no guarantee we'll find anything edible. The Rd'dyggians called this world habitable. That just means we can breathe there. It doesn't mean we can survive there long term."

Firebrandt's shoulders slumped. "So, our choices are go to Earth, where we might lose everything we have or go to this distant planet where there's nothing to have."

Roberts grimaced. "That about sums it up."

"It sounds as though Earth is the best option after all." The captain walked toward the holographic display. "I'm the one who'll have to face the consequences. Roberts, the admiralty would pay your medical expenses, place you on a new ship. Suki, you could go to Ceres, reconnect with your parents…"

Suki led Firebrandt aside, grabbed him by the shoulders, and gazed into his eyes. "Did you forget? My mom disinherited me for running with pirates. Roberts won't leave your side. Is that really the best option for us to move forward?"

"I would be cut off from my accounts. They'd probably seize my assets, but I could sell the ship, such as it is, and get money for us to survive," he said. "We'd have options."

"Why are you a pirate?" Her fingers dug into his shoulders.

He shook his head. "Privateer, my love."

"Whatever. Answer the fucking question."

"I'm a pirate because I want the freedom to choose my own course."

"Will you have that freedom on Earth?"

"But you and Roberts…" he protested.

"Would die as surely as you would," she said. "We chose this life as much as you did. If I am to die, let me die with dignity." Suki's brown eyes started to glaze over. "We may find death on a frontier world as well, but at least we'll have made an effort at survival. Returning to Earth is just suicide."

The captain shook himself free from Suki's grip and stalked to the command deck's stern. He sat down at Lowry's gunner's rig and stared at his reflection in the blank monitor. He considered his childhood dreams of finding fame, fortune, and glory aboard a privateer. He'd come so close. Was he the man he imagined he'd become? What would that man do?

Roberts and Suki approached. Firebrandt looked up at his first mate. "I know what Suki wants."

"We've fought the good fight, old friend." Roberts' eyes

had a faraway look. "We've had some amazing times and pulled off some jobs people will talk about for years to come. That wouldn't have happened if we'd played it safe."

The captain nodded. "Think you can make a course for the frontier world's jump point?"

Roberts gave a sharp nod. "Absolutely."

"Then let's go." Firebrandt smiled as he considered a new type of freedom. At that moment, he wondered whether his mother had manipulated him into this exact choice. He shook his head to clear the paranoid thoughts. They had materials to barter. They could make other choices, but he liked this one. Going to a frontier world would give him the time he needed to figure out his next move. Connecting with Rd'dyggians could allow him to connect up to the galactic banking net and other online resources to help himself and the crew.

The deck plates rumbled as Roberts activated the thrusters. Because only one thruster pack remained, the ship didn't feel quite right.

Suki stepped forward to the wheel console. Roberts showed her what needed to be monitored and how to keep the ship on the programmed course. She piloted the ship to its new destiny.

Even with a single thruster pack, the ship accelerated to 0.8 times the speed of light. Two hours after the journey started, a green light flashed. Suki called Roberts over. He showed her how to reverse thrusters and bring the ship to a stop. "We're at the jump point." He grabbed the rail on the side of the wheel console with white knuckles.

"Are you sure you're good to do this?" asked the captain.

Roberts looked to Suki then to Firebrandt. "I'm good to go."

"I don't know where we're going," said Firebrandt. "All I know is we're on our way. Let's do this thing."

"Strap in." Roberts executed the first jump commands, which in turn sounded the jump warning.

The captain grinned, realizing no one else could hear the alert. Suki strapped herself in at the engineering console while Firebrandt took the functional gunner's rig.

Roberts strapped himself in at his station and continued

the jump sequence. Computer would have executed all the steps in a single thought. If all went well, the thrusters would fire after the jump and they would find themselves en route to the planet. Roberts checked and double-checked the sequence. If he had made a mistake typing a critical command, the ship would never reappear within three-dimensional reality. It would continue riding a wave moving perpendicular to all three spatial directions until it damped out somewhere between galaxies where their atoms would break up and be scattered into oblivion. Roberts executed the sequence.

The *Legacy* sidestepped into the fourth dimension, moving faster than light from one node of a great wave group to another. Reality ceased for the people aboard ship. Senses continued but time was no longer a referent. The colors of the rainbow slammed into their bodies. Sound was too bright. The ship grew and shrank, burst apart and reassembled. Reality resumed.

Roberts' head hit his console with a thunk. It seemed the stresses of the jump and pain from his wrist were too much to bear. The main holographic viewer had gone dead again. Suki sat motionless, her eyes glazed and her mouth open. She stared into the dead holographic tank. Firebrandt bent over, placing his head between his legs as he fought both fainting and nausea. A gentle nudge told him the ship's thrusters had kicked in.

Firebrandt forced himself to stand and leaned on a chair. While there were few limitations to interstellar travel with the EQ jump, they had just made a long bound to the far side of the galaxy and the effects took a while to wear off. He stumbled around to Suki and touched her shoulder. She screamed, tried to stand and realized she was still belted in. She clawed at the restraints. When free, she ran back to the head in the corridor just outside the command deck. Firebrandt grew nauseous as he listened to the retching sounds of breakfast coming back up. He took several deep breaths and walked toward Roberts.

Firebrandt placed his hand on his friend's back. "How are you doing?"

Roberts stirred, then jumped, blinking a few times. "Better than Suki ... I think." He looked at the holographic viewer, his eyes narrowing. "It's dead. I thought I had programmed it to come on as we came out of jump."

The captain looked at Roberts' holographic display. He pointed to a line of code. "You did." He walked over to a panel on the wall next to the holoviewer and opened it, releasing a smoke cloud. "We fried the network interface." He walked back to the pilot's console and tapped the manual override button. The holoviewer came to life.

They approached a yellow star. Firebrandt located the planet on tracking sensors and adjusted the ship's course.

"Point of no return." Roberts' holographic display showed Quinnium reserves too low for another jump. "Good-bye civilization."

Suki returned to the command deck. She had cleaned up, but still looked almost as haggard as Roberts. She stepped up to Firebrandt, and leaned on him for support as they watched the viewer.

Roberts went back to the mess and retrieved a water jug. He returned and passed it around.

An hour later, the planet appeared in the viewer. Roberts read statistics from the computer screen. "Diameter, 655 million centimeters. Surface gravity is 1.05 times Earth normal. Intensity of light from the star on the surface is so close to Earth's it hardly matters. Rotational period is 25.89 hours. Revolutionary period is 414 local rotations."

A bluish green ocean and broken white clouds dominated the planet's surface. Underneath the clouds were scattered dark landmasses. A single oblong moon that could be a captured asteroid orbited the planet. White continents sat at each pole.

Firebrandt maneuvered the ship into orbit. As they swung around the planet, they saw large continents in opposite hemispheres. There appeared to be four smaller continents, each about the size of Australia.

"It's beautiful." Suki had grown more stable, but she still clung to Firebrandt. "What will we call it?"

"According to the ship's database, the planet's name is G.S.C. 47689329 III," said Roberts.

"That's no name for a planet." Suki twirled the end of her hair. "It's got to have a real name."

"Why don't we name it after the three of us?" Firebrandt flashed her a whimsical grin.

"You mean Mori-Firebrandt-Roberts?" Suki shook her head, perplexed.

"Awkward." The captain's brow knitted. "How 'bout we shorten it to Mo-Fi-Ro?"

Suki wrinkled her nose as though the word smelled bad. "El-Su-Ca?" she countered.

Firebrandt frowned. "What if we mix up given names and surnames? What about Su-Fi-Ro?"

Roberts checked a reading, then cursed. "I hate to intrude on your romantic thoughts, but we're low on fuel. We won't be able to maintain orbit for much more than another hour or two."

Firebrandt whirled on his first mate. "That's not enough time. The admiral only left us one launch. We don't have room nor time to load it with the supplies we need."

Roberts sighed. "There are two alternatives. If we begin now, we can perform a controlled atmospheric entry with the ship. We'll need shields to full. The computers can pilot the ship until we're near the ground."

Firebrandt shook his head. "If we take the ship down, it'll never lift off again."

"With no Quinnium, where are we going?" asked Suki.

"What's our second option?" asked the captain.

"We do have enough fuel to put us into a stable orbit." Roberts shifted in his seat. "Whatever we do, we need to decide now."

"I haven't even had time to check if there is fuel for the launch's reactor. If we stay in orbit, we may die here." The captain took a deep breath. "Make your calculations and bring us in. Where will you land us?"

"I'll aim for the first large continent we saw. According to the Rd'dyggian survey reports, there's a large river, just to the east of the continental center. If nothing else, the water should keep us alive for a while." Roberts typed as he spoke.

Suki returned to the engineering station while the captain sat down at the gunner's rig. The electromagnetic shields popped on as the long black ship spiraled in toward the planet.

The erdonium hull designed for super light travel absorbed much of the heat as they entered the diffuse upper atmosphere. The internal graviton field compensated for the worst of the bumpy ride to the surface.

The lights flickered and went out. The graviton generator died. The restraints dug into the captain as he was jostled about. The ship's hull could withstand the motion and the heat, but many of the internal systems could not take long periods of violent, tumultuous motion. The main holographic display went dead again. They were blind as the ship spasmed, jolted by air turbulence. A resounding crash preceded a loud screech just as Firebrandt flew forward into his restraints. A moment later, the ship hit the ground and slid. The force pushed Firebrandt back into his seat.

The thrusters continued to burn. The captain struggled out of his seat and fell more than walked to the wheel. The console vibrated so hard, Firebrandt couldn't make out the buttons. He hit it where he thought the thruster control should be. An annunciator declared his success and Firebrandt would have sighed if he still didn't cling to the side of the console for dear life. Forward momentum carried the ship some distance. At last, it slowed and stopped. The captain slumped to the floor panting, holding the pillar for support. If he let go, he thought he would slide to the wall.

At last, he released the handle and his eyes widened as he did slide toward the wall. He scrambled to his own feet and straddled the boundary between the wall and the deck. The ship was canted some forty-five degrees with respect to the planet's surface. The captain made his way to Suki's seat. He helped her undo the restraint and controlled her slide to the juncture of wall and floor. "I feel fat," she declared as she tried to find purchase.

"It's the higher gravity." Roberts undid his restraints and slid to the junction. The captain helped him to his feet. "Not enough different to harm us, but enough to feel."

They walked down through the ship. It had been hulled amidships due to the sliding. They stepped through the hull onto a grassy meadow. A river, wider than Earth's Mississippi stood before them. The sun was high in a greenish sky. Some animal chirped.

Suki wrinkled her nose. "It doesn't smell right."

"Different organics than we're used to." Roberts sniffed the air. "Alien pollens and a slightly different atmospheric content from Earth." He nodded. "But it doesn't smell bad. Some of this stuff may be edible after all. It's certainly not like the stench we smelled after stepping into the heavy air of the Rd'dyggian dome on Titan, eh?"

Firebrandt nodded. "Thick wet air that's twenty degrees colder than pleasant." The captain stretched in the sunlight. "This is delightful. No wonder the Rd'dyggians turned this over to general colonization."

Roberts looked back at the gaping hole in the ship. He pointed to the empty launch bay, ripped open. He looked beyond the ship. Firebrandt followed his gaze. Wreckage was scattered as far as he could see.

"General colonization or no, we're shipwrecked," said Roberts. "Marooned until someone rescues us or we die."

Suki and Firebrandt sat down on the grass and looked at the river. Right at that moment, he didn't want to think about being marooned and the real hardships they would face if rescue weren't forthcoming. He breathed in the air and thought he could learn to love this planet. He hoped being stranded would be a brief episode and they'd soon return to civilization where he could obtain fine food, wine, and good books. Still, this was a lovely planet to be stranded on and for the first time in many months, he looked forward to the future.

Chapter Three

SURVIVAL

When the adrenaline rush from bringing the ship down wore off, Firebrandt trembled. He closed his eyes, calmed himself and thought of Suki and Roberts. He had no idea how long they would be stranded. The planet looked habitable, but could they subsist on the vegetation or even drink the water without substantial treatment? He took a deep breath, opened his eyes, and looked back at the ship.

Legacy was a long cylinder and it lay lengthwise along the ground. Unlike early rocket ships, the privateer vessel had never been designed to take off and land from a planet's surface. Instead of small decks running top to bottom, its decks ran lengthwise through the cylinder. Firebrandt remembered that old Earth submarines had inspired the design. However, the ship had not landed on its belly. Its decks were canted some forty-five degrees from the ground. They could get in and out, get what they needed, but working inside would be difficult.

Like him, Suki trembled. He reached out and took her hand, then flashed her what he hoped was a reassuring smile. She smiled back at him and he felt stronger.

"First order of business is to get back in the ship and find supplies for making camp, making dinner, and we need to start gathering any equipment we need for our long-term survival. Once we have a camp established, we can attempt to summon help—and avoid attracting those who would imprison us, or worse."

"I'll check the galley," volunteered Roberts. "I can rustle up some provisions for tonight and check for any leaks in our water supply."

"I can go to the cabins and get some bedding," said Suki.

Firebrandt nodded. "Check the hold as well. There should be some canvas and spare plumbing supplies we can rig up into a temporary shelter." He swallowed and listened. He heard more chirping and a faint rustling from the nearby trees. Some kind of animal life inhabited this planet. Whether he, Roberts, and Suki would be hunters or hunted, he didn't know. "I'll check the armory," he volunteered.

With that, the captain stood and helped Suki to her feet. They returned to the *Legacy* and clambered back onto the canted decks. Firebrandt found it most effective to straddle the boundary between the wall and the floor as he hobbled back to the ship's stern. When he reached the bulkhead, he had to pull himself up to the doorway. He waited on the other side to make sure Roberts and Suki could manage the climb.

More muscular than the captain, Roberts grunted and pulled himself through one handed. Once through, he propped himself against the floor and took a few deep breaths. "I'll be okay," he said. "Go on. I'll pull my weight."

Firebrandt grasped his friend's shoulder. "You've done more than enough already. Do what you can and we'll meet outside in a little while."

The captain continued to the ship's stern and entered the armory, where he gathered four hepler pistols and clipped them to his belt. Satisfied for the moment, he left the armory and proceeded astern to the launch bays. The one below him had broken open in the landing. He found handholds on the bulkhead and climbed up to the other side. The panel by the launch bay door indicated power. He tapped it and the door opened. A bolt and a metal brace clattered to the junction of the wall and floor below.

The captain pulled himself into the launch bay. The sleek, red launch vessel had broken free of its magnetic grips and rested against the wall. Dents and scratches showed the craft had banged into the walls on the descent.

He reached the craft's door and entered. He smiled when he activated the launch's main control panel and it came to life. A diagnostic check revealed no hull breaches. It also revealed no fuel in its propellant tanks. No doubt the admiral had drained it during her scavenger hunt. The captain powered down the launch and clambered out.

He made his way forward and found Roberts in the galley. The captain helped him load supplies into a duffel bag.

"We have almost 280,000 gallons of processed water in the tanks," reported Roberts. "Plus we have another 100,000 gallons of unprocessed waste water."

Firebrandt nodded approval. "That should keep us for a while, at least."

He hefted the duffel bag over his shoulder and went forward, followed by Roberts. When they arrived at the hull breach, they found Suki assembling a framework from pipe. She looked up. "I have more materials in the hold. Could you get them, please?"

"Aye, aye, sir!" Firebrandt gave her a mock salute as he set down the duffel bag. He turned to climb back into the ship, then remembered the hepler pistols clipped to his belt. He left those behind, then entered the ship to go to the hold.

Reaching his destination, he frowned at his hidden compartment, breached by the admiral. He hoped the treasures he had stored there were somewhere safe. He knelt beside the items Suki had gathered. He smiled when he noticed a portable biochemical scanner. He'd forgotten about that. He grabbed it and a sleeping bag and went forward again.

As Firebrandt, Roberts, and Suki worked, the sun climbed high overhead, then began its descent toward the horizon. They constructed a makeshift tent from the plumbing and canvas and set up their bedrolls. Outside, they built a fire ring.

While Suki made dinner from ship's provisions, Roberts and Firebrandt took a stroll down to the river with the biochemical scanner. The captain crouched down and held the probe in the water while Roberts activated the computer. His brow furrowed. "There are some biochemicals. Not surprising since there's animal life."

"Anything poisonous?" The captain stroked his beard and looked at his reflection in the water.

Roberts shook his head. "Not obviously."

Firebrandt cupped his hands, dipped them in the chill water and shivered. He brought his hands to his mouth.

"What the hell are you doing?"

"Conducting a field test." Firebrandt sipped the water, pleased at how it soothed his parched throat.

"I don't like it, Captain." Roberts frowned. "We have no idea how the biochemicals on this planet will react with our systems."

"And we've been breathing in a bunch of biochemicals as well." Firebrandt kept his tone level and even. "At some point, we'll need to take a few chances. It's unlikely we'll get help anytime soon. I'd rather know sooner than later about our odds of survival."

"In that case you should have let me drink the water."

"I couldn't ask you…" Firebrandt stood, brushing pinkish sand from his trousers, and looked up and down along the river. The sun had settled on the horizon and red light played across the surface ripples. "This is one big river. It could save our lives."

"I hope that's true." Roberts stowed the probe in its slot on the scanner.

"What should we call it?"

"What? The river?"

"Yeah," Firebrandt nodded. "If we're the first people on this planet we should at least name a few things. It'll help us as we explore the area. Otherwise, we'll end up referring to 'this river' and 'that river.'"

"All right, all right." Roberts shook his head and chuckled. "When the first conquistadors came into New Mexico on old Earth, they called the big river they found, Rio Grande."

"I'm not up on old Earth languages," admitted Firebrandt. "That's Spanish, isn't it?"

"Yeah," said Roberts. "It means 'Great River.'"

"Not very original." Firebrandt grinned and strolled back toward the ship.

"Fits this river more than Earth's Rio Grande," grumbled Roberts. "All right, how about Nuevo Rio Grande, which means New Big River."

"So, if that's the Nuevo Rio Grande, are we in New New Mexico?"

"Don't give me that 'New New' shit like they did all over

New Earth." Roberts cringed. "There's New New York, New New Delhi. I'm still waiting for some jerk to found New New Earth and tack even more News to familiar names." They topped the rise and strolled across the meadow toward the camp where Suki stirred a batch of stew. "How about Nova Granada?"

"A nova's an explosion on a white dwarf." Firebrandt's eyebrows raised in unison.

"I know that. It's also Latin for 'new.' I'm not a damned writer, but even I can do better than New New Mexico," grumbled Roberts. "On ancient Spanish maps, what we call New Mexico was once called Nova Granada."

Suki looked up as the men approached. "Sounds like a good name for this place." She grabbed some bowls and began serving dinner. As they ate, the stars appeared. Firebrandt picked at his meal.

"Is it all right?" Suki narrowed her gaze.

Firebrandt sighed, then forced a smile. "The food is wonderful as is the company."

"But..." prompted Suki.

"Just idle thoughts about seasoning, simmering, and slow roasting." Gourmet meals were the captain's pride. "I'm just thinking that it may be a while before I get to spend time in a proper kitchen."

"You think so?" asked Roberts.

Firebrandt chuckled. "All I know for sure is that I'm not defeated yet."

After dinner, the captain and Suki sat, arm in arm, creating names for constellations in this new sky. At last, fatigue caught up with them and they decided to sleep.

"We should set up watches." Roberts yawned. "There could be nocturnal predators that want to find out whether or not *we're* edible."

"We haven't actually seen any animals," said Suki.

"But we've *heard* a few." Firebrandt pursed his lips. "You two get some sleep." He nodded to Suki. "I'll wake you in a couple of hours so you can take over."

Firebrandt and Suki embraced, then he watched them retreat into the makeshift tent to get some sleep. He checked his hepler, then sat beside the fire and looked up at the stars, wondering about his lost crew.

☠

Firebrandt woke Suki with a kiss. He then dropped into his bedroll. Even before she'd pulled on a coat, he had begun snoring. She knew he was exhausted and concerned about the crew, but something about this world suited him. It seemed a new and welcome challenge.

She picked up a hepler pistol and stepped out to the campfire. She looked up to the stars and tried to pick out the constellations she and Ellison had named earlier. A rustling in the grass pulled her attention from the sky. She narrowed her gaze and spied a creature low to the ground. It reminded her of a lizard, but fur bristled from its back, like a dog raising its hackles. She aimed the hepler in case it decided to charge. With a noise between a hiss and a growl, it turned and scurried off into the woods. She thought she counted six legs. She lowered the weapon and blew out a relieved sigh.

She pulled out her handcomp and browsed dictionary entries about various half-remembered dinosaur species and how they were named. She decided to call the animal a kyonosaur—a dog lizard.

Satisfied with her name for the creature, she hummed to herself for a while and watched time crawl by on her wrist chronometer. She thought about her parents in the asteroid belt and wondered how long it would be before they started to worry about her. Last she'd seen them, her mother had practically disinherited her for consorting with privateers. How long would it be before her parents would welcome her into their lives again? Would she live long enough to see that day? She shuddered at the thought.

Suki allowed three hours to pass, then went in to wake Roberts. His eyes popped open and he scowled, frightening her more than the wild animal. "Time for my watch, I guess." He climbed out of the bedroll, pulled on trousers and left the tent.

Suki returned to her bedroll and fell into a fitful sleep.

She awoke to the smell of bacon. She dressed and emerged

from the tent to find Roberts cooking breakfast. Firebrandt poured boiling water into a cup through a strainer containing ground coffee. The captain handed her a cup.

"Our job for today is to explore our surroundings." He pointed to Suki and Roberts. "I want you two to test the plants to find out if there's anything here we can eat."

"What about animals?" asked Roberts.

"I'm happy to eat anything that won't kill me." The captain flashed a wicked grin as he prepared a cup of coffee for himself. "Presuming we're not talking about intelligent life, of course."

Suki winced at the way he presented the last point as an afterthought. "What will you do?"

"I want to make a more thorough inventory of the ship and see about setting up the distress beacon. We need to figure out what we can do for more permanent shelter and power. The batteries won't last forever."

Roberts narrowed his gaze. "Our options for a beacon are limited. With our Quinnium reserves depleted, we can't send an EQ signal to the Earth Alliance."

Firebrandt sipped his coffee. "You're right. What's more, we're on the other side of the galaxy from Earth on a world claimed by aliens. We're alive now. We should take care not to make our situation worse by inviting the wrong guests to this party, if possible."

After breakfast, Suki and Roberts set out on their mission. Reed-like plants growing a short distance from the river shared many properties with Earth grains. "I'm pretty sure this would sustain us for a while." Roberts grinned. "I think we could even malt it and make an ale."

Suki shook her head. "That presumes there's a life form that mimics the behavior of yeast and will ferment your malted grain."

"Don't need it," said Roberts. "The admiral didn't take all the ale stores from the ship. We can culture yeast from that."

"So, we'd just need to get the cultures to be fruitful and multiply."

Roberts blushed, then pointed to a stand of trees. "I think I see some fruit growing over there." Without waiting for a response, he grabbed the biochemical scanner and marched toward the trees.

Suki fell in step behind the first mate and wondered what he thought. In the Earth Alliance, he could get a new hand and he could return to privateering. He seemed to be handling the trauma well, but how much was adrenaline and how much was the simple need to survive?

They reached the stand of fruit trees. Suki picked a purple orb with rubbery skin. "It looks like a pomegranate, but it feels a little like a citrus." She sat down in the grass cross-legged and cut the fruit open revealing juicy red flesh with an apple-like texture.

Roberts took the half of the fruit sitting on the ground and inserted the biochemical scanner's probe.

"This is a lovely planet," said Suki. "I hope we can survive here. I'm not sure if I want to leave … at least not right away."

Roberts grunted and continued checking readings on the computer. "It should be edible."

She lifted the fruit to her mouth and he lunged forward knocking it from her hand. Her eyes widened. "Why did you do that?"

"This is just a preliminary test," he said. "The DNA structure looks like vegetable matter we can digest, but we won't know until we actually eat it."

"Exactly. That's what I was going to test."

Roberts sighed. "We still have supplies at the ship. I'm hesitant to eat the fruit until we know it's necessary. I don't want you or the captain getting sick and maybe dying."

That gave Suki pause. "I understand, but I'm not sure if I want to go back to the dangerous life of being a privateer. I was always afraid I'd lose Ellison, you, Lowry. You all became my friends, but we had to scrape by so much just to make a living. Part of me just wants to settle down."

"Part of me wants to settle down, too," admitted Roberts.

Suki looked up at him, but couldn't read his expression. "I've always wondered, how do you feel about Ellison? You're so loyal to him."

Roberts snorted. "I've been loyal to him for twenty years." He paused for a moment and seemed to collect his thoughts.

"When I was fifteen, I joined a gang. We shoplifted from grocery stores. We would find ambulances responding to emergencies and grab their painkillers and other pharma. A lot of it, we took to people in need." He snorted a laugh. "We thought of ourselves as real Robin Hoods." He looked down to the ground. "Didn't last, though. Cops caught us. Judge gave me a choice between going to jail or signing aboard a privateer. I took the privateer option and that's when I met Ellison Firebrandt. He understood my pain and helped me become a better person."

Suki edged closer to Roberts. "Your pain? I take it you didn't choose to be a street criminal."

"People only choose a life of crime when the other choices are worse." He took a deep breath and looked away. "Two years before I met Ellison Firebrandt, I saw two men from the Coma Navy rape and murder my mother." His brown eyes glazed over. "I yelled and got one of the bastards in the kidney with my pocket knife." His voice took on a razor-sharp edge. "The other one grabbed me by my neck, threw me over his knee…" At that, his voice cracked. He rubbed his smooth head. "He scalped me." Roberts' voice was almost a whisper. He looked at the stump where a Coma hepler had removed his hand. His face turned ashen. "I don't know who found me or took me to the hospital." He leapt to his feet and took several steps away from her.

Suki stood and followed. She wanted to pull him into her arms and comfort him, but it didn't seem right. "I don't know what to say. I didn't … I didn't know."

"Ellison Firebrandt helped me find purpose in serving a cause beyond myself. He helped me find a reason to go on after the indignities I'd suffered."

Suki stepped forward and touched his shoulder. "You … love him, don't you?"

He shrugged. "I suppose I do."

"Are you jealous of me and him?"

Again, he shrugged. "After seeing sex used as a weapon against my own mother … I haven't been interested." He turned and looked into her eyes. "I'm glad you two have found a measure of happiness."

She stepped back and plucked another fruit from the tree.

She cut it open and handed half to Roberts. "I don't know yet whether destiny will cause us to leave or stay. Whatever happens, I hope we'll stay together."

As she lifted the fruit to her mouth, Roberts put his hand on it. "Let's wash it first in water from our supply. At least let's make sure there's nothing on the skin."

Suki nodded and retrieved her canteen. She rinsed off her section and handed the water to Roberts. He lifted his half of the fruit and took a bite. He grimaced at first, then smiled and nodded. "If anything happens to me, you'll take care of him, won't you?"

"You can bet on it, just like I know you'll be by his side if anything happens to me." She took a bite and savored the tangy-sweet flavor.

"Of course, now that we've eaten this fruit, we may both die…"

"And we both know that Ellison Firebrandt can take care of himself if he needs to," laughed Suki.

Roberts shook his head. "Some days I have my doubts."

"Then we just have to make sure we don't die," she said.

The two finished the fruit, then hiked back to the *Legacy* to report their findings to the captain.

Ellison Firebrandt put a ladder against the floor and climbed up to a cabinet to get a screwdriver and a wrench. When he opened the cabinet, the tools fell out to the deck below. As he climbed down the ladder to retrieve the tools, he realized he could make it easier to work aboard the grounded ship and make more secure living accommodations at the same time.

He grabbed the tools, but instead of going to the communications station on the command deck, he crawled into a workspace amidships and removed the ship's main graviton generator. He set it outside the ship, then began removing deck plate amplifiers one section at a time.

As he carried an amplifier from the ship, Roberts and Suki returned and gave him a report about the fruit and the grain-like reeds. "Sounds promising," he said.

They ate a lunch of ship's supplies and then Firebrandt asked Suki and Roberts to retrieve bits and pieces of hull that broke off the ship as they'd crashed.

"What for?" asked Roberts.

The captain used a stick and drew a crude diagram in the dirt. "I want to set up a platform beside the ship." He pointed to the deck plate amplifiers he'd stacked up. "I can use the graviton generator and the amplifiers to roll the ship so the decks are parallel to the ground."

Roberts shook his head. "That's going to take a lot of our reserve power and you'll burn out the graviton generator."

"We have emergency solar cells. We can recharge our batteries," said the captain. "As for the graviton generator, do you have another use for it now that we're planetside?"

Roberts scowled as he considered the captain's question. "I suppose not."

Over the next week and a half, Suki and Roberts hiked along *Legacy's* path of destruction and retrieved scrap metal. During their forays, they carried the biochemical scanner and tested any fruits or plants they came across. Not all proved good to eat. They lost two days to dysentery, eased somewhat by supplies in the medbay. Afterward, Roberts started a log of plants they could and could not eat.

Meanwhile, Firebrandt assembled a makeshift platform from the pieces brought to him. He welded the pieces together, then bolted the deck plate amplifiers onto the platform.

One day, he looked up to see a small animal perched on one of *Legacy's* gun ports staring at him. The captain thought it looked like a miniature, furry pterosaur. It squawked at him and flew off. The captain's stomach rumbled and he wondered if it would taste like chicken. He thought of the German word for bat—*die Fledermaus*. He had a vague memory that it meant something like "the flying mouse" and thought it suited the hairy creature.

That night, they dined on pork chops from the ship's stores plus a salad made of greens from a dandelion-like plant Roberts and Suki had discovered. "I think we'll be ready to right the ship tomorrow," said the captain.

Suki stretched her back. "I can't wait to sleep in an actual bed again." She then cast a glance at the captain. "Once we can sleep inside, will we need to set watches? After all, we'll be able to close the inside doors."

"Good point." Firebrandt considered her question. "So far, none of the animals we've encountered has come too close. I think we'll be able to relax the watches."

"Another reason to celebrate," she said. "A full night's sleep at last!"

The next day, Firebrandt connected the graviton generator to the deck plate amplifiers, then ran power cables from the ship's battery to the generator. He activated a control program on his handcomp and had Roberts review the parameters.

Roberts made some adjustments to assure the captain had compensated for Sufiro's gravity.

At last, Roberts nodded and handed Firebrandt the handcomp. The captain activated the controls and the ship shivered and quaked. Some hull plates began to warp and distort and for a moment, Firebrandt feared the ship was stuck in place and wouldn't roll. Just then, the cowling flew off a gun port and crashed into the deck plate amplifiers sending up a shower of sparks. The captain thought for a moment the whole thing would overload.

After a long, tense moment, the ship rolled a few degrees. Firebrandt cut power. The ship rolled just a little further, then hit the scaffolding and stopped.

The captain blew out a relieved sigh.

He ran to the hole in the ship's side with Roberts and Suki at his heels. They looked inside. They would have to climb in and out of the ship now, but the decks were parallel with the ground.

Suki grabbed Firebrandt into a tight embrace and Roberts pounded his knee with his hand. "Outstanding," he said.

"We've still got a lot of work to do," said the captain, "but this gives us a much better base of operations."

He had Suki give him a leg up and he clambered into the ship. He soon found a ladder in the storage area and brought it back for Suki and Roberts. They climbed aboard. The captain and Roberts went back to the engine room and confirmed the batteries were almost depleted.

They found the manual winches and deployed the emergency solar cells. Roberts wiped sweat from his brow. Within the hour, the batteries charged at a trickle. "They're not charging as fast as I'd like," grumbled Roberts.

"The solar cells are designed for use in space. The planet's atmosphere absorbs some percentage of the sunlight. Also, one bank of solar panels is under the ship, so we only have three banks deployed." Firebrandt shrugged. "It's still better than nothing."

"All correct." Roberts nodded. "It'll get worse if we have a cloudy stretch. We've been damn lucky the weather's been mild since we crashed."

"The question is, do we have enough power to fire up the emergency beacon?"

Roberts checked the power meters and shook his head. "It would put us close to the red line. Most of our power goes to maintaining food storage and we want to be able to charge weapons. I wouldn't advise it yet."

Firebrandt cursed under his breath. "Barbara Firebrandt won't defeat me this easily." The captain led Roberts back to the hole in the ship's flank. He looked out toward the river. "The way I see it, we have ample backup power. We just need to figure out the best way to connect it."

For the remainder of the day, they tidied the ship. They returned books to their shelves and tools to their cabinets. They repaired burned out components, focusing on those they needed for survival.

That night, they retired to their cabins. Suki sat on the captain's bed in a short robe. Loosely belted, it revealed a tantalizing amount of cleavage. "What I've missed the most is privacy," she said.

The captain knelt on the bed between her legs and unbelted the robe. "I could have ordered Roberts to take a long walk."

"The ground is awfully hard," countered Suki.

"It's not the only thing that's hard."

She swatted his naked shoulder and tried to suppress a giggle.

"Seriously," he said, "I would have been happy to be the one with my back to the ground if you'd asked."

Instead of waiting for a response, he teased her nipple with his tongue. She responded with a sharp intake of breath. "I think this primitive planet's affecting me. I want you more than ever."

He turned his attentions to her neck. After a moment, he brought his mouth to hers and she guided his penis to just the right spot. Tired as they were, the sex was sweet and satisfying, but all too brief. Their energy spent, they drifted off to sleep in each other's' arms.

The next day, Firebrandt awoke, dressed, and walked to the galley. There Roberts chased a fledermaus, pancake clasped in its jaws, outside. "I suppose we'll need to seal the hole in the ship's side after all."

"In the original Nova Granada, they built houses with adobe bricks. They're just mud and straw. We have plenty of both here. I can calculate a good ratio using the computer."

"Sounds like a plan," said Firebrandt. "And I bought a book about power generation a while back. I know it discusses water wheels."

Suki entered the galley as Firebrandt spoke. She still wore the short robe from the night before. If not for his growling stomach, Firebrandt might have decided to lead her back to the cabin. She grabbed a plate of pancakes and sat down next to him. "Making plans for a hydro-electric generator is more my specialty, or Roberts'." She poured syrup on her stack of pancakes. "After breakfast, I'll go take a dip in the river and wash up, then go find your book while you start digging mud for bricks."

Firebrandt scowled as he buttered his pancakes. "So, does this mean you're the captain now?"

She lifted his chin and gave him a kiss. "With just three of us, does anyone really need to be in charge?"

Chapter Four

HOMESTEAD

Suki went down to the river to bathe. The water at once chilled and revitalized her. As she swam with the current, one of the six-legged animals approached the bank and eyed her warily. She caught onto a root and took a close look at the kyonosaur. Fur covered the creature even though it reminded her of a reptile. She estimated it was the size of a monitor lizard or a Gila monster from Earth. It leaned over the water and drank, then scurried back toward the tree line with its strange, waddling lizard-like gait. It paused for a moment, looked at her and seemed to wink before it disappeared into the trees.

She climbed out of the river and let the air dry her skin. Alone on the planet with Firebrandt and Roberts, she didn't worry about who might see her. If strange alien reptile-mammals had fantasies about her, so be it. She donned her robe and strode back through the grassy field to the ship. There she found Roberts and Firebrandt discussing the best ratio of mud to straw for the bricks and how to form them to a uniform size.

She sought out the book on hydroelectric power and began to read. She found a design for a water wheel she thought they could build with the resources at hand. She input the parameters into the computer, then decided to consult Roberts about the details.

Over the next few days, Roberts and Suki took turns working on plans for the adobe structure and the water wheel.

When not at the computer, Suki helped Firebrandt dig up mud and mix it with dried grass from the surrounding meadow. They poured it into forms they had constructed from local timber.

Besides working on plans, Roberts used the ship's scanners to measure the planet's axial tilt. Without satellite imagery, rain storms sometimes caught them off guard, but he wanted to be ready to close up the ship before winter's onset.

Three and a half weeks after crashing on Sufiro, they had placed the first layer of adobe bricks. Roberts managed the project as architect. He directed Firebrandt and Suki to cut down trees and shape them into load-bearing supports.

"I don't know if I like my first mate giving me orders," said the captain.

"There's only three of us," Suki reminded him. "This isn't about power. It's about trusting the person with the most expertise."

Firebrandt grunted. She knew he wanted to find out what had become of the crew. He also knew the only way he could help them was to survive long enough to restore contact with civilization. He didn't resent his first officer, but he bristled at the prospect of the passing time.

Two more weeks passed and they completed the first floor, covering almost a third of the hull breach. They disassembled the structure Firebrandt used to support the makeshift gravity winch and used the metal to make an upper floor.

They fell into a routine. Get up in the morning, make breakfast, and get to work. Suki made bricks throughout the day. Firebrandt lay and mortared the bricks in place. Roberts started work on the water wheel and converting one of the engine turbines to work with the wheel.

One morning, Roberts called them into the command deck to chase away a kyonosaur. At one point, it backed into a corner, hissed and snapped at them. Suki had them back away. Once they gave it room, it fled to the outside.

As they returned to their tasks, Suki noticed Roberts limped. She waited until Firebrandt had gone outside to dig up more mud for bricks, then followed the first mate to the engine room. "Are you okay?" she asked.

He shrugged, then held up his missing hand. "You mean besides this?"

Suki put her hands on her hips. "Just now, you were limping."

"It's nothing," he said. "I just banged my toe into the computer station when we chased that stupid kyono ... lizard ... whatever you call it."

Suki didn't quite buy it. She'd seen Roberts shake off worse injuries in less time. Then again, he didn't have a crew of blood-thirsty pirates—okay privateers—to impress. "All right, just be careful. It's not like we have expert medical help out here."

Again, Roberts held up his missing hand. "Believe me, that's one thing you don't have to remind me about."

Two months after their arrival, they topped the adobe structure with a roof. When finished, the three stood back and examined their work.

Legacy had once been long, black, and sleek. She had jumped from star to star with ease. Now, the cylindrical ship sat scarred and matted with what appeared to be a two-story, mud-colored growth protruding from its side. "It's not pretty," said Firebrandt, "but it's home."

"I think it's beautiful." Suki admired the work, proud of their accomplishment.

With the adobe structure completed, Suki and Firebrandt helped Roberts with the water wheel. He'd completed most of the parts. All together they assembled the wheel and the supports based on the first mate's plans. They connected it to a shaft and gears made from plumbing supplies, machine stock, and even metal cannibalized from the ship itself.

At last, they unloaded the engine turbine Roberts had refurbished to work on water power. They managed to hoist it out through the damaged launch bay and they rolled it on logs to the river bank.

"It's too bad someone destroyed the graviton generator," grumbled Roberts.

"I didn't hear you complaining when we got to sleep inside the ship two nights ago with a thunderstorm raging outside," countered Firebrandt.

They lifted the water wheel into the river and propped it up with supports. Once done, they connected the wheel to the turbine's shaft, then removed the support pillars. The wheel creaked and groaned as though the river would tear the flimsy wooden structure apart, but it turned. Roberts checked the output with his handcomp. It produced ample electricity. Suki cheered. A moment later she shivered and hugged herself. The wind seemed cooler than normal.

She looked over at the nearby trees. Leaves turned orange, red, and brown. "What's wrong with the trees?"

Roberts held up the handcomp and showed her a holographic projection of sunsets he'd filmed. With each loop, the sun moved farther south. "It's called autumn," he said.

Having grown up on an asteroid and living most of her life in space ships, Suki hadn't really experienced seasons before. Even life on Epsilon Indi 2 had been an urban existence. All she knew was that the air turned colder and hotter as the seasons changed.

"We should construct a shed to house the turbine." The captain's words were more a suggestion than an order.

After building the house, the turbine's shed proved a simple task. Once complete, they used their hand lasers and dug a trench to the ship. They lay wires alongside plumbing and then buried it all.

The ship had electric power and fresh water the night snow first fell on the humans of Sufiro. Electric heat supplemented the wood-burning fireplace in the homestead's adobe structure. They were secure with food stocked in the hold. They still had the ship's stores as well as fruit and vegetables they had acquired from the countryside. The snow continued for three days.

On the third morning, Suki awoke next to Firebrandt and studied his features. His face had thinned and his beard had a few gray strands. It suited him. She had been trying to find the right time to talk to him about some important issues. She steeled her nerves and stroked his beautiful, long red hair. "You know, I worry about Carter," she said once his eyes opened and they'd kissed.

"In what way?" asked Firebrandt.

"I worry that he's lonely. We have each other. He has no one."

Firebrandt blinked twice and sat up. "Has he ever told you about his mother?" Suki nodded. "Those were Coma pirates. They've violated him twice now. I'm not sure if he'll ever get over it."

Suki folded her arms across her stomach and glared at the captain. "If anything, I think he may need even more affection."

"What brings this on?" he asked, gently.

"Remember soon after we met, I captured the *Legacy* and tried to return home?"

"How could I forget?" The ship had fallen into the hands of a New Earth battle cruiser. Although Suki had gotten them into the situation, she had also rescued them.

"Roberts was the first crewmember to stand by my side." She glared at him. "Even before you." She tried to find the words to convey her feelings. "I'm not sure I love him, but I fear he might leave if the opportunity arrived and I'm not sure what that would mean for us."

"We can't force him to stay if he doesn't want to," said the captain.

"No, we can't make him stay," agreed Suki, "but I want to know, do you love him?"

Firebrandt opened his mouth. He seemed lost for words.

"I'm pretty sure he loves you," she said.

Firebrandt cleared his throat. "I would never hurt him."

"Sometimes it's easy to hurt someone without realizing it, especially when love is involved." Suki put her arms around the captain. "I just wanted you to be aware."

"And that's why I love you." Firebrandt returned Suki's embrace.

"There's something else."

Firebrandt sat back and waited for her to speak.

"Ellison … I'm pregnant."

Suki's announcement lent new urgency to activating the emergency beacon. Firebrandt gathered his small crew around the galley table.

"Between the solar cells and the water wheel, we now have reserve power," said Firebrandt. "It does no harm to let the beacon run. Someone might answer who could bring us supplies and take us to facilities if an emergency strikes."

"And how do we pay for supplies or transport?" Roberts

stood from the galley table and limped over to a carafe. He brought it back to the table and poured coffee for the three.

Firebrandt glanced at Suki. "We'll find a way." Firebrandt lifted the coffee cup. "If we gain access to the networks, we'll have access to our bank accounts. They were slim when it came to the day to day operation of a privateer vessel, but for the three of us..."

"This all presumes our accounts haven't been seized," said Roberts.

Firebrandt sighed. "We have skills. At the very least, you and I could work in exchange for help."

Suki bristled. "Having a baby won't make me helpless." Her eyes darted to Roberts for a moment, then back to Firebrandt. She sighed. "There's no guarantee anyone will respond, is there?"

"None at all." Roberts sat down.

"All right. Why not?" said Suki. "Set the beacon."

A week later, Firebrandt trudged through snow, slush, and mud to check on the turbine by the river. A whooshing sound attracted his gaze skyward. He shielded his eyes with his hand.

A launch descended—and from the profile, the captain could tell it was alien. He turned and splooshed back toward the homestead. When he arrived, he threw open the door. "Company's coming!"

Roberts appeared first. He limped through the door and looked up into the sky where Firebrandt pointed. "That's a Rd'dyggian launch."

Suki entered the main room. "Someone's responded to the beacon already?"

"Yeah," said Firebrandt, "and I'm not sure it's a good thing." He pointed to Suki. "Go to the armory, get some weapons and stand by, out of sight. Let Roberts and I vet these guys."

Suki opened her mouth as though she would argue, but finally nodded. She went upstairs and into the ship. Firebrandt and Roberts followed her and changed from casual work clothes into slacks and jackets. As a privateer vessel, the *Legacy* didn't have uniforms per se, but Firebrandt had insisted that his officers maintain a uniform dress code for formal situations.

The launch landed in the meadow a hundred yards from the homestead. Firebrandt and Roberts went outside to meet the visitors.

An orange being stepped from the craft. Shaped like a human, but larger, he wore a silver jump suit with a blue sash. Firebrandt recognized him as a command officer. His hands were massive with four pointed fingers and two thumbs. He had no hair, but tiny purple appendages that resembled a bushy mustache wriggled in front of his mouth. The creature was a Rd'dyggian warrior. Firebrandt bent in a low bow and greeted him in a guttural, hissing voice.

"Not bad," said the Rd'dyggian using a translator unit. "Not many humans can speak Rd'dyggian. I am impressed." As a general rule, Rd'dyggians did not give complements. Had the captain made a good first impression or did the Rd'dyggian know humans could be susceptible to flattery? "I am captain of a scout ship. I am called Arepno. We detected your emergency beacon and decided to investigate."

"We are honored to have you." The captain bowed again. He indicated the door and invited Arepno inside.

"It appears you have settled here." Arepno, eyed the house. "You are aware this planet is Rd'dyggian?" He shifted his weight from foot to foot as he spoke—a Rd'dyggian trait. It helped their depth perception.

"Yes," said Firebrandt. "We understood the planet was open to general colonization."

"Still, one should contact the Rd'dyggian government before settling." Arepno followed them into the main room and the three sat.

"We didn't know." Firebrandt opened his hands, gesturing apology. "Our ship was damaged, our Quinnium reserves were gone. Our only choice was to make a crash landing and attempt to make a home here. Without Quinnium, our EQ transmitter won't work."

Arepno studied Firebrandt, then Roberts. "How long have you been here?"

The question caught the captain off guard. He'd lost track of time.

"Just over six months," answered Roberts.

Firebrandt stepped in and told the story of the crash and how he and Roberts had survived.

Arepno's near-constant swaying ceased, indicating the Rd'dyggian's surprise. "You are truly impressive. This planet is too hot and dry by Rd'dyggian standards." Arepno tugged at his collar. Firebrandt gestured to Roberts, who climbed the stairs into the ship and soon returned with drinks.

Arepno reiterated how impressed he was with Firebrandt's knowledge of Rd'dyggian culture.

"So," said Firebrandt, "what brings you to Sufiro?"

"Is Sufiro the human name for this world? According to our records its only designation is a number in the Generic Star Catalog." Arepno's swaying turned into a fidget.

"Sufiro is *our* designation for this planet." Roberts passed glasses of water around.

"We are on a long exploratory mission," said Arepno. "We need food and water. May we please exploit some of your planet's resources?"

Arepno's legs bounced and his head bobbed. Rd'dyggians never lied well.

"Arepno." Firebrandt enunciated the syllables. "I've heard your name. You're a privateer, not a civilian." Arepno stood and drew his gun. Firebrandt sat still. "Put your gun away. We are retired privateers ourselves."

Arepno looked from one to the other. "I can kill you."

"Your capacity for killing does not frighten me." The captain folded his arms. "I'm prepared for death."

"You speak like a privateer but you have the same name as the admiral who pursues the galaxy's privateers. I do not think I should trust you." Despite his words, Arepno's fidgeting slowed to a gentle sway.

"I know Barbara Firebrandt," spat the captain. "She's the one who did this to my ship." The captain pointed to the room's far wall, the *Legacy's* damaged hull. "She scattered my crew and took my first officer's right hand."

Arepno looked into Firebrandt's face. "You were this ship's captain?"

Firebrandt nodded. "I was."

"An Alpha Coma cruiser pursues my ship. Help me

elude capture and I will help you."

Firebrandt considered the Rd'dyggian's words and his body language. At last he gave a sharp nod, then suggested a plan. The Rd'dyggian would order his crew to abandon ship and seek cover on the large continent opposite Nova Granada. All launches would be returned to the vessel in orbit. No escape pods would be used. It would look like another ship had come and picked up the crew. "We'll keep our emergency beacon on, which should draw your pursuers here."

"Clever." Arepno sipped the water. "But how will we return to our ship?"

"There is a functional launch aboard *Legacy*," explained Firebrandt. "All it lacks is fuel."

Arepno swayed for a moment. At last, he set the glass down on the table beside him. "A good plan." Then he waved his gun at Firebrandt again. "If you deceive us, I will come back and kill you and take your house and supplies."

Firebrandt bowed. "So be it."

Later that day, the Rd'dyggian crew landed near the homestead. They brought fuel packs and anti-gravity hoists. Firebrandt and Roberts helped them unload the *Legacy's* launch. They inspected the craft and repaired a few minor systems. Roberts reviewed the craft's operation with the Rd'dyggian crew.

Satisfied the plan could work, the aliens commanded their launch to return to the ship in orbit while they flew off to the other continent.

Suki joined Firebrandt and Roberts as the launch departed. "This may be obvious," she said, "but if the Rd'dyggians can control their launches remotely, why do they need ours?"

Instead of answering, Roberts asked a question. "What's the first thing you'd do if you found an abandoned ship?"

"Check the launches, look for pre-programming and check to see if they're active and listening for a recall signal."

Firebrandt nodded. "Now you're thinking like a pirate."

"I hoped that was all behind us," she muttered.

The captain nodded agreement, then pointed to the grass scorched by Arepno's launch. "Speaking of thinking like a pirate, we better hide the Rd'dyggian landing marks." They grabbed a pair of shovels and set to work.

By the end of the day, dark clouds rolled in and fresh snowfall further obscured the landing site. Roberts stood beside the window and rubbed his arm. "I've never been so grateful for more snow."

The snow lasted just one night, but it left a nice, even layer on the ground, which would have been perfect, except that Arepno's pursuers didn't arrive for two more days. Again, the sun had been out and the snow turned slushy. The captain could tell where the Rd'dyggian launch had been, but hoped that was only because he knew where to look.

Firebrandt, Roberts, and Suki emerged from the homestead in time to see the hatch open on the Alpha Coman launch.

The captain's mouth fell open when Nicole Lowry emerged wearing an Alpha Coma Navy captain's uniform. Suki took a step forward and smiled.

Lowry nodded to the three of them. "When we entered orbit, we registered *Legacy's* emergency beacon, but I didn't quite believe it was really you until now."

Firebrandt stepped forward and held out his hand. "It's good to see you, Ms. Lowry." He paused and made a show of studying her epaulets. "Captain Lowry ... Working for the enemy, I see."

Lowry frowned. "Admiral Firebrandt gave us a simple choice. We could join her and hunt pirates or we could rot in an Alpha Coman brig." She patted her arms and glanced around. "It's cold out here. May we go inside to talk?"

Firebrandt took her meaning. They were monitored next to the shuttle. There may be nanoprobes as well. Suki held her hand toward the house.

Lowry followed Suki inside and they sat around the table. Roberts brought coffee. "We didn't expect an Alpha Coma ship to respond to our emergency beacon." Firebrandt sipped his coffee. "It's only a standard broadcast. This soon after we started it, you would have needed to have been in the system to pick it up. Why are you here? Were you looking for us?" In fact, the captain wouldn't put it past his mother to send someone to hunt them down.

Lowry shook her head. "Are you aware there's a Rd'dyggian pirate ship in orbit?"

Roberts swallowed too fast and coughed. The captain couldn't tell if it was a genuine accident or if he tried to cover his lack of surprise. Either way, it gave him an opening. "Our scanners were damaged in the crash," lied Firebrandt. "We've been making plans to plant a garden in the spring. It hasn't given us time for idle stargazing."

Lowry narrowed her gaze.

"Do you think they'll try to raid us?" Suki's eyes widened.

Lowry had been Firebrandt's boatswain and his best gunner. She had an eye for detail and she was patient. She wouldn't strike unless she had a good target. "According to their logs, they abandoned their ship three days ago. They didn't use lifepods and all their launches are aboard."

"Did they have engine damage?" Recovered from the coughing fit, Roberts sipped his coffee again.

"Their EQ engines are intact, but they had thruster damage," admitted Lowry.

Firebrandt admired that. If Lowry hadn't fired the guns herself, she had acquired a good gunnery officer. Limited thruster control meant the Rd'dyggians would have a difficult time making it to jump points. The knowledge also gave the captain more to bargain with.

"They must have called for help," said Firebrandt. "Another Rd'dyggian ship must have picked them up."

Lowry scowled but didn't seem to have an argument to make. After a moment, she sipped her coffee, then set the cup down. "The *Hunter* isn't equipped for rescue operations, but we could send word to Alpha Coma and have them send another ship."

"Alpha Coma is the last place I want to go." Firebrandt's words came out with a razor's edge.

Nicole Lowry leaned forward. "I know you see what I did as a betrayal ... but Computer has been in a vegetative state since the admiral disconnected him from *Legacy*. Last I knew, Kheir el-Din is still awaiting trial. If you came with me, maybe you could help them."

The words struck Firebrandt like a physical blow. The

captain fought not to wince. He wanted to help them, but knew if he went with her, he would be jailed and even more helpless than he was stranded on a planet. Lowry was in a better position to help the crew than he was. Even so, he suspected she needed assistance. Firebrandt glanced over to dust motes drifting in a sunbeam and wondered whether nanoprobes also hovered, relaying their words to his mother's ears. Firebrandt had to play this carefully. "I dare say helping them is now your job ... *Captain*." Firebrandt emphasized the last word. Suki and Roberts stared at him, but the more he considered his words, the more he knew he'd made the right decision. On Alpha Coma Berenices, he could be compelled to testify against his friends. On Sufiro, he remained a shadowy mystery. Lowry could get Computer medical help. She could pay bribes to reduce Kheir el-Din's sentence. He had to gamble he read her correctly. "I think you should return to your new masters now."

Lowry nodded. Firebrandt thought he detected a faint grin before her expression turned neutral again. He stood and led Lowry back outside to the launch. Before Lowry ascended the ramp into the craft, Suki ran forward and pulled her friend into a hug. "I'm glad to see you again. I wish the circumstances had been better."

Nicole returned the hug, then stepped back. "You can still come with us."

Suki looked back at Firebrandt and stepped away from Lowry. "This isn't the time."

Lowry nodded and ascended the launch's ramp. At the door, she turned. "Ellison, do you want me to tell your mother you're safe?"

Firebrandt shook his head. "I suspect she knows already."

Lowry turned around and the launch's door slammed shut behind her. Firebrandt, Roberts, and Suki entered the homestead and heard the craft ascend into the sky.

Suki reached into a pocket and blinked in surprise at a scrap of paper. She handed it to Firebrandt. "I think that's Nicole's handwriting, but what are the numbers?"

Firebrandt glanced at the paper, then handed the slip of paper to Roberts. "Looks like bank routing numbers," remarked the captain.

Suki's brow furrowed. "What would she give us that for?"

"I daresay she's looking to help our friends as much as we are," suggested the captain.

"Or she's laying a clever trap," said Roberts.

"Either way, let's be careful and hope the Rd'dyggians can help us." Firebrandt turned to Roberts. "She'll need to put on a good show of watching the planet. Better not send for our friends until we know she's gone. Let's keep the external cameras running and monitor the skies for the next few nights."

"So, we have time for idle stargazing now?" Roberts lifted an eyebrow.

"Not so idle, I daresay," mused Firebrandt.

High resolution video of the night sky revealed parallel light streaks moving overhead for two more nights. Lowry and her *Hunter* remained near Arepno's ship, waiting and watching. At last, on the third night, the parallel light streaks became one.

Roberts pointed to the screen. "I think she's gone."

"Either that, or she's assumed a position above or below the Rd'dyggians." Firebrandt pursed his lips. "Let's give it a couple more days."

Three days later, Firebrandt signaled Arepno. Within the hour, Arepno landed *Legacy's* launch. He grasped Firebrandt's hands. "Our pursuers have left the system. I owe you a large favor, friend human."

"Can you take us with you?" asked Firebrandt. "We have access to funds. We could pay for passage."

The Rd'dyggian's mustache wriggled. "No. We do not return to human-friendly sectors for some months. Also, we would have to report you as illegal occupants of our territory. This would not be an advantageous course of action, though we can take steps to correct that if you do not come with us." Arepno looked over at Roberts' hand. "We can, however, help you now."

The Rd'dyggian took Roberts back to his ship. The next day, Roberts had a new right hand. "It's made from cloned tissue," explained Roberts. "Fully functional!"

"You have earned it." The Rd'dyggian captain made an attempt to imitate a smile. "I am especially pleased that you helped us repair our thrusters. I will see that your homestead is not molested."

Moreover, the Rd'dyggian captain left them fuel for the launch and restocked their medical supplies.

"I thank you." Firebrandt bowed low.

"You have saved my life and my cargo," said Arepno. "More importantly, you have saved my crew. If you need anything, call."

Roberts, Suki, and Firebrandt watched Arepno's launch ascend into the sky.

Firebrandt turned to Roberts. "Were you successful?"

"I gained access to four of our accounts. I isolated one and gave Lowry limited access. If she's still on our side, we've helped the crew."

"If not?" asked Suki.

"I've limited the damage she can do to us," said Roberts.

Firebrandt held Suki's hand. Suki reached out and took Roberts' new hand. The sky grew dark and the air cold. The three returned to their peaceful homestead.

Chapter Five

THE SETTLERS

Blossoms on fruit trees and fragrant green stalks growing beside the river heralded spring's arrival on Sufiro. Roberts made a picnic lunch and set it up outside. Firebrandt and Suki joined him. Suki's stomach had rounded into a slight bulge, revealing a promise not unlike that of the nearby fruit trees.

Firebrandt lifted a sandwich, took a bite and, like a good ship's captain, considered his crew's status. "It's been what? Three months Earth time since we activated our distress beacon and the only responses came from pirates looking to escape their pursuers followed by those same pursuers." He shook his head. "We need to face the fact that we may have to make a long-term life here." Firebrandt scowled. "I'm a space farer, not a homesteader. It would seem my mother wanted to humiliate me, either by sending me hat-in-hand to planets where I wouldn't be welcome or stranding me here." He raised his fist. "I will not be humbled. If we're stuck here, we're going to do it right and make the best life we can."

"We've made a good start." Suki pointed to the adobe enclosure attached to the ship and the water wheel. She lifted a potato crisp. "We have food aboard to feed fifty pirates for a year and there are only three of us ... well, soon to be four."

"Hmmph." Roberts grimaced. "True, our stores will last for a while and we've taken steps to make sure our preservation systems won't fail, but they won't last forever."

"We have just a few varieties of fruit we can eat on the local trees," noted Firebrandt. "While it looks like we can make a passable flour from the local reeds, it'll be a small amount."

"We could use the launch to explore more of the planet,"

suggested Suki. "Maybe we can find some more trees and plants to harvest."

Roberts held his stomach. "Sampling plants at random sounds like a bad idea. We shouldn't squander what fuel we have."

Firebrandt snorted a laugh at Roberts' discomfort. "I agree, we need to be careful about what we sample and we shouldn't take the launch too far, but I think exploring more of the continent is a good idea."

Once they finished lunch, they gathered supplies and readied the launch for a journey. Roberts performed a full systems check. Firebrandt turned off the emergency beacon. They didn't want any unwanted visitors to arrive at the homestead during their absence.

That evening, Firebrandt went to his quarters aboard the *Legacy* and packed some of the dwindling stockpile of tobacco into his pipe. Alone, he walked down to the river and smoked. He worried about his crew and hoped he'd done the right thing, trusting Lowry to help the crew. He also worried about their child and how long it would be before the child would know anyone aside from the planet's three adults.

Footfalls alerted the captain to another person's presence. Roberts stepped up and put his new hand on Firebrandt's shoulder. "What're you thinking about, Captain?"

"I grew up in Johannesburg and in a mining habitat on an asteroid. I came of age on spaceships. Making a home on a rural planet … raising a family…" Firebrandt lifted the pipe to his lips and took a puff. "This isn't what I imagined my life would become."

"We don't seem to have much choice." Roberts shrugged.

"We could keep the beacon going, stay put, hope for rescue," mused the captain. "Save the launch for emergencies." He crouched down and grabbed a handful of sand and let it pour through his fingers. "Is my thirst for adventure driving this expedition? Is it really the best thing for us?"

Roberts shifted from one foot to the other, then folded his arms, as though reaching a decision. "We're privateers. We're here. This is our world. Let's learn what we can. Who knows?

Maybe it's information we can sell or barter." He flashed an alarming, death's-head smile.

Firebrandt considered that as he continued to crouch and smoke the pipe.

"Whatever we find, we'll need to return. We'll reactivate the beacon then," said Roberts.

Firebrandt nodded. He finished his pipe, tamped out the spent tobacco, and stood. "You know, I'm looking forward to this adventure."

"So am I," said Roberts as the two returned to the homestead.

The next day, Suki and Roberts joined Firebrandt aboard the launch. The captain made a clean liftoff. As he looked down at the homestead, a tear came unbidden. The *Legacy* with its adobe addition and surrounding structures had come to feel like home and he found he would miss it, even if he was only leaving for a few days. Suki reached over from the adjacent seat and touched his arm. He sniffed, smiled, and took her hand. He felt like a fool. The captain squeezed Suki's hand, then checked the computer map. He turned toward the northwestern coast.

Within an hour, they reached an immense coastal mountain range. They followed the range along the continent's west coast until they came to a dazzling white cliff wall. Roberts scanned the rocks and found them to be limestone, similar to the white cliffs of Dover on Earth. After a while, the cliffs rolled into a plain and a river emptied into the ocean. Firebrandt followed the river back inland a hundred miles until they came to grassland dotted with bushes. He set the launch down.

The river was smaller than the Nuevo Rio Grande. Firebrandt had hoped the tall, wild grass would have grain-like properties, but Roberts shook his head when he tested it. "Like Earth grass, this has too much silica. It wouldn't necessarily kill us, but we'd have a difficult time digesting it."

Suki scanned their surroundings with binoculars. She lowered them and pointed. "There's a small herd of animals about two hundred yards that way. They seem really interested in some bushes over there."

The three walked through the grass, quiet as they could until they saw the animals well. They reminded Firebrandt of the kyonosaurs near the homestead, but these were fatter, rounder animals with long snouts. They ate berries from the bushes.

After a time, the animals moved toward the river, looking for water. Roberts scanned the berries, then plucked one, washed it, and ate it. His face pinched up. "Tart," he said, then he swallowed it down. "Not bad, though." He made notes in the handcomp's field journal.

They paused for lunch, then continued their journey to the southwest. There, they found a black sand desert. When Roberts tested the sand, it proved to be basalt. He pointed to some low hills in the distance. "Those were probably volcanoes long ago and the lava rock has eroded to sand over the centuries."

The three explorers flew over the desert, looking for cactus-like plants which might bear fruit. Instead, they found thorny bushes and flowering plants with spiny bases. "They remind me a little of mesquite and yucca," remarked Roberts.

"Anything we can eat?" asked the captain.

Roberts shook his head and they returned to the launch.

As the sun reached the horizon, they left the desert and entered a dense wetlands area. Suki checked the map. "I think this is where the Nuevo Rio Grande lets out into the ocean." They found a dry island in the delta to set the launch down and make camp.

Dense flowering plants that resembled a purple broccoli or cauliflower grew on the island. Roberts tested the plant. "It has much in common with Earth's cabbage family. I think there's a chance this could grow near our camp." Suki and Roberts harvested plants to sample in a few days.

That night as they ate dinner, a creature emerged from the river. At first, the creature reminded Firebrandt of a crocodile or an alligator. It had jaws much like those terrestrial animals and short legs. However, the animal kept emerging from the river until a second, third, fourth, and even a fifth pair of legs followed. Now the captain thought it resembled a python or an overgrown centipede and realized such a creature might need to eat quite a lot to sustain itself.

They gathered their supplies and moved inside the launch before the entire creature had emerged from the water. Inside, they finished their dinner then set up blankets between the seats for sleep. The three found themselves packed in, nice and cozy. Suki, in the middle, put her arms around the two men. "Our baby is fortunate."

"Fortunate? How?" Roberts lifted an eyebrow.

"She'll have two fathers to teach her how to survive on this rugged world."

Firebrandt turned as best as he could. "She? And since when do we know we're expecting a she?"

"I won't call our child 'it' and my great aunt always said a mother's first child is the same sex as the grandmother's first child."

Firebrandt looked over Suki to Roberts. "Is that true?"

Roberts shrugged.

Soon, the three fell asleep.

The next morning, the crocothon, as Firebrandt dubbed it, had vanished. They continued further along the coast until they spotted snow-capped mountains in the distance. The captain flew toward them, hoping to find spring runnoff that fed plants they could examine.

They landed in a grassy meadow near a forest. They loaded up packs with scanners and food and set out on foot. They found more trees with blossoms on them. They marked the location on the map, vowing to come back and investigate in a few months and see what fruit grew on them.

They continued until they found a stream flowing through the forest. Roberts stopped them and pointed across the river. There, a creature covered in some downy material that seemed not quite fur, but not quite feathers drank from the water. Its mouth was beaked like a bird, but it had paws and a long tail like a cat.

"It looks like a griffin from mythology," remarked Firebrandt.

The creature looked up at the words. It unfurled long wings and launched itself over the stream.

"Look at that beast's cranial capacity," exclaimed Roberts. "Do you suppose it's intelligent?"

The creature stalked toward them.

"I don't think we should hang around and find out." Suki

reached out and took both of their hands and they backed away from the animal, which continued to follow them.

"We mean you no harm," said Firebrandt.

The creature stopped, inclined its head, then reared back on its haunches and unleashed a fearsome scream.

Roberts drew his hepler just as the creature pounced. He fired and the creature fell dead just beyond them. He holstered the weapon and scanned the carcass. After a moment, he looked up and shrugged. "I don't know how it'll taste, but I think it's edible."

Aside from the fruit trees, the forest didn't prove lucrative. Firebrandt sampled a small portion of the griffin and said it tasted like gamy chicken.

"Even if it stays down, I don't know if I want to raise these things," commented the captain. "Still, I can think of some nice sauces that would make this much more palatable."

They settled in for a peaceful night. On the third day, they reached the southern tip of the continent they'd dubbed Nova Granada and worked their way up the east coast. There they found more promising berry bushes.

Just before sunset, they turned the launch westward and settled on a low hill for the night. Firebrandt stepped out and stretched stiff muscles. The sun lay on the horizon, casting long shadows. Orange light danced on the surface of a nearby river. He sighed and sat on the soft grass. He hugged his knees. Suki and Roberts came out and joined him.

He looked from one to the other. "A year ago, we scraped and scrounged for every job we could get just to survive. I was happy to attack ships to advance my career and earn recognition for my accomplishments. I'd been trained that dying for Earth was the greatest honor a man could have." He shook his head. "I never understood what dying for Earth meant until I came to a primitive planet on the galaxy's far side. I don't want to die for Earth, but I feel like I'd die to protect Sufiro."

Suki moved closer to him and put her arm around his shoulder. "I don't plan on you dying. I want you to be around for our daughter." She cast a pointed gaze at Roberts. "You too, Mister. Do I make myself clear?"

"Yes, ma'am," said Roberts with a chuckle and a half-hearted salute.

Firebrandt turned and gazed into Suki's eyes. "Have I ever told you about Captain Avery, the ancient seafarer from Earth known as the successful pirate?"

Suki shook her head.

"I think I may be more successful than him."

"How so?" asked Roberts.

"He had riches and no one caught him, but he always lived in fear." He looked from Suki to Roberts. "Me? I have a family and even if I never leave this world, I don't feel trapped. I feel free."

"Does this mean you've given up on being rescued?" asked Suki.

The captain shook his head. "Not at all. I just know that when I return to civilization, I want it to be on my terms. I want to show our child the galaxy and give her—or him—the opportunity to build a happy life."

"So, what's next, Captain?" asked Roberts.

"I think it's time to go home and turn the beacon back on. After that, we'll take life one day at a time."

Firebrandt, Roberts, and Suki returned home to find a family of fledermice in the homestead's chimney. Not certain what would be the best way to evict them, the captain hoped they would clear out before they needed the fireplace in the winter.

They found the native purple cauliflower to be digestible. Medical scanners showed it to be nutritious. Firebrandt couldn't quite identify the flavor, but Suki thought it reminded her of Brussels sprouts.

Roberts returned to the site of the plants and collected seeds. He returned and they dug a small garden patch. They consulted photos from their expedition to estimate how far apart to plant the vegetables.

Around midsummer as the fruit on the nearby trees started to ripen, Firebrandt returned to the south where they had found the other fruit trees so he could sample the fruit and bring back any that proved good to eat. He returned with three crates of fruit he'd picked.

The purple Sufiro cauliflower proved more abundant than they could eat. As autumn arrived and the air turned chill, Firebrandt decided to burn it in the fireplace. The pungent smoke drove off the fledermice and the captain smiled, pleased with himself. He experimented with cooking the cauliflower and found he liked it best boiled and served with dried meat from their stores.

Suki had the baby later that autumn. Firebrandt held Suki's hand and read poetry from the ship's library during her labor. The meter of the words helped Suki concentrate on breathing. Roberts worked the medical scanner and stood by, waiting for the baby to appear. Each time a contraction struck, Suki's face distorted with pain. Her face reddened and sweat streamed down her forehead.

Firebrandt wiped her face with a cool cloth. Roberts brought ice for her to chew. As each pain hit, she groaned at the captain and shuddered. After a long night, Suki grabbed Firebrandt's long, red hair and they yelled together as she pushed. He looked into her face to avoid seeing the blood at the other end of the table, even though he had no trouble with blood during battle. Certainly, the birthing experience proved as intense as any battle he'd experienced. Yet blood from his own beloved was too painful to look at.

When the baby cried, Firebrandt forced himself to look. "It's a girl," Roberts announced. Scans over the summer had proven Suki's prediction right, but Roberts made the age-old announcement anyway. He took the baby and cleaned her, wrapping her in linen from the crew bunks. Firebrandt sat down, his chest hurting. Suki had pulled out a large clump of chest hair.

Roberts brought the little girl to her parents. Suki took her and held the baby to her breast. Firebrandt dabbed the sweat from Suki's brow. "So," said Roberts. "What's her name?"

Firebrandt and Suki looked at each other. "She's a little bit of each of us," said Suki.

"Suki Firebrandt?" suggested the captain.

"Suki Carter Firebrandt," amended Suki.

"That's an awfully big name for someone so small." Roberts smiled. Unlike his usual smile, this one was warm and inviting.

As if responding to Roberts' good-natured comment, the baby let out a blood-curdling yell. "My," exclaimed Suki, shaken from her exhausted euphoria. "What a fiery temperament."

"Her name may be Suki Carter Firebrandt, but I think we'll call her Fire." The captain stroked his mustache as he stared transfixed at the baby girl.

Night fell and Sufiro slept. Inside, Roberts, Firebrandt, and Suki fell into their own peaceful slumber, awakened from time to time by cries from a fiery small one demanding attention.

A week after Fire's birth, Firebrandt and Roberts harvested the last of their first year's cauliflower under a gorgeous green-blue sky while Suki tended the baby indoors. Something flashed in the sky and Firebrandt tried to find the source. His gaze settled on a contrail. "Get the binoculars," he called to Roberts.

Roberts set his basket down and hustled to the homestead. He returned a moment later with the binoculars. Even fixated on the contrail, Firebrandt noticed his friend's limp. He frowned and took the binoculars, then focused on the object responsible for the contrail. A launch descended some distance from the homestead. Firebrandt passed the binoculars to Roberts.

"That's an old one," he said. "Human design, and she's been around for a while."

Both men had seen the design many times in their early days serving Earth aboard privateer vessels. Shaped like eggs, they were nicknamed "tumblers." Covered in heat shielding, they plummeted into an atmosphere, and landed on their broad ends so they could launch back into space. Marines making assault landings used them most, along with pirates making hit-and-run raids on outposts. Even through the binoculars, the craft's hull looked dark and worn, as though it had been through many descents.

"I don't like the looks of this," said Firebrandt. "I'd better go check it out. Get inside and arm yourself and Suki."

"Aye aye, sir," said Roberts.

Firebrandt watched him go and considered following, but decided he didn't have time to lose. He grabbed a walking stick from beside the door and set out down the river valley. Given the landing vessel, he could imagine pirates picking up their distress signal in a nearby system, then noticing it stopped. If he'd seen that and hadn't noticed the signal's return, he might well have investigated, hoping for profitable salvage. By all appearances, this launch came from Earth—not Rd'dyggia or Alpha Coma Berenices.

He found the launch sitting on its landing gear a little over two miles from the homestead. Streaks of heat damage obscured any paint or logos that might have once adorned the craft. He counted ten men and women milling around the craft's base. They wore old, worn but clean civilian clothes. These were not marines and probably not pirates. They studied their surroundings and talked among themselves. One pointed to the river. Another pointed to nearby fruit trees.

He decided to take a chance and stepped from the bushes, hands visible.

One man looked around at the others, then stepped forward. He had black hair and a thin mustache. "This is a surprise. We didn't expect to find anyone on this planet." Firebrandt estimated the man was around his age.

"My name is Ellison. My ship crashed here about eighteen months ago, Earth standard time." The captain decided not to reveal too much before he knew more about these people. Still, he held out his hand.

The man grasped it in a firm grip and shook. "My name is Espedie Raton. The Rd'dyggians have started taking applications from humans interested in starting a colony here." He looked back at those who accompanied him. "Our life on Earth … it wasn't much. We're looking for more."

Firebrandt nodded. The launch made sense now. A cheap tramp freighter would carry these to ferry cargo and passengers. A few such launches could carry enough people and supplies to start a small settlement. Encouraging the Rd'dyggian government to solicit settlement may have been Arepno's way of helping.

"The captain said scans indicated this was a good, fertile valley, well suited to our needs," said Raton.

"It is that," said Firebrandt. "Welcome to Sufiro."

"Sufiro?" asked Raton with a wry smile.

"That's right."

Raton narrowed his gaze. "So, is Ellison your only name?"

The captain decided to take a chance and tell the whole truth. "I'm Ellison Firebrandt."

Raton backed up a step and Firebrandt noticed the others fell silent and stared at him.

"The famous pirate who disappeared?"

Firebrandt smiled, but Raton did not seem reassured. "I was a privateer captain until I crashed. I've been surviving on ship's supplies and I've tried my hand at planting a crop of local vegetables."

"It sounds like your presence could be fortuitous. You could help us identify local plants we could use."

"Did you bring seeds from Earth?"

"We did, and a few animals." Raton smiled.

Firebrandt sensed no deceit from this man and it pleased him to see new, friendly faces, though he wondered why Raton trusted him so readily. "I've been marooned here with two members of our crew. We made a homestead at our crash site less than an hour's walk upriver. This whole valley is good for farming. You and your people would be welcome."

Raton went back to the others and huddled with them for a few minutes. The captain heard murmurs of interest and agreement. At last Raton strode to the launch, where a bored-looking man in a gray transport-service uniform sat on the step awaiting further instructions.

Raton spoke to him, then turned back to Firebrandt and beckoned a woman over. The settler introduced the woman as his wife, Carmen. "We want to see your homestead, Captain Firebrandt, and meet the others in your party. If all is as you say, we'll proceed with our plans."

"And if not?" Firebrandt narrowed his gaze.

"This is a big river," said Raton. "There are other rivers on this continent. There are other continents on the planet. We

can find another place to settle and we can defend ourselves."
Raton narrowed his gaze.

The captain nodded. Raton wasn't so trusting after all.
Firebrandt led the way back along the river to the grounded
Legacy. Sweat poured down the settler's faces after the walk
over rugged terrain. Despite the strenuous walk, Raton's eyes
flitted from the adobe structure to the garden surrounded by a
wooden fence.

Firebrandt went to the door and knocked. "It's the captain,
all's clear. I have guests." He opened the door. Inside, Roberts
and Suki stood with lowered sidearms. The captain nodded to
them and they set the weapons on a shelf. Firebrandt introduced
his guests and described their intentions as they dropped into
chairs at the table. Suki excused herself and returned with a
pitcher of water.

"It seems this valley provided succor to you and your
friends in a time of need," said Carmen. She lifted the glass of
water and took a drink.

Firebrandt lifted his eyebrow at the archaic word. "Yes, I
suppose you could say that."

"We come here from El Paso, on Earth. Espedie and I have
been living in a cargo container for the last five years." Carmen
shook her head. "Espedie made good money with his ... courier
service, but he never made enough to rent an apartment, no
matter how much we tried to save. We're looking for our own
place of succor in an uncaring galaxy."

The captain noted the pause when Carmen mentioned
Espedie's past employment. He suspected he had more in
common with the settler than he first imagined. Before he
could respond, a cry from the ship interrupted them. Roberts
excused himself and went to check on the baby.

"Do you have any experience with farming?" asked Suki.

Espedie took a sip of water, then nodded. "Many in our
party worked as laborers in Martian farm domes."

"We also have a few asteroid miners in our party," said
Carmen. "Maria Lopez worked the hydroponics facility on
Vesta."

"It sounds like we might be able to help each other after
all," said the captain.

Just then, Roberts returned with Fire. "She has a clean diaper, but I think it's feeding time." He handed her to Suki.

Suki lifted her blouse and the baby latched onto her breast.

"And who is this little one you neglected to tell us about?" asked Carmen.

"She's our daughter," said the captain. "We call her Fire."

"How did you hear about Sufiro?" asked Roberts.

"One of the asteroid miners, Roger Babst, has family in El Paso," explained Espedie. "He returns when he's off duty. He overheard the supervisors discussing this planet. The Rd'dyggians hoped to find some industrialists to develop it..."

Firebrandt could fill in the rest. The Rd'dyggians hadn't found the world appealing, but if humans settled, the Rd'dyggians could charge their own taxes and make a profit from the planet anyway. However, the planet was too far from the Earth Alliance to establish profitable factories. The *Legacy* hadn't detected anything to mine that didn't exist in abundance much closer to Earth. When Arepno had suggested opening the planet up to small farms, it must have proved a way for the Rd'dyggian government to cut their losses.

"We pooled our money," said Carmen, "and hired a tramp freighter. We bought some used farm equipment and prefabricated structures."

"We have camping gear." Espedie rubbed his arms. "But it seems like we picked the wrong time of year for a camp-out."

"It is late autumn," said the captain. "Invite your party to come here. Have dinner with us. There are crew bunks in the old ship. You can sleep warm and well."

"We won't impose upon you, Captain Firebrandt." Espedie waved his hands in protest.

Roberts grinned. "Please, be our guests. This has been a lonely planet. Our baby has been a welcome addition, but we appreciate new faces. We have plenty of food and even a local ale to sample."

Espedie smiled, then took a drink of the water. "All right, you've convinced me." He reached out and took Carmen's hand. "We'll accept your gracious invitation."

By that time, Raton and Carmen looked refreshed from their hike. They left to retrieve the others. Before nightfall, the launch dropped down outside the homestead and the people poured out. Roberts and Firebrandt prepared a meal of Sufiro cauliflower and broiled kyonosaur steaks. Over ale, Firebrandt told how he lost his crew and came to be marooned on Sufiro.

"Firebrandt sufrio grande miseria," said Raton after hearing the story. "Roberts and Suki, too. I'm sorry to hear your Ms. Lowry went to work for the admiral who stranded you."

"Sufrio?" It was Firebrandt's turn to ask.

"Suffered … the planet's name is so close to the Spanish word that I thought you knew. It seems fitting given what you've been through," explained Espedie.

A while later, Firebrandt, Roberts, and Suki assigned quarters to Raton's party. Once they had settled in, Roberts left the homestead and walked outside and joined Firebrandt who stared up at the stars. "It feels good to have people back on the ship," said the first mate. "I hadn't realized how much I missed that."

"Yes." Firebrandt turned and focused on the mud-colored wall. "But they will soon build their own houses. They will soon have their families." Firebrandt walked over to the fence enclosing the garden. "These settlers are just the first. Someday, farms will fill the valley—perhaps extending from the swamps and bayous in the south all the way to the northwest mountains." He looked toward the stars. "It was a nice planet while it was ours."

Roberts put his hand on Firebrandt's shoulder. "It still is a nice planet. It still is ours."

"But for how long?" The captain sighed. "How long will it stay out of Earth's hands now that people know about Sufiro?"

"Just a few months ago, you worried about our isolation. Now you're worried about the people joining us. Maybe you should make up your mind." Roberts released a hollow laugh.

"I have no desire to see this place ruined like every other planet man has tromped on. Sufiro is the home I didn't know I sought. Even if we return to space, I want Fire to know the planet." The captain blew out a sigh. "These people don't worry me. They're like us, tired and beaten people looking for solace. They can't abide what's happened to Earth any more than I can. But what happens when the others come?" Firebrandt looked at the ground and kicked the dust.

"The time has come," said Roberts, "to think about the shaping of a world." Roberts patted Firebrandt on the back and led him inside.

The next day, the settlers began work on their homesteads. They stayed with Firebrandt and Roberts while they built their houses. Elfrida Grimm had experience with electrical plants. She designed a more efficient water wheel with a wind back-up station. Everyone worked together to build an efficient power plant in a few weeks. Everybody in the community took turns making food for others. Carmen and Espedie enjoyed helping Firebrandt and Suki care for their daughter. Firebrandt caught Carmen whispering to Espedie about how she wanted a child of their own to raise in their new home.

The settlers brought a working EQ transmitter. Roberts asked for some time. Given that Firebrandt provided power, the request was granted without question. Roberts adapted some old algorithms and broke into the Alpha Coma network. He learned Kheir el-Din, Computer, and the rest of *Legacy's* crew who had not joined Alpha Coma's military had been remanded to Earth's authorities.

"It would seem Mr. El-Din is serving as first mate aboard the *Argo*," reported Roberts.

"A good ship," remarked Firebrandt. "We should send congratulations."

"Already seen to," said Roberts.

Over the winter's course, a small town grew along the river with Firebrandt's homestead on the rise above. The homesteaders erected silos and barns to collect the crops the homesteaders hoped to plant in the spring. The captain and Roberts claimed a parcel of farmland near the river. The town, now called Succor by all the settlers, stretched five miles south of Firebrandt's homestead, beyond the settler's original landing site. This gave everyone plenty of room. They all came to respect each other and value each other's privacy. The law of the land was simply that anyone could do what they wanted in their way as long as it didn't hurt anyone else.

They often met at Firebrandt's house for dinner. The settlers shared the captain's concern about the future. Firebrandt soon found himself respected and treated as the settlement's leader.

On one hand, he liked it. A part of him missed the status that came with being 'the captain.' And yet, he'd grown used to sharing the responsibility of decision making with Suki and Roberts. He was glad after the dinners finished and he could sit with just his two closest friends and discuss what decisions needed to be made and what they would need to do if more settlers arrived.

The recent construction unearthed many small burrowing creatures that resembled Earth's arthropods. As winter came on, those creatures sought new places to burrow for the cold season. Roberts found he had to be careful with what he left out in the kitchen. Fledermice were no longer his biggest concern. Instead ant-sized, scuttling crab-like creatures would get into the vegetables. He set out sticky tape to catch them.

One day, in the heart of winter, Firebrandt started a pleasant blaze in the fireplace. He sat down in an armchair he'd pulled from his cabin. Snow fell outside and all seemed peaceful. Suki walked in holding Fire. She sat on the couch and breastfed the baby. When finished, she laid out a blanket Carmen Raton had crocheted. The three dozed off together, warmed by the fire.

"What the hell is that?"

Suki's words stirred the captain from his nap. A bug that resembled an Earth cockroach with two curly antennae crawled along the blanket toward the baby. Suki knelt down and scooped it up, then stood and walked toward the door to throw it outside. Just as she reached down to grab the door handle, she yelped.

Firebrandt jumped up and joined her. The creature's antennae had unfurled and now penetrated Suki's skin. She cursed, but kept quiet to avoid waking the baby. Firebrandt grabbed the creature and extracted it from Suki's hand, tossed it to the ground and stomped on it. Its armored carapace made a loud crunch and it oozed a foul-smelling blue-green ichor.

As the day went on, Suki's eyes glazed over and her skin paled. She said she couldn't feed the baby. The captain fed the child from a bottle, then Firebrandt asked Roberts to analyze what was left of the bug near the door. The captain stroked his mustache as he watched Roberts limp off to his task. An hour later, Roberts returned, his face drained of color. He motioned for Firebrandt.

"How is she doing?" asked Roberts.

Firebrandt shook his head. "Not well."

"The baby?"

"The baby's just fine." The captain looked down at his feet.

Roberts sighed. "That bug, whatever it was, had traces of a toxin in it that could kill an army."

Firebrandt fell against the wall for support. "Then Suki and the baby?"

"The baby will be fine as long as the toxin didn't enter her system." Roberts' brow creased. "I wish there was an easy way to say this, but Suki's lucky she's still alive."

A tear trickled down Firebrandt's cheek. He sniffed and wiped it away as anger overtook grief. "She's in pain. Can't you find an antidote?"

Roberts shook his head and frowned. "Our only hope is for it to pass out of her system." The two men held each other for several moments. "Go to her, Ellison. She needs you."

"She needs you, too," said Firebrandt.

"The baby needs someone." Roberts choked back a sob.

That night, Firebrandt sat up with Suki, holding her hand. He fought back tears several times. When she slept, he didn't fight, but he kept quiet so as not to disturb her. A few minutes past midnight, Suki's eyes opened, she sat up in bed and screamed. Firebrandt ran to her. Her body didn't yield, as though every muscle had suddenly contracted, including her heart. Firebrandt grabbed her. She was still warm from fever and being under the blankets. "Suki!" he yelled.

Roberts ran into the room. He examined Suki, but there was nothing he could do. The baby began crying. Firebrandt yelled Suki's name again. The baby yelled in response. The captain turned to Roberts. "The baby," he said.

"Aye aye, sir." Roberts limped from the room to tend to the child.

Firebrandt held Suki's body for what seemed like hours, swaying back and forth. Roberts left him alone for a while. The captain wept until Roberts returned and pulled him loose from the body and escorted him back to one of the crew bunks. Roberts helped him in and covered him with a blue woolen blanket. Too tired to resist, he fell into a fitful slumber. Occasionally he awoke and cried into the pillow. He didn't leave the bed for twenty-six hours.

At last, the captain awoke too drained for tears. Clean clothes hung beside the bunk. He put them on and eased his feet into his boots. In the galley, Roberts rocked the baby in a cradle Maria Lopez had built. His face drawn and eyes red, he stood and brought some pastry to the captain. "How is she?" Firebrandt pointed to the cradle.

"She cries for her mother's milk, but I coax her into taking the bottle, sir," said Roberts. Without looking, he reached out and took a pastry.

"And her mother?" Firebrandt bit the pastry and swallowed it down without tasting it.

"I built a coffin from one of the storage lockers. I wasn't sure what kind of funeral you wanted for her."

"We never discussed it." Firebrandt shook his head. "For me, I guess I always expected to be buried in space. I guess all privateers do." He flashed a wistful smile despite the emotional pain. "Burning up in a decaying orbit around a distant planet always sounded like a beautiful ending to me." He sighed. "But that's not what she wanted. She loved this planet and wanted to stay here. That desire kept me from working harder to escape."

"We haven't set aside space for a cemetery in Succor." Roberts pursed his lips. "We can cremate her and scatter her ashes in the river so she can explore the planet. She'll be part of this planet forever."

Numb, Firebrandt nodded.

The next day, the settlers helped Firebrandt and Roberts stack wood. In the dead of winter, no flowers grew near the homestead, but Carmen, Roger, and Elfrida made colorful paper flowers. They dotted them around the stacked wood.

Espedie and Roberts carried the coffin from the ship. Reverently, they lifted Suki's body onto the wood. The captain held little Suki Firebrandt while Roberts lit the flame. The baby cried. A distant kyonosaur howled. The fire crackled. The wind carried the smoke and ash to the sky from whence Suki had come.

Chapter Six

NEW GRANADA

Another spring arrived, but the blossoms on the trees didn't lift Firebrandt's mood. Succor's farmers plowed fields and planted crops. Firebrandt and Roberts took turns watching the baby and taking lessons from the farmers. Maria Lopez and Espedie Raton gave them seeds from Earth along with fertilizers to help the crops grow.

As they turned over the earth, Firebrandt found two more arthropods like the one that had killed Suki. He ground each of them under his boot heel as though exacting a personal vengeance. Roberts found the strips of adhesive he used to capture the crab-like arthropods in the galley sufficed to keep all bugs out of the house if placed by the doors and windows. The deadly arthropods proved rare and they never caught another in the house.

One day while hoeing weeds, Firebrandt unearthed a third deadly arthropod. He lifted his foot to crush it, then stopped. He removed his glove and used it to scoop up the creature. He took it into the homestead.

Roberts emerged from Fire's room and held a finger to his lips. "I just got her to sleep."

Firebrandt nodded and motioned for Roberts to follow him to *Legacy's* science lab, where the captain dumped the arthropod into a plastic container. "Is there any chance we can eliminate these things?"

Roberts frowned as he knelt down and peered into the transparent container. "They're a real nuisance, aren't they?"

Emotions surged within the captain like magma under an active volcano. His eyes grew moist. He willed himself to remain calm as he answered. "They killed Suki." The words sounded more clipped and angry than Firebrandt intended.

Roberts stood upright and sighed. "I could engineer a nanococktail to target their reproductive systems. They would die off within a generation or two." He shook his head and frowned. "The problem is, we don't know exactly what place these creatures serve in the ecosystem. They could prey on insects that would damage the settlers' crops as well as our own."

The captain dropped into a chair and blew out a breath as though Roberts punched him in the gut. "If we destroy the creatures that killed Suki, we could condemn the colony to failure."

"I can't rule it out," said Roberts.

Firebrandt rubbed his eyes. "Can we afford to let someone else die?"

Roberts scowled and walked around the counter. He pulled up a chair and sat down. "They're not that common and they seem content to live underground." Roberts hesitated, as though trying to decide what to say next.

"I worry about children encountering these things." Firebrandt's breath caught. "I've already lost Suki. I can't afford to lose Fire."

Roberts took a deep breath and released it. "I can use the ship's sensors, scan for these things, see if I can better map their behavior."

Firebrandt nodded. "Do it."

As Roberts stood to leave, Firebrandt grabbed his arm.

"Is it a mistake to remain on Sufiro?"

Roberts sat down again and waited for the captain to say more.

"We have access to an EQ transmitter. We can signal Earth now. The admiralty might want to question me. They might send a ship…"

Roberts shook his head.

Firebrandt's brow creased. "You don't think they would?"

"Oh, they might send a ship for you, but what would that mean in the long run? Court of inquiry, no ship to command, dropped at some Earthside port to fend for you and your daughter. It would be your childhood story all over again."

"At least she wouldn't be in danger," snapped Firebrandt.

"From a bug that's only killed one person who didn't recognize the threat?"

"That bug killed Suki!" Firebrandt leapt to his feet and stalked to the far wall.

Silence filled the space after the outburst. "Yes, the bug killed your lover and a loyal crewmate. Yes, you're worried about your daughter, but I don't believe running back to Earth is the answer. You have people right here who need you."

Firebrandt snorted. "What, Espedie Raton? Elfrida Grimm? We need them more than they need us."

"Really?" Roberts lifted his eyebrows. "You attribute none of their success to your leadership and experience?" When the captain didn't answer, Roberts continued. "Besides, it's not just them. I'm talking about Fire and me. We need you and I think we'll be happiest if we stay put, even if it means occasionally reliving Suki's loss."

The baby's cries echoed through the ship's corridors.

"You'll excuse me." Roberts limped away and left Firebrandt to ponder his words.

Later that night, Firebrandt and Roberts walked in silence along the sandy riverbank while Fire slept at the homestead. Soft static from the handcomp monitoring the baby's room reassured them. The oblong moon sat high in the sky, casting a pale light over the landscape. "I've been thinking about Captain Avery," said Firebrandt, at last.

"The so-called successful pirate you mentioned when we explored the planet?"

"The same." Firebrandt looked to the stars. "He was successful until he returned home to England to sell his diamonds. The diamond merchants bought the treasure for a fraction of its worth, claiming they would turn him in to the authorities if he complained." The captain looked into his companion's eyes.

"You've decided to stay." Roberts narrowed his gaze.

Firebrandt nodded and put his arm around his friend's shoulder. The two turned and walked back toward the homestead. "Suki loved this world. I dreamed of being a successful privateer. I now understand the dreams aren't incompatible. Staying here fulfills both dreams."

"We're both successful, my friend," said Roberts. "We have the most beautiful daughter in the world."

"We?" Firebrandt raised his eyebrows.

"I would give my life for your daughter … for our daughter. I'm in this for the long haul."

The next day, Firebrandt moved out of his quarters aboard the ship and into the adobe structure he'd built with Suki and Roberts. The addition had windows and the morning sun streamed in, reminding him of the other homesteaders and his reason for being on the new world.

A few days later, as the captain rocked Fire to sleep, he considered his own parents. He remembered his last adventure with his father, when they had gone on a quest for an ancient Rd'dyggian treasure galleon in the home system. He smiled. The profits from that venture had allowed his father a comfortable retirement.

Then, Firebrandt's thoughts turned to his mother. The captain hated the Coma Navy and the tyranny it represented. He resented his mother for being a willing participant. Still, as Fire cooed on his lap, his gut clenched. Had there been different ways to handle the encounter with his mother? Was there a reality where he could have joined her and gotten to know her? Could she have taken them all back to Alpha Coma where Fire could have been raised comfortable and safe? Now the baby would never know her mother and she may never have an opportunity to be anything besides a farmer.

Firebrandt found Roberts in the galley the next morning dressed for work in the field. The former first lieutenant limped to the table holding a coffee carafe.

"Your limp is getting worse," remarked the captain. "What's going on?"

Roberts shook his head and for a moment Firebrandt thought he would refuse to answer. At last, he poured a cup of coffee and took a sip. "Arthritis. The bones in my feet are starting to decay."

The captain's stomach clenched again. Just as he'd convinced himself staying on Sufiro was the right answer, some other problem appeared. "We should contact the Rd'dyggians. They should be able to treat you."

Roberts held up his artificial hand. "Rd'dyggians may be able to replace limbs, but they don't suffer from joint inflammation. Their own bodies don't attack them like our bodies can. They have no treatment."

Firebrandt considered options as he poured coffee for himself. "Earth, then."

Roberts sighed. "We've discussed this. You shouldn't go back. I won't go back, either." He sipped his coffee and then sat back. "Arthritis is like cancer. It can be treated, even fixed if you can afford it. Unless you have more money squirreled away than you've told me about, my fate is sealed."

"You're in for a lot of pain, my friend." The captain sighed.

"Pain, I can tolerate," said Roberts. "Just promise me one thing."

"Name it."

"No matter how bad it gets, don't use my pain as an excuse to give up on this planet or on the settlers who rely on you. I'd have to work through this even under different circumstances."

"You've got my word," said Firebrandt.

Roberts had started investing their funds. Arthritis was an evasive, tricky disorder, but the captain vowed to do what he could for his friend. He took Roberts' hand and cherished the strength he found. Together, they could endure whatever this planet—this universe—would throw at them.

☠

Firebrandt finished his chores on a hot, clear day. He looked back at the river and thought a swim sounded like the perfect way to cool off. He returned to the *Legacy* where Roberts sat by a table. Fire crawled toward him making babbling noises. He picked her up. "How's my fiery one today?"

"She needs a diaper change," said Roberts. "I do believe it's your turn."

Firebrandt scowled.

"Do it and I'll make a pitcher of succorade." Roberts referred to a refreshing juice made from the citrus-like fruit that grew near the homestead. The horticulturist, Maria Lopez, had dubbed it succor fruit after the town's new name. Espedie Raton coined the term "succorade," enjoying the pun he made on a drink whose name combined the synonyms "succor" and "aid."

"You're on." The captain took Fire to the changing table in his room and removed the wet, cloth diaper and applied a clean, dry one. He would have preferred modern diapers but they didn't have a way to manufacture them or dispose of them.

Once he changed the diaper, Firebrandt placed her on the floor, then removed his sweaty clothes and donned swim trunks. He retrieved Fire from the floor. "We'll teach you to swim, soon, but I think we'll start with a more placid pool than the river."

He went outside and found Roberts pouring two glasses of succorade. Firebrandt returned his daughter to the grass and picked up the glass as four people strolled up the riverbank.

The captain recognized Espedie Raton, but not the three people with him.

Firebrandt glanced at Roberts. "I think we may need some more glasses."

Roberts nodded. "Should I arm myself?"

The captain scrutinized the strangers with Raton. "Wouldn't hurt, but conceal it. I don't think we're dealing with anyone dangerous here."

Roberts gave him a curt nod, picked up Fire, and entered the homestead.

Two of the people who approached with Espedie wore trim, business suits. The man wore gray while the woman wore a deep blue. The clothing seemed incongruous on people walking up the river. The third stranger seemed less out-of-place. She had short, mussed hair and wore black trousers, a gray shirt, and a khaki utility vest. Firebrandt placed her as captain or crew from a tramp freighter.

The woman in the blue suit stepped forward with her hand out. "I'm Mary Hill and this is Floyd McClintlock." She inclined her head toward the man in the gray suit who looked Firebrandt up and down with a disapproving gaze. "We're from

Earth, but we've heard this planet is open for colonization."
She then introduced the woman as Captain Sally Kowalski,
commanding the freighter that transported them.

Firebrandt stood and shook the woman's hand. "What
brings you to this world in particular?"

"Earth ... stifles us," said McClintlock. "Mary and I
sold hovers." He referred to hover cars, standard ground
transportation on most worlds. "You see we're from the Iowa
Citystate where we belong to the Church of the Creator's Word.
We don't work on Sunday, yet the government still taxed us for
working on days our business was closed."

Firebrandt blinked. He knew a little about the Church of the
Creator's Word. They had attempted to blend many doctrines
from Earth's Abrahamic religions. Roberts cleared his throat.
He stood in the doorway, holding some glasses on a tray.

"Maybe we should go inside where it's a little more
comfortable," suggested the captain. He led the way. Roberts
served them succorade while he strolled back to his room to
grab a shirt. Fire lay contended on a rug, occupied with some
homemade blocks and worn, plastic pieces salvaged from the
ship's engine.

Firebrandt returned a moment later and joined the group at
the table. "So, am I to understand you're here as missionaries?"
Firebrandt lifted an eyebrow.

"Not at all," said Hill. "We want to find a place to create
a township where we can raise our children without bad
influences."

"We want a place where government doesn't impose its
will on us," chimed in McClintlock. Hill shot him a glare.

Firebrandt knew many religious groups throughout history
had attempted to impose their will on people. Sometimes that
meant women hadn't been allowed to operate vehicles. Some
groups thought government-mandated vaccinations for the
community's health stifled freedom. He'd even heard of religious
groups insisting on public-mandated prayer, even in cases
when not all the society's members shared the same religion.
"So, what exactly are you looking for?" Firebrandt gestured to
the two new settlers. "Are you two looking to join us?"

"There are over five hundred of 'em aboard my ship," said

Captain Kowalski. "Plus, enough plascrete and prefab buildings to make a sizable township."

"We have horticulturists and biologists," said Hill. "We plan to farm what crops we can. We have a few animals from Earth. We understand you've identified a few local animals that could be domesticated as well."

"We also brought trade goods." McClintlock sipped the succorade. "I thought we could trade for some local goods, start a regular shipping run with Captain Kowalski here."

Firebrandt looked at the captain. "You wouldn't happen to have any tobacco, would you?" He couldn't help notice the disapproving looks from Hill and McClintlock.

The freighter captain pulled a pouch from her utility vest. "I have a source."

Firebrandt smiled. His own supply had dwindled. What's more, a regular trade route could mean medical supplies, both for Roberts and for Fire should the need arise. Perhaps such newcomers wouldn't be a bad thing. "All right, then. Why are you talking to me? Sufiro is a big planet. I can't prevent you from finding your own town site."

"They wanted to see you." Raton spoke up for the first time since the group had arrived. "They said they wanted to see the planetary governor."

"But I'm not..." Firebrandt started to protest, then stopped himself. He knew the current settlers looked up to him as a leader. In their small, close-knit community, that didn't mean much more than having a house big enough to host meetings from time to time and he did chair those meetings. As a ship's captain, he knew how to moderate discussion and he had no problem making decisions when he needed to, though he had gotten into the habit of consulting Roberts before he made the decision final. "Here's the deal," he said at last. "I think trade is a good thing. I think more people on the planet with more expertise would also be good." He shook his head. "We've been small enough to keep government informal and I like that."

"I have a simple proposal." Hill folded her hands on the table. "We establish our colony about sixty to seventy miles upriver from you. We'd be close enough to go back and forth via hover, but far enough apart we don't have to share most governing responsibilities. If we have a matter that requires input from both parties, we appoint a representative to meet and discuss our issues."

Roberts leaned in. "You've given this a lot of thought."

Hill blushed, then brushed a strand of dark hair from her face. "I actually had considered running for office back on Earth, but our business never raised sufficient funds for me to organize a campaign."

Firebrandt narrowed his gaze. It seemed a little too convenient for an ambitious person to come to a new world where they could make themselves the government. "So, what do you plan to call your colony?"

"We're from Iowa," said McClintlock. "We'll call the town New Des Moines."

Roberts groaned. If the newcomers noticed, they gave no indication.

"What do you call the continent?" asked Hill.

"We call it Nova Granada. Centuries ago, it was the Latin name for New Spain on Earth."

McClintlock chuckled. "That sounds a little intimidating. Can't we just call it New Granada?"

Firebrandt opened his arms. "Call it whatever'n hell you want to call it."

The baby fussed. Roberts walked over and retrieved her. "It's time for her afternoon bottle," he explained.

"May I hold her?" asked Mary. "My son, Rocky, is ten years old. It's been a while since I've had a chance to hold a baby."

Roberts looked to the captain, who nodded. The first mate brought the baby over, then went to the galley to prepare a bottle. Fire quieted in the woman's arms, and appeared fascinated by the new face.

"You have a good way with children," remarked Firebrandt.

"You seem surprised." McClintlock sat back and folded his arms. "I know our faith makes you uncomfortable. I can see it in your eyes, but we're parents and we want a good future for our kids. I learned about this planet on a news broadcast after I spent a horrible day selling hovers. The air was stifling. I had a hard time breathing, even though I knew my Dairtox injections were up to date. The idea of a planet not choked with people seemed like a fantasy." He reached over and tickled Fire under the chin. She laughed and reached for his hand. "I want to raise my children, Clyde and Anne, on a nice planet. I want them to have fields to run in, trees to climb. The only planet like that is Alpha Coma Berenices…"

"And no one from Earth can afford to go there," said Hill.

Roberts returned with the bottle and handed it to Hill. She adjusted Fire's position and the baby latched on.

"I don't see Alpha Coma as an 'ideal world.'" Firebrandt's voice turned cold.

"Neither do we." McClintlock shook his head. "It's a technocracy where everything is strictly regulated. We don't want that any more than we want to impose our religion on you."

"Of course, you'd be welcome to attend services." Hill slipped the words in.

Roberts rolled his eyes, but Firebrandt nodded. "I might well visit your church one day." He leaned forward. "But let me tell you something. I started my career as a privateer. I'm happy for you to come to Sufiro and improve your quality of life. However, the minute you try to take over, impose your will on people who don't want it, I have no problem taking the land from you." He pointed at McClintlock and then at Hill. "Believe me, I've faced far worse odds than five-hundred colonists from Earth."

"Mark my words." Hill met the captain's gaze. "It will never come to that."

"What we want isn't different from what you want." McClintlock flashed a nervous smile. "We want to raise our children as we see fit and give them an opportunity to be the best people they can be."

Firebrandt had no argument. He stood and the others followed suit. He reached out and shook their hands. "Welcome to Sufiro."

Spring and summer flew by for Ellison Firebrandt. Learning to farm and raising a daughter who changed almost daily absorbed his thoughts and energy. He fell into bed exhausted. Often, he fell asleep before he had a chance to look to his side and miss Suki.

Still, every time Fire reached a new milestone, he wished for Suki's presence to share their daughter's growth. He ached for Suki when Fire took her first step and spoke her first words. He wished Suki could stand beside him as the sun set on uniform, healthy fields. He would have appreciated Suki's help chasing away the fledermice who dug up seeds and young sprouts.

As it turned out, kyonosaurs preyed on fledermice. Roberts put out food from time to time to encourage a pair of the reptile-like animals to remain near the field. Once he did that, fledermice ceased to be a problem.

Summer's end meant harvest approached. Firebrandt and Roberts prepared their supplies. After dinner, the captain settled into an armchair, lit a pipe filled with tobacco purchased from Captain Kowalski, and opened a book on his handcomp. The book was the first published on Sufiro. Written by a journalist named Nicholas Johns, it told the story of the New Des Moines settlement. Firebrandt shook his head as he looked at the photos and read the descriptions of how the people from Iowa built a life in humanity's newest frontier. As he read about the harsh conditions, the captain thought there were far worse places in the galaxy to live than Sufiro.

He set his pipe aside and moved on to the next paragraph.

Next thing he knew, Roberts stood beside him, shaking him awake. The handcomp had fallen on the captain's chest and light now streamed in from outside. "I must have been more tired than I thought."

"A call just came in from Floyd McClintlock up in New Des Moines. He said an official from Alpha Coma Berenices III has arrived and wants to meet with you." Roberts handed Firebrandt a coffee cup.

The captain blinked as he sipped the coffee and tried to wake up enough to comprehend the words. "Alpha Coma? I thought the Iowans didn't like the Alpha Comans any more than we did. Why can't he just send this official packing without involving me? We have crops to harvest."

"This official is Admiral Barbara Firebrandt."

Firebrandt fought not to spit out the coffee he'd just sipped. Instead, he swallowed it down fast and began coughing. Roberts patted him on the back until the cough subsided. At last Firebrandt took a slower sip and steadied his nerves. "Admiral Barbara Firebrandt is here, on Sufiro, right now?"

"In the meeting hall at New Des Moines." Roberts sat down next to the captain. "I've taken the liberty of preparing the launch. It's outside the ship and ready for a flight. Do you want me to come with you? I'm sure Espedie and Carmen would be happy to watch Fire for the day."

Firebrandt shook his head. "No, I'll go on my own. I can't imagine this will take long." The captain finished his coffee, then strode into his old quarters aboard the ship. There he showered and changed into a more formal suit, including black trousers and a jacket with a white shirt. He examined himself in the mirror. His beard had filled out in the last year and his hair had lengthened. He tied the hair back and gave the beard a light trim so it didn't look so shaggy. He took a deep breath and decided he could delay no longer.

He stopped by the galley for breakfast and hugged his daughter. He noted Roberts' sympathetic gaze and wished Suki were there to lend support.

Firebrandt strode through the ship, down the steps into the adobe homestead and outside. He climbed in the launch, performed the preflight checks and lifted off. The flight upriver was pleasant enough. He passed two farms before the land became wild and uncultivated as the day he, Roberts, and Suki had crash landed. The greenery to either side, the river below, and the clear blue-green sky above did little to calm his nerves though.

New Des Moines sprouted from the landscape like an unexpected weed. Cultivated fields surrounded plascrete structures. Two prominent buildings dominated the village square: the Church of the Creator's Word and the town meeting hall. At the outskirts sat a small space port with a radio beacon. On the tarmac squatted a sleek, shiny Alpha Coma launch. Firebrandt landed alongside.

As he clambered from his craft, a carryhover pulled up and

Floyd McClintlock stepped out. "Roberts told me to expect you. I thought I'd give you a ride to the meeting hall."

"Much appreciated."

McClintlock seemed much more relaxed in his gingham shirt and denim pants than he had on that first day at the homestead. He still wore his blond hair short and he shaved, making Firebrandt feel all the scruffier.

They drove to the meeting hall. New Des Moines remained small enough not to require a full-time city staff. Still, the meeting hall had an office for a mayor and chambers for a city council. New Des Moines hadn't yet elected a mayor, but McClintlock told Firebrandt he'd find the admiral in the mayor's office. "It seemed the most appropriate place for a visiting dignitary."

Firebrandt snorted at the word dignitary. He exited the carryhover and walked up the steps. He had visited the meeting hall just once before, but he recognized the mayor's office because two Alpha Coman flag officers guarded the door. The captain tried to remember if those were the same two flag officers who had accompanied his mother two years ago when she had raided the *Legacy*.

Two years. Had it only been two years?

It felt like a lifetime.

Firebrandt looked at the two officers. "Ellison Firebrandt," he said. "I'm expected."

The two officers stepped aside. The captain knocked.

"Come." The voice had a razor edge.

Firebrandt entered and faced his mother. She looked much as he remembered. Steel gray hair pulled back in a ponytail, much like he wore his hair. Sharp, steel-gray eyes penetrated him. As a child he had thought she could read his mind with those eyes. As an adult, he thought she tried to read his soul. *Good luck with that,* he thought.

"It's good to see you, my son," she said.

The captain nodded. "Likewise." He strove not to choke on the word. Just then, he noticed a second person in the room. A nervous, young, science officer with thinning, blond hair. "What brings you to our fair planet?"

"I came because I have a proposition." The admiral clasped her hands behind her back. "This planet, Sufiro, is in

Rd'dyggian space. In principle, the Rd'dyggians will protect you in an emergency, but I suggest that it would be more advantageous for you to petition to be a protectorate of Alpha Coma Berenices."

Firebrandt clenched his teeth. "Why would Alpha Coma's protection be a benefit? You're farther away than Rd'dyggia."

The corner of the admiral's mouth lifted as she rounded the desk and took a seat facing the captain. "You're not Rd'dyggian. If military intervention were ever required, I suspect you'd be low priority for their navy. On the other hand, as a human world, we'd be more than happy to extend services to protect this world."

Without awaiting an invitation, Firebrandt sat and faced his mother and the unnamed scientist. "And exactly how does this world benefit Alpha Coma?"

At that, the admiral indicated the scientist. "Allow me to introduce Peter Stone, a science officer aboard my flagship, the *Diadem*. He scanned the planet and made some remarkable discoveries."

Stone swallowed and launched into an explanation. "This world has some rather odd geological anomalies. The structure resembles a planet formed closer to its host star than Mercury in Earth's system. We see evidence of crystalline structures rather similar to those worlds."

Firebrandt narrowed his gaze, fascinated despite his discomfort. "How do you think this happened?"

"I suspect Sufiro formed close to its star, then some catastrophic event threw it into a wider orbit. The same event may even have given Sufiro its small moon." Stone gave a dismissive shrug.

"Is there a danger? Is Sufiro's orbit stable?" Firebrandt leaned forward.

"It is now, at least as far as we can tell." Stone held up his hand. "The important part is how closely this world resembles phase-locked worlds where we find erdonium."

Erdonium. That explained the interest. Firebrandt pursed his lips. A complex crystalline metal, erdonium was a critical component in space vessel hulls. It formed on phase-locked planets near their suns—planets humans couldn't occupy without expensive gear. Although aliens from harsh environments didn't monopolize the erdonium trade, they could mine and sell it much cheaper than say humans or Rd'dyggians. "So, does this mean Sufiro has erdonium?"

Peter Stone wrung his hands. "We'd have to launch subsurface probes to tell for sure." His manner exuded a sleaziness the captain didn't trust.

Firebrandt nodded. "That's why you want us to be an Alpha Coma world. You can't fire subsurface rockets into our ground without Rd'dyggian permission."

"We'd still need your permission if this were an Alpha Coman world," interjected the admiral.

"We don't want, or need your help." Firebrandt shook his head.

"Really?" The admiral's eyes widened. "At the very least, I would have thought you'd be grateful to me."

"Grateful?" Firebrandt fought to avoid shouting the question. "Why should I be grateful to you?"

The admiral clenched her teeth. "Surely by now you've worked out that I had made sure you had a world to land on. I hoped you would start a new colony, stay out of trouble. I'm just as surprised as you that this little rock turned out to have some potential value."

"I don't want it to have value." Firebrandt sat back. "If it has value then more people will come and it'll become just another crowded human colony world. I want to stay off the radar."

"You're already on the radar." The admiral stood. "Colonists have found this place and more people will arrive. At some point, someone else will reach the same conclusion we have. True, you might put it off ten years or twenty, but mark my words, it will happen."

"That's ten or twenty more years than you're offering." Firebrandt stood and matched his mother's gaze. "As for being grateful, coming here cost me the person I love most."

Admiral Barbara Firebrandt had the decency to look shamed for just a moment. "Yet, I don't see you leaving. This would give you that opportunity. You could even come to Alpha Coma and raise your daughter there. You could send her to the best schools."

The captain spared just a moment to wonder who had told his mother she had a granddaughter. It could have been anyone including Floyd McClintlock or Mary Hill. It didn't matter. "What happened to my crew?"

She cast him a sidelong glance as though she suspected he already knew the answer. "Your boatswain came to work for me. She even came to this world, so I'm surprised she didn't find you. Or did she?" She studied Firebrandt for a moment.

The captain struggled not to reveal any thoughts.

"The rest served their time and went home to Earth, as I promised."

Ellison Firebrandt walked around the chair and reined in his emotions. He grabbed the chair's back and looked up, facing his mother again. "You abandoned me as a child. Why should I believe you would have my back now if I gave you what you wanted?"

"Because I love you."

"I don't know if I believe that."

For just a moment, Firebrandt recognized hurt in his mother's eyes. For just a moment, he regretted the pain he believed he caused. Then her gaze hardened and the calculating officer and politician returned. "I don't have to go through you. Hill and McClintlock will listen to Alpha Coman money and influence."

Firebrandt shook his head. "If you didn't have to go through me, why am I here? Until today, you didn't know for certain whether I was alive or dead. It's time for me to harvest my crops. I've been away from my family too long."

With that, Firebrandt turned on his heel and strode from the office.

Part II: Tejo

The Years 2948-2952 Earth Standard Calendar

"Howbeit, he sent word unto the Emperors through their ambassadors that in no wise would he pay the tribute, nor would go to Rome for the sake of obeying their decree, but rather for the sake of demanding from them what they had by judicial sentence decreed to demand from him."

—Geoffrey of Monmouth, *The History of the Kings of Britain*, Book IX, Chapter 20

Chapter Seven

DISCOVERY

Espedie and Carmen Raton's son, Manuel, lay atop a blanket looking up at the stars. Next to him was his best friend and the most beautiful woman he knew, Suki Carter Firebrandt, daughter of Ellison Firebrandt and Carter Roberts. Manuel knew she once had a mother named Suki Mori, but that Suki's name had all but vanished into the past, recalled on those rare occasions when the older generation told stories of bygone days. The woman next to him called herself Fire.

A low-power forcefield enclosed them in a tent-like bubble. It kept fledermice and other pests away. Over the years, kyonosaurs had learned to avoid humans. Arthropods like the one which killed the legendary Suki only appeared during the spring planting, and even then it seemed as though the population diminished over time.

Manuel reached out and took Fire's hand. She smiled and kissed his forehead. She snuggled a little closer and looked skyward again.

"What do you think about when you look at the stars, Fogacita?" His nickname for her meant "little campfire." The nickname captured his feelings about her—warmth with a hint of danger.

"I see a universe full to the brim with possibility," she said. "I see a universe I want to explore."

He grunted. "I see a lot of cold, empty space."

"There are also a lot of stars."

"And those stars have planets with people who aren't so nice."

She squeezed his hand. "Some people are nice."

He snorted. "I'm glad my parents came to Sufiro. If people aren't nice here, you can find another place to live and ignore them."

She giggled. "Don't you want to see the galaxy's sights? The Trapezium in Orion, the Great Cathedral in Shangri La, the Tharsis Volcanoes?"

He turned and gazed into her deep, brown eyes. "If I could, I'd follow you anywhere, Fogacita." As he spoke the words, his stomach churned. Her father had arranged passage to Earth aboard a freighter scheduled to arrive within the next two or three days. If he could, he would follow her, but his parents didn't have the money to send him to Earth and, while he wouldn't mind visiting, he didn't really want to live there. He liked Sufiro and wished Fire wanted to stay as much as he did. "There's lots to explore right here on this planet." He'd spoken the words before. He didn't expect them to persuade her.

"I know," she said. "I'll return one day and explore them with you."

His heart soared at the words, even though he knew he should hold his feelings at bay. He knew Fire well enough to know that if she returned, it would be just a short visit before she flew off somewhere else. But, maybe he'd be able to follow then, just for a while.

A bright object cut a path across the twinkling star field. Fire caught her breath. "Do you suppose that's the freighter *Nantucket* entering orbit?"

"It could be." He sighed the words. "I'd hoped we would have a few more days before you flew off to Earth."

"My poor Manuel." She placed her hand on his chest and unbuttoned his shirt. "Even if the ship has just arrived, it's not like I'll be leaving tomorrow and it's not like I'll never be back."

Her warm hand drifted down to his abdomen. It comforted him, like a hot water bottle. Her hand drifted even lower and for a time, Manuel didn't think about how much he would miss Fire.

Later that night, Fire crept into the homestead. Her father sat in an easy chair, his head back and snoring. On his lap, sat a handcomp with a novel he had been reading. As she latched the door, he jolted awake.

"Ah, there you are," he said.

She cringed and thought he might ask where she had been.

"We received a call from the freighter *Nantucket*. They've arrived and have started making preparations for their business here."

"Sounds great." It meant the time had come to pack up and say proper good-byes to her friends before she left. She looked around the room and realized she would miss the house she grew up in.

"Apparently," continued her dad, "the *Nantucket* has a commission to send some probes down to the other major continent."

"After all these years?" Fire's eyebrows came together. "The Rd'dyggians gave them permission?"

"So they say." Ellison Firebrandt stood from the chair and stretched his back. "We've been invited aboard to see the operation tomorrow. Do you want to come along?"

"I wouldn't miss it."

The captain walked over and embraced his daughter and kissed her on the head. "That's my girl." He strode toward his room. "We'll depart at sunrise."

Fire groaned. She climbed the stairs, into the old ship. She had claimed her dad's former cabin for her own. She liked the way he'd decorated the room and the solid walls gave her privacy. She took a shower and then dropped into bed. She looked over at a smiling hologram of her mother and said "good night" just before she fell into a solid slumber.

Her alarm sounded far too early the next morning.

She dressed and went to the galley where Roberts had made breakfast. She hugged her other dad. He smiled and groaned as he sat at the table. Roberts had arthritis and despite treatments imported by family friends such as Captain Kheir el-Din, his joints had worsened. It amazed her he could still move around as well as he did. He'd long ago given up work in the fields, leaving that to Firebrandt and hired hands, but he still did chores around the homestead.

Firebrandt arrived a few minutes later, dressed in the

black trousers and coat he wore when he captained the *Legacy*. Working the fields kept him trim and the uniform still fit well. Fire hoped she would age as well as her dad, but a lump formed in her throat as she wondered what her mom would look like now.

They finished breakfast and went to the launch. "I've completed all the pre-flight checks," said Roberts. "You should be good to go."

"Thank you, my friend." Firebrandt clasped Roberts' hands, then led his daughter into the launch. Fire strapped herself in as her father confirmed the launch's readings. A few minutes later, Roberts signaled he had returned to *Legacy* and they were cleared for departure.

Fire's pulse quickened as her father fired the thrusters and they bolted skyward. Gravity pulled her into the seat and her eyes watered, but she forced herself to look forward. Firebrandt had only taken his daughter to space once before for her sixteenth birthday. Sufficient fuel to achieve orbit was expensive. Still, she never forgot the first time she had looked down on Sufiro's blue-green waters and cloud-strewn continents from space.

Once they reached orbital velocity, Firebrandt throttled back the launch and they took a turn around the planet. Half an hour after launch, the captain pointed. "There she is."

Fire had to squint to see the black star vessel against the black backdrop of space. After a few minutes, sunlight glinted from the hull so she could make it out more easily. "It resembles the *Legacy* from here."

Her father grunted. "I think the *Nantucket* may be the same class ship. They were popular with a number of companies and private ship owners. The Mao Corporation used to buy them for cargo ships."

"The *Legacy's* armed. Do these freighters have guns as well?"

"They do indeed." Captain Firebrandt laughed. "Remember what I used to do for a living. Ships like the *Nantucket* need to be able to defend themselves. I doubt she's as heavily armed as the *Legacy*, though. I upgraded my ship's guns a few times over the years when money permitted."

Even though she grew up aboard a grounded privateer vessel and occupied her father's quarters, Fire still had a hard time picturing her dads as vicious pirates. She smiled at the thought of her dad with an eyepatch and a tricorn hat. The idea of Roberts hobbling along with a peg leg seemed a little too likely, though.

At last they came alongside the *Nantucket*. A woman signaled and gave them docking instructions. People sometimes used the word 'mating' to refer to one ship attaching itself to another. Fire thought the process seemed much gentler and less frenetic than mating. It was more like a gentle kiss.

They unstrapped their harnesses, went to the airlock and opened the hatch. A young woman in a crisp, tan corporate uniform greeted them. A simple black patch with a golden sun adorned her upper arm. Above it blazed the word, 'Mao.' "Captain Ellis has invited you up to the command deck. I would be happy to escort you."

Fire quirked an eyebrow at the captain's surname, so similar to her father's given name.

"Please lead the way," said Firebrandt, even though the corridor beyond the airlock proved similar enough to the *Legacy*, Fire knew they could find their own way.

The woman led them to the command deck in silence. Captain Ellis stood next to the wheel console, hands on hips and stocky legs set wide. He wore a blue uniform, like the rest of the bridge crew and not the tan of the deckhand who met them. Cut short in the Navy style, his auburn hair somehow looked as though it blew in an unseen wind. His long mustache gave the impression he scowled. He examined the readouts in the holographic tank at the command deck's bow.

Their escort cleared her throat and Ellis turned. Fire's breath caught. The captain wasn't much older than she was. He held out a beefy hand to Firebrandt. "Captain Jerome Mycroft Ellis, commanding the *Nantucket*."

"Captain Ellison Firebrandt, retired." He inclined his head toward Fire. "This is my daughter Suki Firebrandt. She'll be your passenger when you return to Earth."

The captain took her hand in a self-assured grasp. He smiled, revealing dimples on either side of the long mustache and Fire's knees threatened to give way. "Mycroft?" She arched an eyebrow. "I take it your parents were Arthur Conan Doyle fans."

"It's an old family name." The captain turned toward a woman at the auxiliary command station. "This is my first officer, Leila Pfister." She nodded to the new arrivals. The captain addressed her directly. "Ms. Pfister, please have Mr. Stone meet us in my cabin."

Fire noticed her father's creased forehead and brief frown, as though he recognized a name but couldn't quite place it.

Ellis turned to face Firebrandt and Fire again. "Would you care to accompany me? I'll show you what we plan to do and make sure the plans meet with your approval." The way he said it didn't sound like he needed her father's approval at all, but treated this as a courtesy.

The captain led the way off the command deck and down the corridor. As they reached a junction, a young man whipped around the corner and rebounded off the captain. He took several steps backward and flushed red. Unlike the crew, he wore a yellow shirt and black trousers. Fire estimated the young man was a little younger than her, maybe Manuel's age, but he seemed much spindlier and didn't carry himself with Manuel's self-assurance.

"Watch where you're going, son," said the captain, even though he was, at most, old enough to be the boy's older brother.

"Yes, sir." The boy trembled

The captain smiled and his dimples appeared again. "Mr. Stone, I would like you to meet my guests, Captain Ellison Firebrandt and his daughter, Suki." The captain turned to face Fire and her dad. "This is Samuel Stone. His father is the geologist who put this mission together."

"Pleased to meet you both." He held out his hand. "You can call me Sam."

Sam's hand reminded Fire of clammy fish from the Nuevo Rio Grande. She struggled to maintain a pleasant expression.

The captain dismissed the boy with a nod and then continued along to his cabin. "I'm sure someone on the command deck told him I had left. He likes to watch the operations, but I don't allow passengers on deck during maneuvers." He must have referred to her father's docking. She doubted the *Nantucket* did much actual maneuvering during the operation. It just needed to maintain station while her father docked the launch.

When they reached the captain's door, a short, bald man in a business suit met them in the corridor. He reminded Fire of a potato. Her father narrowed his gaze. "Peter Stone?" he said. "From the Alpha Coma Berenices Navy?"

"Formerly of the Alpha Coma Berenices Navy," corrected the potato man in a grating, high-pitched voice. "I left almost fifteen years ago to start my own geological consultation company. I've made many people quite rich over the last decade and a half."

Fire detected something unspoken in Peter Stone's words. He'd made many people rich and now it was his turn.

Captain Ellis looked from Firebrandt to Stone. "I gather you two have already met."

"We have." Firebrandt faced his daughter. "Mr. Stone came to Sufiro with … your grandmother a number of years ago. He had a theory there might be erdonium deposits in No-man's Land." He referred to the large continent opposite New Granada. It earned its name from the hard rock and scrubby vegetation that dominated the land mass and made it unsuitable for agriculture. Fire knew her dad had no love for her grandmother. She had never met Barbara Firebrandt and based on her father's stories, she never wanted to. The admiral's interest in the continent may have also contributed to its unflattering moniker.

Ellis led Firebrandt, Fire, and Stone into his cabin. Fire cast a cursory glance around the room. It unnerved her how similar this room was to her own room on the planet below. Her father had paneled his cabin in wood and placed stained glass over the windows, but otherwise, the rooms were almost identical.

Ellis brought up a holographic globe of Sufiro and zoomed in on No-man's Land. The continent wasn't entirely uninhabited. A few evangelical Christians fled religious persecution in certain sectors of the Gaean Alliance and settled a sandbar along the continent's west coast. Lush vegetation had taken hold near the ocean, much like Florida on Earth. The settlers called their town Roanoake.

"Do you mind if I smoke?" Ellis opened a wooden box on his desk and retrieved a cigar.

"As long as I may as well." Firebrandt retrieved his pipe from his pocket.

Although she liked the smell of her father's pipe, Fire wrinkled her nose. Together in the small space, the cigar and pipe smoke almost overwhelmed her. Still, she decided to stick it out while Ellis explained the plans.

"We want to fire four subsurface probes into the continent at these spots." Ellis pointed at the holographic globe with his cigar. "They're pinpoint probes and they'll be well away from any settlements."

"What happens if one goes astray?" asked Firebrandt.

"I'll shoot it down myself," said Ellis.

Firebrandt smoked his pipe for a moment, considering that. "And what if I don't give my consent?"

Ellis pursed his lips around the cigar. "We're here with the Rd'dyggians' blessing," he said at last. "If we don't see this through, I'm sure they'll want you to explain your reasons for denying the probe."

"If I refuse this test, rest assured I'm perfectly capable of providing reasons that will satisfy the Rd'dyggian high command." Firebrandt faced Stone. "So, what do you get out of this? Is this just a way for Alpha Coma Berenices to lay claim to Sufiro after all these years?"

"You're well off the galactic net here, so you may not have heard your mother is long dead." Peter Stone spoke the words with surprising bluntness. Fire searched her dad's face for a reaction, but saw none. "No, I'm here on the Mao Corporation's behalf. I brought them my hypotheses and they wanted to learn more."

"Discovering a mineral is not the same as establishing a claim." Firebrandt took a puff from his pipe. "On most worlds within the Gaean Alliance and the Confederation of Homeworlds, you must take possession to claim mining rights."

"I intend to do just that." Stone smirked. "My hope is to return to Sufiro with you and recruit people to help me explore and lay claim to any erdonium deposits we find."

Fire's brow furrowed. "So, what does Mao Corporation get from this deal?"

Ellis's charming smile reappeared. "By contract, Mao will get fifty percent of Mr. Stone's claims."

Fire strolled around to the captain's desk. An old, brown map of an island hung on the wall. The legend read Nantucket. Fire wondered if he'd posted the map because the island had the same name as the ship, or if it held a deeper significance for him.

Her father folded his arms. "You've been convinced there's erdonium under No-Man's Land for almost twenty years. What if you're wrong?"

"I admit it's a high-stakes game." Stone's grin was more shark-like than charming. "I'm ready to bet I'm right and we can get at the erdonium. If so, I could become a wealthy man." He walked over to Firebrandt and put his hand on his shoulder. "It could bring good fortune to many people on Sufiro, too. This time it's not for Alpha Coma's benefit. It's for Sufiro's."

"And yours, apparently." Fire flashed a smile.

Stone didn't respond to that.

Ellis looked from Stone to Firebrandt. "Do we have your permission to see if Mr. Stone is correct?"

"All right, I'm game," said Firebrandt.

Ellis left his cigar on an ashtray on the desk. Firebrandt checked to make sure his pipe had gone out and then stuffed it in his pocket. The four strode to the *Nantucket's* command deck.

When they arrived, Leila Pfister acknowledged them. "We're ready to launch the probes." The holo display's glow enhanced her angular features.

Fire scanned the deck while her father, Captain Ellis, and Peter Stone reviewed the details of the probe's targeting solution. She'd been on *Legacy's* command deck many times and it was strange to see such a similar room so populated with people. Computer consoles sounded alerts and notifications.

Sam Stone stood off to the side, taking everything in. Fire motioned for him to come forward. She pointed at the holographic display. The *Nantucket's* orbit carried it over the planet's night side. She explained that the dark landmass was called No-man's Land.

"It looks weird," said Sam. "Most planets I've seen have pinpricks of lights where the cities are."

"There are no cities in No-man's Land except along the coast." Fire shrugged.

"My dad wants to change that. He thinks there's erdonium there."

"So I've heard."

At the front of the command deck, Captain Ellis, Peter Stone, and her father broke from their huddle. The captain pointed to the gunner's rigs. "Launch probes one and two."

On the screen, two arcs appeared, connecting the *Nantucket's* bow to the planet below. They showed the course of the first two probes.

"Probes on target, no deviation," reported Ms. Pfister.

"Excellent." Ellis turned around again. "Fire probes three and four."

Two more arcs appeared in the holographic tank showing the probes' courses.

"Probes one and two have penetrated the surface. Probe one is 250 meters under the surface. Probe two made it to 375 meters." Pfister's fingers danced over her console. The hologram zoomed in closer to the continent, showing the first probes' impact sites. "Probes three and four have now penetrated the surface. We should have probe telemetry analyzed in a few minutes."

"What do surface scans show?" Peter Stone walked around and stared over the first officer's shoulder. Fire decided if she were Ms. Pfister, she would smack the pushy bastard.

"All we see are common rocks—feldspars, basalts, and so forth—typical of any terrestrial planet in the galaxy," reported the first officer.

Ellis beckoned Stone away from the console. Fire decided she liked the captain just a little more because of that. The captain looked around at his guests. "May I offer you some coffee while we're waiting?"

Firebrandt nodded. "I'll take some," said Fire. Peter and Sam Stone declined.

Ellis stepped over to a dispenser unit and retrieved three cups of coffee. He handed one to Fire, then another to her dad. He took the third to Leila Pfister. Another reason to like this captain. He considered others before himself.

Pfister sipped her coffee and smiled at the captain. Fire's teeth clenched. Was this jealousy? She sipped her coffee and forced herself to relax.

"We're getting telemetry from the probes now," reported the first officer.

"Put it on the main display," said the captain.

"Well, that's interesting." Peter Stone stepped toward the display.

Sam walked up to his father. "What? What do you see?"

"There's a surprising quartz deficit given the amount of basaltic rock and granite on the surface." Peter Stone rubbed his chin.

Sam's shoulders slumped, but his father gave him a hardy pat on the back. "Buck up lad, this is just what we expect."

Pfister turned back to the console and grinned as she expanded the scan radius. She shook her head and whistled, then displayed the results in the holographic viewer. Ellison Firebrandt's gray eyes widened. Fire set her coffee down on a console. "Is that even possible?"

Peter Stone broke out in a wide grin that bordered on a leer. "Would you please save these results to my personal directory? I'll need them for the operation's next phase."

Fire looked back at the holographic display. Underneath No-man's Land lay sheets of erdonium. The metal tended to form on planets close to their suns. While the metal could be manufactured starting at the molecular level, it had always been significantly cheaper to buy it from those who mined it.

Captain Ellis stepped up to Peter Stone. "Congratulations. It seems you were right after all."

Ellison Firebrandt gulped his coffee, then approached Stone and Ellis. "I would like a word … in private."

"We can go to my quarters." The captain led the way. Stone and Firebrandt followed. Fire trailed behind, then looked over her shoulder to see if Sam followed. His gaze remained transfixed by the holographic display. She saw no reason to pull him away and hurried after her father.

When they reached the captain's cabin, Ellis invited everyone to sit. The captain sat behind the desk. Stone took the seat opposite the captain. Firebrandt sat on a couch facing both men. Fire sat beside him.

Firebrandt folded his hands and looked at the deck as he began. "Congratulations, Mr. Stone. This is a big discovery." He looked up and met the geologist's gleeful gaze. "I advise you to tread carefully in the claim process."

Stone's brow furrowed. "Of course, I intend to use best mining practices. I won't unleash a torrent of particulates and pollutants into the atmosphere like they did in the early industrial days on Earth, if that's what concerns you."

"I'm glad to hear it." Firebrandt sat back and removed his pipe from his pocket, but he didn't light it. He just looked at it as though the object helped him focus his thoughts. "Discoveries of this magnitude attract attention. Many people with their own agendas will come, hoping for their share of this discovery."

If possible, Stone's grin widened. "I'm counting on it, sir."

Firebrandt looked up, gaze narrowed. "Those same people will insist on certain ways of doing business. Those business practices ruined the lives of many people who found their way to Sufiro. However, there are people on the planet who can help you build a business that's fair for all."

"I trust you'll introduce me to those people." Stone tilted his head.

"Why not come down to the planet with us tonight?" Fire interjected. "You can meet Espedie Raton and his family."

Firebrandt turned and quirked an eyebrow at his daughter.

"Can you think of anyone else who can both organize people and understands the issues you're talking about?"

"I suppose not," Firebrandt lifted the pipe to his lips for just a moment, "but we should ask him first."

"Ship's communications are at your disposal." Ellis looked from Fire to Stone. "We will need to arrange a landing point for your equipment."

"If he's willing, Espedie will be a good resource to help you make those arrangements," affirmed Firebrandt. "As Fire says, he would be a good person to help you put together a team for the expedition."

"As I understand, these arrangements are likely to take a few days." Fire flashed the captain what she hoped was a charming smile. "Perhaps you would care to join us as well, Captain Ellis. You could have dinner with us tonight and then help make plans tomorrow."

Firebrandt narrowed his gaze. "Let's start by talking to Espedie."

"Presuming these plans fall into place, I can contribute to the meal," said Ellis. "My cook makes a delightful quohog chowder."

Fire leaned forward. "What's a quohog?"

"They're a type of clam. Like me, they're from Nantucket."

"I wondered." Fire grinned then blushed under her father's scrutiny.

"I think you'd better take me to your communication's station so we can make arrangements." Firebrandt returned the unsmoked pipe to his pocket.

Stone stood. "If you'll excuse me, I need to pack and transfer data onto my handcomp. Let me know the plans when they're arranged." He left the cabin as Firebrandt, Fire, and Ellis stood.

Ellis turned to Firebrandt. "Is it true you were once a pirate?"

Firebrandt scowled. "I was a privateer."

Ellis laughed. "If I come down to the planet, promise to tell me some stories from those days."

Firebrandt sighed but smiled and clapped Ellis on the shoulder. "It's a deal."

Chapter Eight

SEDUCTION

Manuel Raton hopped into the carryhover's passenger seat. His father started the motor and they drove to the landing pad just east of Firebrandt's homestead. Manuel's father had said they would have guests, a geologist named Peter Stone and his son, Sam. This Sam was about the same age as Manuel. He didn't quite know how he felt about that.

For the last four years, he'd attended school in New Des Moines. There had been several kids his age there, but when the school day ended, he had been able to leave them behind and return to Succor where he had been the oldest boy and son of a community leader. He had recently graduated, and with Fire leaving, he would be the oldest of the first generation born on Sufiro living in Succor. He knew kyonosaur packs had leaders the animal specialists called alphas. He often considered himself a kind of an alpha. Another boy his age in his territory seemed like a challenge in the making.

They pulled up to the landing pad and found Roberts waiting. Espedie nodded to Firebrandt's first mate. Roberts greeted the two new arrivals in turn. It still seemed a little strange for the older generation to greet him as an equal, but he liked it. Manuel gave him a nod.

Legacy's launch came into view followed a moment later by a bright blue Mao Corporation launch. The two small landing vessels sat down side by side on the pad. The door on *Legacy's* launch opened and Fire emerged. Manuel imagined himself striding over, taking her in his arms, and giving her a big, romantic kiss that would make her want to stay with him forever. In reality, he knew if he followed through with the

110

fantasy, she would kiss him back, they would both blush and she would still leave aboard the *Nantucket*.

What actually happened was that Fire and Manuel gawked at each other while people emerged from the landing craft. One was stocky in a blue uniform with gold epaulets and sporting a mustache that rivaled his father's. Manuel gathered the stocky officer must be the ship's captain. Fire stole glances at the young captain from time to time and he wondered what that meant. A bald man around his father's age emerged next, wearing a business suit. That must be the geologist. A teen, who must be the geologist's son, followed.

Espedie and Roberts stepped forward and introduced themselves. Listening to the conversation, Manuel realized he had been correct in his assessments. Taking the lead from the others, Manuel walked up to the other teen and held out his hand. "I'm Manuel."

The teen looked up from his handcomp and sniffed. He gave Manuel's hand a half-hearted shake. "Sam Stone, pleasure to meet you." Despite the words, Manuel didn't sense much pleasure from Sam.

One of Captain Ellis's crewmembers pushed a hover cart with the Stones' luggage. Espedie directed them to load it in the carryhover's bed. "Carmen's getting a room ready for you and your son," said Espedie to the geologist.

"I hope it's no trouble." Mr. Stone's response sounded forced. "We can always stay at a hotel."

Espedie laughed and the geologist's forced smile became a genuine scowl. "There are no hotels in the fine city of Succor," explained Espedie. "The closest hotel would be in New Des Moines, but I guarantee we have better hospitality."

Peter Stone looked dubious, but nodded. He walked over and spoke to Captain Ellis for a moment before returning. Espedie climbed in the cab. Mr. Stone gave the carryhover a doubtful look then climbed in on the passenger side.

"Where do we ride?" Sam's eyes held real interest for the first time since he'd emerged from the launch.

"We'll ride in the back." Manuel climbed up on the sideboard and pushed himself into the vehicle's bed. Sam looked at him with uncertainty. Manuel held out his hand and helped Sam into the carryhover.

"Aren't there any seatbelts?" Sam looked around.

"Nope," said Manuel. "Just don't fall out."

The carryhover lurched forward. Manuel's gaze lingered on Firebrandt's homestead. Ellison Firebrandt, Captain Ellis, Roberts, and Fire were deep in conversation as they strolled toward the old pirate craft. Manuel hoped Fire would glance his way, but her eyes seemed fixed on Captain Ellis.

Manuel turned to face Sam. "So, how do you like our planet?"

"This is the most primitive planet I've ever visited." Sam shook his head. "I've never seen so many trees growing wild and so much grass in one place."

Manuel tried to imagine a world where no room remained for grass and trees. He supposed someone who grew up in New Des Moines might see the world much that way, but even Sufiro's largest settlement was surrounded by miles and miles of wild land. You'd almost have to stay in your house the whole time to avoid seeing nature.

"What do you like to do?" asked Manuel.

Sam smiled for the first time since arriving. He held up his handcomp. "I just bought Haunted Space Station 5."

Manuel narrowed his gaze. "You bought a space station?"

"No, you idiot. It's a game." Sam laughed.

Manuel didn't like being called an idiot. Handcomps required expensive energy and computer games never seemed as much fun as playing with friends.

Something softened in Sam's expression. "I like computers. Being aboard the *Nantucket* was great. All those computers surrounding us, doing calculations and displaying information, made me feel like I'd entered a video game." He laughed again, but this time Manuel caught a nervous, self-conscious lilt. "What do you like to do?"

"I like to play ball," said Manuel. "I like to go hunting with my dad."

"Hunting?" Sam's eyes widened. "You mean with real guns?"

"That's right."

Just when it seemed as though the two might be hitting it off, the carryhover pulled up to the Raton's house. Manuel hopped out of the carryhover and helped Sam clamber to the ground. Manuel and Espedie grabbed bags. Sam's gaze drifted back to the handcomp. Mr. Stone grabbed one bag and followed Espedie inside.

Over the next half hour, they helped the Stones settle into the spare bedroom. Manuel's mom and his brother, Juan, set the table for dinner. She made chiles rellenos with a side of local squash and seasoned, puffed corn that several settlers called hominy, but his parents called posole.

Sam tasted the chilies and his eyes widened. He gulped half of the glass of water, then tried the squash, but made a face. In the end, he settled on eating the posole.

Manuel found himself drawn to the conversation between his dad and Peter Stone. They discussed the discovery of erdonium on the continent people called No-Man's Land. "I want to put together a team of people to lay claim to the deposits," explained Peter.

Carmen narrowed her gaze. "And how much would you pay these people?"

"I don't have much up-front money," admitted Peter, "and what I do have will be needed to build infrastructure."

Carmen began to interrupt, but Peter held up his hand.

"I can guarantee the erdonium is there. We have the scans to prove it. I can provide mining jobs to all those who accompany me with a share in the company's profits. All I ask is that those who come along provide food and supplies to support the expedition."

Espedie leaned forward. "You're asking farmers to give up their land where they're making a good living to follow you and become miners for no money."

"For no up-front money." Peter sounded a little irritated. "We're talking about a share of profits in an erdonium mine. The people who follow me won't just get paid, they'll get rich."

Espedie sat back and rubbed his chin. "Okay, can you show me the proof?"

Peter looked at Sam. "Could you get my handcomp from the bedroom?"

For the first time since dinner started, Sam appeared interested in the conversation. He left the table, went to the spare bedroom and retrieved his father's handcomp. A moment later, Peter pulled up a chart from the *Nantucket* showing erdonium sheets under the surface of No-man's Land.

Juan let out a long, low whistle. Even Manuel's mom invoked the names of two saints. "It's like a pirate's buried treasure," she whispered at last.

"You have equipment?" Espedie raised his eyebrows.

"I have equipment. I just need supplies and manpower."

"Let's talk more after dinner," said Espedie.

Fire willed herself not to stare at Captain Jerome Ellis, who sat at the head of their rectangular dining table. Her father sat at the end opposite Ellis while Roberts sat across from her. Upon returning to the homestead, Fire went to her cabin and changed into a form-fitting red dress cut to accentuate her curves. Woven from a local fiber, the cloth could appear as many shades of red, depending on how the light hit it.

Firebrandt still wore his black jacket and the trousers with a blood-red stripe down the side. Fire noticed that having been outted as a privateer, he had added a brass pin with a skull over two crossed swords. She wondered whether he did that to honor Captain Ellis or to intimidate him.

Roberts also wore a black jacket and trousers. His trousers had a purple stripe and he wore a matching purple sash over his shoulder. For dinner, he whipped up a lovely fried fish accompanied by fruit salad, which tasted delicious alongside Captain Ellis's quohog chowder.

Firebrandt regaled Ellis with tales from his days as a privateer captain. He told how he had met Fire's mom on Epsilon Indi II and how they had outsmarted a drug lord. He then told how the drug lord had lain in wait for them, posing as gun runners on a satellite. Fire admired her father's bravery and wished she'd had the opportunity to know her mother.

"It sounds like you did pretty well for yourself," said Ellis. "How in the world did you end up marooned here?"

"An admiral from Alpha Coma Berenices laid a trap for me. She armed a freighter to the teeth and filled her holds with marines and took my ship."

Ellis's eyes widened and he grinned. "That was Admiral Barbara Firebrandt wasn't it?" He snorted a laugh. "Your mother who brought Peter Stone here the first time is also the admiral who stranded you."

Fire blew out a breath as her father stiffened in response.

Roberts cleared his throat and cast Firebrandt a meaningful look. The first mate stood and refilled wine glasses. Firebrandt sipped the wine, closed his eyes, then took a deep breath.

"Yes," he said at last. "Admiral Barbara Firebrandt was responsible for stranding us here."

Ellis sipped his wine and had the good graces to look downcast. "I'm sorry, I didn't mean to offend you, Captain. It just helps me understand your shock at Stone's return. I can see why you would be reluctant to work with someone so connected with the admiral."

Fire folded her hands and looked at Ellis. "Does this understanding make a difference in your job?"

Ellis sighed. "I suppose not." He took another sip of wine. "That said, there is another puzzle that doesn't make much difference to my job, but I wondered if you would answer."

Firebrandt narrowed his gaze and gave a curt nod.

"Where in the world did the name 'Firebrandt' come from?" He shrugged. "Did you have an activist in your family's history who decided to add a 't' to the end of the word 'firebrand'?"

Tension broke as Firebrandt and Roberts both laughed. Fire looked between Ellis and her father, intrigued by the question she'd never thought to ask. "Do you know the answer?" she prompted.

Firebrandt shrugged. "My dad told me an ancestor shoveled coal on old steamships. When it reached temperature, he would call, 'Vuur brandt,' which means 'Fire is burning!' After a while, that's just what they called him. Over the centuries as English and Dutch merged, it became Firebrandt."

Fire smiled and turned her attention back to Ellis. "I take it family histories intrigue you."

"They do indeed," said Ellis. "My family is filled with sailors and ship captains. Edward Ellis captained the whaler *Madaket*. His son commanded a ship called the *Orion*."

A knot formed in Fire's stomach. "Was the *Orion* also a whaler?"

"It was," admitted Ellis. "Whaling was the major industry on Nantucket in the seventeenth and eighteenth centuries, but when the danger to the whale population became known, the family took an active part in stopping the whale hunts. We pride ourselves on being a long line of captains, not that we hunted whales. My ancestors sailed every ocean on Earth. Later, the family commanded space vessels. You may have heard of Howard Ellis, captain of the *Hawking*."

Roberts' brow furrowed. "*Hawking* was the first ship equipped with an EQ generator, wasn't it?"

"*Einstein's Folly* was the first," Ellis corrected. "But the *Hawking* was built just two years later and the first with a full exploratory crew aboard." Pride sparkled in the captain's eye.

Fire looked toward the wall, her brow knitted. "'Nantucket! Take out your map and look at it. See what a real corner of the world it occupies; how it stands there, away off shore, more lonely than the Eddystone lighthouse.'"

Ellis smiled, revealing his exquisite dimples. "That's from Melville, isn't it?"

"*Moby-Dick*." She nodded, then looked at him and concentrated. "'And thus have these naked Nantucketers, these sea hermits, issuing from their ant-hill in the sea, overrun and conquered the watery world like so many Alexanders.'" She inclined her head. "'Let America add Mexico to Texas but remember that two-thirds of this terraqueous globe are the Nantucketers.' So, too, remember that ninety-nine percent of all space belongs to the Nantucketer."

Ellis laughed and clapped his hands. "I guess you figured out that I'm proud of my home."

Fire lifted a spoonful of chowder to her lips, swallowed it down, then smirked. "Your ship's name, the map in your office, the quohog chowder ... you talk of puzzles. That one wasn't difficult."

"All right, you have me there." Ellis held up his hands in

mock defeat. "You also have a hell of a memory if you can recite chunks of Melville like that."

She smiled. "I looked up the passages before dinner."

Roberts cleared his throat, stood, then collected dirty plates. "I do believe we have some business to discuss before we call it a night."

"That's right." Firebrandt led Ellis and Fire to the sitting room in the homestead's adobe addition. There, Firebrandt brought up maps and Ellis retrieved his handcomp and brought up manifests. Roberts soon joined them. Fire hovered around the periphery and listened with interest, even though she had little to contribute.

Once they had discussed the routine deliveries and Ellis relayed data to Ms. Pfister aboard the *Nantucket*, they turned their attention to No-Man's Land.

"A lot will depend on who Peter Stone recruits to claim the erdonium," said Firebrandt. "I imagine the best course of action would be to deliver Stone's heavy equipment directly to the sites he wants to claim. He can then take personnel and vehicles over the ocean to those sites."

Ellis nodded. "Given mass and fuel, I suspect that would be cheaper than shuttling those people across in launches."

Firebrandt yawned, then looked at the time. "It's getting late. I think I should turn in." He turned to Fire. "Can you show our guest to his quarters when he's ready to call it a night?"

"I can." Fire walked up to each dad in turn and gave them a kiss goodnight.

She turned back to Ellis, pleased that her affection for the two men who raised her didn't appear to shock him.

"So, what do you plan to do when you get to Earth?" asked Ellis.

"I've arranged to tour some universities. My dads have some money set aside for my education." She flashed a smile at the captain. "And what do you plan to do when you get back to Earth, Captain Ellis? Will it just be turn around and go right back on another mission, or will you have some time off?"

"Please, call me Jerome." He unbuttoned his collar. "I will have a little time off. I have a home on Nantucket. I'll go back there and recharge my batteries. Go to the beach and wiggle my toes in the sand."

"That sounds nice," said Fire.

"Nantucket today isn't much different than it was in Melville's time." He shrugged. "In some ways, it's not much different than Succor ... except it's an island in the ocean. I think you'd like it. If you have time when we arrive on Earth, I'd be happy to show you around."

"I'd enjoy that." Fire smiled

Jerome looked down at his handcomp. "You should show me to my room," he said. "It's getting a bit late, even by ship's time."

"We're putting you up in the old first mate's cabin ... not far from my room." She wondered if her comment implied more than she meant. A quick glance at Jerome's face didn't reveal that he took any unintended meaning in the disclosure.

She led him back past the old star cruiser's galley and into the crew quarters. She passed her room and stopped at Roberts' old quarters and opened the door. Before he entered, she stepped up and put her arms around him. She was almost as tall as him and she thought she might drown in his eyes.

He leaned forward and kissed her. She pulled her head back and laughed.

"What's so funny?" He lifted an eyebrow.

"Your mustache tickles."

"If you want, I'll shave it off. I'm not that attached to it."

"Don't you dare." She pulled his head close again and they shared a much longer kiss. A fire burned in her belly and she almost laughed again as she considered her fire stoker ancestor. Jerome's crotch grew hard and she wanted to take him inside and consummate their now obvious and mutual attraction. She also knew how strange and complicated some humans made sex and knew she should get to know more about this Jerome Mycroft Ellis before she proceeded too far.

He gently pulled back. "I look forward to getting to know you better in the coming weeks, Ms. Firebrandt." Jerome's voice had turned husky.

"Likewise, Captain Ellis."

He reached down and gave her another, brief kiss, then stepped backward into the cabin and shut the door.

Suki Carter Firebrandt hummed and forced herself not to skip back to her own cabin.

☠

The next morning, Manuel Raton rolled out of bed, stretched and yawned. The smells of kyonosaur bacon and coffee lured him out to the kitchen. There, his mother and father prepared breakfast. His dad wanted Manuel to plow the field. This would allow Espedie to take delivery of the new wind generator arriving from the *Nantucket*. Manuel thought Juan should plow the field since his brother enjoyed it much more than he did, but Juan had school that day and would have already left on the hover transport for New Des Moines.

Their guest, Peter Stone, sat at the kitchen table. There was no sign of Sam. Manuel guessed he had slept in, having no responsibilities. Stone looked at Manuel and smiled. "I understand your friend, Suki Firebrandt, will go to Earth aboard the *Nantucket*."

"Yeah." Manuel grabbed a cup of coffee. "She's planning to scout universities and continue her education."

Mr. Stone pursed his lips and nodded. "What about you? I gather you just graduated from high school. Do you have plans to go to college?"

Manuel shrugged. "I want to study criminal investigation, but we don't have any colleges or universities on Sufiro yet."

Stone narrowed his gaze. "So, you'd have to go Earth as well."

Manuel tried not to show his disappointment with his parents standing there. "We don't have enough money for me to go to Earth. Captain Firebrandt has all kinds of money squirreled away in accounts from his days as a privateer. He couldn't touch most of it for a while after crashing here. Now that he has access to the galactic banking net again, he has money to send Fire to school."

Carmen set a plate of fledermaus eggs, kyonosaur bacon,

and toast in front of him. "It's not our business to discuss the finances of others."

A knot formed in Manuel's stomach. Indeed, he knew better. Some kind of detective he'd make.

Peter Stone held up his hand and smiled. "Good Captain Firebrandt's finances aren't my concern. My expedition is funded. I just need people who will go with me to No-Man's Land and lay claim to the erdonium there."

Carmen placed a plate in front of Stone. "You're asking people to give up everything they have, contribute their food stores, and put in a lot of hard work..."

"In exchange for a handsome reward," finished Stone.

Espedie and Carmen joined Peter and Manuel at the table. Espedie took a bite of eggs and swallowed it down with some coffee. "So, what about your son, Mr. Stone? He's around Manuel's age. Won't you send him to college?"

Stone took a deep breath, then blew it out. "That's why I'm here. I've been a geologist all my life. I've earned enough in my consultancy to afford a good school if he took out some loans, just like I did. He wants to study business and finance. If he's successful, he could do quite well." He paused and took a sip of coffee. "However, I knew I could do much better. Instead of giving my savings to an institute of higher learning, I've put it into this expedition. Now, I'll be able to send him to school free and clear plus retire in comfort."

Carmen narrowed her gaze. "So, you decided to gamble on your son's future."

Peter Stone leaned forward and pointed to the sky. "Captain Ellis and I threw the dice aboard the *Nantucket* yesterday morning. At this point, I know the erdonium is there. All I need is some help. I would appreciate your assistance, but if you're not interested, I'll go to someone else here in Succor. If they can't help, I'll go to New Des Moines."

Carmen opened her mouth to speak, but Espedie put his hand on hers. "There's still a gamble. What if someone is hurt, or even dies? We know little grows over there. What if we discover toxic chemicals leaching into the groundwater? What if we can't grow anything?"

Peter Stone nodded and seemed to consider those points

as he dug into breakfast. "That's why I want the best people I can find," he said at last. "I want medical techs. I want expert equipment operators. If we can't create self-sustaining cities, we'll need help from the farms back here in New Granada. We need that help to begin with and it'll still create an influx of capital." Stone turned to face Espedie. "No matter at what level you help me, you'll get more money to send Manuel to school. If you join up as a partner, you'll do as well as I will."

"And why would you want my dad as a partner?" Manuel had finished breakfast and folded his arms.

"Because others will have the same questions." Stone shrugged and turned to Espedie and Carmen. "If they see your conviction, they'll help much more readily. I'm anxious to get started. I know the erdonium is there. We just need to claim it and make the best mining operation we can. If we don't claim it ourselves, the Mao Corporation will be back within the year and they'll do the job instead. They won't support the farmers here in New Granada and they won't worry about creating a sustainable colony in No-Man's Land. They'll be happy to strip mine the continent and who knows what that would mean for New Granada."

Stone fell silent and resumed eating breakfast. Carmen and Espedie stared at each other. At times like this Manuel wondered if his parents shared a psychic link. At last, Carmen faced Stone. "Okay, we'll go in with you and we'll set up a meeting tonight to see who else can join us."

"What about the farm?" asked Espedie.

"What about Juan?" countered Manuel. "He wants to be a farmer. He knows plowing and planting and harvesting. He even enjoys it! You could leave the farm to him while you explore."

"And what about you, young man?" Carmen narrowed her gaze.

Manuel bristled at being called "young man" even though he knew his mother just teased him. "I want to go with you. I wouldn't miss it. I want to see the new continent." It wasn't going to see Earth with Fire, but it was the next best thing Manuel Raton could think of.

☠

Fire spent the next week sorting through twenty-one years' worth of belongings and deciding what should accompany her in two small cargo bins. Clothes and personal items were obvious. She already stored a library of books, music, and photos on her handcomp. She packed a teddy bear Roberts made for her when she was four. She wondered if she would see a real bear on Earth, or meet the galaxy's most advanced race, the Titans, who also resembled teddy bears.

Her dads said Espedie and Carmen Raton had interested several people from Succor in accompanying them to No-Man's Land. After the first meeting, they had gone to New Des Moines to recruit more people. They had rented a warehouse and now stockpiled the supplies they needed. She laughed to herself and thought it wouldn't be right to keep calling it No-Man's Land if they succeeded and she wondered what they would call it.

Her handcomp beeped. She picked it up and read a message from Manuel Raton. He wanted to meet her that night in the woods, "for old times' sake." She sighed, but smiled and said she would be there.

That night she walked out the front door and told Firebrandt she would be back before long. She strolled between the homestead and the garden toward the trees and considered how much she would miss this simple idyllic place. She would miss running to the river, peeling off all her clothes, and going for a swim whenever she wanted to. She would miss quiet nights with Manuel.

She found Manuel in the clearing under the forcefield with a plate of tacos. He lowered the forcefield for a moment and she entered. "I know you've been packing," said Manuel. "It's hungry work. I thought you'd appreciate a snack."

"That's very thoughtful." She leaned over and gave him a kiss.

The two sat under the electronic canopy and snacked on the tacos while watching fledermice dive for bugs in the moonlight.

"So, when will you and your folks be heading to No-Man's Land?"

Manuel shrugged. "Mr. Stone says the way things are

going, we should be ready in a few days."

"Sounds like you'll leave right after me. Captain Ellis says he wants me aboard in two days," said Fire.

Manuel narrowed his gaze. "That Captain Ellis, what do you think of him?"

"He's nice," said Fire. "I like him. He reminds me of my genetic dad, but younger. And he has dimples."

She laughed, but Manuel didn't join her.

"They say we marry our moms and our dads. And his name? It's so similar to your dad's."

Fire gave him a playful swat on the shoulder. "I never said anything about marrying him." She let her eyes drift off to the stars. "He did offer to help me get settled in on Earth and show me around his home on Nantucket Island."

Manuel leaned over on his elbow and looked up at Fire. "Would you ever come back and ... I dunno ... marry me?"

"Is that a proposal?"

He blushed and stammered, then grabbed a taco and took a bite to cover his embarrassment. She took pity on him and didn't make him answer. Instead, she said, "You're not my dad. Somehow you're more ... dangerous." She shot him a meaningful look.

That made Manuel sputter even more. "More dangerous than a pirate?" he managed at last.

"Jerome Ellis may remind me of my father, but you remind me of yours and I think he has some secrets. I wouldn't be surprised if you have a few by the time your journey to No-Man's Land is finished."

"Don't worry, Fogacita. I will save all my best stories for you."

"I'm counting on it." She kissed him again, then thanked him for the tacos and returned to the homestead.

Two days later, she stacked her two storage bins in the homestead's sitting room and then sat with Roberts and Firebrandt, waiting for the signal indicating the *Nantucket's* launch would be arriving to pick her up.

A knock on the door startled them. Espedie Raton entered. He gave Fire a warm embrace, then sat down in an empty chair. "What brings you here?" asked the captain.

"Peter Stone says we'll be ready to depart for No-Man's Land the day after tomorrow. It's been busy. I thought I'd take a break before I make sure Juan is all set to take over the farm." He pointed to Roberts and Firebrandt. "You two are sure you don't mind looking in on him from time to time?"

"Not at all," said Roberts. "It'll be our pleasure."

"So," asked Fire, "have you thought about what you'll name No-Man's Land if you decide to stay there and settle?"

"Name it?" Espedie laughed. "It already has a name!"

"Yeah, but it won't be No-Man's Land anymore." Fire flicked a strand of long hair over her shoulder. "There'll be men there, and women too for that matter."

"She has a point." Firebrandt stroked his beard. "Aside from the Roanoke colony, the only people who have visited that continent in all these years are the Rd'dyggians we helped during our first winter on Sufiro."

"We could call the colony Roanoke," mused Espedie.

"Bad luck." Roberts stood up and went around the corner to where they kept a refrigerator. He returned with four beers and passed them around. "Roanoke on Earth was a lost colony. They disappeared within five years of settling."

Espedie laughed. "Yeah, but it hasn't been so bad for the people in our Roanoke. They've been there over a decade!"

"I still say it's the Rd'dyggians who have claim to that land." Firebrandt sipped his beer. "As far as I'm concerned, they can keep it."

Fire and the three men lifted their beers in unison. "To the Rd'dyggians."

Firebrandt set his beer on the table. "If you succeed in digging up erdonium, you could name the continent Erdon after Pierre Erdon of Earth or after Alrecca the Titan who was the first being in the known galaxy to discover erdonium."

"Why not name the continent T'Ggo?" Fire took another sip of the beer, smacked her lips, then set it down on the table next to her father's. She liked Roberts' beer but didn't want to drink too much before getting underway.

"Tayho?" asked Espedie. "What the hell's a Tayho?"

"T'Ggo, not Tayho," corrected Fire.

The way Espedie shook his head, she realized he didn't hear

a difference. "T'Ggo was the Rd'dyggian who first discovered erdonium, or T'Gganoq in her language."

Espedie took a long swallow of his beer. "Still sounds like Tayho to me. I'd spell it like in Spanish, though. T-E-J-O."

A chime from Fire's handcomp interrupted them. Captain Ellis would land in five minutes. Espedie and Roberts helped her carry the cases out to the landing pad. They looked up to the sky. The launch descended and then settled just across from them. The door opened and Captain Ellis stepped out.

Fire's heart seemed to skip a beat. She wanted to go to him. Instead, she turned around and embraced Ellison Firebrandt hard. "I love you, daddy. I'll miss you."

"I'll miss you, too." The two held each other for a long time. She then let go and reached out and embraced Roberts. When she let go, she gave Espedie a hug as well. As she suspected, hugging Espedie reminded her of hugging Manuel, except he had a lot more stubble. She stood back and hoped no one saw the smirk on her face.

Firebrandt sniffed. "Remember," he said, "your life is your own. Never do anything because someone else wants you to do it."

"I will," said Fire. "I won't ever forget." With that, she strode to the shuttle. She embraced Captain Ellis and didn't want to let go, afraid that if she did, she would run right back to her dads. At last, she willed herself to let go. She looked up into his eyes and they exchanged a brief kiss.

If her dads had comments, they kept them to themselves. Firebrandt and Roberts loaded the cargo bins, then stepped from the shuttle with a wave. Jerome indicated she should take the co-pilot's seat.

"It has the best view."

He sat next to her and activated the landing boat's thrusters. She looked down and watched her dads and Espedie wave. A funny feeling struck her and for just a moment she thought she would never see Espedie again. It was all the more notable because she had no such thoughts about her dads. She dismissed the feeling as nerves and turned her eyes skyward.

Chapter Nine

EXPLORATION

Peter Stone, Espedie Raton, and one hundred twenty-two other men and women chartered an ocean-going ship to the continent known as No-Man's Land. For the most part, those ships ferried goods between New Granada, Roanoake, and the island-continent of Little Sonora which was the only government on Sufiro the Gaean Alliance recognized. The three small governments formed a trade coalition to run all shipping from headquarters based in the Gato Archipeligo.

Stone, Raton, and their party sailed aboard an efficient, fast vessel called *Queen of Sufiro* from Nouveau Baton Rouge near the swampy delta where the Nuevo Rio Grande emptied into the Great Ocean. The ship used turbosails, which a sea captain named Jacques Cousteau had designed a thousand years before on Earth. The turbosails augmented the ship's engines.

One night, Manuel Raton strolled the near-silent decks before he returned to the cabin he shared with his parents. He found them by the deck rail, holding hands and gazing up at the stars. He joined them and wondered where Suki was now.

"Is this what space travel is like?" asked Manuel.

Carmen chuckled and put her arm around Manuel's shoulder. "We came here aboard a tramp freighter with no windows, mijo. A sharp, oily smell clung to the air."

Manuel wrinkled his nose. "Sounds like the engine room."

"Yeah, mix in the aroma of poor sewage treatment and you've got it." Espedie's gaze never left the stars above. "I feel more like a space traveler from a romantic story right here than I did as the passenger on a real space ship."

Carmen squeezed Manuel's shoulder. "You should get some sleep, mijo."

Manuel sighed. He knew his parents wanted to be left alone. He wondered what they would talk about. After a moment, he thought they might want some privacy to make out. The idea sent a shiver down his spine. He returned to the cabin, changed into pajamas, and climbed into his bunk where the ship's gentle rocking lulled Manuel to sleep.

The next day, Manuel awoke to the sound of his parents' gentle snores. He climbed down from the bunk, dressed, and went to the galley for breakfast. There, Sam Stone stared at his handcomp while he shoveled food into his mouth with his free hand. Manuel grabbed some cereal and coffee from the buffet table, then sat down across from Sam. Manuel had never eaten manufactured cereal before. On the farm, the closest thing available had been a cooked cereal made from locally raised grains.

"So, what is Earth like?" asked Manuel.

Sam glanced up and blinked, as though noticing Manuel for the first time. He shrugged. "It's crowded. There are people everywhere. Not like here."

"What do all those people do?" Manuel took a bite of the cereal and savored the crunchy, sweet mouthful.

Sam paused the game. "Same as everywhere, they create programs to make things, they sell things. A lot of people work in jobs serving other people."

Manuel leaned forward. "With all those people, how bad is the crime?"

Sam folded his arms and sneered at Manuel. "On a podunk planet like this, do you even know what crime is?"

Manuel narrowed his gaze. "We have crime all right. People get drunk, get mad, shoot at each other. Every now and then someone tries to steal livestock from someone else. Traffic has picked up in New Des Moines and Nouveau Baton Rouge. Where there are laws, people try to find their ways around them."

Sam barked a laugh. "Man, that's nothing! On Earth we have criminal gangs smuggling pirated drugs and software. We have bankers who steal from their clients. Don't get me started on sex crimes." All at once, Sam's mirth turned into a leer. "Say, did you and that pirate captain's daughter ... you know..."

Manuel's cheeks burned and although he knew just what Sam asked, Sam didn't need to know. Manuel decided to change the subject. "Sufiro's getting big enough, it could use some organized law enforcement."

Sam folded his arms. "Well, first you need laws to enforce. That's something Earth has plenty of. So many, they contradict one another. I think my dad is glad to be in a place with fewer regulations."

Manuel considered that as he took a bite of the cereal. "Is your dad thinking about doing something..."

Sam laughed and waved the question away. "It's nothing like that. It's just on Earth, there are laws and regulations covering everything. They practically tell you how to eat your cereal and how to wipe your butt. Not only do they regulate what you do, they tax the cereal going in and going out."

"That's gross." Manuel's appetite diminished as he visualized Sam's description.

"The point is there are so many taxes and statutes, it's difficult for anyone on Earth to make money."

Manuel glanced at Sam's handcomp. "I didn't think you concerned yourself much with money."

Sam shrugged. "Why not? After all, money's survival."

Manuel considered that. Growing up, most transactions he had witnessed were among people exchanging services and bartering with one another. Sure, they used money in New Des Moines and his dad and mom bought things, but money had never seemed an essential ingredient for life. "Money's not survival," he said at last. "Survival's easy as long as you know people and you know the land."

Sam snorted and turned his attention back to the handcomp.

Jerome Ellis led Suki Firebrandt to a forward section of the *Nantucket*. Pushing a button, large, metal shutters irised open. Light from several billion suns swept an arc across the sky before them. Fire's mouth dropped open as Ellis led her toward the window. The arc bulged in the center, then swept off in either direction as though it wound around the ship. Raven colored swaths of dust twisted through the stellar band. Off to one side of the bulge sparkled two oval clouds, like cotton candy decorated with glitter. "The galaxy's center," explained Ellis. He pointed to the cotton candy-like clumps. "Those are the Magellanic Clouds, our galaxy's two nearest neighbors."

Fire stared at the sight in wide-eyed wonder. "I've seen the galactic bulge before, but never like this."

"You're in space, no atmosphere to get in the way," said Ellis. "The closest I've ever come to this view from a planet was in the Andes on Earth."

"It's beautiful." She allowed her eyes to wander the panorama.

"I brought you here because I've enjoyed the last two weeks with you on the ship," Ellis looked at the deck and shuffled his feet.

Suki had also enjoyed the last two weeks with Ellis. They'd had meals together and she had watched him work on the command deck. They had visited in his quarters and had discussed books and movies they enjoyed. They would reach Earth before much longer and she didn't want the voyage to end. She looked up and met his gaze.

"I have an important question, and I couldn't think of a better setting in which to ask it."

Fire looked into the captain's eyes, both anticipating and dreading the coming question. Jerome Ellis had loaned her numerous books he enjoyed. Many involved one character winning another's heart. Had he won her heart?

"Suki Carter Firebrandt, would you marry me?"

Fire swallowed hard, then turned away to look at the stars. She thought about her parents who had loved each other yet had never married. What would marriage to a space farer like Jerome Ellis mean? Would she travel with him everywhere he went, or would they have their own, separate adventures, meeting on Earth or other worlds from time to time? Both options appealed to her and both options presented problems. "Nantucket, the Andes ... so much to see and that's just on Earth. I still need an education beyond the books from my father's library ... and yours." Fire reached out and took Ellis's hand. "Jerome, I have grown to love you and I won't abandon you. But I won't marry you … at least not yet."

"If you love me…" Ellis dropped his hands to his side.

"If you love me, you will let me go to college first. I have to find my own career. Then we can discuss whether or not my career fits in with your career."

Ellis shrugged. "I understand. But what if…"

"What if I meet someone else? I might be tempted to have my way with them." Fire grinned at Ellis's shocked expression. "Still, they'd have to work hard to be someone I'd want to spend the rest of my life with more than you."

"Then, may I take that as a provisional yes?" The words seemed to catch in Ellis's throat, as though the answer might not be something he wanted to hear.

"Take it as 'ask me again in two or three years' and we'll see where our lives have taken us."

Ellis looked back to the stars. "Would you at least take me back to my cabin and console me in my disappointment?"

Fire reached around to the control, closed the door and punched in the lock code. "I'll console you right here, my captain."

☠

The Queen of Sufiro deposited Peter Stone and his people at Roanoake. Manuel Raton disembarked with his family. Espedie walked over to Stone, who spoke to a man in an official-looking uniform and a woman in a hard hat. The two settlers from Roanoake cast suspicious glances at the dozens of people disembarking all at once.

Espedie affixed a vocal amplifier to his throat and waved to attract the team's attention. "Let's all form up over here. Mr. Stone is arranging hotel rooms for us for the night while the ship's crew offloads our hover transports and equipment."

"Do you suppose this little shit-hole town even has rooms for a hundred people?" Sam's voice caused Manuel to jump.

He tried to cover his surprise with a laugh. "I don't think they know what to expect."

Carmen looked over at Sam and Manuel. "These people have strong religious convictions—even stronger than the people who settled New Des Moines. Respect them. Be nice."

"If they have such strong religious beliefs, why did they come to such a wild planet out on the frontier?" Sam's tone challenged Carmen in a way Manuel wouldn't dare.

"Sometimes the best place to make your own laws is a place that doesn't have any to begin with." Carmen concluded the statement with a curt nod.

Sam sneered, but Manuel thought his mom had a point. Once Stone had signed all the appropriate papers, he called Espedie over again. A moment later, Espedie directed all the people to walk between two nearby buildings and across a street to a concrete, steel, and glass structure which resembled a 25th century building more than a modern plascrete structure.

Manuel followed his father into the old hotel and watched as an efficient desk clerk handed keys to Mr. Stone. Stone passed them to Espedie, who called out names. Married couples shared rooms. Other rooms were given to teams of three or four people.

Once Espedie distributed all the keys, he pushed a button beside an old-fashioned elevator and they went up two floors and entered a musty-smelling room with two beds, a desk, and a bathroom with stained tiles.

While he didn't agree with Sam that Roanoake was nothing but a shit-hole, he didn't understand why the town had enough rooms for such a large group. He borrowed his mother's handcomp and looked up information. Although Roanoake was the only large town on the continent, there were several farms and a couple of small fishing villages on the peninsula with it. Farmers, it would seem, used the hotels on market days.

With nothing to do in the room besides stare at the handcomp, he decided to go out for a walk. His mother told him to meet them at the hotel's restaurant in an hour for supper.

Manuel found Sam out on the street. "I wanted to see if there was anything to do around here," said Sam.

"Me too," agreed Manuel.

Sam picked a direction and started walking. They came to a large open plaza, big enough to house a farmer's market. A young woman strolled past, wearing a long-sleeved, black dress and a bonnet. Despite the heavy clothes, Manuel appreciated her curves and smiled. He considered approaching her and introducing himself, but she scowled at him and picked up her pace.

"I guess you're not quite the lady's man you fancy yourself as being." Sam laughed.

"I think you scared her off," snarled Manuel.

Finding little else to do, the two returned to the hotel to meet up with their families.

The next morning, the group from New Granada convened at a warehouse near the docks. They loaded their gear and supplies into the hovers. Espedie walked over to Manuel. "I have a hover that needs a driver. You want to take it?"

"Any passengers?" asked Manuel.

When Espedie mentioned it would be Sam Stone, Manuel grimaced, but agreed. Sam grated on his nerves, but he was the only person in the group around his age.

Using his amplifier, Espedie instructed the group to drive single-file through town and reconvene before crossing the gypsum desert.

Manuel sat behind the hover's control console and started the propulsors. Sam tossed a backpack in the backseat next to some other gear and climbed in. He turned on his handcomp and ignored Manuel for the time being. Soon the vehicles began to move. They passed the large open square and numerous brick houses. The houses gave way to low, scrubby vegetation, which stopped when they reached a barren, white expanse of gypsum sand. If not for the heat waves wafting into a clear, blue sky, it resembled a snow mass. No wonder most people dubbed the rest of the continent No-Man's Land.

Manuel's father and Mr. Stone consulted their handcomps. A moment later, Espedie called out distance and bearing. Manuel glanced over at Sam.

"Yeah, yeah, I got it." Sam paused the game and inserted the numbers into a map program.

Manuel followed the other hovers out across the sand. The engines' buzz and the bloop, bleep, bloop of Sam's game were the only sounds that reached his ears. No insects flitted around as they proceeded across the desert.

Half an hour later, Sam released an exaggerated yawn and set the handcomp aside. He turned around and grabbed a water bottle from the back and took a swig. He offered it to Manuel who waved it aside. "We need to conserve our supplies," he said.

"Do you do everything people tell you to do?" Sam folded his arms and glared at Manuel.

"No, not everything." Manuel shook his head.

"We're out here in the middle of nowhere with nothing but a bunch of farmers who want to be miners. There's no cops, there's no traffic besides these people. Why don't you open this baby up and see what she can do?"

"Are you serious?" Manuel narrowed his gaze. "This thing's just an old clunky hover."

"Yeah, but why not see how fast she can go?"

"All right, but don't say I didn't warn you." With that, Manuel pushed the acceleration lever forward and their hover shot forward past all the others.

From time to time, Sam shouted out course corrections. They approached a sand dune. Manuel adjusted course and speed, shot upwards, then banked off the dune. The two young men started laughing as they dropped from the sky and shot forward again.

Three hours later, the desert sand turned into a rugged, rocky field. A few strange, tall plants that resembled cactus grew here and there. Sam called out another course correction and Manuel turned right toward a tall red outcropping. Manuel veered to the side and they caromed into the rocky projection.

Manuel and Sam were thrown clear as the hover tumbled end over end across the rocks scattering supplies until it clattered to a stop. Manuel groaned and sat up. He'd torn his shirt and pants, but aside from some scratches seemed unharmed. He ran to Sam and shook him.

To his surprise, Sam started laughing. "That was awesome!"

Manuel couldn't help it and he laughed as well.

Half an hour later, though, they still sat on the ground and grew hungry. They stood and gathered the supplies. Sam found a few packages of protein snacks and handed a pair to Manuel. Manuel gobbled them down.

At last, a hover carrying Espedie, Carmen, and Stone arrived. They picked up the boys and rescued the salvageable supplies. "You boys, had me worried sick," said Carmen. "You could have been killed!"

Before they got underway again, Espedie pulled Manuel aside. Manuel braced himself for a lecture. Espedie put his hand on his son's shoulder. "I saw how you bounced that old hover off a dune. I'm impressed. I didn't think these things could go that fast." He laughed.

Manuel responded with a nervous chuckle. "Sorry I destroyed the hover, dad."

"Well, some losses are expected, but this was your one chance and you blew it. It'll be a while before you earn another chance."

That evening, the expedition arrived at the site where Peter Stone expected to find the first erdonium deposit. As promised, they found several shipping containers from the *Nantucket* at the foot of a wide mesa. Green and purple scrub brush dotted the landscape.

Manuel helped his father and mother set up their tent. "I'm surprised there's no crater here. Didn't the *Nantucket* fire probes from orbit?"

"They did," said Carmen, "but they don't have to be in this area to triangulate on the erdonium deposits' locations."

Manuel nodded as he walked backwards. He stumbled over a purple bush and cursed. Several thorns hid among the rubbery leaves. Espedie walked over and checked for poison using his handcomp while Carmen grabbed a first aid kit. Within a few minutes they had him bandaged up. They finished setting up the tent, then went over to the food service carryhover where the cooks rehydrated rations.

Manuel cast a doubtful glance at his food, but took a bite. After the day's adventures, it actually tasted pretty good, even if he couldn't identify what he ate. At the table, people talked among themselves. A man named Adisa Jelani joked about finding a giant "X" on the ground to mark the spot where they should start digging.

☠

Two weeks after Peter Stone and Espedie Raton had left for No-Man's Land, Ellison Firebrandt decided he should check in and see how well the claim process proceeded. He called early in the morning, estimating Raton should not have fallen asleep yet. When Espedie answered, his hologram was translucent and riddled with static. Sufiro had few communication relay satellites and none had been tuned to relay signals from the middle of the distant continent.

"How's the search going?" asked Firebrandt.

Espedie snorted a laugh. "It's been hard work. The last thing I expected was that we would be blowing holes in the ground with old-fashioned dynamite. I thought we'd use Quinnium to clear the scene."

Firebrandt shook his head. "No one uses weaponized Quinnium, not even pirates."

Espedie's brow furrowed. "Are you sure about that? I thought I read a story about terrorists threatening to use Quinnium weapons on Zahar a couple of years back."

"Terrorists, maybe," snorted Firebrandt. "The problem with Quinnium is its inherent unpredictability. It sounds great for your application—the tachyon blast just makes a bunch of material disappear. Sometimes, the matter vanishes forever. Other times, though, the matter reappears a few hours in the future, sometimes intact and sometimes scrambled beyond recognition. A crew working in a crater blasted by a Quinnium charge could find themselves buried alive." The captain released a sigh. "I'm actually relieved to hear that Stone isn't using Quinnium. Somehow I wouldn't be surprised if he thought it would get him to his goal faster."

"Well he is working people really hard." Espedie shrugged. "Each day begins with the demolition team setting off a charge. Once the dust has settled, he sends in the heavy equipment operators to clear the big debris. After that, he sends in the geologists to examine the material in the crater, with the rest of us serving as labor to move stuff around. By the time dinner comes along, we're tired and grimy and ready for bed."

"I'm sorry to call you so late," apologized Firebrandt, "but I wanted to make sure you and the rest of your team were doing well."

Espedie waved the apology aside. "We're doing fine, and it's not all tedium. Actually, the very first morning after we arrived, someone went out and painted a big orange 'X' on the ground where we were supposed to dig. Everyone got a big laugh out of that."

Firebrandt laughed. "Any idea who did that?"

Espedie looked over his shoulder. "Oh, I have a pretty good idea."

"You can't prove anything," came Manuel's voice. He wasn't close enough to Espedie's handcomp to be picked up by the holographic scanner.

"Next time you handle a spray can, remember to wash the orange paint off your hands," chided Espedie.

"I should let you get some sleep," said Firebrandt. "If there are any problems, or you need help, you know where to reach me. Roberts and I can be over with the launch in just a couple of hours."

Espedie smiled. "Thank you, my friend, but I doubt there are any tricks Stone can pull that an old dog like me hasn't seen before."

"Somehow, that doesn't surprise me." With that, Firebrandt signed out.

After five harsh, frustrating days, a great, ragged crater sat at the foot of the mesa. The entire team grew discouraged. Manuel ached to move on to another site, hoping to see more of the continent.

On the sixth day, Manuel shoveled rock and looked for the telltales they'd been told to watch for. Mr. Stone walked up with his handcomp nodding and mumbling to himself. "This is good," said Stone. "Very good indeed."

Manuel stood straight. "Good? I still don't see any erdonium."

Stone patted him on the shoulder. "I have a feeling you will. If not today, we'll get there tomorrow. This layer we're working on has a measurable quartz deficit."

Manuel blinked at Stone and wondered what a quartz deficit had to do with finding erdonium.

"This is exactly what the *Nantucket's* scans showed," muttered Stone as he walked away.

Even though Stone had not directed the words at Manuel, he smiled. He knew Stone wouldn't be so pleased if he didn't think they were about to find what they sought.

The next day, the dynamite charges were set. The first time the charges had been set, Manuel had covered his ears, expecting a fearsome blast. Instead, the dynamite had released a dull "whump" followed by a great billowing dust cloud.

Once again, the charges were detonated and a slight roll went through the ground as though a giant had thumped the Earth. After the dust settled, the force beam dozers rolled in. Within the hour, they started pulling up gleaming, black rocks.

Peter Stone grabbed Espedie and had him call a halt to the dig so he could examine the new rocks. Manuel followed them out to the dig site, as did several other people in the party.

Mr. Stone used his handcomp to study the rock. "Excellent," he muttered. "This rock wasn't sheered in the explosion."

Manuel and Espedie looked at each other and shrugged.

"It's not carbon and it's not diamond." He nodded. "There's no question it's metal of some type." He called out to a geologist named Shawna Danvers. She brought a kit with chemicals. Opening it, she dropped first one chemical on the rock, then another.

Manuel frowned. Neither chemical did anything. Whatever the rock was, it seemed to be a dud.

"Erdonium," whispered Stone. He stood and held the rock high overhead. "Erdonium!" He shouted the word. "We found it!"

Danvers examined data on her handcomp. She walked up to Espedie and showed him the seismic readings recorded during the morning's blast. "There's erdonium underneath the mesa and extending for miles around."

That night, the crew broke out bottles of champagne and beer along with an assortment of distilled spirits. Espedie pulled out a bottle of tequila he'd brought with him from Earth and poured shots for Manuel and Carmen. He lifted a toast and they all drank. Manuel drank a second shot and his head began to swim. He wandered away from his parents as a few people retrieved instruments and began to play a jaunty tune.

Shawna Danvers asked Manuel to dance and he took her up on the offer even though she was much older than him. Once the dance finished, he continued to wander through the camp. As far as he could tell, the only person not celebrating was Mr. Stone. Manuel found him filling out forms and talking to someone in professional clothes—perhaps a clerk—on the portable teleholo unit.

The clerk's eyes bugged out. "Erdonium, on Sufiro!" he exclaimed.

"Yes." Stone flashed a smug grin. "The geological analysis is appended."

"Indeed." The clerk examined a screen Manuel couldn't see. "Everything is in order, but this find is phenomenal."

Manuel decided to leave Stone to his work. He returned to the dancing geologists, but discovered that Dr. Danvers found another partner. He continued on and found Sam sitting alone playing games on his handcomp. Manuel decided not to bother him. He wandered back to the tent and fell into an uneasy slumber.

The next morning, he woke to Mr. Stone's voice in the tent.

"Espedie, we need to keep moving. We need to claim the other sites."

Manuel cracked an eyelid. Stone hovered over his father.

"Go 'way," said Espedie. He turned over, flapping his hand at Stone. "Sleep, my friend. The erdonium will still be there tomorrow."

Manuel had never seen anyone turn as red as Stone. He covered his ears and readied himself for Stone to yell. Instead, the geologist whirled on his heel and left the tent.

Manuel dropped back off to sleep, but awoke that afternoon. He found numerous others in the camp just grabbing breakfast, same as him. Shawna Danvers sat alone. Manuel smiled at her and waved. She blushed, but pointedly avoided his gaze.

Manuel found his father talking to Stone over a cup of coffee.

"So, what are we going to name it?" asked Espedie.

Stone grinned. "How about 'Stone-Raton Mine Number 1'? I couldn't have done this without you."

Espedie sipped his coffee. "Thank you, but that's not what I meant. I meant this land." Espedie gestured at the colorful scrub brush and tall mountains beyond the mesa.

"I thought it was called No-Man's Land." Stone's brow furrowed.

"No," said Espedie. "That's just a nickname. If we're going to settle this place, it needs a real name." Espedie peered into his cup, then stood and retrieved more coffee. "What about Tejo?" he asked when he returned.

"What the hell's a Tejo?" Stone shook his head.

"She's the Rd'dyggian who first discovered erdonium," Manuel interjected.

"The Titans discovered erdonium." Stone's words took on a condescending tone which reminded Manuel of Sam.

"And Erdon is the Earthman who discovered erdonium." Manuel shrugged.

Espedie nodded. "But this is a Rd'dyggian world. I think we should pay tribute to those who discovered this planet." He folded his arms.

Stone sighed. "So what? There are no Rd'dyggian settlements here."

"No." Espedie let his gaze wander to the lazy, white clouds over the mesa. "But, who's going to protect us from claim-jumpers? Certainly not the Gaean Alliance or the Alpha Comans. If anything, they may be the ones who try the hardest to force their way in here."

Stone pursed his lips and frowned. "Okay, name it whatever you want, but how are you going to make it stick?"

"Leave that up to me!" Espedie sauntered off, whistling.

Manuel hurried up and finished his breakfast, then

followed his father to the portable teleholo unit. He smiled, when he noticed Roberts above the unit's dais. "The captain drove to New Des Moines today," Roberts explained as Manuel came within earshot.

Espedie told Roberts that they'd found the erdonium and staked their claim. "Also, I've talked it over with Stone. We want to name the continent Tejo. It was Fire's suggestion."

Roberts' eyes narrowed. "Don't you mean T'Ggo?"

Raton shook his head. "No one can say that! We'll go with Tejo, spelled 'T-E-J-O.' It's easier to pronounce. Besides the Rd'dyggians know we can't pronounce half their words anyway."

Roberts smiled. Manuel knew that any human spelling of a Rd'dyggian word was just an approximation. T'Ggo's spelling attempted to convey the sound and accent. "I'll pass that along to the captain," said Roberts.

"Thank you, old friend," said Espedie. "Time for me to go."

Espedie stood and patted Manuel on the shoulder. It was time to get to work.

☠

When Suki Firebrandt arrived on Earth, she had a difficult time finding a university that would accept her. Her diploma had been granted by a frontier school no Earth college recognized. At the schools that would let her take entrance examinations, she had mixed results. She performed well in writing and mathematics, but poorly in Earth history—especially recent history.

At the University of Arizona, she lost her temper at the Dean of the College of Arts and Sciences. "You might have a wonderful school here, but what the hell good does it do if no one can get an education?"

"We have our standards." The dean assumed a smug expression and raised his hands in mock apology.

Fire couldn't stop her rising temper. "Standards be damned, I just want to learn." She regretted the words as soon as she spoke them.

He stood and lifted his chin, so he looked down his nose at her. "Perhaps some remedial school will take you."

Just then, she understood her dads much better. If she had carried a hepler pistol, she would have been tempted to blast the smug smile off the dean's face. Instead, she turned and stormed from the office. In the hallway, she collided headlong with a tall, young man sporting a buzz cut. He dropped his pack and papers.

"Whoops." Fire scrambled to help the university student pick up his scattered belongings. "I'm so sorry."

"That's okay." The young man held out his hand. "My name's Ed Swan, I'm a law enforcement major."

"Hi Ed." Fire's expression softened. "Suki Firebrandt." She shook Swan's hand then finished helping with the papers.

"You're not related to Barbara Firebrandt, the famous admiral, are you?" Swan asked as he sorted papers, then shoved them into his pack.

"My grandmother." Fire shrugged. Without her father around, she figured it was safe to discuss her extended family.

"I bet you could tell me some pretty wild stories about her days in the military. Talk about law enforcement!"

"I don't think my fathers would see it as law enforcement," said Fire, under her breath.

"Fathers?" He arched his eyebrows.

"Only one is my genetic father," explained Fire. "The other helped him raise me."

"That's more detail than I expected. Do they love each other?"

Fire considered that. "Yes. Yes, I believe they do."

"What's your major?" Swan stood and led Fire to a spot in the shade.

"Nothing … at least not here." She folded her arms and cast a glance back at the dean's office.

Swan invited her to a nearby coffee shop. She ordered an iced mocha while Swan ordered black coffee. "How can you drink that in this heat?"

He laughed. "Living in Tucson, you get used to it."

Swan and Fire discussed her life and education on Sufiro and how that seemed to present problems for her finding a college to attend. She told him she sought a school either in North America or Europe because they had the longest histories of academic prestige. "Prestige my ass," said Swan. "When I'm done, I'll have been here at least six years. What'll that get me? I'll probably just be a cop on the street."

"I'm sure you'll go far." She sipped the iced mocha.

"Now, you want a good school? From what I hear, you may want to go to South America. Those schools have been around almost as long as the ones here in North America."

Images of the Andes and Jerome's stories of the Southern Hemisphere's beautiful cities came to mind. "Maybe I'll do just that." Fire smiled.

Once Swan finished his coffee and excused himself, Fire checked her handcomp. After a short search, the University of La Serena in Chile caught her eye. She noticed they ran an astronomy museum on Cerro Tololo, which had once been an important astronomical observatory. She filled out the online application and sent it in, hopeful she'd found a good path forward.

In Tejo, Espedie assigned five people to stay behind at the mesa, while the remaining team members packed up and moved all the equipment and supplies to the next site. The second site proved to be a grassy valley. The farmers tested the grass and found it to be inedible. While Tejo had plants and ground water to support them, so far none of those plants would support life.

On the dig's third day, a large animal pack surrounded the ragtag camp. The animals themselves were the size of lions and resembled hyenas. Their low-slung bodies reminded Manuel of New Granada's kyonosaurs.

Espedie joined Manuel and watched the creatures. "They'll go away if we ignore them." Despite his words, Espedie retrieved his old-fashioned projectile rifle from the family's tent. He preferred it to pulse beams such as heplers in unknown circumstances.

Espedie waved to indicate that the people should go about their business. "Just take it slow and easy. Don't run or make any sudden moves toward them."

Manuel watched as Mr. Stone approached, fingering a hepler's wooden handle. Manuel tried to decide whether the animals were carnivores, herbivores, or omnivores. He didn't think enough plants grew to sustain large herbivores. Then again, he didn't think the plant life they encountered would be sufficient to sustain enough small herbivores to feed a pride of lion-like carnivores.

One of the animals lifted a foot.

Stone raised a trembling arm and fired a pulsed energy beam from his Hepler 225, missing the animal. The animal rumbled a sound halfway between a growl and a jackhammer's roar. Stone fired again. This time his aim proved true. The pulsed beam hit and bounced off. The animal charged. With a squawk, Stone turned and tried to flee.

"Shit," muttered Espedie as he cocked the ancient gun. He raised his rifle and tracked the animal. The animal leaped. Espedie fired. A deafening explosion echoed through the countryside. A flock of winged animals, like fledermice but smaller, lifted off in a black cloud from the tall grass. The blast startled the lion-hyena pack and they ran off. The limp animal dropped onto Stone, covering him in putrid-smelling yellow blood.

It took Espedie, Manuel, and Shawna Danvers' combined strength to remove the animal from Stone, who gasped for breath. Manuel examined him and discovered nothing but scratches and abrasions—no deep wounds.

"I told you to leave them alone." Espedie grasped Stone around his pudgy wrist and hefted him upright.

Stone recovered his breath. "I could have been killed."

"Most animals on Sufiro have tough hides. Heplers just annoy them." Espedie smiled as he handed the hepler back to Stone.

Stone's face flushed red as he glared at Espedie. "Your sense of humor can be irritating you damned hick."

Espedie pushed Stone back to the ground. "You sit there until you can be civil. I just saved your fucking ass."

If anything, Stone turned an even deeper shade of red. "Don't forget who runs this expedition."

"Trust me, I haven't." Espedie spoke through gritted teeth.

Manuel couldn't remember a time he'd seen his father so angry. "I know who organized all these people and all these supplies. I also know who has been sitting in the shade watching men and women work and waiting for results. I know whose son has been playing games and whose son has been digging."

Manuel's cheeks warmed, but he didn't dare interrupt.

This time, the color drained from Stone's face. "Sorry, I'm tired and didn't think." He raised his hands in apology.

Once again, Espedie offered his hand. "I know you're doing your part reporting the claims and doing the paperwork necessary to open the mines, but don't you dare say anyone here isn't doing their share. Everyone has been working their asses off and they'll keep working their asses off as long as they see there'll be a reward."

Stone swallowed. "I'm sorry." He grasped Espedie's hand and stood up. Espedie and Manuel helped him get the blood cleaned up and the abrasions tended. Shredded from the fall, Stone's clothes reeked of the creature's blood. They decided it was better to burn them than try to clean them.

That night, Manuel lit a roaring bonfire. Stone tossed his clothes into the blaze. Many people had seen the fight between Espedie and Stone. Carmen spoke for them when she said, "This is good. You two are burning away the bad blood."

"I'm grateful you saved my life," said Peter. "I'm grateful you're along to help me."

Espedie offered Stone a shot of tequila and the two men drank. Instead of leaving to work on the computer, Stone stayed beside the bonfire and sang with the others.

Manuel looked over his shoulder. Sam hung back and watched for a while before he disappeared into his tent.

After that night, the expedition proceeded with only minor glitches and the occasional equipment failure. In the end, Peter Stone and Espedie Raton claimed six large erdonium deposits in Tejo. Three would stay with Stone and Raton. The other three would go to the Mao Corporation. Stone filed the claims in Little Sonora and volunteers remained at each site.

Peter and Espedie decided to establish their first mine at the site in the grassy valley. A river flowed nearby and it seemed the easiest site to develop given the supplies on hand.

They may not be able to grow crops in the hard ground, but they had fresh drinking water. What's more, Shawna Danvers estimated the deposit under the grassy valley was the largest of all.

Manuel helped Espedie and Carmen build a new adobe house. Other people built close to the new homestead. Manuel noticed the houses were closer together than those in Succor, even closer than those in New Des Moines, but this town was devoted to mining, not agriculture. Once Montgomery Sheppard opened a general store and trading post, the settlers dubbed the town Tejo City.

One night, Manuel checked his handcomp for messages. He learned that Suki Firebrandt had enrolled in the University of La Serena and spent hours at the astronomy museum on Cerro Tololo staring at the stars. She learned about Earth history and told him how much she enjoyed her mathematics and physics courses. He sighed, wondering what the future held for him.

He called his little brother on the teleholo. When he answered, Juan looked much older. He'd grown a mustache and slicked back his hair.

"How's it going, bro?" asked Manuel.

"We're getting ready for a great harvest. We've got carrots, onions, and tomatoes from Earth plus a lot of the purple Sufiro cauliflower mom and dad like."

"You're sending some of those vegetables our way, right?"

"I'll bring the shipment over myself," said Juan. "After all, I want you guys to meet Armanta."

"Armanta?" Manuel furrowed his brow. "Who's Armanta?"

"She's a girl from New Des Moines. She's been helping on the farm."

"Yeah, I think my brother's been sowing a few more seeds than carrots and onions," teased Manuel.

Juan at least had the good manners to blush and not say more. "So, what will you be doing now that there's a mine and a new town?"

"There's a small volunteer police force starting up," said Manuel. "I thought I'd join and learn what I can from the people who were real cops. Plus, dad insists I need to learn about the mining business." Manuel stuck his finger toward his mouth as though he would gag on it.

"Can't be any worse than the business part of farming." Juan laughed. "That Mr. Roberts is a strict teacher."

"Someone's gotta keep you in line." Manuel laughed. "Listen, I gotta go, but we'll talk soon. Take care of yourself, bro."

Juan gave his brother a wave and they signed off. Manuel sat back and sighed and wondered what the future would bring.

Chapter Ten

BETRAYAL

Peter Stone shipped a small load of erdonium ore to Earth and used the profits to build an office building in Tejo City across from the general store. Espedie Raton recruited several people from the claim expedition to work as supervisors. He sent the supervisors to New Granada to recruit more people to work in the mines. He promised fair wages and good living conditions.

Growing up on Sufiro, Manuel knew how difficult farming could be. He'd experienced the long hours tending crops and animals, fitting in school work when he could, then dropping into bed, exhausted at day's end. He had never become addicted to games like Sam because there had been no time. They'd had few luxuries because all his father's profits had gone into buying more seed, animal feed, and supplies to keep equipment running. Manuel had no complaints about life on the farm, but he knew many people would be glad to give it up for a regular, predictable salary and time off to call their own.

Espedie and Peter taught Manuel accounting and payroll. His eyes tended to glaze over within an hour and he would ask to be excused to go on a volunteer police patrol of the town. Sam managed personnel and enjoyed matching the right people to the right positions. Manuel thought those duties must be like a game to Sam.

As miners arrived in Tejo City and started work, Manuel found the accounting chores more interesting. He reported the numbers to his father, who oversaw shipments off world. The more shipments went back to Earth and its colonies, the more money came in and the easier it became for Sam to fill jobs.

147

Even though the job grew more interesting, Manuel still took half days off to patrol streets, then go into the desert to practice target shooting. Learning about heplers and projectile weapons became a passion. He longed to travel to a police academy on a colony world or Earth itself to learn better technique.

One day Manuel sat back from the computer and rubbed his eyes. He looked over at Sam. "I'm ready to knock off for the day."

Sam scowled and looked at the clock, then turned around and faced Manuel. "It's not even lunch time. You might try putting in a full day some time."

Manuel shrugged. "The work's getting done, isn't it?"

Sam frowned. "I suppose so," he conceded.

Manuel leaned forward. "Say, why don't you come with me? You like those games where you shoot things. Ever tried your hand at the real deal?"

Sam fidgeted and looked as though he would make an excuse, but after a moment he grinned. "All right, you're on!"

They took Manuel's hover out to the desert. When they reached a suitable spot, Manuel placed cans atop rocks, then strolled back to the hover. He gave Sam a lesson in how to use the hepler safely.

"I think I got this." Sam aimed the hepler at a distant can and fired. The pulsed beam careened past the can and rock, blowing sand several feet into the air.

Manuel laughed. "Not bad for a first try."

Sam clenched his teeth and fired off several more rounds. Each shot missed by several feet and pockmarked the ground.

Manuel put his hand on Sam's arm. "Easy there. This isn't a game where you keep shooting until you hit something. Let me show you." Manuel took careful aim and fired. The pulsed beam knocked the can off the rock.

"So what?" Sam sneered. "It's not a skill you can use in the office. Why should I care?"

"There's more to life than business, Sam." Manuel holstered his pistol. "Maybe you might want to go hunting some day. Maybe you'll want to defend yourself. Maybe you just want sunshine and fresh air."

Sam kicked at the sand, then glared at Manuel. "If I help my father build our business, I'll be rich. I can afford all the food I want without hunting. I can hire guards to defend me. If I want sunshine and fresh air, I can lounge around a pool."

Manuel shook his head. "That kind of success can be an illusion. You become addicted to those luxuries. What happens when they go away?"

Sam narrowed his gaze. "One day, Tejo City will be a center of commerce and the mining empire we're building will be a galactic power. Now, you can shape up your act and we can build Stone-Raton Mining together, or you can keep leaving the office on your own and I'll buy you out and Stone will be the only name people will know."

Manuel sighed. "I don't care about power. I want to lead a good life and find a way to contribute to this world and this galaxy."

"Nice ideals." Sam pulled a handcomp from his pocket and looked at the time. "You should take me back to the office. Lunch hour is over."

☠

Suki Firebrandt received a message from Jerome Ellis reiterating his invitation to visit him on Nantucket. He had a month-long break between assignments that coincided with the university's autumn break. On the break's first day, she caught a transport from La Serena to Boston. A monorail carried her from Boston to Hyannis where she took a boat to the island itself.

She enjoyed the wind whipping through her hair as she stood on deck and crossed the gray water. Soon, Nantucket appeared on the horizon, like a plush green mat sitting on the ocean. She remembered recent history lessons and knew sea level rise in the twenty-first century had threatened the island. She didn't know how this little sandbar had survived. Had it been submerged and then rebuilt when the waters went down again? Was it more like Seattle where the residents built a new city atop the old? She knew the answer would be interesting no matter what.

The ferry slid into Nantucket's harbor. She smiled as they passed the stubby Brant Point Lighthouse. At one point, such structures had been essential to navigation. Now satellites alerted vessels to hazards. She wondered if she could get inside a lighthouse and see it for herself.

Jerome met Fire at the dock. She dropped her bag and the two embraced and shared a long kiss. She stepped back, held Jerome's arms, and looked into his eyes, feeling welcome. He retrieved her bag and they walked up through Nantucket's cobblestoned main street.

"I thought we'd take your stuff to my house, then I can give you a tour," said Jerome. "Are you hungry?"

"Not yet." She noted all the gray shingle and brick, so different from La Serena and its whitewashed walls. They no longer built with adobe there, but her current home resembled Sufiro much more than this place. Her eyes roved over antiques for sale in the shop windows.

They turned a corner onto a residential street and she sighed contentment as she breathed in the scents of flowers and herbs. It may be autumn in La Serena, but it was spring on the northern hemisphere island of Nantucket.

They passed a sign for a place called the Maria Mitchell Association. It included a red brick building with an observatory dome among gray-shingled houses. A woman with gray hair stepped from a one-story building across the street and called out to Jerome. He turned and walked up to a white, picket fence. He introduced Nancy Collier, the Maria Mitchell Association's director.

"Who was Maria Mitchell?" Fire narrowed her gaze.

"America's first woman astronomer," explained Ms. Collier. "The association is devoted to nature, history, and astronomy." The director turned to face Jerome. "I just got off the teleholo with Minister Takami of the Alliance. He says probes in the Atlantic show an increase in petrochemicals and he suspects a leak in some old capped well, but they haven't been able to pin it down. Do you suppose you could talk to Richard and find out if he knows anything?"

"If I can find him, sure." Jerome gave Nancy's hand a pat and led Fire to his house, just a few doors up from the building with the observatory dome.

"Who is Richard?" Fire asked.

"He's an old friend. Would you like to meet him?"

She smiled. "I'd be delighted to meet any of your friends."

They deposited her bags in Jerome's living room. He offered to give her the full tour later, then turned around and left the house. Fire followed him back to the docks and wondered if this Richard lived on a houseboat. Instead, Jerome led her to a small boat tied up at the pier. He helped Fire aboard and then untied the boat. He fired up the propulsors and slid out into the bay.

Fire stepped up to Jerome, who stood behind the boat's wheel. "I just got here. Don't tell me we're leaving already."

Jerome flashed a reassuring smile and revealed those wonderful dimples. "We won't go far. I just spoke to Richard yesterday and I know where he's hunting. We should be able to find him."

Fire shook her head. "Hunting? Don't you mean fishing?"

Jerome shrugged. "I suppose you could say that. Mostly he eats squid."

The boat circled the island and then shot out to sea. Jerome focused on the compass and automated navigation. Fire left him and moved to the boat's bow. Unlike the ferry, this small boat heaved and rocked with the water's motion. The propulsors' quiet hum did little to compete with the wind rushing by the boat. She held onto the boat's forward rail and laughed as her long hair blew straight back.

An hour later, Jerome brought the boat to a stop. Fire looked around. No other boats sat atop the water, nor could she discern any other structures. "So, was this just an elaborate ruse to get me out here alone? You could have just asked." She laughed.

"Just wait." Jerome retrieved two translator units from a box beside the wheel. He placed one over his ear and handed the other to Fire.

He draped his arm around her shoulders and she leaned into him. Fire's legs wobbled and she couldn't believe she had such a crush that her knees would go weak just from a man's embrace—albeit a nice, attractive man's embrace.

Then, she realized it wasn't her legs. The boat itself wobbled. A moment later, water spouted just off the boat's side drenching both Fire and Jerome. A gray form rolled through the water just beside the vessel and a rapid clicking, almost like static, sounded.

A voice spoke from the translator. "The cycle continues."

"The cycle continues," intoned Jerome, almost like a litany. "The hunt is the art, old friend, and I hear an old human artifact may be leaking waste and interfering with your hunt."

"You have heard correctly," said the creature, which Fire now realized was a sperm whale. The whale rattled off coordinates which Jerome transcribed onto a handcomp.

"I promise, humans will come out and fix the leak." With business concluded, Jerome introduced Fire. "Richard, may I present my friend, Suki Carter Firebrandt? Fire, this is my dear friend, Richard."

"Charmed." Fire meant it. She wanted to reach out and touch the whale, but wasn't sure if that would be rude.

"Are you also from Nantucket?" asked the whale.

"I'm from a planet called Sufiro," said Fire. "It's on the far side of the galaxy."

"Whales know not the ways of space." The whale rolled over so that a single eye looked up at Fire. "Are the oceans of Sufiro damaged like the oceans of Earth?"

Fire shook her head. "The oceans of Sufiro are beautiful. I wish I could show you."

"I would enjoy seeing, if you could find a way."

Fire considered that. "Let me see what I can do."

"The cycle resumes." With those words, the whale dove into the depths.

"The cycle resumes," echoed Jerome.

Suki removed the translator. "Richard?" She arched an eyebrow. "As in Dick? Like Moby?"

"I didn't name him." Jerome shrugged. "Richard is an old Norman name, which means brave ruler. Still, he's listened to many narrated classics. I wouldn't be surprised if he's listened to Melville. He would appreciate the irony."

"Is there a reason whales have never traveled into space?"

Jerome shrugged. "They've never expressed an interest

and it would be quite an engineering challenge building a craft that could carry them."

Fire looked to the place where Richard disappeared below the waves. "What if space could be brought to whales? Do you think Richard might be interested?"

"I don't know. You'd have to ask him." Jerome narrowed his gaze. "What do you have in mind?"

"I was just reading in one of my classes how Rd'dyggians have adapted their neural interface units to be able to project images directly into the brain." Fire grinned. "I wonder if it would work on whales."

"Do you know any Rd'dyggians?"

"My dad has a friend named Arepno…"

"Sounds like quite a project." Jerome activated the propulsors and turned the boat in a wide arc and set a course for Nantucket. "In the meantime, let's get the info about the well to Ms. Collier and then go find some dinner. I don't know about you, but I'm starved."

Fire looked down at her drenched clothes and laughed. "I hope we plan to change first." She then looked ahead and began to think she could love this Nantucket just as much as Jerome did.

Mary Hill reviewed plans for a new housing project on New Des Moines's outskirts. She served as the city's mayor and longed to create a continental government, but so far, all she had managed was to get each of the continent's cities to send representatives to quarterly meetings she hosted. She sighed and tried to focus on the plans. New Granada held so much potential if people would just pull together. She could help contractors get lumber from the north, she could better negotiate water usage rights, and better distribute job services throughout the continent.

Her teleholo chimed, interrupting her thoughts. She answered and blinked when Espedie Raton's torso appeared above the dais. "Good afternoon, Ms. Hill. I hope you don't mind my call."

Hill shook her head. "The interruption is welcome. I hear congratulations are in order. You and Mr. Stone have done an outstanding job setting up a mining industry in No-Man's Land."

"The continent is called Tejo, now."

She smiled and huffed an amused snort. "Tejo, of course."

"At the moment, two different companies manage six mines spread across the continent along with town sites to support them." Espedie leaned forward. "Peter Stone and I realize there needs to be a civil government to coordinate road construction and law enforcement and assure both companies operate on a level playing field. He asked if I knew anyone who could do that and you were the first person who came to mind."

Hill tried to decide how much to reveal about her hopes for the planet. "What you suggest is quite interesting, but you can't snap your fingers and make a government happen. I know that more than anyone."

"Would you mind traveling to Tejo City to meet with Peter Stone? He can fill you in on our plans and needs, and perhaps suggest ways we can help launch a government."

Hill shook her head and sat back. "Out of the question, I won't serve as the puppet governor for one company in a two-company country."

Espedie waved his hands. "It's not like that at all. We want independent civil moderation of any disputes. Moreover, we need a civil infrastructure. We can't afford to have two companies setting up businesses and accommodations at cross purposes."

Hill pursed her lips and nodded. "All right. I'll talk to Stone. I make no promises, but I'll listen to what he has to say."

"Great. When would you be able to travel to Tejo City? We can send a shuttle transport for you."

Hill checked her calendar. "I could go tomorrow."

Espedie checked something outside of the scanner range. "We'll send a transport to the New Granada Space Port. Is the fifth hour after midnight too early?"

Mary considered the time difference between New Des Moines and Tejo City and realized a later flight would arrive quite late at night. She could always catch a nap on the shuttle. "I'll be there." She signed out and tapped her fingers on the desk. After a moment, she placed a call to her longtime business partner, Floyd McClintlock. He appeared over the teleholo dais wearing a suit. "How's business today?"

He shook his head and frowned. "Slow. The new model hovers just aren't selling."

"I thought they'd be a big hit, nice and sporty..."

He laughed. "We don't have the roads for nice, sporty hovers. People want big tough vehicles they can take through the grass and underbrush."

"Tell me about it." Mary leaned forward. "Listen, I just had a call from Espedie Raton of all people. He says Peter Stone wants to set up a government in Tejo."

McClintlock shrugged. "Makes sense to me. They'll want some infrastructure and having a government would allow them to join the Gaean Alliance, which would have definite trade advantages."

"I know all that, but I've tried to do the same thing here in New Granada for years and no one from the other towns listens. They're happy with their loose association." Hill rolled her eyes.

"Many people who came to New Granada feel Earth's government burned them." McClintlock shrugged. "They've been taxed and regulated to the point they can't live life the way they see fit. I seem to remember that's the reason we packed up and moved here."

Hill snorted and remembered when McClintlock proposed moving to Sufiro and then her first meeting with the pirate, Ellison Firebrandt. Even so, life on Sufiro had been good to her and Sufiro's branch of the Church of the Creator's Word prospered. "The way I figure, it doesn't hurt to hear what he has to say."

"A lot of people who went to Tejo came from New Granada," said McClintlock. "If you were to run a campaign for a continent-wide office, I'm sure you'd do well."

"I'm concerned Peter Stone might try to assure that outcome. What's more, he might consider me on his payroll." Hill sighed.

"Listen to what he has to say." McClintlock smiled. "I know you'll make the right decision." He signed out.

Hill called up the housing development plans, made some comments, then sent them back to the developer. She then went home for dinner with her son, Rocky, and a chance to think more about meeting with Peter Stone.

The next day, she awoke in the predawn hours and drove her hover to the New Des Moines space port. A Stone-Raton Mining shuttle sat on the tarmac as expected. She climbed aboard and they made a two-hour sub-orbital flight around the world to Tejo City. They entered the city's airspace at 1900 hours local time. The shuttle pilot pointed out the mine and the town site. The town's neat, grid-like arrangement impressed her.

The shuttle sat down at the space port and she stepped out. Sufiro's sun lay close to the horizon. A cool breeze wafted through her hair. A tangy, oily smell tickled her nose and she missed the aroma of vegetation. Despite that, the plascrete, glass, and metal spaceport facility impressed her. Peter Stone emerged from the building and extended a chubby hand.

She shook his hand and he led her through the building to a waiting hover. As they rode through town, she appreciated the houses and their neat yards and she grew sentimental for New Des Moines's early days.

The hover pulled up to a small, two-story office building. They climbed the stairs and entered a comfortable office with a picture window that looked out over the city. Lights turned on around the town and flood lamps illuminated the spaceport and the mine. The lights also washed out the sky, keeping her from seeing the stars.

"You've gone to considerable effort to bring me here," Mary folded her arms.

Stone indicated a seat, then he offered her something to drink. She asked for a cup of coffee. Stone activated an intercom and ordered the coffee along with water for himself.

"Espedie has explained a lot of it to you. As for the rest, we want a legitimate government, Earth recognition, everything done right and proper."

Mary nodded. "Those are good goals. I've been trying for years to build infrastructure and a relationship with Earth, but

I keep meeting resistance in New Granada. Why do you think I'll succeed here?"

"The people who came here with me are the people who realized New Granada can't offer them the lives they wanted. Many of those people came from New Des Moines. They know you. If we get the word out that you're working to build a government, I think they'll support you."

A knock at the door interrupted them. A thin man entered and delivered Stone's water and Hill's coffee. She took a sip and nodded approval. "This is from the rain forests on Alpha Coma, isn't it?"

"I import it at great expense, but I can afford it now." Peter smiled.

She took another sip of the coffee and evaluated Stone. "You say 'we' can get the word out. Do you mean Stone-Raton Mining would be my official sponsor?"

Stone shook his head. "That's not my goal at all." He leaned forward. "I've spoken with the Mao Corporation. It's in their interests for Sufiro to be an official Earth colony as much as it's in my interests. We'd contribute equally to your efforts."

"At some point there would have to be elections," Mary eyed Stone over the coffee cup, "unless you plan to set up a dictatorship."

"Elections are a given." Stone set the water aside. "The thing is, both companies have an interest in a government. Neither of us have the time or experience to create this government. That's why we need you."

"Can I recruit whomever I choose to help me?" Mary sipped her coffee.

"I would recommend recruiting people from each of Tejo's six town sites, to assure the process of creating a government is fair and no one accuses you of following one party's interests." Stone steepled his fingers.

"When do you want me to start?" She set the coffee cup on Stone's desk.

"Right away, if possible."

Mary stood and walked to the large picture window and looked out at the nice, orderly town. She had shaped New Des Moines into such a place, but she hadn't succeeded with the rest of New Granada. She could make a clean start in Tejo. "I have six more months left in my term as mayor."

"Is there a conflict of interest in serving as a town mayor and also helping Tejo form a government?" Stone shrugged and stood beside her. "You could always ask your partner Floyd McClintlock to help you. A branch of your hover dealership would go over well here, I think. I heard you have those sporty new hovers in..."

Mary sighed. "I'm interested. I'd like to sleep on it."

"We can get you a hotel room here in Tejo City."

"I'd rather sleep on it back in New Granada." She looked down into Stone's eyes. As far as she could tell, he was just what he appeared, a geologist who struck the paydirt he longed for. Now, he realized more needed to happen to secure his legacy.

Before he could answer, a knock sounded at the door. A man who resembled a younger, taller, thinner version of Stone peaked around the door. "Sorry to interrupt, I didn't know your meeting hadn't finished."

Stone waved the apology aside. "I was just going to call for a driver to take Mayor Hill back to the spaceport."

The young man smiled. "I can drive her. No problem at all."

Stone held out his hand to the younger man. "This is my son, Sam."

Hill shook hands with him. "Are you sure about taking me to the spaceport? I thought you wanted a word with your father."

"It can wait until we're home," said Sam.

"All right." Stone nodded. "I'll call the shuttle pilot and have him stand by."

Hill shook hands with Stone and told him she'd be in touch later in the week. Sam escorted her downstairs to a nice hover outside.

"I'm curious," said Sam. "Aside from the people of New Des Moines, how would you characterize New Granada's populace?"

Mary Hill looked at Sam Stone. The father had proven easy to read; the son much less so. "Drifters." She climbed in the hover and continued as he took the controls. "People looking for a new life."

"People who left old lives behind." Sam started the hover. "People of questionable moral turpitude."

Mary kept her expression neutral. "I suspect that's true in many cases."

"Wouldn't it be good if such people could be helped? I can see a path where such people could become productive members of society instead of ... lawless stalwarts." He pulled out of the parking area and turned onto the street.

Hill turned to face the younger Stone. "Tell me more."

☠

Manuel and Espedie Raton knocked on Peter Stone's door. "Come in," called Stone.

Father and son entered the room and took two chairs opposite the desk. Stone stood at the window looking out at Tejo City from the second-floor window. All around town, construction crews worked on buildings to serve the town's fast-growing population.

Stone turned around, a proud smile on his face.

Another knock sounded at the door. Sam Stone entered a moment later without awaiting his father's response. He swaggered into the office and threw himself into the one open chair opposite his father.

Peter nodded to Sam, then sat behind the desk. "Mary Hill has negotiated a deal with Transgalactic Space Lines to create special rates for anyone choosing to move to Sufiro permanently."

"That's great news," remarked Espedie. "That should help us get more people to work the mines."

"Yeah, great," grumbled Sam. "It helps Mao Corporation just as much as us, and they already have lower costs than we do. What would help us more is if she could get those damned tariffs that the Erdonium Trade Federation insisted on lifted." He pointed at Manuel. "For that matter, it wouldn't hurt if you paid those farmers from New Granada less."

Manuel scowled. "They're skilled labor and you know it.

They're worth the money we pay them. Many bring technical skills. Those without skills are still strong. We get more work per man than Mao Corporation does."

"You have the statistics to prove it, don't you?" growled Sam.

Peter held up his hands. "I didn't call you here to start a fight."

Manuel shrugged. "The only way we could pay less than Mao Corporation would be to force people to work for next to nothing."

Sam's eyes sparkled. He turned toward his father. "You know, many New Granadans have criminal backgrounds. What if we told them the choice was work for us, or we report them to the Gaean authorities?"

Manuel rose from his chair. "That would be extortion."

Peter stood up, his face flushed red. "Sit down, Manuel. How dare you think I would even condone such a thing?"

Manuel sat down and folded his arms. "I'm never sure what to think. When laws benefit the company, they're good. When they benefit someone else, they're bad."

"That's the way of the world." Sam sneered.

Peter opened his mouth to speak, but no words came out. He dropped into his chair and put his head down on the desk. "So much to worry about." His breath came in short, shuddering bursts.

The sneer vanished from Sam's face. He rushed forward. "Dad!"

Manuel and Espedie hopped to their feet. Manuel pushed past Sam and then helped Espedie lower Peter to the floor.

"He's not breathing," muttered Espedie. He pushed his fingers into the geologist's fleshy neck. "It's hard to tell for sure, but I don't think there's a pulse."

Manuel pointed to Sam. "Call a doctor." He then started chest compressions. Espedie shot to his feet and darted into the hallway. Sam hadn't moved. When Espedie returned, he carried an automated defibrillator.

"I called Doc Greene. She's on her way." Espedie started the defibrillator. It gave them instructions. Espedie opened Peter's shirt and applied the two electrodes. Manuel sat back.

The machine delivered a shock and instructed them to continue compressions. Espedie took over from Manuel.

Sam dropped into his father's chair and watched.

At last Doc Greene arrived. She waited for the defibrillator's next cycle, then shooed both Espedie and Manuel back. She pressed a stethoscope to Stone's chest, then touched a probe to his head and checked a handcomp. She huffed out a deep breath, then stood and faced Sam.

"I'm sorry, Mr. Stone. Your father's gone. Cardiac arrest."

"Gone!" Sam's eyes went wide. He leapt to his feet and grabbed the doctor's arms. "What do you mean gone? If this weren't some hick planet on the ass end of the galaxy, you'd take him to the hospital and revive him. I'll give you money, profit shares, even. Just bring him back."

"I'm sorry," said Doc Greene. "Even if we had Alpha Coma's most up-to-date facilities, I couldn't revive him. He has no brain activity. He's gone."

Sam opened his mouth to say more, but Manuel grabbed his arm and hustled him out to the hall. He turned around long enough to see his father kneeling beside Peter Stone, making the sign of the cross. "Good bye, my friend."

Six months after Peter Stone's untimely death, Manuel still maintained the Stone-Raton Corporation's books. He had earned enough money to move out of his parents' house.

Manuel entered his office one morning juggling an electronic key, a cup of coffee, and a handcomp. Somehow, he managed to get through the door and deposit the items on his desk without spilling them. He activated his computer and brought up the latest figures for productivity, worker compensation, materials and equipment cost, and income.

At first glance, all looked fine, as it always did. Mine output had steadily increased as had profit. He placed one chart over another to get it out of the way. As he did, he blinked at the translucent holograms. He took a sip of his coffee, then double checked that he plotted profit and output on the same scales. He rubbed his chin. Profit increased at a faster rate than output.

He checked the materials' cost. That increased at a rate similar to output. Then he looked at payroll. The line was much flatter than the others. He sat back and drank more coffee.

He almost let it go, assuming the miners just grew more productive with time. If true, they gained experience at a phenomenal rate, especially at the Stonestown mine. Manuel collated the data, checked individual reports from all the mines, put it on his handcomp and took another drink of coffee before taking the data to Sam Stone.

After Peter's death, Sam inherited his father's partnership. Despite a lack of formal education, Sam proved an adept manager and profits had increased since his father's demise.

Manuel showed his charts to Sam, who nodded and grunted at appropriate points in the narrative, but never looked surprised. "The numbers would make sense if Stonestown hired about fifty new miners," said Manuel, "but those extra employees hadn't been reported for some reason."

Sam shrugged. "If true, wouldn't they have drawn more from company funds to pay those people?"

Manuel squirmed. He had checked that. "I would think so, but I don't see how…"

Sam waved Manuel's concerns aside. "It looks to me like the workers and managers at Stonestown should be commended for a job well done."

"Even so, the numbers don't add up. Are they not paying overtime as they should?" Manuel shook his head.

"I don't see the problem here. We're making a sizable profit. The supervisors and the miners at Stonestown are doing a terrific job." Sam leaned forward and folded his hands. "I think you've been working a bit too hard. You used to like going out into the desert for some target practice. Why don't you take some time off?"

Manuel sat up as a thought occurred to him. "Hey, why not send me to Stonestown? If they've found a good way to ramp up productivity, shouldn't we apply that to all the mines?"

Sam frowned. "I have the reports. I'll decide what we do at the mine sites."

Manuel narrowed his gaze. "Aren't you and my dad partners? Doesn't he have a say?"

"I'm telling you, as a friend, don't pursue this." Sam's voice assumed a hard edge.

Manuel realized he'd run up against a proverbial stone wall. He decided to change tactics. "No problem, just trying to do my job." He held up his hands. "You know what, you may be right. I should take some time off."

Sam relaxed and flashed a broad smile. "You won't regret it."

Manuel collected his belongings, deposited them in his office, then drove to his father's house. He showed Espedie the data.

"I noticed that as well," said Espedie. "When I spoke to Sam, he offered to buy my share of the company."

Manuel ran numbers through his mind. "He can't have enough money to buy you out. We've been profitable, but not that profitable."

"I haven't told you much about what I did to make a living before I came to Sufiro." Espedie sighed and looked to the ground. "The details don't matter. What matters is that Sam knows. All these years, he's been digging through records, learning who I ran errands for, what I bought and sold. It's all in the past, but he suggests if I dig too deep, he'll reveal it … or worse."

Manuel ground his teeth. "Dad, that's extortion. He can't get away with it."

"He's made a decent offer for my share of the mines. I'm half tempted to take him up on it. We've made some good money, had some good adventures, but I'm ready to move back to New Granada."

Manuel stood and patted his father's shoulder. "Something's not right. I don't trust him. Somehow, I think if you accepted his offer, he'd find some way to renege on the deal."

Espedie met Manuel's gaze. "I don't really care about that. I made plenty so far."

"I still don't like it and I'm going to get to the bottom of this." With that, Manuel went home. As Sam suggested, he took some time off work and let his stubble grow out for a few days, then he packed a bag and bought a ticket on the overland airship to Stonestown. He dressed in some grungy clothes. On the ship, he looked like another miner seeking a new job.

Manuel enjoyed the airship ride from Tejo City to Stonestown. It was his first time aboard such a craft and he marveled at the view through the windows. The land rolled like a snapshot of ocean waves. In places, mountains thrust up. Wind and water eroded some mountains into mesas. As he passed over the countryside, he thought about Fire and her life on Earth. Last he knew, she'd completed her physics degree and she would complete her history degree in less than a year. He considered how much he'd earned in the time since the mines opened. He could travel. Maybe he should just quit and go to Earth after all, but then what?

When the airship arrived in Stonestown, Manuel took a room at a hotel, then went out to the mine site. He barely recognized the place. By the time the original expedition had reached Stonestown, all the sites looked alike to him.

The mine site resembled the site outside Tejo City—all except for a large building near the mine entrance. He walked to the gate and presented a standard worker's clearance card. The guard waved him through. He strolled toward the mine entrance, then veered toward the strange building. In the back, he found a ladder to the roof. He climbed up and looked in a window to see a room lined with bunk beds—a dormitory.

Since when did Stone-Raton mines house people on site? He continued up to the roof and waited in an air conditioner unit's shadow. The machine clanked and banged as though failure was imminent. It couldn't be producing much airflow below.

When the evening whistle sounded, a half dozen men in official-looking uniforms herded a few dozen miners from the entrance. Instead of walking toward the main gate, they went to the dormitory. One man fell to his knees and called for water. A uniformed man dragged him upright and shoved him toward the dormitory.

Manuel fell back against the air conditioner unit. He wanted to go to the mine's local office and demand an explanation. Being Espedie Raton's son, he might even get one, but then what?

Sam Stone had all but threatened him and his dad if he didn't leave things alone. What's more, his law enforcement training told him not to rely on first impressions. He had two choices. He could stay and investigate further, or he could return to Tejo City and confront Sam. If he remained in Stonestown, he would be missed and Sam may take action against him anyway. He decided to return to Tejo City.

On the return airship journey, he remained in his cabin and thought how best to confront Sam. When he arrived, he climbed down the ramp, went home, showered, shaved and went into the office.

He knocked on Sam's door. "Well, you look rested. Are you ready to get back to work?"

"Almost." Manuel sat down across from Sam. "I took a little trip and visited our mine at Stonestown."

Sam's smile melted.

"There's a dormitory on site for at least one shift of miners. I don't find any on-site housing on our books," pressed Manuel. "It doesn't look good. Someone on the outside may think you're using slave labor."

"Slave labor?" Sam's eyebrows rose. "That's crazy! No one condones slavery in the Confederation."

"What about the Tzrn or the Alpha Centaurans?" asked Manuel.

"But those are aliens." Sam waved Manuel's objections aside. "No one in the Gaean Alliance advocates slavery."

"No one openly objects to it, either. It's been over eight hundred years since it's been practiced on Earth. It's never stopped if you consider migrant labor on Mars."

"Is that what this is about?" Sam chuckled. "Migrant labor? Yes, we have adopted a migrant labor pilot program at Stonestown."

"Food and housing? Are you even paying them a minimum living wage?"

Sam shook his head. "There is no minimum wage in Tejo."

Manuel shuddered. "Where did these people come from?" He thought he knew the answer and he doubted the people came from off world.

Sam stood and walked around to the front of the desk. He sat down and stared into Manuel's eyes from a height. "I warned you not to pry into this. What's more, you have no authority here. Your dad already agreed to sell his share of the mines to me."

"What?" Manuel stood so he looked down into Sam's face. "Just when did this happen?"

"Two days ago." Sam shrugged. "Apparently while you were out and about looking into things that don't matter." Sam stood and looked Manuel in the eye. "You are welcome to stay on as an employee of the company."

Manuel stormed from the office and went home. He poured himself a shot of tequila and downed it, then poured another. At last he stopped trembling. He would call his father in the morning and figure out what to do next.

When he awoke, he showered and shaved, then activated the teleholo and entered the code for his father. When he didn't get an answer, he sent a message to his father's handcomp. Two more hours went by without an answer. He tried the teleholo again and finally decided to drive over to his father's place.

He knocked on the door. When he didn't get an answer, he let himself in. His father sat in the recliner, face blank and skin waxy. He checked his dad's pulse. Not finding one, he shouted for his mother. He found her lying on the kitchen floor.

Manuel fell to his knees and released a sob.

He then pulled himself together and called Doc Greene. She arrived half an hour later and scanned Espedie and Carmen's bodies. "You've heard of the Succor whip arachnids, haven't you? They dig them up from time to time in New Granada."

"You mean those burrowing things that killed Suki Mori all those years ago?" Manuel narrowed his gaze.

The doctor nodded. "It seems your mom and dad were both stung."

"Do those things even exist in Tejo?" Manuel shook his head. "I thought they needed soft ground, not the hard rock we have around here."

"I guess we'll have to be more careful." With that the doctor turned away to call the morgue.

Manuel moved into the dining room and logged into his father's bank account. No one had touched the money ... yet. He then made a call to Ellison Firebrandt. He breathed a sigh of relief when his dad's old friend answered.

"I remember you told my dad to call if anything happened," said Manuel.

Firebrandt nodded.

Manuel relayed the events of the last few days to the old privateer captain. "I think I'm taking my life in my hands if I stay here."

Firebrandt scowled. "I think you're right. I only know one person killed by those arachnids." The former pirate captain's voice hitched. "I can't believe one somehow got in and killed both your mother and father. Something is going on." The captain sat back and retrieved a pipe from his pocket and lit it. "Give me the relevant account numbers and I'll make sure Roberts secures your funds. I'll bring the launch and get you this afternoon."

Manuel read the account information to Firebrandt, then closed the connection. He went out to the living room where he found medical technicians covering his mother and father's bodies with blankets. Manuel said a silent good bye and vowed he'd find a way to make Sam Stone answer for his crimes.

☠

In Chile, Suki Carter Firebrandt received a long message from Manuel Raton. He told her what had happened to his parents and that he had returned to New Granada. He had moved to Nuevo Santa Fe where he found a job as deputy sheriff.

She called him on the teleholo. The man who appeared looked tired and haggard—no longer the carefree boy she remembered from her youth. "How are you?"

"I'm well, Fogacita," he said. "I've been taking classes in the evening. I think I may even run for sheriff later this year. I think I have what it takes."

"Why in the world did you move to Nuevo Santa Fe?" She knew little about the settlement other than it sat up near New Granada's northern mountain range.

"The valley here is green and pretty. It's a real balm after the barren wastes in Tejo." He shrugged. "The people settling here seem to appreciate the experience I gained helping my dad and Peter Stone build Tejo City. It's a place I can call my own like my dad called Succor his own."

"Good for you." Fire forced a smile. "What are you doing for fun these days?"

He shrugged. "Target practice." He brightened. "I've been reading. I finally picked up *Moby-Dick*."

She quirked an eyebrow at the choice and thought it might be just a touch too appropriate.

Two days later, Fire received a call from the Rd'dyggian, Arepno. His image materialized over her teleholo unit. "There is a philosopher called G'Liat. He has agreed to meet with you to discuss the prospect of a conversation with the whale Richard."

"Can he use Rd'dyggian neural interface technology to show him space? To show him the oceans of Sufiro?" Fire leaned forward in anticipation.

"I believe he can," said Arepno. "I can provide him the imagery."

"When can we go meet him?"

Arepno consulted something out of the scanner's range. "I can pick you up in one Earth week's time."

Fire checked her own calendar. "Okay, I have a lot to get ready. I'll be in touch soon."

For her senior thesis, Fire proposed to conduct an in-depth interview with Richard about whale history using Rd'dyggian neural interface technology. It would allow her to get details and nuance no other researcher had gained through human-based translators. In return, the Rd'dyggian neural scanner could be used to give Richard a taste of what could be seen out in space.

She contacted Nancy Collier, the director of the Maria Mitchell Association on Nantucket and told her she planned to visit in a few days to meet with Richard and get his permission to continue with the interview.

"While you're here, you could interview for a job as well," remarked Collier.

Fire's brow furrowed. "What job would that be?"

"I'm thinking about retiring." Collier's eyes seemed to sparkle. "You've developed a rapport with the whales and you know old telescopes from your time in La Serena. It seems like you'd be a good match for all the association's missions."

"I'll consider it on one condition," said Fire. "I don't want to be tied down to one island on Earth. I want to be able to travel."

"By now you of all people should know Nantucketers are rovers. It doesn't matter whether you rove the oceans of Earth or the sea of stars. Islanders wander."

"Then let's talk when I get there."

Collier smiled. "I imagine you'll want to see your friend Jerome Ellis while you're here, too."

"I do. I have a ... proposal for him." Fire grinned and terminated the call.

Chapter Eleven

POWER IN UNITY

People had been disappearing from the township of Nuevo Santa Fe on the planet Sufiro. The newly minted sheriff, Manuel Raton, intended to put a stop to it. He patrolled the streets in his hover. Only the hum of its propulsors kept him company. Tracking down the kidnappers would be much easier if he could use nano-surveillance drones, but the ores in the valley's surrounding mountains blocked the signals and the strong winds swept them out of town, never to be heard from again, rendering them not just useless, but an expensive loss.

Nuevo Santa Fe's geology and climate were two important factors in his decision to settle there. It meant Sam Stone couldn't easily monitor his whereabouts. Someday, somehow, he believed Stone would have to come to him.

He scanned the houses. A few were modern plascrete structures, but most were made from local materials such as adobe or even wood from the nearby pine forests.

He turned a corner and saw a carryhover parked in front of Hoshi Matsumoto's house. The man repaired farm equipment and didn't own a carryhover. Raton tapped his vehicle's accelerator, then killed the propulsors, drifting by Matsumoto's house in silence. The carryhover's cargo area stood open and empty, as though someone had made a delivery, but the porch lights were off, Matsumoto's door was closed, and no deliverymen were in sight—and it was after midnight.

Raton allowed the hover to drift across the next cross street before applying the brakes and letting his vehicle settle on the ground. He hopped out and strode back to Matsumoto's house. He knocked. When no one answered, he tried the door and found it unlocked. Drawing his hepler pistol, he entered. All appeared neat and orderly. A light shone beside a chair and a book lay face down on an end table. He peered through a door into the kitchen, then turned on his flashlight and crept down the darkened hall to a bedroom at the back of the house.

He pushed open the door and the hairs on the back of his neck stood on end. Hoshi Matsumoto lay trussed up on the bed like a calf, silent and still. Dead or tranqued, Raton couldn't tell. He pushed aside the momentary flashback of finding his mom on the kitchen floor.

"Empty your hands and reach for the sky." The cold voice came from the shadows at his right.

He shifted his gaze just enough to see a pistol. Raton dropped his weapon and the flashlight, then raised his hands.

Someone jumped on him from the left, grabbed his arms and pulled them down behind his back. Raton closed his hand into a ball and pressed a control stud in his palm, sending a stun pulse through his sleeves, knocking the assailant who held him backwards.

Raton dove for the floor as the gunman in the shadows fired, scorching the floor inches from his head. He grabbed his hepler and flashlight, then aimed into the shadows. The shooter had vanished. Footsteps echoed from the hall.

The sheriff rolled over and checked the stunned man—out cold, at least for the time being. He leapt to his feet and ran after the other suspect. As he reached the yard, the carryhover pulled away, setting the neighborhood dogs barking. Raton ran to the street, hoping he could see a license plate on the retreating carryhover. Even if he couldn't make it out, perhaps his bodycam would catch an image.

The carryhover turned a corner and disappeared from view. He considered giving chase, but he needed to check on Mr. Matsumoto and he wasn't sure how long his assailant would remain unconscious.

He jogged through the house, rolled his attacker over and zip-tied his hands together, then stood and checked on Mr. Matsumoto. The repairman had a steady pulse and his chest rose and fell as though in a deep sleep. Only tranqued, as he had hoped.

Raton reached for his radio and called in medical and police backup. While waiting, the sheriff knelt down and found his assailant had a wallet.

Raton scanned the man's ID with his handcomp. A weight settled in the pit of his stomach. Mr. Gordon Lassiter was an employee of the Stone Corporation.

The revelation couldn't have come at a worse time. The next day, he planned to meet with Mary Hill, governor of Tejo. The Earth Alliance levied heavy tariffs on goods from both continents and she wanted to present a united front as she demanded Earth's council reduce the burden so they could better compete against other markets.

Raton rubbed his hand through his hair. Mary Hill had refused to investigate his parents' murders claiming there was no evidence to contradict the coroner's report of accidental death by arthropod sting. What's more, she feared pursuing Stone would damage the Stone Corporation, doing harm to Tejo. Now he had proof the Stone Corporation had been abducting people to work in the mines. It made him glad the company no longer carried his name.

The assailant—Lassiter—began to stir and Raton resisted the urge to kick him.

Sirens broke upon the sheriff's consciousness. He heaved a sigh and went out to meet them. He could think more about his meeting with Mary Hill once Lassiter was safely locked up and the paramedics had tended to Mr. Matsumoto.

Mary Hill watched the surrounding countryside as her hover limo carried her through the pass into Nuevo Santa Fe. She had things to discuss with Manuel Raton that wouldn't be prudent over a hololink. No matter how secure the connection, there were people who could listen in. It seemed quaint to travel overland, but the same ores that interfered with Raton's nano-drones also interfered with the sensors that would allow for safe computer-guided, high-velocity air travel into the valley. Unfortunately, the pass made the possibility of ambush seem all too likely in light of the botched personnel extraction.

She tried to brush her concerns aside. In the year since he left Tejo, Raton had never blamed her for his parents' deaths. Why start now?

"Troubled?"

Mary blinked and looked over at the creature sitting next to her in the back of the hover limo. Var Gwenyu came from a small, phase-locked planet orbiting Proxima Centauri, the smallest star in the Alpha Centauri system. From a distance, a Centauran might pass for human. They had a head, stood upright on limbs, and had a trunk with another set of limbs. They had two tentacles for each human arm or leg, giving them a total of eight limbs—like an octopus.

Var spread languidly on the seat. When Mary first saw the Proxima Centauran, she thought him hideous, but her feelings changed as she grew to know Var. A warmth filled her belly and her cheeks flushed.

"Just letting my imagination run away with me." Mary chuckled and slid closer to Var.

She tended to think of Var as male, but Centaurans had no strict gender. Each individual carried both eggs and sperm. Centaurans could not fertilize themselves, and it would be a bad idea even if they could. Mated Centaurans sometimes picked one individual to be mother for life. Other couples took turns.

"You seem unduly worried about this meeting." Var draped a tentacle around Mary's shoulder. "Manuel Raton must agree Earth's tariffs are egregious. Allying with you is the best way to put an end to them."

Mary sighed, uncertain whether Manuel could be counted on to view the situation as logically as Var. Earth imposed tariffs on goods from Sufiro even though the planet had one resource no other Earth colony possessed—the mineral erdonium. Until Sufiro, the only worlds with erdonium were those close to their stars like Mercury or the hot side of Proxima Centauri. The problem was that all of Sufiro's erdonium was in Tejo and a single continent had no sway over Earth's senate.

New Granada had no unified government recognized by Earth. She needed the continent united and allied with Tejo to give her power to negotiate. Manuel Raton was popular and wealthy. He could make that happen. "My relationship with Manuel Raton is … complicated," said Mary at last.

"More complicated than our relationship?"

Mary laughed. "Our relationship is good and … interesting, but it's hardly complicated."

Var came to Sufiro representing Galactic Erdonium. They bought the third largest stock share in the Stone mines, making them part owners. In that way, Var was like a prince, sanctioning the work of the upstart humans who mined a resource they had never before controlled in quantity.

"Something beyond the political and financial ramifications of this meeting troubles you." His tentacle worked its way down the front of Mary's blouse.

She slapped at it playfully and it retreated.

On Earth, Mary had sold used hover cars. She read people well and that ability helped her make the best deals. The people who bought hovers from Mary had always gone away happy, even when she had sold a vehicle for well over its value.

The hover limo cleared the pass and Mary noted Nuevo Santa Fe's ramshackle houses. Personnel extraction was not slavery. The Stone Corporation gave people a good place to live and good food to eat. To her mind, that made a better life than scraping by in a rude dwelling with no amenities.

Var's tentacle returned and flicked over her nipple. She turned and smiled. Meeting Var had been nothing like love at first sight. Rather, she'd resented the off-world corporation's meddling. Over time, Var had made deals, maneuvered, and bluffed people in ways that had made her take a second look at this alien.

And she warmed up to Var's appearance—mollusks could be cute, right? His warm, brown eyes melted her heart and he could adjust his muscle tension to be firm in all the right places while still being soft and cuddly.

"I've known Manuel Raton since he was a boy." Mary put her hand on Var's chest and felt his heart beating. "Our relationship hasn't always been an easy one."

"Ah," Var imitated a human nod—difficult since Centaurans didn't really have necks. "You refer to his father's death."

Centaurans weren't telepathic—no race in the galaxy

was—but they could be extraordinarily empathic.

"It was an accident. He can be made to see that." Var spoke softly, reassuring her.

"I hope that's true." The details didn't concern her. Either Espedie's death really had been an accident or Manuel could be made to see the death as an accident.

She snuggled into him while one of his lower tentacles worked its way up her skirt and she lost herself in his caress. She lost track of time, but came back to her senses when the chauffeur cleared his throat, holding the door open.

Mary affixed a stern expression, buttoned her blouse, straightened her skirt, and walked into the Nuevo Santa Fe Sheriff's Office.

Manuel Raton displayed a hologram of Gordon Lassiter, the man he'd captured while on patrol. He then pulled up the scan of the carryhover he'd watched speed away from the crime scene. He enhanced the image of the license plate and ground his teeth—a rental from New Des Moines.

He looked up as Chief Deputy Li Chang knocked and poked her head around the door. "Mary Hill and Var Gwenyu to see you, Sheriff."

Raton frowned but nodded. "Show them in."

Hill wore a broad smile as she entered the room. She looked much as he remembered her—about five-foot-five with short hair. Although he'd seen her graying hair in holovids, her face looked much craggier in person than he expected. She opened her arms, as though expecting an embrace. "Manuel, it's been too long."

"Mary, we have a problem." He inclined his head toward the hologram of Lassiter. "People have been mysteriously disappearing for the last year and I know they're being taken to work in Tejan mines." The sheriff dropped into a chair without approaching closer. "I know you want to find a way to put our difficult past behind us, but this has got to stop."

Hill's smile only faltered a little as she clasped her hands in front of her. "It's possible Stone Corporation has ... overreached, but your best chance at bringing a case like this to trial is by joining with me rather than opposing me."

Raton narrowed his gaze and decided he would listen to her argument. "The Stone Corporation and the Tejan government are virtually inseparable," said the sheriff. "Joining you would be like an admission that kidnapping New Granadans was okay."

Mary shook her head. "If we're united, then under Earth Alliance law you can prosecute—" her eyes darted to the hologram "—Mr. Lassiter and file suit against the Stone Corporation for damages. If we're not united, then you're like an independent world. You could declare war, but how far would that get you against Tejo, much less the Earth Alliance?"

Raton sighed. "Look, I know why you've come to me. I'm sheriff of New Granada's second largest township. To make the unification deal you're proposing stick, I'd have to get the backing of the other townships, effectively running for the presidency, a job that doesn't even exist here." Which would get me out of your hair. He left that last part unspoken.

Var Gwenyu leaned forward. "That power would put you in a position to seek justice."

Raton felt himself drawn into the alien's seductive brown-eyed gaze. He shook his head. "Maybe that's true, but hell, I'm only twenty-two years old. Who would elect me president?"

"You don't give yourself enough credit. You're a natural leader. If you bring a strong platform, people will listen." Mary stepped toward Raton. "Your people live in poverty. I need you on my side if we're ever going to get Earth to take us seriously and negotiate in good faith with us. It's the only way we'll make things better on Sufiro."

Raton frowned and folded his arms. He knew she had her own agenda. Despite that, he didn't see how the people who'd elected him would fail to benefit. He also had to admit that he kind of liked the idea of running for a presidential office. He could do far more good than he could as sheriff. He could deal with Hill as an equal and he would be in a better position to expose Stone Corporation's policy of kidnapping New Granadans.

"All right, what do we need to do to make this work?"

"The first thing you need to do is hold off prosecuting Gordon Lassiter."

Raton's brow furrowed, not liking her opening hand, but he had his own card to play. "I'll consider it, if you'll promise to get the Stone Corporation to end the kidnappings."

☠

Two weeks later, Manuel Raton sat at home sipping tea. A team of friends and advisers had just departed. All had supported the idea of him running for New Granada's presidency. As sheriff, Raton could investigate Lassiter's ties to the Stone Corporation, but even if he found ties, what could he do?

The investigation could continue while he ran for president. If the investigation bore fruit, the high office would give him more power to end the abduction of New Granadans and bring those already taken back home. They had discussed ideas and worked out strategies. Although he knew he needed to get some sleep, his thoughts buzzed with possibilities.

The door chime startled him. He turned his head, expecting to see a misplaced coat or a forgotten handcomp. With neither in evidence, he shrugged and walked to the door.

When he answered, he shuffled back a step or two, surprised to see the Centauran, Var Gwenyu. The alien wore a shimmery, form-fitting one-piece suit that accentuated his—no her, definitely her—curves.

"What brings you here?" stammered Raton. "With Mary Hill on her way to Earth, I thought you would be busy in Tejo."

Var gently pushed Raton back inside and closed the door behind her. "We're being manipulated, you and I."

Raton frowned. "I know. I'm being careful."

"Not careful enough," said Var. "Like you, I believed Mary Hill was working to make things better on this world, but I have discovered evidence that she's being manipulated as well."

Raton pursed his lips and nodded. He gestured for Var to sit and offered a drink. She took a glass of wine. "What have you discovered?"

"When I came here with Governor Hill, she seemed ill at ease. I decided to investigate the cause." Var took a sip of wine, as though to steady her nerves. "I started looking into Earth law. As you know from the incident with Gordon Lassiter, Stone Corporation has been quietly engaged in a policy of personnel extraction, grabbing workers from New Granada. It's illegal, but the corporation gets away with it because New Granada has no unified government to pose a challenge."

Raton shook his head. "Mary—Ms. Hill—has kept her word. The kidnappings have stopped."

"Only because it suits Sam Stone's long-term goals. There's an old clause in the Earth Alliance laws not invoked for over a century and mostly forgotten. If New Granada is part of the Alliance, then any industry deemed necessary for military success can conscript people openly in time of war."

The sheriff dropped onto the couch next to Var. "Stone wants Mary to institute forced conscription to fill the mines?" He poured a glass of wine for himself and took a gulp. "Of course, there would have to be a war."

"In a galaxy as big as ours, there's always a war somewhere."

Raton set the glass down and put his face in his hands. "What else have you learned?"

"In time of war, the possessions of any non-humans may be confiscated without compensation. My corporation is a major stockholder in the Stone mines. Stone could pressure her to eject me and seize my holdings. My company would lose not only its profits, but its initial investment."

Raton looked up. "Surely the Alpha Centauran Hegemony wouldn't stand for that."

Var snorted a laugh that would have been cute if not for the suppressed bitterness. "What would they do? Declare war? There's always war somewhere." Two of Var's tentacles inched behind Raton and began massaging the tension from his shoulders. An image of Fire flashed to his mind, but she had married Jerome Ellis. He didn't have to feel guilty about Var's attentions.

"She wanted me to hold off prosecuting Lassiter. She said it was to foster a spirit of amity. Is there something else?"

"His credentials are fake. Gordon Lassiter is not an employee of the Stone Corporation—or at least not a traditional employee."

"What do you mean?"

"He's a mercenary from Prospero. Corporations don't hire mercenaries. Governments do. The truth of his identity would prove collusion between the government and the Stone Corporation. The fact that Tejo has been hiring mercenaries from a world outside the Earth Alliance would threaten Sam Stone's plans."

Raton nodded slowly. Mercenaries explained how Mary could stop the kidnappings so quickly. She was the one paying their salaries. He picked up the glass of wine and settled back into Var's warm embrace. He expected her to be squishy and cold like an octopus, but she was warm and firm like a woman. It had been too long since he'd lost himself in Suki Firebrandt's embrace.

"How did you learn that Lassiter was a mercenary? Surely those aren't files Mary leaves open on her computer."

"She has called a name at the height of ecstasy—the name of a former lover, I believe—Morgan. Knowing that, the password was not hard to decrypt."

Raton decided he didn't want to know more just yet and took another sip of wine.

Mary Hill's yacht, the *Prydwen*, jumped into normal space at a way station at Tau Ceti. One more jump and they'd reach Earth. Her handcomp pinged as messages came in from the way station. She picked up the pad. About halfway down the list of messages, she saw one from Var. The Centauran was so good to her. She hated that Var would probably lose his position after Stone seized Galactic Erdonium's stock, but she hoped Var would see she had no choice.

Her mouth fell open as she read Var's letter. "With regret," wrote Var, "I must return home so I may work to assure Galactic Erdonium's interests. I understand you believe you feel compelled to cooperate with Sam Stone, but I plead with you to reconsider. He doesn't care about anyone but himself."

Mary's breath caught. She felt betrayed but something in Var's words pricked her conscience.

She poured herself a glass of brandy to calm her nerves. Everything she did was for Tejo and for Sufiro. On Earth she'd only owned a small business. On Sufiro, she'd risen to a continent's leadership and was determined to give back and make life better for everyone on the planet.

She turned her attention to the news feed. She took a sip of brandy, but nearly spit it out when she read that Manuel Raton had brought charges against Gordon Lassiter.

She set the brandy snifter down with a trembling hand. She never had any animosity toward Manuel. His talents were wasted as sheriff of a small town on the far side of the galaxy. She wanted to see him succeed.

She also believed New Granada's people deserved a better life. Sam Stone provided food and shelter to those people extracted. He promised they could earn enough to buy nice homes in the city. He allowed visits by elders from the Church of the Creator's Word to minister to their needs. Why couldn't Manuel see this was a better path for people than letting them struggle as farmers?

Mary blinked, then grabbed the brandy snifter and downed another gulp. Manuel putting Lassiter on trial would unravel Stone's plans. Knowing Stone, he would act and he wouldn't care who got in his way—and Manuel would almost certainly get in the way.

She had to go back and try to keep the situation from spiraling out of control. She looked at the date displayed on her handcomp. It was only a day before her meeting on Earth.

She strode forward into the yacht's cockpit. The pilot looked up and nodded. "Ma'am, we'll be ready to make the final jump to Earth in about four hours."

"How long would it take to go back to Sufiro and return to this point?"

The pilot's brow furrowed and he frowned. He punched data into his computer, then double checked the results. "I'd allow four days round trip."

Hill performed a few mental calculations. "Get me Senator Costello."

"Yes, ma'am," said the pilot.

By the time she returned to the executive cabin, the senator's hologram sat in an empty chair, waiting to speak with her. "I'm looking forward to our meeting tomorrow," he said.

"I'm sorry, Senator, but I'm going to have to ask to reschedule. Something's come up and I need to return to Sufiro."

Senator Costello looked down and shook his head, as though disappointed. "I'm sorry to hear that, Ms. Hill. I'm afraid the hearing time is locked in. We can't change things at this late date."

"Oh?" Mary arched her eyebrows as though shocked. "I'm so sorry to hear that. I fear we may have to raise the price of erdonium. We already have to charge more than I'd like to compensate for the Alliance's tariffs. If you can't afford it anymore, I'm sure I can find other buyers. Alpha Coma Berenices has expressed interest."

Senator Costello blanched. "How long do you need?"

"Oh, not long," she said. "Do you think you can reschedule our meeting for next week?"

He looked at an unseen display to his left and frowned, but nodded. "It'll be difficult, but I think we can make that work."

"Delighted to hear it and I'm very sorry to have created this inconvenience."

Mary terminated the connection, then sighed. She had helped to create this mess. She prayed to the Creator that she could help clean it up.

☠

Ellison Firebrandt's hologram appeared above the teleholo in the sheriff's office. "I just received a message from Shawna Danvers over in Tejo. Sam Stone canceled several important meetings this afternoon and a ship registered with G.S.C. 101243 landed in Tejo City's spaceport a couple of hours ago."

Manuel shook his head, not recognizing the number.

"Gunrunners and mercs," said Firebrandt. "I encountered them a few times in my privateer days."

Manuel pursed his lips, understanding.

"There's something else. Roberts picked up the *Prydwen's* transponder signal in orbit."

Manuel's eyes widened. "Really? Mary Hill wasn't due back on Sufiro for another week."

Firebrandt snorted. "I think you got her attention by announcing Lassiter's trial."

"I wanted her attention." Manuel sat back and sighed. "I just figured she would call me so we could talk before she met with the Earth Alliance. What do you think she's up to?"

The captain stroked his mustache. "Stone certainly wouldn't want Lassiter to testify, but killing him outright would force you to probe even more."

"So Stone, at least, wants to get him out of my custody. A jail break." Manuel's brow furrowed. "And Mary?"

"Don't judge her too harshly." Firebrandt leaned forward. "I think she's actually made an effort to keep Stone from acting on his worst impulses. The problem is, Stone has a way of getting people to do what he wants."

"Like getting my dad to sell his share in the company right before killing him."

Firebrandt nodded.

"All right, I'll get my people ready for whatever Stone and his band of mercenaries has in mind." With that, Manuel terminated the call.

Manuel could see no reason for Stone to delay putting a plan to extract Lassiter from jail into action. His people would strike as soon as they could get to New Granada. He expected the mercenaries to make their play in the pre-dawn hours the next day. The only advantage he had was the geography-driven weather which made it dangerous for spaceships to land in his town. That meant any attack would come overland through the pass.

He gathered his deputies and filled them in on the situation. Two would guard Lassiter's holding cell. The rest would spread out through the pass. "Avoid shooting. Take them alive, if possible," ordered Manuel.

"Capture them?" Schulze's brow wrinkled. "Why?" The big man shrugged.

"The more mercenaries we capture, the more it builds our

case." Manuel studied his deputies' faces and nodded. "Any other questions?"

They shook their heads. "Go get some sleep and we'll meet back here at midnight."

As the deputies departed, Manuel fell back into his chair. He'd tried to talk Var into staying. Var could fight for her people better from a position of power on Sufiro than from a faraway corporate office. Manuel wondered if she'd used intimacy to manipulate him, or if there had been genuine feeling. He wondered whether or not he would ever see Var Gwenyu again.

The sheriff shook off the melancholy and went back to a cot he kept in a dark corner of the office. There, he fell into a restless slumber until the first of his deputies—reliable, mountain-like Schultze—returned. Soon, the rest of the team had assembled. They pored over the map one more time, checked their equipment and moved out.

Raton drove out to the pass with his chief deputy, Li Chang. The quiet woman chewed her thumbnail as her eyes roved the rocks of the pass, illuminated only by starlight. Raton and Chang left the hover car near a crook in the river that ran through the pass and hiked up a gully to get a better view of the road. The pass served as a conduit for chill northerly winds discouraging the vegetation that covered the surrounding mountains. Raton pulled up his collar.

As Raton took a position behind a boulder, Schultze's voice came over his handcomp. "I see something moving, but can't make it out. I think they're in stealth suits."

The Tejans had enough money to afford the expensive camouflage. Optical sensors on the suits transmitted images from one side to the other. If the person wearing the stealth suit stood absolutely still, it was almost impossible to see them.

A moment later, a pair of bright flashes flared up from Schultze's position. Raton spat a curse as he peered up over the rock and tried to distinguish the silhouettes of his people from those of the spindly trees that clung tenaciously to the sandy soil.

The sheriff tapped his handcomp and spoke to Schultze's partner. "Jones, what do you see?"

There was no answer. A moment later, another flash appeared from the same direction. "Got one," growled Susan Jones, "but not before they vaporized Schultze. I'm going to subdue him before he wakes up."

Raton waited several tense minutes for Jones's report. A fireball erupted from her position. Apparently, the mercenary had been wired. Raton wondered if the merc knew he'd been made into a human bomb to keep Sam Stone's secrets.

The sheriff tapped the handcomp, broadcasting to all his deputies. "Until further notice, don't approach fallen suspects. My capture order is rescinded."

Raton scanned the terrain with a pair of binoculars. Wind blew through the pass, setting the thin grass rustling. His hair blew into his eyes and he shivered. He blew in his hands to warm them, then scurried around the boulder, trying to get a better view.

Another set of flashes erupted in the distance, but no report followed.

"I think I see something," called Li Chang. She ran forward and disappeared into a gully. His heart pounded as he surveyed the landscape. A moment later, Chang reappeared, but disappeared again behind a hill.

Light flashed from behind the hill and a tremor rolled through the ground.

"Chang!" called Manuel.

He ran toward the gully.

"I'm all right, boss," called Chang. "Someone in a stealth suit took out one of the mercs."

Raton's brow furrowed as he crossed the gully. A shimmering form bobbed near a cluster of rocks just ahead. Raton took aim and squeezed the trigger. The figure dropped down, flattening the tall grass.

The sheriff scrambled up the slope toward the person, who pulled themselves to their feet. Apparently, he'd only struck a glancing blow. Up close, he could make out the figure's female form. He covered her with his hepler pistol. She stood upright and pulled the hood from her suit—Mary Hill.

"I'm here to talk to you. These men are under orders to extract Lassiter at all costs. Let them do their job and go. It'll diffuse this situation, then we can go to Stone together and work something out."

Manuel shook his head. "I'm not interested in working with Stone."

"There's power in unity, Manuel. We can make things better."

Raton caught a shimmering out of the corner of his eye. A stealth-suited mercenary lifted a hepler pistol. "Mary, get down!" he called as he dove for the ground.

Mary whirled toward the mercenary, who fired. She crumpled to the ground.

Li Chang targeted the stealth-suited mercenary and dropped him. She then hit the dirt before the mercenary's bomb exploded.

Once the dust cleared, Manuel rose to his feet. He walked over to Mary and looked down into her lifeless eyes. A tear rolled down his cheek. "Power in unity? Power for whom?" He reached down and closed her eyes.

Part III: The War

The Year 2973 Earth Standard Calendar

"There is many a boy here today who looks on war as all glory, but, boys, it is all hell. You can bear this warning voice to generations yet to come. I look upon war with horror."
—William Tecumseh Sherman from a speech to the Grand Army of the Republic Convention, August 1880

Chapter Twelve

THE CLUSTER

A board the star cruiser *Astrolus*, tactical officer John Mark Ellis trudged to his berth after a long shift. He yanked off his jacket, hung it in the locker, grabbed a book of poetry, then climbed into the upper bunk. Once there, he activated a privacy force field and turned on a fan. He opened a cupboard over the bunk itself and retrieved an old wooden box. From it, he took a cigar. He inhaled its aroma, then snipped off the end and lit it. He savored the taste, then lay back, thinking a brandy snifter would make the evening perfect. Well, to be honest, he also would have preferred reclining in an easy chair back home on Nantucket, but this was nice for an evening on deep space patrol.

He opened the book at random and smiled when he read the title. "Whales Weep Not" by D.H. Lawrence. His mother had given him the book on his tenth birthday. She'd told him the book came from her father's library. Mark couldn't imagine how a bloodthirsty pirate like Ellison Firebrandt would enjoy poetry.

Mark inhaled more smoke from the cigar and then blew it out. He glanced at the poem and remembered his father blushing when he asked what the word "phallus" meant. Jerome Ellis had changed the subject to how humans learned to talk to whales, who in turn already communicated with the Confederation of Homeworlds.

"Is it true creatures like whales float through Jupiter's clouds?" Mark had asked at the first opportunity.

"Indeed, yes." Jerome had sat down and lit a cigar. "There are many ancient, powerful, and hot-blooded creatures among the stars. More, I'm sure, than we know."

A pounding on the wall beside the berth interrupted Mark's memories.

"I know what you're doing in there," called engineer's mate Janelle Shoukry. "You've got the light on; I can see the smoke shadows swirling around."

"Is that any way to address a senior officer," grumbled Ellis.

"The air scrubbers have to work overtime to clear the air every time you light one of those damned things, *sir*." Ellis could not mistake the sarcasm she spit out with the last word.

"It couldn't make the ship's air smell any worse." Ellis wrinkled his nose as he considered how odors like stale plastic, sweat, oil, and ozone pervaded the ship's atmosphere. He had good reasons for retreating to his bunk once in a while with a good cigar.

"Sir, may I remind you that tobacco is illegal on Earth?" Shoukry's voice shifted from sarcastic to exasperated.

"Outdated laws," grumbled Ellis. "The Dairtox we take to breathe Earth's polluted air keeps tobacco smoke from being the health hazard it had been centuries ago. As long as the force field's on, I can do whatever I want in here. You know the regulations."

Shoukry didn't answer. Instead, her locker slammed shut. A moment later, a low bass beat, not quite audible, thrummed from the bunk below. He sighed. She had activated her own force field and now listened to some loud, driving music. He considered pounding on the bottom of his bunk, but doubted she would hear or respond even if she did. He sighed and turned to a Shakespearean sonnet. He amused himself reading it to the music's almost-inaudible beat.

A chime from the overhead speaker interrupted his thoughts. The thrumming from below stopped mid-beat. A woman's voice sounded over the intercom. "Attention, this is Executive Officer Shankar. The Old Man wants all officers on the command deck immediately."

Ellis knocked the hot cherry from the end of his cigar into the incinerator chute, then deactivated the force field. He climbed down from the upper bunk and donned his jacket. A moment later, Shoukry emerged from her bunk. She wrinkled her nose, but didn't say a word. Barefoot, Ellis padded toward the command deck.

Spaceflight, even at its peak, had never been well funded on Earth. Small, outdated ships comprised the Gaean Navy. The largest ships had three decks. When off duty, ships' crewmembers slept in bunks lining the upper deck's inner hull. Officers' bunks were just a little larger than the berths of enlisted personnel and they could be sealed off with a privacy force screen. Only the captain had a space big enough to be called a "cabin." Ellis glanced into Captain MacPherson's quarters as he passed—just a bunk, a fold-down desk, and a chair on rails.

Ellis strode onto the command deck and stood next to the gunner's mate who manned the tactical station in his absence. Shoukry appeared a moment later, buttoning her jacket. She walked over to the engineering station. Captain Angus MacPherson occupied a large, black chair on an elevated dais in the command deck's aft quarter. The executive officer, Karen Shankar, stood beside him.

Naval captains had, for centuries, been called "the Old Man." Over half the captains in the fleet were women and most captains were under fifty years old. Spacers often joked "the Old Man" was neither, but Angus MacPherson fit the description well. A forty-year space veteran, the captain's white beard framed a hard, lined face.

Three more officers entered the command deck. As they found places to stand, the captain pointed to the ship's communicator. "We just received an urgent message from Earth," explained the captain as the wraith-like woman turned to her console and executed a command.

"Earlier today, the star cruiser *Courageous* encountered an unknown star vessel." Ellis recognized Admiral Marlou Strauss's voice. "The vessel was larger than any we've encountered. Even the Titans say they've never encountered its like.

"*Courageous* attempted to make contact. The alien ship ignored her signals. The two ships faced each other for nearly an hour. At that point, the captain reported his intention to scan the vessel. We have not heard from the *Courageous* since then.

"We have been trying to reestablish contact. So far, no luck. The alien may have interpreted the scan as a hostile act and attacked *Courageous*. They may be damaged, even destroyed. I want *Astrolus* to investigate. Render aid if possible. Coordinates of the *Courageous's* last transmission have been beamed to your pilot. Good luck."

MacPherson glanced around the command deck, making eye contact with several officers in turn. "We'll be at jump point in forty-five minutes. Get some scran, then assume action stations." Serving under Captain MacPherson, a sailor soon learned scran was old British Isles slang for food.

Ellis nodded, then followed Shoukry. His mind whirled as he tried to imagine the giant vessel the *Courageous* encountered. He tried to think what they would do if the other star cruiser had suffered critical damage. *Astrolus* didn't have room for many survivors. He hoped the silence indicated little more than a destroyed comm system. He stopped at his bunk to grab boots.

Shoukry smirked. "Thank the odd gods of the galaxy for alerts. At least now the air filters may make it a few more days before I have to replace them."

Ellis snorted a laugh as he pulled on his boots. "Air filters are cheap compared to speakers." He appreciated the momentary distraction from the upcoming rescue operation. "And where's that 'sir'?"

Shoukry cupped her hand beside her ear. "What did you say? Can't hear you. Guess I was playing my music too loud. At least I wasn't smoking a damned smelly cigar."

Ellis shook his head and the two continued on to the ship's mess. There, the cook dropped plates piled high with something covered in a lumpy brown goo.

Shoukry sniffed it then glanced at Ellis. "I thought your cigars smelled bad."

Ellis shrugged. "You know Cookie's philosophy, cover it with enough gravy and we won't know what we're eating."

The cook pointed at Ellis. "Better be nice to me, sir, or tomorrow it'll be purple."

"Oh yum. Fruit flavor." Ellis patted his stomach and winked.

"You only wish the algae tanks would give us fruit flavor," said the cook as he left to retrieve more plates.

As Ellis ate, the captain's voice came over the intercom. He gave a succinct mission summary in his deep, sonorous brogue. Ellis nodded as he listened. The captain laid out the plans in such a straightforward manner, it sounded like just another job. The tactical officer ate the meal, which actually wasn't bad. It reminded him of mashed potatoes and beef chunks in gravy, even though he knew it started in protein vats and algae tanks.

Cookie gathered up the dishes as the pilot's voice came over the intercom. "We have reached jump point. All hands assume your stations. All hands assume stations for jump point."

Shoukry gave Ellis a nod and the two walked forward to the command deck. Shoukry took a seat at the environmental systems' monitor while Ellis relieved the gunner's mate at tactical. He checked all ship's weapons systems, then checked force field and power reserves.

From the raised dais, the captain ordered the jump. Reality collapsed on itself. For a moment the ship screamed, then it sang. At last, it fell silent. Ellis closed his eyes and held his stomach for a moment. When his stomach settled, he glanced back at Captain MacPherson, who sat, unfazed. Only white knuckles gripping the command chair's armrests betrayed discomfort.

"Ship hull integrity normal," croaked the pilot, sounding as though he still struggled with nausea.

"Ship's weapons operational, sir," reported Ellis.

"Environmental systems nominal, sir." Shoukry's voice trembled.

More reports came in from around the deck.

"Ship's communication systems operational, sir." The communicator touched her forehead. She had a brain implant that allowed her to control any ship's system in an emergency. Back when Ellis's grandfather was a privateer, such officers controlled numerous systems as a matter of course, but those officers often lost the ability to distinguish between the real world and the world within the ship's network.

"If communications are working, where's my damn

picture?" MacPherson gestured toward the holo viewer.

The communicator activated a control and an image formed. The command deck officers gasped in unison. A large clump of iridescent spheres dwarfed the smaller, cylindrical *Courageous* in the hologram. The image transfixed Ellis and seemed to speak to some dark, unused corner deep within his brain. "There are many ancient, powerful, and hot-blooded creatures among the stars," mused Ellis, under his breath. "It's a cluster."

The executive officer narrowed her gaze. "What did you say, Ellis? If you have a report, speak up."

"Cluster," echoed the captain. "It's as good a name for the alien as any until we learn more." MacPherson sat forward, resting his chin on his fist. He studied the hologram for a moment. "How large is the Cluster?"

Shankar checked her screen. "Approximately two hundred meters in diameter overall. The outer spheres are fifty meters in diameter. Reflectivity from the star in this system indicates the spheres are quite smooth. I'll have to commence active scan to learn more, sir."

MacPherson held up his thick hand. "Don't. What's the status of the *Courageous*?"

Shankar scanned their sister ship. "*Courageous* has been hulled, sir." Ellis looked back at the XO as routine pings and beeps sounded from ship's stations breaking the uneasy silence. "I detect hull breaches on every deck and in every section. I read no life signs."

"Lifeboats?" MacPherson's gaze never left the hologram.

"None used, sir. They're all accounted for on the ship."

"Damn it all to hell." MacPherson's fist pounded the command chair's armrest. "Communicator, try to contact the cluster ship. Use all known languages. Use ship's lights to flash a prime number sequence at it if you have to. Just try to get them to talk to us."

"Aye aye, sir." The communicator sat back, using her brain implant to try to contact the alien. After a moment, she shook her head. Indicators on Ellis's console alerted him that ship's lights had been activated. Perhaps she was trying the captain's suggestion. "No response, sir," she reported at last.

"Dead slow ahead." The Old Man stroked his white mustache.

The ship's pilot nodded and activated thrusters. As they eased forward, the alien ship vanished.

"Full stop," ordered the captain. "Where is she? Where is the Cluster?"

"Temporal-Gravitational waves indicate she has something like an Erdon-Quinn engine aboard, sir." Shankar shrugged. "She jumped."

"But to where?" The Old Man chewed his lower lip. After a moment, he sat up, straightening his uniform jacket. "Take us over to the *Courageous*. Communicator, copy their sensor telemetry to our computer. I want the captain's logs as well. We need to know what happened."

"Aye aye, sir," responded the pilot and communicator in unison.

As the *Astrolus* approached the *Courageous*, Ellis studied the attack pattern. The ship drifted, all dark, including the EQ generator which should glow a vibrant blue when functional. Neat holes, resembling open mouths, gaped from the ship's sides. Ellis brought up the image on the tactical display and overlaid a grid. He shook his head. "Those blast points are too precise for any ship I know."

"Hmmph." The captain studied Ellis's screen. "Let's see what the sensor analysis shows."

"I have the records from the *Courageous*, sir," reported the communicator. "I'll display the log in the holo viewer."

The Old Man gave a curt nod, then folded his arms. In the holo viewer, the alien ship reappeared, only now they watched the image as it would have appeared in *Courageous's* viewer. A green beam flashed into existence from a forward sphere. Ellis jumped even though he knew it was a replay. The beam winked on and off like a strobe light.

"Switching to hull camera," reported the communicator. The green beam moved down the ship's hull. "*Courageous* took these images two minutes after she scanned the alien."

"What do the scans of the alien vessel show?" MacPherson's gaze never wavered from the viewer.

"Nothing, sir." The communicator shook her head.

MacPherson edged forward. "What do you mean nothing? The scan had to reveal something."

"Nothing more than we learned from visual analysis, sir." The communicator turned to face the captain.

"Any energy readings to indicate electromagnetic shields?" The Old Man stood, hands behind his back.

"Nothing, sir."

MacPherson looked at each duty officer in turn. "Opinions?"

Shankar sighed. "For all we know the scan damaged the Cluster and its crew interpreted it as hostile."

"Perhaps," said Shoukry, "but the cluster ship sure seemed undamaged."

Ellis shook his head. "For that matter, sir, we have no evidence the Cluster is even a manned vessel."

"You mean it might be an unmanned probe?"

"We have no evidence to the contrary, sir."

MacPherson sat down and faced the viewer. "Communicator, get me command," he ordered.

Sam Stone's private yacht entered Saturn's orbit. He gazed through the viewport at the beautiful world. He could just make out faint dust spokes within the glistening rings. On the planet's surface, a white oval rotated among the golden clouds. Stone realized he watched a powerful storm, but it seemed peaceful and lazy from orbit. As the ship continued along its trajectory, Stone spotted the planet's largest moon, Titan. His tongue flicked a new, foreign object behind his upper lip. He was still adjusting to the diamond he'd had set there—a small concession he made to his own vanity.

Earth's ambassador to the Confederation of Homeworlds, Valentin Lifshitz, had summoned Stone to Titan for a meeting. Although he traveled in his official capacity as governor of Tejo, the meeting could prove quite lucrative for the Stone Mining Corporation. Stone smirked as he contemplated the tiny moon. When humans first reached out into space, the last place they expected to find intelligent life was in their own solar system. They were even more surprised to find Saturn's moon housed a vast confederation of alien species shrouded from human eyes and probes by technology they didn't begin to understand until the late twenty-first century.

Stone knew the Titans had little interest in commerce. This perhaps helped to explain why the confederation's capital went undetected for so long. It did not serve as a hub for transport or cargo vessels. Most ships visiting Saturn's largest moon belonged to those who had business with the Titans, who in turn served as mediators between the galaxy's governments.

The Titans had been space travelers for over two thousand years by the time humans discovered them. Once a species achieved interstellar travel, the Titans invited them to join their loose confederation. The planets that joined maintained their sovereignty. The system worked quite well, in part because interstellar war was impractical for most civilizations. A few Titan ships explored the galaxy, but most Titans seemed content to remain on their cold moon.

Stone's yacht entered Titan's thick atmosphere. As it neared the surface, interlocking pressure domes grew visible. They housed representatives from the galaxy's known worlds. Soon, the yacht reached the human compound. It settled onto a platform and a gangway extended to the craft. When the airlock cycled, a tall rail-thin man with silver hair boarded the yacht and extended his hand.

"Valentin Lifshitz, a pleasure to meet you in person."

Stone clasped the ambassador's hand and patted his shoulder.

"Likewise. You've arrived just in time. The meeting is about to commence."

"Please lead the way." Stone retrieved a briefcase and followed Lifshitz into the dome. They stepped up to a kiosk which scanned the ambassador's retina, then Stone's. It pinged and Lifshiftz led them outside the terminal building. Despite a surface temperature almost 180 degrees below freezing, the air inside the human dome proved quite pleasant. The air circulation system provided a gentle breeze. Stone looked up through the translucent dome to see Titan's atmosphere of nitrogen, methane, and hydrogen roiling overhead.

The ambassador led Stone to an office building. "You are

familiar with the *Courageous* incident?" asked the ambassador as they entered an elevator.

Stone frowned. "Yes, I read the report on the journey. Bad business. Has anyone learned more about this … Cluster?"

Lifshitz shook his head. "In the last few days, the Rd'dyggians, the Alpha Centaurans, the Tzrn and the Zahari have lost ships. The attacks all resemble what happened with *Courageous*."

Stone's heart raced and he fought to maintain a neutral expression. "Then we're looking at war?"

Lifshitz sighed. "War? We don't even know what this thing is. All we know is that we need to stop it." The elevator reached its floor and Lifshitz led Stone to a conference room. The ambassador indicated a chair and Stone sat.

Across the table, the hologram of a seven-foot tall orange being in flowing robes appeared. The Rd'dyggian ambassador eyed Stone while his purple mustache wriggled. A moment later, a spider-like creature's hologram appeared followed by an Alpha Centauran's hologram. Stone blinked as he recognized the Alpha Centauran—Mary Hill's old paramour, Var Gwenyu. The next ambassador to appear was an amoeba-like Zahari from a water-covered super earth. Each ambassador sat—or in the Zahari's case, drifted—at an identical table in their own dome.

The final hologram to appear reminded Stone of a massive silver-gray teddy bear wearing an orange sash. She was Teklar, matron of the Titans. She glanced around the table, nodded and sat in an enormous chair. "This meeting is called to order." Stone shuddered when he saw her razor-sharp teeth, even though he knew Titans only used them to eat water and methane ice. "We have convened today to discuss the so-called Cluster which has destroyed ships from each of your worlds."

"It is clearly an act of war." The Rd'dyggian Ambassador pounded a massive six-fingered hand against the table. Stone allowed himself a slight grin. Others agreed with his conclusion.

The spider-like ambassador from Tzrn tapped four legs in impatient syncopation. "Clearly? I don't think this situation is clear at all. We don't even know if we're dealing with one ship or an entire fleet."

Ambassador Lifshitz shook his head. "It's inconceivable that it's just one ship." He activated a button on the table displaying a hologram of five red glowing points scattered around the galaxy. "This shows where each encounter occurred. There is no way a single ship could reach so many points in the galaxy in just one week. It goes against all the laws of physics we understand."

Var Gwenyu rested his—or was it her?—head on a tentacle and grinned. "Your people thought the Raz'pohod field, what you call the Erdon-Quinn drive, violated the laws of physics until a milliorbit ago." Given that Proxima Centauri orbited its central stars every 547,000 years, a milliorbit was, in fact, a rather significant span of time. She—definitely she now—cast a pointed glance at Stone.

Lifshitz leaned forward. "When the Cluster retreated from the *Astrolus*, it made an Erdon-Quinn jump. We're not discussing unknown technology. We're talking about physics we all understand."

Teklar held up a paw and made a rumbling noise equivalent to a human clearing their throat. "We have strayed from the meeting's objective. The Cluster has destroyed nothing but ships. Why hasn't the Cluster shown interest in inhabited planets?"

The ambassador from Zahar wriggled. "Perhaps the Cluster's objective is to drive us from interstellar space, to keep us on our respective worlds."

Var Gwenyu placed two tentacles on the table and leaned forward. "That would end all commerce across the galaxy."

"And cut off our colony worlds," said Lifshitz.

"May I make a suggestion, Madame Ambassador?" The Rd'dyggian folded his hands and addressed Teklar.

The ursine matron nodded.

"We must defend ourselves against a common aggressor." The ambassador's purple mustache-like growth grew taut. "I concede we don't understand what they intend. However, I think we should unite our fleets and pool our resources as we search for a solution to this problem."

"And who commands the united fleet?" Lifshitz scratched the bald spot on the back of his head.

The Rd'dyggian held out his hands in a human-like gesture. "As we have the most experience with military matters, I believe we should."

The conference chamber exploded with cries of "Outrageous!" and "Never!" A roar silenced the outburst. The ambassadors turned their attention back to Teklar. "Uniting the fleets is a good idea, but uniting them under one planet's authority is unacceptable."

The Rd'dyggian's mustache grew agitated.

"I suggest a board comprised of admirals from each planet represented," suggested the ambassador from Tzrn.

"Indeed a good suggestion." The ambassador from Zahar swam around her chair. "They could manage the resources from the Confederation's worlds and oversee strategic ship deployment."

Teklar looked from the Alpha Centauran ambassador to the spider-like Tzrn. "As we knew before today's meeting, more ships will be needed to address the problem of the Cluster. I know your worlds can increase erdonium production in a short time presuming reasonable resources are allocated." She turned her gaze on Stone. "Ambassador Lifshitz tells me the humans on Sufiro now have substantial capacity for erdonium production as well. Is this true?"

Stone folded his hands. "We will do everything it takes to make the galaxy safe again."

Var Gwenyu glared at Stone. He ignored the Alpha Centauran and regarded Teklar. Titans were peaceful to a fault, but the matron seemed all too ready to make war on the mysterious alien. Her fur bristled, as though she feared the Cluster.

"Very good," said Teklar. "Prepare a report on how soon you could increase your production and what resources you require from the Confederation. I expect you to account for the Mao Corporation's needs as well as your own company's."

"Of course, Matron." Stone bowed his head in deference.

She glanced around the table. "Thank you for your presence today." Again, she looked at Stone. "I would speak with you alone."

Stone wondered why he was the only planetary governor at the meeting. Perhaps he would now discover the reason. The other ambassadors' holograms vanished one by one. Lifshitz stood. "I'll wait for you outside."

Once Lifshiftz closed the door, Teklar stood and lumbered over to Stone. "Do you know a human called John Mark Ellis?"

Stone narrowed his gaze and thought. "The only Ellis I ever knew commanded the ship that transported my father and me to Sufiro twenty-five years ago. I think his first name was Jeremy, or maybe Jerome. I don't recall a John Mark Ellis."

"John Mark Ellis is Jerome and Suki Firebrandt Ellis's son."

Stone arched an eyebrow as he remembered the pirate's daughter. Manuel Raton had a thing for her once upon a time. "I met the parents, but I don't know the son. Why do you ask?"

"Based on his record, he shows ... strong leadership skills and ... remarkable insights." Teklar walked around the chair and stood beside Stone. "We think he may be a good candidate to be a captain in a united Confederation fleet."

Stone held out his hands even as he suspected Teklar didn't reveal the whole truth. "If he's like his father, he'd make a competent ship's captain. His mother ... seemed nice."

Teklar lumbered back to the head of the table. "You know the family. Perhaps inquiries could be made."

"I will see what I can do." Stone thought he sensed anxiety from the Titan, perhaps related to the earlier fear. He began to suspect Teklar knew more about this Cluster than she said. Perhaps Ellis had learned something that worried her and Teklar had hoped he knew more about Ellis than he did. "Is there anything specific you want to learn about Ellis?"

"I want to know if Ellis would make a good appendage ... for the Confederation."

Stone smirked at the strange expression, but nodded. "If I learn anything, I will let you know."

Without another word, Teklar's hologram vanished.

Stone tapped his fingers on the table and considered the best way to increase erdonium production. Over twenty years ago, he had introduced Mary Hill to mercenaries and encouraged her to induct New Granadans to bolster his labor force. She had worked toward uniting Tejo and New Granada to make the activity legal. Once Manuel Raton had uncovered the plot and Hill had died, those plans had been set aside. Revisiting those plans would give him an edge over the Mao Corporation and allow him to meet erdonium demands at competitive rates.

He returned to his shuttle and opened a channel to Clyde McClintlock. Clyde had originally settled Sufiro with his parents and now oversaw the Tejo National Guard. Since Mary Hill's plans to unite Tejo and New Granada through diplomatic channels hadn't worked, he wanted to be prepared to use force.

☠

One month after Sam Stone's return to Sufiro, Manuel Raton sat in his house in Nuevo Santa Fe reading opinion pieces about the Cluster and the new Confederation fleet being assembled to address the threat. In one month, over two dozen vessels had been destroyed. The Cluster had sent no signals and the attacks seemed random.

Across the planet, both the Mao Corporation and the Stone mines stepped up production. The Confederation voted to fund new Earth ships as part of its campaign to learn what the Cluster was and stop it, even if it meant destroying the alien.

Manuel yawned, then removed his shoes and padded toward the bedroom. Just as he pulled off his shirt, the teleholo chimed. With a curse, he threw the shirt back on and answered the call. Above the unit's dais appeared his sister-in-law's face. Tears streamed down her cheeks. "Manuel, you've got to help me. It's Juan. He vanished."

"Slow down, mija. What do you mean vanished?"

"We're getting ready for planting. He's been plowing the fields all day. He came in, had dinner and dropped into bed exhausted. I cleaned the dishes and then joined him. A little while later, I heard shouts. I thought some kids were out to cause trouble, so I rolled over and tried to go back to sleep. That's when I noticed Juan had left the bed."

"Where did he go?"

"I don't know," shouted Armanta. She composed herself and blew her nose. "I don't know, mijo. I looked everywhere. I even went outside. It looked like someone had a wrestling match in our yard. My flower beds were trampled and there were footprints everywhere. Someone must have come and taken Juan away."

A cold chill settled into Manuel's gut as he considered what Sam Stone stepping up erdonium production might mean. He thought all that was behind him. "I promise I'll do everything in my power to get him back, Armanta. You have my word."

She nodded. "I know you will. Thank you." Forcing a brave smile, she terminated the connection.

"Fuck!" Manuel stormed into the kitchen. He retrieved a bottle of mescal and poured a shot. His hand trembled as he lifted it to his mouth. He downed the shot, then poured another. His head swam, but the liquor calmed the rage enough for him to think. How the hell would he stop Stone a second time?

Chapter Thirteen

SHOWDOWN

Deputy Sheriff Edmund Swan navigated his hover through a hazy orange sky in Southern Arizona's Tucson sector. In the distance, a factory belched purple smoke. The orange and purple met in a swirling green eddy. He remembered old photos which showed a deep blue sky looming over a desert covered by mesquite, grass, and tall saguaro cacti. Now, he didn't even know where a cactus could grow.

The hover's navigation system informed him to turn right between two buildings, then descend in the next block. He followed the directions, then sounded the siren to make sure no one loitered below. He drifted down to the ground at a narrow alley's inlet. He made a few notes in his handcomp.

A message came in. He took a look at it and grinned. He'd just been accepted for a job he'd applied for on the planet Sufiro. He sighed. He'd applied on a whim and didn't know whether he wanted to move to a primitive world halfway across the galaxy or not. He had a home in Southern Arizona and a routine, but the planet captured his imagination from the time he first heard about it during a chance meeting with the daughter of the pirate who founded the world.

He opened the hover's canopy and climbed out. Although he didn't expect trouble, he drew his sidearm before going down the alley. He smelled the body before he reached it. Bile rose in the back of his throat. He approached and found a teen-aged boy sprawled on the ground atop a brown stain of blood and other bodily fluids, a deep knife wound in the gut. The odors of decay and fecal matter intermingled with each other.

Swan looked around and tried to understand what had happened. He suspected a drug deal gone bad. He scanned the body with his cybernetic eye and detected traces of Aquilan love crystals. Running an identification check, he found no priors.

His stomach couldn't take the smell any longer. He stepped over to a nearby dumpster and vomited. His vision blurred and his hands trembled. He hated this aspect of the job. He looked down and spotted a vomit-splattered bag. He put on a glove, held his breath, and extracted it with two fingers. His cybernetic eye had detected more Aquilan love crystals. Was this coincidence or evidence? He'd save it just in case.

As he returned to the hover, flashing red and blue lights attracted his gaze skyward. The coroner arrived. Swan led the coroner and her assistant to the body. While they worked, he returned to his hover and filled out a report. As he read it over, the coroner and her assistant brought out the sheet-covered body on a hover sled. "We have all we need," said the coroner.

Swan nodded. He closed the hover's canopy and ascended. Half an hour later, he reached the sheriff's station. Sheriff Wilmot awaited him at the evidence lockers. She took the transparent evidence container from him and scowled. "Is that your vomit?"

Swan sighed and nodded. "I'm sorry, I thought I was clear of the crime scene."

She handed the container over to the clerk, who cross-referenced it with Swan's report.

"You know, if not for your sensitive stomach, you'd be my best deputy," said Wilmot.

"Thank you, ma'am."

She shook her head. "Don't thank me yet, I have another crime scene for you to check out."

Swan's shoulders slumped as he reached a decision. "No, ma'am. I'm done with Southern Arizona. I just received a job offer as Tejan Marshal on Sufiro."

"Sufiro? From everything I've heard that's the ass end of nowhere. Why would you want to go there?" Wilmot folded her arms.

Swan shrugged. "To be honest, being in the middle of nowhere is the appeal. There are only about five million people on the whole planet." Swan flashed a wistful grin. "The sky may be a little green for some people's taste, but I think I could get used to it."

The sheriff narrowed her gaze. "You'll get bored."

Swan chuckled. "I hope I do. Maybe I'll keep enough lunch down to gain some weight." He patted his stomach.

Wilmot sighed. "I don't suppose I can talk you out of this."

"I can think of ways, but I hope you won't. I want to see a place that's a little like Southern Arizona in the old days before it became nothing but urban sprawl, factories, and domed farms."

She snorted. "The good ol' days when Wyatt Earp and Doc Holliday rode around shooting it out with the Clantons? Is that really any better?"

"I hope Sufiro isn't like that," said Swan.

She held out her hand. "All right, I wish you luck, Marshal Swan. And congratulations on your new job." They shook. "If we need you to testify in this case…"

"I'll be just a holo call away." Swan walked away, a nervous flutter in his stomach. He wondered if he was being too impulsive. He had romantic ideas about a world with a low population density, but the sheriff was right. Frontier worlds could be rough places. He supposed if it proved too much to handle, he could always return home.

☠

A week later, Edmund Swan floated near a starliner's window. Most starliners traveling to the galaxy's far side ran without graviton generators to conserve fuel. Then again, the ship was so old, rust-stained, and battered, Swan wondered whether the graviton generators would even work if activated. He watched Sufiro rotate beneath him, fascinated by the white clouds, blue-green oceans, and scattered landmasses. He compared the view to a map on his handcomp. He identified both New Granada and Tejo. His breath caught as he anticipated the shuttle flight to the larger landmass where he would assume his duties as the chief law enforcement official. The oily-chemical air he inhaled stung and he coughed, longing for the fresh air below.

The ship's intercom pinged. "Passenger Edmund Swan, please report to the ship's teleholo station for an incoming call."

Swan's brow furrowed. He wondered who would call him at the ship rather than messaging him through his handcomp. He left the observation area and pulled himself along a corridor until he reached a booth just outside the ship's bridge. An officer in a tan uniform met him. "Edmund Swan?"

Swan nodded. The officer led him into a small, private alcove. A moment later, a hologram of a man with black hair and a long black mustache appeared. "Mr. Swan, my name is Manuel Raton."

The soon-to-be marshal thought someone must be playing a prank on him. "The Rat" had developed a reputation not unlike the gunfighters of the Old West who fascinated Swan. Twenty years ago, Raton once ran for New Granada's presidency. For some reason, that bid ended after an incident involving Tejo's governor. "What can I do for you, Mr. Raton?"

"I'm sheriff of a township called Nuevo Santa Fe," Raton explained. "I've heard you're Tejo's new marshal. I have … a favor to ask."

Swan lifted his eyebrows. "You have a favor to ask me?"

"My brother disappeared a little over a month ago." A hologram of a man who resembled Raton appeared. Clean-shaven, the man seemed happy, less care-worn than his brother. "I have reason to believe he's somewhere in Tejo."

"Tejo's a big place." Swan shrugged. "Can you tell me more?"

Raton shook his head. "I don't know where to start. That's the problem. All I know is that Tejo recently ramped up their erdonium operations. Last time that happened, agents from the Stone Corporation abducted New Granadans to work in the mines. I know it sounds crazy, but if you give me your network address, I'll send you my records."

"If you suspect kidnapping, you should press charges." Swan sat back and folded his arms.

"Whoever is behind this is being careful. I don't have evidence … yet." Raton shook his head. "All I ask is that you look over the data I do have. If you happen to come across my brother, please let me know."

The intercom interrupted them. "Shuttles for Sufiro will be leaving in thirty minutes. All departing passengers, please report to the shuttle bay."

"Look, I have to go." Swan leaned forward and typed an address into the console. "Send me your data and I'll look. If I learn anything, I'll be in touch."

"Thank you. That's all I ask."

Raton terminated the call. Swan sat back and rubbed his fingers through short, bristly hair. He gathered buzz cuts, like the one he sported, were fashionable in Tejo. His handcomp pinged. A message arrived from Manuel Raton. He would go to the planet, then review Raton's data.

At the very least, it didn't look like boredom would set in anytime soon. He went to his cabin to retrieve his luggage before going to the shuttle bay.

☠

Sweat trickled under Swan's gray suit the minute he stepped from the shuttle onto the tarmac in Tejo City. He could have tolerated that if not for the tiny insect-like creatures swarming nearby, attracted to his sweat. He wished such tight suits were less fashionable both because he feared the sweat would work its way through the cloth and the tight suit made his bulging sidearm stand out too much.

A short, thin man with dark brown hair buzzed short strode toward him. Like Swan, the man wore a fashionable gray suit, but without the bulge that betrayed a pistol's existence. Swan recognized him from his holographic job interview as the Tejan lieutenant governor, Rocky Hill.

"How are you doing, Mr. Swan?" The man spoke rapidly, like a used hover salesman. He locked Swan's hand in a death grip. Before Swan could answer, the man continued. "It's good to meet you in person."

"Pleased to meet you as well."

After a moment, Hill released Swan's hand and led him to a hover outside the shuttle port. Swan looked forward to

his first views of Tejo City. There had been no windows in the
starliner's shuttle. As they ascended, Swan grew dismayed.
Instead of the quaint, rural settlement he expected, a vast urban
metropolis surrounded him. Swan realized most of Sufiro's five
million people must live in Tejo City.

"What do you think of our little town?" Hill's question
startled Swan.

"It's not what I expected." He fought to tamp down his
disappointment.

"I'm sure it's not like Earth cities, but we're growing each
and every day!" Swan wondered if Hill ever stopped smiling.

In the distance, an airship drifted away from the city. He
remembered his office inspected cargo and regulated air traffic.

Hill piloted the hover toward a plascrete skyscraper.
Instead of descending toward a parking structure, the
lieutenant governor ascended to a docking ring near the roof.
Once the hover docked, the lieutenant governor and marshal
entered a large office. Swan's feet sank into the deep blue
carpeting. An air conditioner ran, making him grateful for his
jacket. Several valuable but uncomplimentary paintings hung
on the walls.

Tejo's governor, Sam Stone, stood up from behind a large
wooden desk. The governor smiled, making Swan think of a
shark evaluating its prey. A diamond set in the man's right front
tooth contributed to the impression. The governor dismissed
Hill with a brief word of thanks then invited Swan to sit.

Hill opened his mouth as though he had something to say,
then patted Swan on the shoulder and left. As Swan sat, he
noticed the desk's edge was inlaid with gold. Valuable baubles
surrounded a jade-colored computer terminal atop the desk.
Swan sank into the plush upholstery.

"Impressive, isn't it?" Unlike Hill, Stone's voice sounded
cold and calculating.

Swan nodded, more from a sense of duty than agreement.

"Sufiro has become an important place in the galaxy. Our
city is growing and I think you're the right person to help us
keep the peace."

"I intend to do my best, sir." Swan's voice sounded hollow
in the large room.

"I expect no less." Swan noticed a note of menace in the man's voice. "We supply almost half the erdonium necessary to build the galaxy's star ships. Our operation is a priority for galactic security. You've heard about the Cluster?"

Swan nodded.

"We had to ramp up production tenfold to meet demand for new ships to search for it. Earth wants ships to fight it if they can catch it. That means many new jobs which have attracted people from the other continent." Stone sat back and folded his hands. "What do you know about New Granada?"

Swan's mind flashed to his conversation with Manuel Raton. "Ellison Firebrandt settled New Granada almost forty years ago..."

"A known criminal," interjected Stone. "Go on..."

"Agriculture grew up around New Granada. Twenty-five years ago, give or take, you and your father arrived and discovered erdonium here. That's what put the planet on the galactic charts."

"Now, don't get me wrong. I'm not prejudiced or anything, but you need to watch out for the Grenades. They're trouble makers." Stone folded his arms.

"Grenades, sir?" Swan cocked his eyebrow.

"Grenades. You know—New Granadans. They're damned explosive over there." Stone leaned forward. "We hired you because you come from Southern Arizona. You've seen what poor people living on the streets can be driven to. They steal. They get angry at the system when it doesn't provide them jobs or they can't pay for medical care. We want to make sure our migrant population remains settled and doesn't cause trouble."

Swan lifted an eyebrow. "You have a large migrant population here?"

Stone shrugged. "Not by most standards, but some migrants get out into the city. They claim they were forced to come here and that we don't let them go. Of course they're welcome to go whenever they want to, but despite their protests they seem to hang around and cause trouble. Some try to stow away on the airships to make trouble elsewhere. If they wanted to move, they could just buy a ticket on a passenger transport."

Swan considered what Raton told him about Tejans abducting people to work in the mines. He could imagine people brought against their will would want to help their friends. He could also imagine disappointed people causing trouble when a new place wasn't as good as they expected. "I'll be sure to look into the situation and do what I can to stem problems before they occur."

"That's what I like to hear," said Stone. "You should also get to know Clyde McClintlock. He's in charge of our National Guard. He's a good resource should you run into a problem beyond the purview of the marshal's office."

"Sounds good." Swan made a mental note of McClintlock's name. "Would it be possible to see my office now?"

"Good." Stone winked. "I like a man who's ready to get right down to business." He stood and led Swan through the door and down a long corridor. They entered an elevator and went down ten floors. They came out facing a sliding door with a sign that read, "Edmund R. Swan, Marshal, Republic of Tejo."

Swan entered an office almost as large as Stone's, but without the gaudy decor. He said a silent prayer of thanks when Stone excused himself to attend to other business.

Swan seated himself behind the desk and activated the computer terminal. Several messages already waited. The first informed him that his baggage had been delivered to his apartment and showed its location. Several messages offered tours of businesses and official agencies. A message offering a tour of the Tejo City mines caught his eye. He instructed the computer to arrange for a tour at the end of his second week. He figured that would give him time to settle in.

With the preliminaries dealt with, he turned his attention to the on-going police investigations. He read the reports, sent a few queries, and acknowledged his approval of the rest.

After reading the messages, Swan sat back, and rubbed his eyes. He decided the best thing to do would be to introduce himself to his deputies then retreat to his apartment where he could get some well deserved sleep.

☠

As the first week progressed, Edmund Swan adjusted to his new job. At first, Tejo City proved to be a disappointment. The sky already had an orange cast, a little like Southern Arizona. In both cases, dust and pollution mixed to create the color. Unlike Southern Arizona, Swan discovered accessible parks just outside the city in the mountains. Because there was so little natural growth in Tejo, Earth plants had been imported and nurtured. The oases consoled him. While Tejo City might not be as perfect as he'd hoped, it was still an improvement over his former home.

The people also seemed an improvement. Swan's neighbors in his apartment complex made a point of saying "hello" and checking in with him. Likewise, his deputies impressed him. They stayed on top of the few criminal cases in process and he found little need to intervene. He thought it somewhat puzzling that none of them had been promoted to the marshal's post. During his interview, Sam Stone had told Swan they wanted someone who could navigate Earth's legal system should the need arise. So far, Swan hadn't seen any reason that would crop up.

Swan contacted Colonel Clyde McClintlock and introduced himself. The National Guard's commanding officer seemed nice enough, but Swan wondered how much field experience the colonel actually had. At least an inexperienced military official meant Tejo hadn't suffered any serious military threat in recent years.

After lunch on his second week's last day, Swan found a calendar reminder for the mine tour on the computer. He smiled to himself, looking forward to learning more about Tejo City's primary industry. He checked to see whether any investigations needed his attention. Seeing no problems, he signed out for the day and left word with the clerk that he would be out and could be paged through his handcomp.

Swan drove his hover to the mine. At the gate, the security guard checked his credentials and waved him through. An airship tethered to a mooring post offloaded supplies. He found a place to park and entered the main office. The mine's shift supervisor met him and handed him a hard hat. "Safety first," he said.

Swan donned the hat and followed the man back outside and then into the mine entrance. They picked up an anti-gravity cart and rode down through a smooth, laser-cut tunnel. Out of the sun and surrounded by mountain rock, the temperature dropped. Lights ran overhead, keeping the brown and red rock around them well illuminated.

They soon came to a point where a half dozen robust miners dug into the rock with laser drills and loaded the tailings into robotic carts, which carried the material back to the surface for mineral extraction.

"As you can see," said the shift supervisor, "we use the most modern equipment. Our miners are among the most skilled in the galaxy."

Something bothered Swan. He examined the rock wall with his cybernetic eye and frowned. He detected traces of gold, silver, and copper—all somewhat valuable and all with industrial applications, but by no means the mine's most valuable asset. "I thought erdonium was black."

"It is." The supervisor smiled. "Of course, encased in the rock, it's not always apparent."

"It would be to me." Swan pointed to his mismatched eyes. Most people who had cybernetic eyes colored the new one to match the old. Swan never bothered. Given that his eyes dilated differently, he never thought he fooled most people. Besides, he liked having one brown eye and one steel-gray.

The shift supervisor spoke to a miner in a hushed tone. He returned a moment later. "As it turns out, the erdonium is played out here, but there's still gold, silver, and copper."

Swan nodded. "So I noticed. Can we see where they're extracting erdonium? I was really looking forward to that part of the tour."

The supervisor smiled. "Let me check to make sure we've got a work site that's safe for visitors." He pulled a radio from his belt, but walked further down the tunnel.

Swan heard the query, but couldn't make out the answer. The marshal understood about visitor safety, but something nagged at him and he couldn't put his finger on it. It seemed the shift supervisor worked a little too hard to keep something quiet. Also, shouldn't a shift supervisor know which areas were safe and which weren't?

The supervisor returned. He climbed on the cart's seat and asked Swan to join him. "They're extracting some erdonium just ahead." He started the anti-gravity cart and they continued forward, passing another tunnel that descended to a lower level. Swan thought he could hear heavy machinery rumbling.

"What's down there?"

The shift supervisor stopped the cart. "More erdonium extraction, but they're boring into hard rock. Lots of dust and it could be quite dangerous if we're not behind the forcefield."

As the supervisor spoke, the machinery clunked to a stop. Swan thought he heard shouts.

"It sounds like trouble." Swan hopped off the cart. An electrical pop resounded through the tunnel followed by a scream. Swan started down the tunnel, but the supervisor cut in front of him. "Sir, you can't go down there. It's not safe."

"It sounds like there's been an accident. I'm a marshal. It's my duty to respond to emergencies."

"I assure you, we have all the emergency response personnel we need, including some members from your own department."

Swan thought he could make out raised voices followed by another sizzling pop. The marshal tried to sidestep the supervisor, who didn't give way. Swan reared back and delivered a roundhouse punch into the man's jaw. He crumpled to the floor. As Swan ran down through the tunnel, the overhead lights grew less frequent and the floor less even. He guessed explosives had blasted the tunnel, but it had not yet been laser-smoothed. Another scream followed an electrical pop which resounded through the tunnel.

When Swan reached the outlet the hair on the back of his neck stood on end. A deputy marshal named Dodge held a four-foot transparent rod with a hand grip. The device, inspired by twentieth-century cattle prods and known as a disciplinarian, could be used to inflict pain to any human body part. Dodge stood over a whimpering man with long, dark hair and dirty, tattered clothes.

"What the hell is going on here?" Swan pointed to Dodge. "Why aren't you at your patrol station?"

Dodge shrugged. "The erdonium mines *are* my patrol station."

Swan pointed at the disciplinarian. "That's not standard issue. Drop it."

"The mining company issued this to me. It's the only way I can get these Grenades back to work." Dodge spoke the words as though faced with a mundane challenge.

"Since when does Tejo sanction torture as a work incentive?"

"Look, all I know is that the mine has a bunch of these Grenade migrants and they have a quota. If they fall behind, I gotta keep them moving." The disciplinarian buzzed and crackled as Dodge waved it through the air.

"Put that damned thing down!" Swan unsnapped his holster and gritted his teeth.

"Make me put it down." Dodge stalked toward Swan.

The marshal drew his hepler pistol but Dodge continued forward, pointing the disciplinarian at his superior. New Granadan miners gathered around. Swan fired the pistol. The hepler's beam struck the disciplinarian. The crackling rod exploded and Dodge fell backward, hitting the ground with a splat. Swan knelt beside his deputy, whose face resembled burned and bloody ground meat.

The marshal ran to the opposite wall and vomited into a crevice. He rose up on his knees, then fell back into a sitting position.

A miner handed a rag to Swan. "Thank you for your help," said the miner.

Swan took the rag and wiped his mouth. "What in the hell is going on here?"

"Enforcers like your friend over there have been abducting us from our homes in New Granada and forcing us to work in the mines so they can supply the erdonium needed to combat the Cluster."

Swan's brow furrowed. "Abducting you? Governor Stone said you were coming over in droves to take jobs."

"Like anyone actually wants to live in barracks on a barren continent," grumbled another miner.

Swan heaved a deep sigh. "The question is, what do I do

about you now?" He rose unsteadily to his feet and pointed to the injured New Granadan. "How is he?"

A woman knelt beside him. "He's hurt pretty bad, but I think he'll make it."

Swan balanced himself on the wall. "You can't stay here and I'm guessing my superiors want to keep this quiet." He remembered the airship docked at the surface. "I think I may know a way to get you home, but we'll need to hurry."

Swan gathered the miners around and formed a plan. He helped carry the wounded New Granadan up the tunnel. Burdened as they were, the ascent took almost half an hour. By the time they reached the bright, laser-cut tunnel, the shift supervisor had vanished, but several of the miners Swan met earlier blocked their way.

Swan and the New Granadan who helped him, placed the wounded man on the ground. The marshal drew his hepler and pointed it at the gathered miners. "Let us pass."

"You're in a lot of trouble," said a bearded Tejan.

"Who do you think you are?" shouted another Tejan. "Savior of the Grenades?"

"Clear out!" Swan's grip on the hepler pistol tightened.

A Tejan woman with short hair crept to Swan's left. The marshal's cybernetic eye narrowed and he fired an energy pulse, striking the wall near her. She stopped in her tracks.

The Tejan miners stared at the scorched wall. "He's crazy," muttered one. "He'll kill us," said another. In the confusion, Swan rushed them. The New Granadans followed. Swan spotted a hover cart. He ran toward it and activated the controls. The New Granadans placed their wounded friend inside, then hopped in.

Swan lifted his hepler as the Tejan miners approached. "You're going to stand right there and watch us ride out of here, now aren't you?"

One man lunged forward. Swan fired at the ground in front of the man, knocking him on his back. The other miners stood still. Swan steered the hover cart toward the mine's entrance.

At the entrance, three deputy marshals waited. Beyond them, Swan could see the airship at the mooring tower. A gangway extended from the cargo area to the ground. Swan stopped the cart right at the mine's entrance and hopped off. He looked at the New Granadans. "Someone needs to take the controls. I'll distract the deputies. You all get aboard the airship. I'll join you as soon as I can."

The woman who tended the wounded man clambered out of the cart and took the controls.

Swan shouted over to the assembled deputies. "I'm Marshal Swan. I order you to drop your weapons and let these people go."

One of the deputies fired. Swan dove behind a crate and returned fire. He used his eye to estimate distance to the deputies. It projected a target in his field of view that followed the gun's motion. He fired, hitting a deputy in the leg.

The other two hit the dirt. He motioned for the cart to go. Before it left, a New Granadan jumped out and joined Swan. One deputy stood and ran for cover. Swan fired, dropping him in his tracks. As he did, the other deputy opened fire, destroying the crate in front of Swan. The marshal spat a curse, then retreated back to the mine entrance. This gave the remaining deputy time to get behind an erdonium ore cart.

The New Granadan looked at Swan. "I could draw his fire."

Swan indicated the dead deputy. "That's what that guy tried. You saw how far it got him."

"But you have a cybernetic eye," protested the New Granadan.

Swan shook his head. "That tactic was being used long before cybernetic eyes. You'll only get yourself killed."

The New Granadan nodded. "I wish there was something I could do."

Swan took a moment to overlay an image from the eye's memory on the dirty, scruffy man before him. "You're Juan Raton, aren't you?"

"That's me. How did you know?"

Before Swan could answer, a hepler pulse hit the cave entrance scattering pebbles.

Swan and Raton fell back.

"He's inexperienced." Swan nodded toward the hepler fire. "We'll get out of this."

Five minutes later, the deputy grew impatient. He darted

out from behind the erdonium cart. Assisted by his eye, Swan locked on and fired. The deputy dove out of the way.

Before the deputy could get his bearings, Swan gestured for Juan Raton to follow. As they ran for the airship, Juan repeated his question from earlier. "How did you recognize me?"

"I promised your brother I'd look for you. I guess I succeeded."

Edmund Swan and Juan Raton ran up the airship's gangway and found the ship's officers facing the New Granadan miners. Swan opened the wallet containing his badge. He sought out the person with the most braid on their shoulder. "I'm Marshal Edmund Swan of the Republic of Tejo. I'm confiscating this airship to take these trouble-making New Granadans back home."

A woman with shorts and a button-down shirt nodded. "We don't want any trouble with Tejan law enforcement. We'll do whatever you say."

"Glad to know someone around here will, ma'am. You're a credit to your country." Swan holstered the hepler and placed the wallet in his pocket.

☠

The airship flew unmolested toward New Granada. Talking to the ship's captain in the gondola, Swan learned that Governor Stone had little power to attack an airship. Tejo had few large transports and if Stone downed one for any reason, it would trigger a strike among the other captains, effectively shutting down commerce between cities.

"So, will helping us cause trouble for you?" Swan lifted an eyebrow.

The captain shrugged. "I know those deputies you fought. Bad 'uns they were. There's been word of people being smuggled to Tejo. I don't like it. I don't know if they used airships or some other transport, but if I've been a party to human smuggling, I can only hope this helps to make it right again."

Swan narrowed his gaze. "So, are people being smuggled to all the mines."

The captain considered that, then shook her head. "No, sir.

Mostly I've only heard about it happening in Tejo City, Raton Mesa, and Stonestown."

"The sites controlled by Stone Corporation, but not Mao."

The captain nodded. "That's right, sir."

Swan smiled at the captain and went aft. He found Juan Raton in the galley. The former Tejan marshal grabbed a cup of coffee and joined his new friend. "So tell me," said Swan. "How did your brother come to be known as 'the rat'?"

"It's our name, Edmund." Raton smiled. "In the old Earth language Spanish, 'ratón' means rat or mouse."

"I'm sure there's more to the story than that…"

"The rest of the story involves a gun battle." Juan scratched at the stubble on his chin. "Twenty years ago, Manuel caught a Tejan abducting our people for work in the mines. Manuel always said he should have shot the bastard, but he took him to jail instead."

"Why kidnap New Granadans?" Swan shook his head. "From what I can tell, there are plenty of people to work the mines. It makes no sense."

"Back then, it was about profit." Raton frowned. "Now, it's about keeping the Confederation happy. Tejo doesn't want them going to another planet that supplies erdonium."

Swan frowned, but nodded. "Please go on with your story."

"Well, the Tejans didn't like the fact that their compadre had been thrown in jail. They sent an extraction team through the Camlan Pass near Nuevo Santa Fe to get him out. Manuel and his deputies holed up like pack rats to fight them off."

Swan sipped his coffee. "I don't suppose a former Tejan governor named Mary Hill was involved in that."

Raton considered his answer for a moment. "She tried to stop the extraction team, but the mercenaries shot her."

Swan set his coffee cup down. "Why did she try to stop the extraction?"

Juan sighed. "No one's really sure, but I think she believed the situation had spiraled out of control and if it proceeded, things would get worse."

"You think her conscience bothered her about the situation?"

Juan shrugged. "I think she cared about the people involved and realized Stone actually didn't."

Three days later, Edmund Swan sat in a small adobe house in Nuevo Santa Fe. The aroma of chilies and garlic cooking swirled around him. He had been living around automated food dispensers for so long, he forgot how delightful kitchen aromas could be. In his hand, he held a beer brewed by people from the town called Succor.

Swan's host stepped through from the kitchen. He placed a plate of enchiladas at the marshal's place. "This looks amazing." Swan's mouth watered.

"Be careful," came his host's calm, deep voice.

Swan had already scooped up a large mouthful of the enchiladas. His eyes bugged out and sweat beaded on his forehead.

Swan's host sat down and grinned.

"Is this the real reason they call you 'the rat?'" Swan croaked at last.

"Drink your beer," said Sheriff Manuel Raton. "I cook with a local pepper. It's as hot as a habanero, with all the flavor of New Mexican green chile."

Swan wiped the sweat off his brow. "You could have warned me."

"I did." Raton sampled his own dinner.

As Swan ate, the flavors began to emerge from under the spices. A wave of wellbeing washed over him. "You know. This ain't half bad once you get used to the heat."

"Sufiro is like that." Raton sipped his beer. "It's a good place to live. It's beautiful in its own way. Unfortunately, the Tejans make it painful."

"Is everything you cook a metaphor?"

Raton shrugged.

Swan took another bite. "There's a history between you and Stone, isn't there?"

Raton sat back. "Yes. When I was young, Sam Stone's father arrived. Like the rest of us, he sought a new beginning.

My father, mother, and I went with him to lay claim to Tejo's erdonium deposits."

Swan rested his chin on his closed fist. "Sounds like a success story."

Raton gritted his teeth. "It would have been a success story if he hadn't sullied this world." Raton stood and threw his napkin into the chair. "It would have been a success story if his son had not taken our people and used them for slave labor whenever he needed to make a bigger profit or impress galactic leaders. It would have been a success if Stone had not killed my father and mother." Raton stormed over to the far wall. "When we were children, I did my best to befriend Sam Stone." He pounded the wall with his fist. "I learned the hard way that Stone does not make friends. He uses people." He took a deep breath, then stepped back to the table. "Thank you for bringing my brother home, but you have now betrayed Stone and he will not let that go. Make no mistake, he'll send people to erase what he sees as a mistake. He will do everything in his power to assure you don't leave this world alive."

"I'm sorry. I didn't mean to put you in danger."

Raton shook his head and chuckled. "You misunderstand. I welcome this fight. I just want you to understand what's at stake and make sure you're willing to fight as well."

Swan sat back and wiped his mouth. "I now realize Stone manipulated me into the mine tour so I could testify that my deputies never mistreated or abused anyone. He didn't expect me to notice things I wasn't supposed to. You can count on me to fight with you. I saw what they're doing to the people in the Tejan mines."

That night, Swan rolled and tossed on the cot. When he did manage to drop off to sleep, images of miners filled his dreams. He dreamed of Sam Stone stalking toward him with a disciplinarian. The marshal sat up in bed and let out an involuntary yelp. His knuckles turned white as he gripped the sweat-soaked sheets.

Manuel Raton stood next to the bed and handed Swan a hepler pistol. "They're coming."

Swan dressed and followed Raton outside. The sheriff had two hepler pistols and he wore two crossed bandoleers with reserve energy packs. Slung on his back was an old-fashioned rifle, like ones Swan had seen in museums. He understood they fired lead-cased cartridges.

Swan looked around the horizon. Nearby, scrub-covered foothills rose into tall mountains bisected by a narrow pass. "Is that the infamous Camlan Pass?" Swan pointed his hepler toward the barren break in the mountains.

Raton nodded.

Swan's stomach growled, making him wish for breakfast. He walked around the house's perimeter. Nuevo Santa Fe sat cozy in the valley below them. If not for the approaching fight, Swan would enjoy living in this place. Green trees climbed the mountainsides, much nicer than Tejo's scrub-covered rocks. Swan continued his walk until he returned to Raton's side. "How many will the Tejans send?"

"Stone will want to keep this quiet." Raton examined his rifle. "We're both a problem for him, but he doesn't want to create a galactic incident. He'll bring enough to do the job, but no more. I'm thinking half a dozen or so. A dozen at most"

Swan lifted his eyebrows. "Think we can handle so many?"

Manuel gave a curt nod. "My deputies are on the way, too, but they got a late start. Stone masked his approach better than I expected. It'll be more of a race than I like."

"Why haven't you and Stone confronted each other before now?" asked Swan.

Raton shrugged. "Once the abductions stopped twenty years ago, the only reason to press matters would be to seek justice for my parents, but he was too well protected..." As Raton spoke, a vibration turned into a low hum. A dust cloud billowed up between the house and Camlan Pass. Swan's cybernetic eye could just discern three hovers in the midst of the dust cloud. The hovers broke formation. One went to each side of the house, while the third faced them. Each craft kicked up more dust as it landed. As the dust settled, the hover doors opened. Four Tejan deputy marshals stepped from each vehicle. A fifth person stepped from the larger vehicle in front of them—Sam Stone. Swan took a distance bearing and realized he stood just outside a hepler pistol's effective range.

Stone grinned, the diamond in his tooth catching the morning sunlight. He reached up and touched a device at his throat. "Give it up, Raton! All we want is Swan! Turn him over and we'll leave you in peace!" He wore a voice amplifier, making it sound like the governor stood right next to them.

"Peace?" Manuel Raton called back. "There was once a time when we had peace. We might even have been friends. Why did you discard that?"

Stone shook his head. "Friendship…" Stone's voice cracked. "Friendship is for children. I had a business to run. You could have participated in the Tejan dream. I tried to convince you. You just had to work at it."

"Then I would have been equally guilty of abducting my friends and my family." Raton sneered.

Stone shrugged. "You could have convinced the New Granadans to come of their own accord. We always gave them food and shelter. Working in the mines is no harder than farming. As I see it, you have to share some blame for the situation we find ourselves in today."

Raton snarled. "You would have used me that way?" The sheriff gripped his rifle. "Tell me, old friend, why did Espedie Raton have to die?"

Stone sighed. "You know the reports showed his death was an accident." The governor reached for a high-powered pulse rifle. "Besides, that's in the past. Give us Swan and we'll be on our way." He sighted along the formidable weapon.

"You had your chance to leave us in peace." Raton lifted his rifle to his shoulder. "This one's for Espedie Raton!" Swan went deaf for a moment and shook his head. Stone fell backwards against the blood-splattered hover. "This one's for Carmen Raton!" Raton fired again. Stone dropped to the ground. The ancient weapon's range impressed Swan, despite his shock.

The Tejan deputies crept toward the house, staying low. Swan gathered his wits and aimed his hepler pistol. He fired. An officer fell backwards onto the ground with a little poof of dust.

Something scorched Swan's shoulder. The marshal yelped and turned. He fired, then ducked below the low wall. Raton fired off two more hepler pulses and ducked down. Swan looked over the wall. The Tejan deputies charged the house. A chunk of wall flew up next to Swan's head. He dove below the wall again.

Raton rose and fired two shots. The red light pulses cut into two more officers. A beam of concentrated light caught Raton in the arm and spun him around and sent him to the ground. Little smoke wisps curled up from Raton's shirt. Swan helped the sheriff into a sitting position. "We're finished, aren't we?"

A loud yell pierced Swan's thoughts. The pulse beams around them stopped. Swan and Raton peered over the wall. Twelve New Granadans ran in from all sides. Raton leapt over the wall. Swan looked around, stunned. These must be Raton's deputies. Almost as soon as the newcomers arrived, silence fell. Swan stood up and looked around. Only New Granadans stood.

Swan rushed over to Raton. "Are you okay?" He examined the sheriff's burned sleeve with his cybernetic eye.

Raton looked down at his arm. "Hurts like hell, but I'll live." Raton turned and introduced his deputies to Swan.

Swan shook each of their hands in turn. "I'm glad you arrived in time."

An older deputy named Li Chang smiled. "Thank you for bringing our families home."

That night Manuel Raton held a party to honor Edmund Ray Swan. Juan Raton brought the New Granadans Swan had rescued along with his wife, Armanta. Swan and the New Granadans knew a war had begun. They also knew they could win it together.

Chapter Fourteen

HOMECOMING

Suki Firebrandt Ellis stepped onto the bridge of the merchant ship *Barbarossa*. Captain Kheir el-Din noticed her and summoned her forward. He pointed to the holographic tank at the front of the command deck. Her breath caught as her eyes swept over the reds and blues of the nebula before them. In the center, sat a faint white dwarf. The whole thing resembled a giant eye looking back at her. Some called the Helix Nebula the Eye of God.

"What an amazing sight." Fire smiled. "It's a little like visiting the ghost of a star that once was. Thanks for the best view in the house."

"I knew you would like it," said el-Din. "One more jump and we'll be back at Earth."

"Thanks again for taking me to the conference on Prospero. I'm glad I didn't have to miss it." Fire, in her role as Director of Nantucket's Maria Mitchell Association, presented a report on the role of astronomy in the development of civilizations at the Galactic Astronomical Society meeting. "A lot of passenger lines are canceling flights because of the Cluster."

The captain nodded. "I have to admit, that enigma makes me uneasy, too. The crew has standing orders to scan a sector the moment we jump in. If they see the thing, they're to jump out immediately."

Fire snorted a laugh. "A big bad pirate captain like you and a former member of my father's crew? I'm surprised you wouldn't take it on yourself."

The captain smirked. "I promised to keep you safe and I don't intend to let harm come to the captain's daughter."

Fire let her gaze drift back to the gas tendrils of the Helix

Nebula, the outer atmosphere of a once sun-like star drifting out into space. She thought about her husband, Jerome, on a shipping run for the Mao Corporation and her son John Mark, on a Navy cruiser. She hoped they were safe.

"Do you mind if I adjust the view?" asked el-Din. "Just for a few minutes while I perform some standard navigation checks."

"By all means."

The captain issued the orders and the view in the tank compressed, showing several nearby stars. The Milky Way cut a swath through the lower left of the field. She recognized the galactic bulge—the center of the galaxy. Stars and dust obscured Sufiro's star, which sat on the other side somewhere. Fire thought about Manuel Raton who helped to expose the Tejan plot to kidnap New Granadans. She couldn't imagine the plot sat well with her father.

Captain el-Din entered the tank and checked a course projection and called up scans of the area. Satisfied, he returned to the deck, next to Fire, and asked the communicator to restore the view of the Nebula.

"So, how's your son taking to life in the Earth Navy?" asked el-Din.

"I don't think he'll be happy until he commands his own ship." A sense of pride brought forth a satisfied smile. "Who would have thought it, though? John Mark seemed so different as a boy. When other children carried handcomps, he carried books. If I were sad or lonely, he would always be able to find a passage that would cheer me up." She sighed. "I wish he could come home."

"Did the other kids tease him because of his old-fashioned books?" Kheir el-Din folded his arms.

Fire shrugged. "He got into several fights, but he always seemed to win." She looked back at the Helix Nebula and sighed. "I think I better turn in. It's been a long week. Thanks again for the view from the best seat in the house."

"My pleasure."

Fire pulled herself away from the view and strolled through the merchant ship's decks to the guest quarters. She entered and undressed in front of the mirror.

She unbraided her long black hair and let it fall over her breasts. She imagined Jerome's hands caressing her body and missed him. She crawled into bed and much as she enjoyed the adventure of travel, she looked forward to returning to her familiar bed. Just as she reached over to turn out the lights, the intercom chimed. "Damn," she whispered.

Fire threw back the blankets, retrieved a bathrobe and padded over to the intercom. "Ma'am, this is the communicator. We're receiving an EQ transmission for you from Mao Corporation headquarters on Earth."

"Go ahead and send it down here," she said.

The hologram of a man she did not recognize appeared. He wore a black suit with a Mao Corporation pin on the lapel. His face was set into a grave expression. "Mrs. Ellis?"

She nodded and suppressed a shiver.

"I regret to be the one to inform you ... the *Nantucket* has been lost with all hands." The man didn't meet her gaze.

Suki Firebrandt Ellis held her hands to keep them from trembling. "How?"

"The ship was destroyed. The damage to *Nantucket* indicates a Cluster ship attacked them."

Fire closed her eyes as her limbs went numb. "Why?"

"As with all Cluster encounters ... we have no answers." The man cleared his throat. "From what we can ascertain, the *Nantucket* did nothing to provoke the attack. If there's anything we can do..."

Fire met the man's gaze. "Give me some time to myself."

The hologram image winked out. Fire put her face in her hands and let the cleansing tears flow.

The star cruiser *Astrolus* leapt into the Gliese 1 star system on its way home to Earth. John Mark Ellis checked weapons systems status and reported to the captain. "All systems nominal."

Once Captain MacPherson gathered all the reports, he nodded. "Stand down from jump stations." He turned to the communicator. "Terminate communications blackout. We're close enough to Earth we can let messages through." He barked for the boatswain who appeared at the captain's side a moment later. "Prepare leave rosters for our crew at Earth. I want everyone to get at least two days to visit family before we depart for Titan to receive our official commission as part of this new Confederation Space Fleet."

Ellis thought the captain sounded skeptical about the new organization. The tactical officer thought coordinating all the galaxy's ships should have been done centuries earlier.

As soon as Ellis's shift finished, he strode to the galley. The teleholo played a news channel. "Erdonium production on the planet Sufiro has fallen by half as workers walk off the job claiming former Governor Samuel Stone ordered laborers abducted from New Granada. The new governor, Rocky Hill, has promised to investigate the charges."

Ellis trudged up to the counter and Cookie handed him a tray. "You look as though someone just died, sir. Is it this trouble on Sufiro?"

"Nothing about Sufiro, but you're right, I do feel like someone's died." Ellis shook his head.

"Your family's from Sufiro, aren't they?"

Ellis shrugged. "Yeah, my mom grew up there, but she left years ago. She makes it back from time to time, but it's so far from Earth, she doesn't get home as often as she'd like."

Cookie inclined his head toward the teleholo. "Still, I could see how the news might play on your subconscious."

"It could just be all the uncertainty about the Cluster. There hasn't been a sighting for weeks now." Ellis carried his tray to an empty seat. Just as he lifted a bite to his mouth, the Old Man's voice sounded on the intercom. "Tactical officer to the command deck."

Ellis finished chewing, then swallowed down some juice and abandoned his tray. He strode forward and snapped a salute when he reached the captain's chair.

The captain returned the salute. "At ease, Mr. Ellis." The captain stood and led Ellis back out into the corridor where fewer people could eavesdrop. "We just received a communiqué from Titan. I'm sorry to inform you the Mao Corporation Freighter *Nantucket* has been reported lost with all hands."

Ellis's knees weakened and he fell back against the wall.

"How did it happen?" In a rush, he remembered who he spoke to. "How did it happen, sir?"

Captain MacPherson shook his head. "Titan says they encountered the Cluster. They tried to increase their distance and leave without making contact, but the ship destroyed them just like they destroyed the *Courageous*. I'm sorry, Mark."

The captain's moist eyes betrayed sympathy and Ellis wanted to excuse himself before he broke down, but MacPherson held up his hand. "I know this isn't the best time, but you'll find secure orders on your handcomp. I gather you'll be reassigned at Titan." The captain held out his hand. "It has been a pleasure to serve with you, Mr. Ellis."

Ellis shook the captain's hand, then retreated to his bunk and activated the personal force field. He retrieved his handcomp and ignored the new message indicating orders. Instead he called his mother.

"Oh, Mark," she said "I have terrible news."

Ellis nodded. "The captain just told me about dad."

His mom's lips puckered and she nodded. A tear leaked from her eye. "I wish I could be there for you."

"I'll be home in a few days."

"Sounds like I'll get there just ahead of you." Her brave smile looked strained.

"Stay safe, mom." Ellis tried to find more words. "Can't wait to see you." His voice caught.

She signed off. The reality of his father's death sank in and Ellis could no longer hold back tears. His head fell back against the wall and he shook as he cried. He regretted that he hadn't been able to tell his father goodbye.

After several minutes, the tears subsided and Ellis grabbed a tissue and blew his nose. He checked his orders and blinked.

He'd been ordered to report to Admiral Marlou Strauss.

Since when did an admiral order a lieutenant to report to her office? He didn't even know how to process that. He saved the orders, set an alarm and lay back. Within minutes, the conflicting emotions overwhelmed him, his brain quieted, and he fell into an uneasy slumber.

☠

Edmund Swan followed a bald man in a hover chair into a large room with tapestry-covered walls and a rough-hewn wooden floor. The man introduced himself as Roberts and instructed him to sit at the room's long table. "May I offer you something to drink?" asked Roberts.

After finding slaves in Tejo City's mines and shooting it out with his own deputies, Swan's nerves were frayed. "Do you have a beer?"

"Be right back." Roberts maneuvered the hover chair up a stairway and through a door into the pirate ship that comprised much of the homestead. He returned a moment later with a dark ale.

Swan tasted the beer and pursed his lips, appreciating the balance of bitter and sweet notes.

"I'll get the captain." Roberts left again.

A moment later, a lithe man with long, white hair tied into a pony tail and a beard trimmed close entered the room. He extended his hand. "My name is Ellison Firebrandt." He smiled.

Swan accepted the man's hand. "Pleased to meet you, Captain Firebrandt." Swan studied the captain with his cybernetic eye. He perspired despite the cool room and his heart beat faster than normal for a man his age. Although he projected confidence, the captain was nervous.

Firebrandt waved Swan back into the chair. "We'll have none of those formalities here." The captain sat across from the lawman. "I am long retired."

"Even so, I'm honored," said Swan.

Firebrandt laughed. "I imagine few people would admit they were 'honored' to meet me." He leaned forward. "I understand you gave the Tejans quite a run for their money."

Swan scratched his head. His hair had grown out from the buzz cut he'd adopted. "I don't think they expected someone like me when they hired a new marshal."

"No, they didn't." Firebrandt flashed a devilish grin. "You proved once and for all they abducted New Granadans to keep productivity high and prices low." The captain folded his arms. "They'll do everything they can to cast your actions in a negative light."

"But surely the Confederation will step in." Sweat trickled under Swan's collar. "They've been shown the New Granadan miners aren't voluntary migrants."

"Son, the Confederation's only concern is stopping the Cluster." For just a moment, the privateer captain reminded Swan of his own father. "They see new ships as the key to locating the Cluster and erdonium's the one thing Sufiro can provide them. That puts the Confederation on Tejo's side." The captain took a deep breath, then released it before proceeding. "I'm afraid few people back on Earth even realize you freed slaves. Tejo's new governor will spin what you did into an aggressive act, slowing the effort to stop the Cluster."

Swan sipped the beer, then lowered it to the table and licked his lips. "Why go to such lengths?"

"The Stone Corporation not only competes with the Mao Corporation, but all the other erdonium mines around the galaxy. If they want to maximize their profits and assure they last, they need an edge. They've seen New Granada as a source of cheap labor for a long time." Firebrandt rubbed his chin. "Twenty years ago, they tried to get the law on their side by uniting Tejo and New Granada, which would allow them to invoke emergency wartime acts. Their failure back then checked Stone's ambition until new circumstances unleashed it again."

"You mean a war with popular support and an opponent who frightens people," interjected Swan.

Firebrandt pointed at the former marshal. "Exactly. If they find a way to unify the two continents, they could invoke emergency wartime provisions and practically declare slave labor legal. Not only would the Confederation not stop them, they would cheer Tejo on." The old pirate captain shook his head. "If I had to guess, I'd say Tejo is planning to invade New Granada. In terms of manpower, they might just succeed in overwhelming us now."

"Is that why you did nothing to free the slaves?" Swan blurted the question out, then regretted it.

Firebrandt stood, put his hands behind his back and paced the room while looking at the ground. He remained silent for some time. At last, he stopped and met Swan's gaze. "You're right. I did nothing, but let me ask this. Who did you expect to meet when you walked in here today?"

Swan considered that. "I expected to meet Ellison Firebrandt, the privateer captain who founded the colony on this planet."

"You're being too thoughtful." Firebrandt grinned. "You expected to see the old pirate captain. That's what everyone sees when they meet me—a man with a criminal past who stole and plundered to make a living. My reputation gets in the way of people seeing me as a respected leader. When the Tejans abducted New Granadans twenty years ago and Manuel Raton stopped it, I thought the story had a happy ending." Firebrandt sat down. "I never expected they would return to their old ways. We must stop the Tejans."

"It would help if Earth or the Confederation recognized New Granada's sovereignty." Swan shrugged.

The captain closed his eyes. "New Granada could have formed a more formal government in the days before erdonium's discovery. We could have kept the planet united." He opened his gray eyes. "I became a privateer and fought for the Gaean Alliance because they had solved all the human rights disasters on the mother planet. Even my father's homeland, South Africa, found peace and relative prosperity."

Swan nodded, remembering history. He had to admit that when Manuel Raton had told him New Granada had few laws to enforce, it had frightened him. He wondered how New Granadans protected individual rights.

"Sufiro taught me that while humans have peace, they aren't altogether free. Suki, Roberts, and I dreamed of a world where people could have both peace and freedom. When I learned about slavery in Tejo, I thought my dream had crumbled to dust." Firebrandt's fist clenched. After a moment, his hand relaxed and his eyes seemed to sparkle. "Then you came along."

Swan sat back, stunned. "What do you mean, I came along?"

"Remember what I said about my reputation?" Firebrandt leaned forward. "You have the opposite reputation. You're a good, just cop here to do a job. I want you to lead the defense forces."

"Me?" Swan stood and walked over to the fireplace and ran his finger over the cold, stone mantel. "I'm no general. Hell, I get sick at the sight of blood."

Firebrandt walked over to Swan. "That's exactly why I want you to lead the fight."

"Because I get sick at the sight of blood?" Swan looked at the old captain as though he'd lost his mind.

"The people of Sufiro don't need some war-hungry hero any more than they need a man with a criminal past. They need a good person who stands for justice."

"I wouldn't even know where to begin organizing a defense," stammered Swan.

Firebrandt grasped Swan's shoulder. "Start with Manuel, he can help you learn about New Granada's people. He also has monetary resources you can use, as do I. Neither of us is quite as rich as the Stone Corporation, but we can buy supplies and pay troops. Put out the word from Nuevo Santa Fe in the north to Nouveau Baton Rouge in the south."

"It won't be easy."

"War is never easy." Firebrandt returned to the table. "I don't want war. I want this conflict over, so we can all get on with our lives." Firebrandt sat down in the chair Swan abandoned. "You see, I don't begrudge anyone in Tejo having and mining erdonium. However, I won't tolerate them taking and using innocent people. I'll do my damnedest to make sure that stops."

"Then you can count me in, sir." Swan heard himself speak the words before thinking through all the consequences.

Firebrandt stood and the two men clasped hands.

The captain led Swan to the door. When it closed behind him, the marshal turned around and studied the house, which, in many ways, told New Granada's story. The house's core was the old gleaming black privateer vessel Firebrandt and Roberts had crash landed in. Adobe bricks composed the second largest part, tying the vessel to the planet. Wooden outgrowths painted a reddish hue seemed newer, yet the forest beyond the house showed no missing swaths of trees. The people who built this house had become the planet's stewards taking no more than they could replenish.

Born of necessity, the house had grown into a virtual palace. From his vantage, Swan could turn around and look across the village called Succor. The houses all nestled along the Nuevo Rio Grande's banks. Swan climbed into the old, battered hover he borrowed from Manuel Raton.

He pushed the starter button twice to no avail. He hopped out, gave it a swift kick next to the propulsor units and the hover drifted off the ground. With a sigh, he pulled himself in and engaged the engine. As he maneuvered the craft along the Nuevo Rio Grande, he took one last wistful look at the pirate captain's home.

The ex-Tejan Marshal drove full throttle, following the wide river. He tried to figure out how New Granada's small population could ever hope to repulse a well-armed Tejan force supported by the Confederation.

As he drove, the scenery distracted him from his glum thoughts. Rolling, grass-covered hills dotted with low scrub surrounded Succor. As he continued north, the terrain became more cultivated. Green hills and cornfields surrounded him. He waved to a farmer riding a hover tractor, pulling a laser plow.

Swan's hover topped a hill crest. He found himself looking down at New Des Moines, a large city by New Granadan standards. On Earth, it would just be a village. New Des Moines had New Granada's only spaceport. Swan thought he would stop off at a tavern, grab a bite to eat and something to drink.

He drove down New Des Moines's central street and parked his hover in front of the Rancheros Tavern. Entering the rough, wooden building through bat wing doors, he had to blink several times for his natural eye to acclimate to the darkness. He sat down at a small, round table that wobbled as he put weight on it. When the server came by, he ordered the burrito plate and a beer.

He glanced around the tavern and noticed several people wearing uniforms from off-world freighter companies. A nearby chair thudded as an eight-foot tall Rd'dyggian warrior sat down. Of the Confederation's citizens, only Rd'dyggians and Alpha Centaurans could survive in the same atmosphere as humans. Despite that, few Rd'dyggians chose human company.

The Rd'dyggian's thick purple mustache moved. Soon a voice followed from a pocket translator: "You look like a man with a problem."

Swan studied the Rd'dyggian whose skin seemed a deeper shade of orange than other Rd'dyggians he'd met. A patch covered one black eye and the warrior wore a listening device in his ear—no doubt associated with the translator.

Swan flashed a nervous smile. "I believe you have me at a disadvantage."

"Not at all," said the warrior. "My name is Arepno." He held out his massive six-fingered hand.

Swan realized the warrior tried to emulate a human custom. The former marshal did his best to accept the Rd'dyggian's enormous hand. "My name is Swan. And brother, do I have a problem."

"Brother," echoed Arepno. He imitated a smile. "I like that. Tell me of your problem."

The server arrived with the burrito plate and beer. Swan downed half the beer as he detailed the Tejo-New Granada conflict to the Rd'dyggian. The Rd'dyggian nodded understanding and sympathy at key points in the story, then fell into silent contemplation.

"Slavery is not honorable," said the warrior at last.

"Do Rd'dyggians even know what slaves are?" Swan asked the question between mouthfuls.

"No." Arepno's mustache wiggled. "Not until I learned about them this morning from an old friend."

Swan blinked twice. He scooped the last of the burrito into his mouth, then studied the Rd'dyggian. "An old friend has already told you this story?"

"I thought everyone knew." Arepno placed his hands on his knees. "Ellison Firebrandt has many friends. My crew and I are ready to help you in your honorable cause, General Swan."

Swan sat back and laughed.

Arepno inclined his head.

"Call me Edmund." Swan waved his hand. "I'll have none of this 'general' stuff."

"My crew and I await your instructions, Edmund Swan." Arepno made a noise Swan recognized as Rd'dyggian laughter.

Swan and Arepno swapped stories until the sun sat. Arepno said Rd'dyggians always swapped stories with new friends.

"It's a human custom as well." Swan smiled.

The lawman could see how Firebrandt could get attached to this large warrior. As the oblong moon rose, Swan made his apologies, explaining he had to get back to Nuevo Santa Fe.

Swan stood. "Can you meet me and Manuel Raton tomorrow?" He drew the Rd'dyggian a map on a paper napkin.

"I will be there." Arepno put his hand to his abdomen in the traditional Rd'dyggian salute.

John Mark Ellis trudged down Nantucket's familiar cobblestone streets. As he passed the old gray houses, he remembered the long walks he would take with his father. Somehow, Ellis didn't feel alone. Whole generations of Ellises had walked these streets. As he drew comforting smoke from a cigar and then exhaled, his ancestors' spirits seemed to manifest for a moment before they dissipated on the sea air.

As Ellis turned up the street leading to his old family house, he noticed a figure standing on the widow's walk that capped the roof. He waved. His mother waved back. The outside of the house had not changed appearance in over a thousand years. Its gray shingles and white-rimmed windows summoned him. He entered the house and glanced around at the curious mix of antiques and modern furnishings. He checked the time on his Navy wristcomp and compared it to a twelve-hundred-year-old chronometer an old family friend named Coffin maintained. The clocks were just two seconds apart.

He dropped off his bag and went upstairs and through a door that led to the widow walk. Back in the days when sailing ships plied the waves, sailors' wives climbed to the wooden structures to watch the harbor for their husbands and sons to return from the sea. By the thirtieth century, many widow walks were merely decorative and would not support a person's weight. Jerome and Fire had kept the structure functional on their house and it provided a great view of the island.

Mark and Fire embraced then walked over to the rail and looked out at the town.

"It turns out, I only have two days at home, then I have to report back to the ship," said Mark.

Fire nodded. "I was thinking about taking a trip home … spend a little time with our family on Sufiro."

Ellis narrowed his gaze. "Is that wise? I hear passenger lines are beginning to limit their services, concerned about the Cluster."

"Kheir el-Din said he could take me."

"He was grandfather's helmsman, wasn't he?" Ellis reached out and took his mother's hand. "I suppose if there's anyone I'd trust with my mom's safety, it's him."

They stood in silence and listened to the breeze rustling the trees and the chirping of birds. "There's one person we need to talk to while you're home," said Fire. "He will want to know about your dad and we're his only source of news."

"Richard?"

Fire nodded.

That afternoon, Ellis consulted his father's records of the old sperm whale's migratory path. Then, they went to the dock and took the family boat out to sea. When they reached the area where they expected to find Richard, they lowered an underwater transmitter and sent out a call.

He didn't arrive right away. Fire and Mark shared a quiet meal, then Mark retreated to his cabin. He touched a control pad next to the bunk. "Music," he said. The dissonant harmonics of twenty-eighth century jazz filled the cabin. He closed his eyes, listening to his father's favorite music.

He considered his encounter with the Cluster and pondered the irony of his chance remark becoming the name used for an unknown alien race. Irrational guilt welled up within him as he realized he'd named his father's murderers.

Somehow, the Cluster must be stopped. The lieutenant winced in pain as he realized he'd clenched his fist too tightly.

The strains of twenty-eighth century jazz faded into Delta blues from the twentieth century. Mark's eyes welled with tears and he fell asleep on the bunk.

The next morning, water spouted next to the boat. Fire and

Mark turned on their personal translators as the 62-foot long spermaceti whale swam alongside, making staccato clicking sounds. The translator converted the clicks to human language. "The cycle continues."

"The cycle continues," intoned both Mark and Fire.

"The hunt is the art," replied Richard.

"It has been a long time, my friend," said Mark.

The whale rolled so he could eye the deck. "Why have you summoned me?"

Ellis took a deep shuddering breath. "We wanted to tell you, my father was killed in space by something we call the Cluster."

"I shall mourn him." Richard's head went below the waves, revealing a wrinkled back. The great tail rose from the water. Mark remembered the D.H. Lawrence poem, "Whales Weep Not," and wondered whether or not the sentiment was true.

Richard surfaced after a minute on the other side of the boat. Fire and Mark crossed the deck and leaned over the railing. Richard rose far enough from the water so Fire could touch him.

"Whales know little of the ways of space," said Richard. "Tell me of this Cluster."

"It is a great ball of silver spheres, bigger than you, bigger than your dead brothers, the blue whales," explained Fire. "They move through space like great vessels. When the peoples of the stars—the humans, the Titans, Rd'dyggians, Zahari— find a Cluster, the Cluster destroys them."

Richard clicked. "The Cluster seems wise. For tool builders the art is the death. Do you know what the Cluster is?"

Kneeling down by the railing, Mark swished the water lazily with his left hand. "People have tried to talk to the Cluster, peacefully. The Cluster began killing all our people."

"Now you know how we feel," said Richard. "Maybe now the tool builders begin to understand." Another great spray came from the whale's spout.

"Maybe I begin to understand at least." Mark pondered the whale's words, heedless of his damp clothes. "We see the Cluster as evil, but maybe they're not."

"But maybe they are," Richard clicked. "Whales know not the ways of space."

"Anyone who approaches the Cluster should not make any assumptions," suggested Fire. "They should open their mind and try to understand the art."

Mark nodded. To a whale, the "art" was the essence of life. Humpbacks considered the song their art. Spermaceti saw the hunt as the art. Mark didn't necessarily agree that humanity's art was death, but he could understand why whales would believe that. To understand the Cluster, one had to understand its art ... its essence.

"The hunt is the art. The cycle resumes." Richard indicated the time had arrived for him to depart.

"The cycle resumes, old friend," said Mark.

"The cycle resumes," agreed Fire.

Richard dove into the water. A moment later, his tail appeared from the waves, as though waving farewell. Fire and Mark waved, even though Richard couldn't see, then turned the boat back to Nantucket.

The next day, Suki Firebrandt Ellis left Earth aboard the *Barbarossa*. Captain el-Din was able to map out an express route that took them to Sufiro with minimal time in normal space, which reduced the likelihood they'd encounter the Cluster. It must have cost him more to make the trip than he charged. Once they arrived, less than a week after departing Earth, Captain el-Din took her to the planet aboard one of the launches. The two climbed out and she walked to her father's house. Memories flooded back as she studied the adobe house alongside a downed pirate vessel. She ran to the old adobe structure and banged on the door. Ellison Firebrandt answered and embraced his daughter. She stood back and looked at him, amazed at his white hair and thin frame.

"It's been too long since I've been home."

"You came home at a difficult time," he said, then noticed el-Din. The old friends clasped hands.

"Was there ever an easy time on Sufiro?" asked Fire as they entered the house.

"I think this may be worse than normal." Firebrandt led them into the old dining room with the wooden table she remembered so well. Roberts floated in on a hover chair.

"It's good to see you both." Fire reached down and embraced her other dad.

Roberts grinned. "With hugs like that, I wish you'd return more often." He activated the chair's propulsors, and went back into the old spaceship. A moment later, he returned with coffee and cups.

Fire held up her hands and yawned. "Thank you, but I need a nap soon."

Roberts poured coffee for himself, el-Din, and Firebrandt.

Fire dropped into a chair and looked from Roberts to her father. "Is it true what they say? Will the worker's strike in Tejo escalate into a war with New Granada?"

Firebrandt released a bitter chuckle. "This isn't just some labor dispute. The Tejans have been abducting New Granadans to work the mines. The hunt for the Cluster is an excuse to press-gang people into servitude."

"You realize Tejo has the Confederation's support?" Kheir el-Din arched an eyebrow. "It's all the chatter on the interstellar frequencies. Tejo says New Granada is interfering with the erdonium trade. The Cluster scares people and they buy into Rocky Hill's narrative."

Firebrandt nodded. "Peter Stone secured a place in popular culture when he discovered erdonium in Tejo. By contrast, people see New Granada as a backwater. The perception makes it hard to get the truth out. Somehow, though, we will."

"When we arrived, I noticed a Rd'dyggian war ship in geostationary orbit over New Granada." Fire's brow knitted. "What's that all about?"

"That's our trump card." Firebrandt sipped his coffee. "They'll defend us and they'll help us get the truth out." He looked to Roberts who nodded, understanding.

Chapter Fifteen

SKIRMISHES

John Mark Ellis reported to the *Astrolus* and traveled with his ship to Titan. Engineer's mate Janelle Shoukry offered her hand. "I hear you're leaving the ship at Titan, sir. Congratulations."

Ellis took her hand. "I'm not sure whether congratulations are in order or not. All I know is that I'm supposed to report to Admiral Strauss."

"It's got to mean a promotion. We're all pulling for you." She shrugged and then patted him on the shoulder. "For one thing, it means the ship's air filters will get a break."

"I'm glad to know I'll be missed."

Later that day, the captain, First Officer Karen Shankar, and Ellis descended to the human pressure dome on Saturn's largest moon. The three walked from the dock to admiralty headquarters. Once there, the captain and first officer peeled off for their own meetings. Ellis checked the directory and found his way to Admiral Marlou Strauss's office. As he entered the reception area, he noted the luxuriant carpet. Expensive paintings adorned the walls. Even wearing a full-dress uniform, he felt underdressed.

The clerk stared at a comp screen and wore a speaker in his ear. Ellis reasoned that he, like ship communicators, must have a chip implant and could communicate throughout the base without leaving his desk. Just as Ellis opened his mouth to speak, the clerk met the lieutenant's gaze. "Admiral Strauss will see you now, Lieutenant Ellis."

Ellis nodded, his lips pursed. The lieutenant paused at the admiral's door, tugged at his uniform jacket, then entered.

The admiral sat behind her desk, eyes glued to a comp

screen much as the clerk's had been. After a moment, the admiral's head turned toward Ellis, though her eyes lingered on the screen. "Please come in, Mr. Ellis."

Ellis stepped forward and saluted. She met his gaze at last and returned the salute, then gestured to a chair. Ellis sat.

Admiral Strauss tapped a button on the desk, then looked back to the screen. A moment later, the clerk entered with a tray. He poured coffee for the admiral and offered a cup to Ellis. Ellis nodded and the clerk poured a cup then left. "Captain MacPherson's report credits you with naming the Cluster."

Ellis flushed red. "Yes, ma'am."

"You've also seen the death and destruction they cause. You know firsthand what a danger they represent." She sipped her coffee.

"Yes, ma'am."

"Between ship losses and the need to respond when Cluster ships appear, we have increased our order for new ships," she said. "Erdonium for ship hulls is at a premium. As you may have heard, shipments from our largest supplier have all but stopped."

"That would be the planet Sufiro." Ellis gave a curt nod.

"Good. You've been following the news. I presume you've heard about the miner's strike and how they blew up a warehouse." She took another sip of her coffee, then set the cup aside. "What you may not know is that striking miners seem to have support from Rd'dyggian privateers." The admiral's eyes narrowed. "Your mother is from Sufiro, isn't she?"

"Yes, ma'am." Ellis's cheeks warmed. "She was born in New Granada to the planet's first settlers."

The admiral nodded. "I don't give a rat's ass for Sufiro or its backwater politics. That is, until the erdonium is affected. I'm giving you a commander's appointment and sending you out to Sufiro. I want you to get the erdonium moving again."

Ellis's heart rate increased. "Commander" was not a rank, but a position a lieutenant filled. Numerous questions popped into his mind, but protocol came first. "Thank you, ma'am."

She gave him a brief nod. "You will assume command of the destroyer *Firebrandt*. She's one of our new ships. I'm giving you wide latitude to settle this dispute. If you have to run off the Rd'dyggian privateer and force the New Granadans to help, I'll back your play. If we have to pay a little more to allow the Tejans to meet the striker's demands, that's fine, too. Just find out why everyone's so upset and straighten it out enough to resume production. If you need backup, we can send a larger vessel."

Ellis shifted in his seat. "Ma'am, are you giving me this assignment because my mother is from Sufiro?"

The admiral leaned forward and steepled her fingers. "I'm giving you this command because the Titans ordered me to."

Ellis sputtered and set down his coffee cup before he spilled the contents on his white uniform. "Why would the Titans order me to go to Sufiro?"

Strauss shrugged. "I hoped you could tell me that."

The commander shook his head. "I don't know, ma'am."

The admiral harrumphed, then sat back. "Let me be frank, Commander Ellis. You're a good officer, but you're young. Based on your record, I think you would stand a shot at command in a few years, but I don't think you're ready yet. Despite that, Teklar, the leader of the known galaxy, called me and insisted you be promoted. I want to know why."

Ellis shook his head. "I would like to know that as well. I've never met Teklar or any Titan for that matter."

Strauss studied the commander for a long moment. At last she seemed satisfied. "Very well, then. Do what you can at Sufiro. Don't be afraid to call in help. If this goes well, it'll be a step toward a permanent promotion to captain. In the meantime, if you learn any reason the Titans are showing a special interest in you, report to me right away."

Ellis nodded. "Believe me, I'm just as interested in knowing the answer to that question as you are."

Strauss stood and Ellis jumped to his feet. "Your ship is being prepped. We'll assign you quarters here on Titan until crew assignments are complete." She extended her hand and Ellis clasped it. "Good luck, Commander."

☠

Edmund Swan scoured the forest a few miles from Manuel Raton's home. He searched the ground for a wild fungus Manuel had told him about. "It's edible and tastes like truffles," Manuel had said. In fact, Edmund had been looking for an excuse to get out of the house. Spreading the word to young men and women that New Granada may need a defense force would be easy. Figuring out how to arm and train this force made his head hurt. What's more, envisioning a major battle made him nauseous. The forest's pine-scented air helped, but not as much as he'd hoped. Edmund shook his head, wondering what Firebrandt had been thinking when he charged him with creating a military.

A rustling sounded from nearby trees. He reached for his hepler. "Damn," he cursed as he realized he didn't have it. Manuel had warned him about the griffins in the woods.

A tall woman with long black hair stepped forward. "Are you okay?"

Swan blinked several times then examined the woman with his cybernetic eye. The pollens on her clothes indicated she had come from Succor. "I'm fine." His mismatched eyes narrowed. "I know you, don't I?"

"You used to have such a pretty pair of brown eyes," she said.

"You're Suki Firebrandt, aren't you?"

"I'm surprised you remember me."

"What you told me about Sufiro when we had coffee in Tucson all those years ago stuck with me. It's part of the reason I'm here now."

"And your advice about schools really helped me." She strode toward him, her hand extended.

Swan shook her hand.

Fire grinned. "Manuel told me you'd be out here."

"It's good to see you again," said Swan. "How the hell are you?"

"I've been better," admitted Fire. "My husband just died a few weeks ago."

"Oh … I'm sorry." Swan glanced away.

"Manuel has been telling me a little about the challenges of organizing a defense against the Tejans." She narrowed her gaze and scanned the forest. "The mushrooms are that way." She pointed.

Swan looked in the direction she indicated. His cybernetic eye could not confirm her assertion, but he followed as she strode off between the trees. "'Challenging' is an understatement. I'm not sure if I'm up to the task."

"Weren't you a Tucson Sheriff's Deputy?" Fire ducked under a low-hanging tree branch.

"Southern Arizona Sheriff's Deputy," Swan corrected. "I organized police investigations and I served as Sheriff Wilmot's liaison with the Planetary Police, but there was an infrastructure in place. I didn't have to feed the officers, clothe them, pay them..."

"I think your first concern is getting them here. If you let them know there's a threat and that there's organization and training available, they'll come. I bet volunteers will help feed them if they know there's a problem. They may even bring food themselves if they know they need to. Pay would be great, but they want to save their homes and their families. You just need to let people know there's a problem. They know Manuel and word is spreading about you." She stepped up and looked him in the eye.

"There's one other problem. I get sick at the sight of blood. That's trouble enough for a cop. What kind of military commander would I make?" Swan thrust his hands deep in his pockets.

"A compassionate one. One who could earn my father's trust." She flashed a grin. "That's not easy to do."

"He really thinks I can do it?" Swan's brow furrowed. "You think I can do it?"

"You got to know where to look, Ed." She pointed to the forest floor. Gray balls on tripod stems covered the ground. "What counts is whether or not Ed Swan believes he can do it."

Swan knelt down and picked a mushroom. He stared at the fungi covering the ground and considered the miners forced to work against their will in Tejo. "Maybe I can."

Together, they picked mushrooms for dinner.

☠

Colonel Clyde McClintlock watched a holographic projection taken from a satellite orbiting Sufiro. A black egg-shaped Rd'dyggian star cruiser hung in stationary orbit above New Granada. Text appeared within the hologram telling the colonel the crew complement along with details about the ship's armaments and defenses. McClintlock shuddered. It could pose a serious challenge to his forces.

After Marshal Edmund Swan helped several New Granadan migrants hijack an airship, Sam Stone and a team of marshals pursued them. When the operation failed and Sam Stone died, the Lieutenant Governor, Rocky Hill, took over. McClintlock briefed Hill about Stone's desire to capture New Granada and place it under Tejan authority. Hill ordered McClintlock to continue mustering forces and stockpiling supplies for the invasion.

Son of the legendary governor, Mary Hill, Rocky had strong support from Tejo's populace. By all accounts, Manuel Raton had killed Stone. Many also blamed him for Mary's death. The time had come to contain New Granada.

As McClintlock watched the hologram, a new ship entered orbit and docked with the Rd'dyggian ship.

"Enhance holographic image," said the colonel to the computer. The ship looked as though it came from a human world, but it was sleek and streamlined in contrast to the bulky, cylindrical Navy ships. "Increase magnification ten-fold," he ordered.

The image of the two ships expanded and the colonel nodded. He put his hand under the new ship's image and made a lifting motion. The image followed his hand above his head. He noted a registry number on the new ship.

"Run registry," he ordered.

"State number," replied the computer's soft, electric voice.

"P 505835." McClintlock paced the room while the computer traced down the number he had given.

Clyde McClintlock and Rocky Hill had been friends since childhood. They both moved to Sufiro with their parents and went to school in New Des Moines. They kept in touch even after Rocky moved to Tejo with his mom. After Clyde graduated from high school, he returned to Earth and joined the Gaean Navy. When he completed service, he returned to Sufiro and settled in Tejo. Mary asked him to organize a Tejan National Guard. Over the last two decades, Clyde had assembled a respectable force comprised of marshals looking for extra income and young people who never imagined they would fight in a conflict on Sufiro.

McClintlock occupied a bunker under Mount Mathews, near Tejo City. He walked around the hologram as though he could gain new understanding by seeing things from a different angle.

"P 505835 is an independent trading vessel from base settlement at G.S.C. 101243," reported the computer at last.

The colonel's adjutant, Major Clarise Ellwood, cleared her throat.

McClintlock pointed to the display. "What do you make of these Rd'dyggians?"

The major approached. "I think they're a distraction."

"A distraction from what?" McClintlock raised his eyebrows.

"There's been a migrant work stoppage at the mine in Stonestown. Our people are on the scene but the migrants just won't work. They put down their tools and sing ballads about Edmund Swan. They describe him as a strong, heroic figure who shows great courage and foresight."

"I don't care about Swan or how they describe him." McClintlock looked back at the hologram. "Computer, what are G.S.C. 101243's primary trade goods?"

"G.S.C. 101243 has numerous factories for household appliances, shop tools, small arms…"

"That's enough." McClintlock looked at his adjutant. "Clear the Stonestown Mine of migrants by any means possible, but keep a guard contingent on them. I don't want them receiving any visitors, especially Rd'dyggian visitors. Am I understood?"

"Sir, if we fire on Rd'dyggians … we could set off a galactic incident." The major clasped her hands behind her back.

"I know, but they're in the same boat. If they fire on us, it'll also start an incident. For now, our people just need to ask them politely to leave." McClintlock sighed and ran his fingers through gray hair. "In the meantime, get me an inventory of our arms plus the number of forces we currently have available.

Once that's done, get me a meeting with Governor Hill. We need to plan strategy and establish a timetable. I fear things may be escalating fast."

Major Ellwood nodded. Her brilliant blue eyes sparkled from the overhead lamp's glow and a hint of a grin crossed her face. She turned on her heel and left.

McClintlock sat down at his desk and tapped his fingers. He didn't like mysteries, especially ones that involved powerful aliens receiving shipments from arms dealers or migrants raising hell.

Edmund Swan and Manuel Raton spread the word throughout New Granada about a possible Tejan invasion. As Suki predicted, men and women traveled to Nuevo Santa Fe. They brought food and camping supplies. The Nuevo Rio Grande supplied water. Swan found the biggest challenge to be assigning people to dig latrines.

Close to fifteen thousand people arrived within a week. All the people who came had originally arrived in New Granada expecting to be homesteaders. They all carried weapons they had either brought with them from Earth or acquired on Sufiro, yet they were not an organized force. Manuel, Juan, his wife Armanta, and Edmund worked to meet all the people and determine the best candidates to serve as team leaders.

Edmund and Manuel reviewed the records and organized the people into platoons. They found a few homesteaders who had been in the Gaean Navy or Marines and assigned them the task of giving lessons to the other volunteers.

A week after the first volunteers arrived and occupied the meadow near Raton's home, Arepno's shuttle landed. Unlike human tech, Rd'dyggian sensors were not blinded by the valley's magnetic properties. Arepno emerged and joined Edmund Swan on a rise that provided a good view of the volunteers' encampment.

"That is one unique force you two have organized." The Rd'dyggian's purple mustache wriggled around the words.

Edmund wondered whether Arepno intended those words as a compliment or an insult. "What brings you here today?"

"My people have been engaged in an adventure." Arepno swayed back and forth.

"Perhaps we should summon Manuel and you can tell us about it."

"That would be a good idea."

Edmund retrieved his handcomp from his belt and typed a message to Manuel. He then led Arepno back to Manuel's house. The sheriff arrived a few minutes later and hung his hat next to the door.

Captain Arepno told Edmund and Manuel that he led a team of Rd'dyggian warriors to the open pit mine at Raton Mesa. "I stared into the mine with both awe and terror. The opened ground showed many wondrous colors—red, orange, and purple among them, but the scale was monstrous. The Tejans have opened the entire mesa top. It reminded me of a wide-open human mouth with the lips sticking out. Grotesque."

Manuel stood and retrieved beers for Edmund and himself. "Can I get you anything, Arepno?"

"No thank you, I brought my own refreshment." Arepno retrieved a can from within his robe's folds and touched the top, which irised open. Mist rose in waves from the mold-green concoction's surface. "I looked into the mine itself. Humans had carved the ground into beautiful symmetries, but slashed those symmetries with roads designed for hover vehicles. Your people seem intent on dominating the planet, much as you dominate your own kind through slavery."

Edmund raised his hand. "It's not us, it's the Tejans who want to dominate others."

"You all have the capacity to dominate others of your own kind." The captain's voice took on a cold, hard tone. Edmund wondered if it was just an artifact of the translator, or if the voice reflected Arepno's feelings.

"This planet does not belong to humans, you know. The planet is Rd'dyggian. We will not tolerate slavery."

"We agree on that point." Manuel lifted his beer, then took a sip.

"We took three sonic grenades to the miners. They laughed and told us it reminded them of a name the Tejans called them." Arepno paused and breathed in the mist from his can. "They used the grenades to collapse the pit's walls and they destroyed the mining equipment. We then gave the miners food and water along with weapons so they could defend themselves."

Edmund lifted his eyebrows. "Those must have been powerful grenades you used, if they only needed three to collapse the mesa walls."

"They were top of the line according to the dealer we met from G.S.C. 101243."

"You gave them human armaments?" Manuel set his beer on the table.

"Of course, giving them Rd'dyggian weapons would be interfering. The Tejans are watching for it." This time Arepno's mustache-like tentacles slipped into the green concoction. When he lowered the can, Edmund noticed less liquid inside.

"But what I don't understand," said Manuel, "is why don't you just rescue the people there?"

"Ah." Arepno held up the forward most finger on his right hand. "That would also be interfering. Interfering with a planet's internal politics is frowned upon."

"But isn't supplying the miners with sonic grenades interference?" Edmund narrowed his gaze.

"Who's supplying miners with grenades?" Arepno imitated a human shrug. "I'm monitoring the surface. Sometimes sensors don't do a good job, so we scout the continents. It's always possible a trooper might drop a grenade near a mine. What the miners do with it is not my concern. If it distracts the Tejan National Guard from invading New Granada, then I feel I have improved security on a Rd'dyggian world."

Raton and Edmund nodded approval. Arepno seemed to have acquired a knack for human idiom. The humans and the Rd'dyggian finished their drinks and went back outside. In the meadow below, two platoons marched up and down alongside the tents. Another platoon had set up targets and practiced with their firearms. Five children sat on the rise and watched the activity. From the words they exchanged, Edmund gathered two of their parents camped down below and they tried to figure out where they were. Edmund then looked up and frowned as he considered the wildflowers and grass trampled in preparation for the conflict—a conflict he knew resulted from a feud brewing for twenty years and touched off by his actions along with those of Manuel and Arepno.

"Each and every person down there will fight for this continent's freedom." Edmund scratched the stubble growing on his chin.

"That may be so," intoned Arepno's translator, "but they are no match for Tejo's National Guard. The Tejan force has been training for nearly two decades." The Rd'dyggian seemed to smile a bit. Edmund thought the smile looked wistful.

"I'm afraid I have to agree." Manuel sighed. "In any conventional military action, they would be wiped out. More modern armaments would help."

Arepno imitated a shrug. "That is no problem. That is being seen to."

"It's what?" Swan narrowed his gaze. "What do you mean?"

"We have connections, Firebrandt and me. We have acquired more than sonic grenades." Arepno paused his near-constant swaying for just a moment, as though expecting a reaction from the others.

Edmund considered what he did and did not know. Although Firebrandt had put him in charge of the defense, the old pirate captain still seemed to be running things behind the scenes. Meanwhile, his new friend, Manuel Raton seemed unconcerned.

Manuel looked from the field to Arepno. "Are sonic grenades the only things your people left behind in Tejo?"

Arepno made another shrugging gesture. "We have managed to sneak transmitters into every mine in Tejo, including the one in Stonestown before Colonel McClintlock ordered them removed from the mine and heavily guarded. All miners can communicate with one another as well as with my ship. The Stonestown miners have told their story. They were singing songs of Edmund Swan when a group of armed soldiers stepped into the group with disciplinarians. They used the weapons on as many of the group as they could touch.

The buzz and crackle of the disciplinarians could be heard long after the singing stopped."

Edmund winced.

Arepno continued. "Most of the miners have stopped working, but some are afraid and continue."

"It's hard to blame them." Edmund folded his arms. "Once you're face to face with a disciplinarian, it's hard to say no to anyone."

"Indeed." Manuel sighed and stroked his thick mustache.

"We also blew up an erdonium warehouse," said Arepno.

Both men gave the captain their full attention. "You did what?" asked Edmund.

"They won't take that for long," said Manuel. "They may use that as justification to bring in Confederation forces."

"We'll see what happens." The large orange being continued to sway back and forth. "Should be fun." Manuel and Edmund exchanged glances.

After a few minutes, Arepno gave a slow nod. "I had better check the cargo systems on the ship. It is possible something else may drop accidentally."

The warrior strode away to his ship. Manuel and Edmund watched as it ascended into the sky. Arepno sent no further communication until several loud thuds woke them the next morning. They each clambered out of bed to discover the noise's source. Six immense crates stood outside Manuel's front door. According to the letters stenciled on the side, each crate contained a thousand hepler pistols and ten times as many energy packs. Edmund Swan's stomach fluttered as the reality of preparing for war settled in.

John Mark Ellis stooped in the launch docked to the *Barbara Firebrandt*. His heart raced and he kept reaching up to adjust the single epaulet, which now sat on his left shoulder instead of the right as it had since his promotion to lieutenant. The *Firebrandt* was a small ship, but it was his to command.

At first, Ellis had been confused about why a destroyer would have been named for his pirate grandfather. It made more sense when he had realized the ship had been named for Admiral Barbara Firebrandt. Despite being related to a former privateer captain, he admired how Admiral Firebrandt of Alpha Coma Berenices had united humanity's legitimate navies against the marginally legal privateers.

The launch's airlock door parted and warm air from the *Firebrandt* rushed in. The ship's computer piped the captain aboard. Ellis stepped forward. A Commissioned Officer B-Grade and two petty officers stood in front of eleven crewmembers jammed into the tiny bay. The B-Com stepped forward and saluted.

"I, Commander John Mark Ellis, by order of the Gaean Alliance and the Admiralty of the Confederation of Homeworlds assume command of the Homeworld's Destroyer *Barbara Firebrandt* this date."

The B-Com had a resounding, deep voice. "I, Francis Rubin, stand relieved. Welcome aboard, Commander Ellis, sir."

Ellis's cheeks warmed when he realized he hadn't prepared a formal address. He cleared his throat. "Well crew, batten down the hatches and secure the tops'l, we're in for rough weather." The crewmembers stifled grins. Ellis nodded to the senior petty officer.

"Dismissed," she barked.

The crew scurried off to their stations.

"Mr. B-Com Rubin, please show me to my quarters."

"Aye aye, sir." The young man led the commander to a small alcove with a forcefield that could be activated for privacy. Within stood a bed and a tiny fold-down desk—typical commander's accommodations on a destroyer.

"Mr. Rubin, please prepare to leave Saturn's orbit." Ellis wanted to show his second-in-command both that he was firm and willing to trust the young man.

"Aye aye, sir. Rubin saluted, then turned on his heel and went ten more feet to the bridge.

Ellis sat on the bunk for a moment, his duffel beside him. He listened to Rubin give commands. Although young and with little experience, he had a firm grasp of his duties. Ellis pondered the reason the Confederation chose to name a mere destroyer after a great admiral like Barbara Firebrandt. As he stood to go to the bridge, the answer occurred to him. Barbara Firebrandt had not been from Earth. In retrospect, it was quite an honor for an Earth ship to be named for a colonial admiral.

Commander John Mark Ellis entered the tiny bridge and noted the stations. B-Com Rubin piloted the ship. The senior petty officer served as gunner. The other petty officer had a recent scar on his head indicating that he was a new communicator. Ellis put his hands on the command chair's back. He looked at the tiny control panel designed for the right hand. The commander nodded, satisfied.

"Request permission to depart Saturn's orbit," barked Ellis.

The communicator touched his forehead, still getting used to the communication's implant. A moment later, he relayed word from orbit control. "Permission granted."

Ellis moved around the chair and sat. "Mr. Rubin, make for jump point to Sufiro. We have erdonium to move."

☠

"It's as though the migrants are coordinating their actions." Clyde McClintlock sat in front of Rocky Hill's desk. "First, they destroyed the warehouse outside Tejo City. Then, they destroyed the mine at Raton Mesa, causing me to send in men to dig out salvage. When a riot broke out at Camp Jones in less than a day, I had to send people there. My forces are being spread thin. It's keeping us from commencing our primary operation."

"Damn it! How?" Governor Hill pounded the desk with his fist. "How the hell is word spreading from one mine to another?" He pointed at Colonel McClintlock. "Among other things, your forces are supposed to prevent that!"

"They're doing their best, sir." The colonel shrugged.

Governor Hill sat back in a large padded chair that emphasized his small frame. It had belonged to his predecessor, Sam Stone, as had many of the other decorations in the office. "The work slowdown is already affecting the Stone Corporation's production figures. The Confederation is sending more business to Mao. Those profits don't stay here on Sufiro."

McClintlock held up a handcomp. "I've been running

analyses. If you let me consolidate all my forces and conscript at least two airships, I can launch our invasion against New Granada."

Hill's feet dropped to the floor and he began pacing the office. "What about the Rd'dyggian ship in orbit. Is it a serious threat?"

The colonel took a deep breath as he considered the question. "It is, but Major Ellwood and I believe we've identified an invasion route they won't expect and can't detect." The colonel used his handcomp to display a holographic map of New Granada along with geological readings.

Hill stopped pacing and placed his hands on the desk, his large ears twitching with interest. "That does look promising, but it's not ironclad. A ship in orbit could still see your forces visually." The governor shook his head. "Right now, we're fighting on multiple fronts. Let's see if we can quell the uprisings at home first. With time, the New Granadans may run out of funds to pay their Rd'dyggian friends."

Colonel McClintlock stood and saluted. "Very good, sir, but there is risk in waiting. I hear the New Granadans are organizing a defense and I do have a way to conceal the airships."

The shorter man tugged on his suit and sat down. "I understand, Colonel. We won't wait too long."

The colonel turned on his heel and left the governor's office.

Chapter Sixteen

DECISION POINT

Colonel Clyde McClintlock frowned as the shrill alarm sounded. Another ship had entered orbit around Sufiro. He adjusted the holographic monitor to view the newcomer. His worry turned to curiosity when he recognized the vessel's Confederation Navy markings. The main hepler gun took up the entire ship's bow. Additional guns bristled from the cylindrical vessel's surface. Small and built for battle, he inferred the new ship must be a destroyer.

The colonel narrowed his gaze. He doubted the small destroyer would intimidate the much larger Rd'dyggian war ship's captain. Still, the destroyer would be well armed and more maneuverable than the big ship. Much would hinge on the captain's experience.

Major Ellwood entered the office interrupting the colonel's thoughts. "Sir, a Commander J. M. Ellis is signaling. He wishes to meet with you and Governor Hill."

McClintlock nodded. "Have you contacted the governor?"

"I have. He wants to meet with the commander this afternoon."

"Okay," sighed the colonel. "I presume he wants to meet in his office."

The major gave a curt nod. "I have taken the liberty of having your driver stand by to take you into town."

"Very good. Tell him I'll meet him at the hover in fifteen minutes." The colonel entered a small side room where he had a cot and a wardrobe with several uniforms. He changed from the field garb into his pressed, gray dress uniform. Only three service medals from his time in the Earth Alliance Navy adorned his left breast. Neither Sam Stone nor Rocky Hill had seen fit to present awards to the Tejan National Guard. Until he deployed troops to the mines, the force's principal duty had been to supplement the Tejan Marshal's office.

The last "crisis" McClintlock's people had dealt with had been a situation where a woman from Alpha Coma Berenices had started a bar fight near the spaceport. The marshal's office had wanted to avoid a situation that had the potential to blow up into a diplomatic incident.

Still, Major Ellwood had referred to the destroyer's captain as "Commander Ellis." The Confederation had not sent an experienced captain after all. This J.M. Ellis would be a lieutenant on assignment. McClintlock's desire for an experienced captain who would know how to deal with the Rd'dyggian threat was dashed. That noted, the colonel didn't feel embarrassed by his lack of decorations. After all, he'd been a senior lieutenant when discharged from the Navy. This new arrival wouldn't intimidate him.

Once changed, McClintlock strode through his command center and entered an elevator, which carried him up to the motor pool. He found his driver waiting beside his hover. The driver saluted and opened the door. McClintlock returned the salute and settled in the back seat. "Take me to the governor's office," said McClintlock when the driver climbed in the vehicle.

"Yes, sir."

The driver lifted off and aimed the hover toward Tejo City. The colonel considered what he would want to see accomplished at the meeting. He wanted the Rd'dyggians to stop helping the New Granadan miners. He didn't think the destroyer could chase the war ship away, nor would it have a marine detachment to help him on the ground. Still, the commander could report back to base and bring help.

The hover docked at the government building near Hill's office. The colonel left the hover, donned his hat, and strode to the governor's office. Hill's secretary announced him and the colonel entered. Hill wore a tailored gray suit and a white shirt with a crystal brooch at the neck.

"The timing of the commander's arrival is excellent." Hill sat, then indicated McClintlock should sit as well. "We should bring him up to speed on our plans to claim New Granada."

"Are you sure that's prudent, sir?" McClintlock hung his hat beside the door, then sat down. "He's just a commander in charge of a destroyer. He won't have many resources to back this play."

"He has the only resources I care about. The admiralty's ears and the eyes of Sufiro's populace."

Before McClintlock could ask Hill what he meant about Sufiro's eyes, Commander John Mark Ellis arrived. He wore a standard duty uniform: a blue jacket over a gray body suit. A silver epaulet hung askew on his left shoulder. Although combed, the commander's hair seemed to have a mind of its own. The governor shook his hand. When the colonel's turn came, he caught a strong odor. It seemed this commander had a taste for tobacco.

The three men sat down and the governor flashed a broad smile. "So, what brings you to our little world, Commander?"

"Erdonium." Ellis folded his arms. "I'm here to find out why production has slowed down."

"Production has slowed down because terrorists have sabotaged our operation." Hill folded his hands and leaned forward. "They collapsed the open pit at Raton Mesa and destroyed a warehouse."

The colonel nodded. "We think the Rd'dyggian pirates are supplying them."

A pained look crossed the commander's features. Something about pirates bothered him. The colonel made a mental note. Perhaps he could use that piece of information.

"Why do you think these 'terrorists' are attacking erdonium mines?" The commander's brow furrowed. "Have they made any demands?"

Rocky Hill shook his head. "Can I offer you a drink? My secretary can bring in coffee or tea. I have a well stocked liquor cabinet if you prefer something stronger."

"Coffee would be fine," said Ellis.

McClintlock frowned. He would have enjoyed an opportunity to sample the governor's fine scotch, but Hill placed the order without asking him what he'd like.

"So, these terrorists haven't made any demands," pressed Ellis.

Again, the governor shook his head. "How well do you know Sufiro's history, Commander?"

"My mother grew up here."

"She must be the same generation as me and the colonel." Hill gave a congenial smile. "Colonel McClintlock and I were both born on Earth and moved to Sufiro with an early wave of settlers. The planet's other major continent is agrarian, but the real money is here in Tejo. The problem is Tejo doesn't support large scale agriculture. Little grows here. It makes no sense for this world to be split in two."

A knock sounded at the door. A moment later, Hill's secretary entered and poured coffee for all three men. Ellis sipped his coffee while Hill added cream to his. "It never made sense to me why this planet isn't unified under one government," said Ellis.

"Exactly." Hill set his coffee cup down without taking a sip. "The time has come for us to unify Sufiro and we want your help."

Ellis narrowed his gaze and set the coffee cup down. "I am here for one reason, to get the erdonium moving. If unifying the planet will make that happen, I'll support it. Tell me how that will help."

Hill smiled. "If we can unify the planet, we can conscript New Granadans under the wartime emergency labor act."

McClintlock worried Hill had overplayed his hand.

The commander's eyes widened. "There have been reports these 'terrorists' claim to be illegally conscripted New Granadans."

Hill leaned forward. "New Granada's legal status has never really been established. They aren't a recognized government. Do you object to legal conscription if it will stop the Cluster?"

"Of course not." Ellis sat back. "Thing is, if the conscription process is in question, I can understand why they'd be upset. You never did tell me why you think the Rd'dyggians in orbit are pirates."

McClintlock leaned forward. "They've made several trips to Tejo and New Granada and they've never once sought permission through official channels."

Ellis shook his head. "On my way to Sufiro, I reviewed

the planet's legal status. On the books, Tejo and the Gato Archipelego are considered human colonies on a Rd'dyggian protectorate world. They can land wherever they want to. I don't see any reason to suspect them of piracy."

"A Rd'dyggian launch landed near the mine before the explosives detonated." McClintlock retrieved his cup of coffee.

"Were any miners killed?" asked Ellis.

"No, they all esca…" McClintlock started. The governor cut him off with a glare. "They weren't on duty. It was night, you see."

"Escaped." Ellis studied the colonel's face. "Why would miners want to escape? Are you confirming the assertion these miners are held against their will?"

The governor beamed again. "I'm sure he meant to say they escaped the explosion." He sat back and folded his arms. "Commander, you seem awfully suspicious for someone who has come to help us."

"I didn't say I came to help you," said Ellis. "I came to get the erdonium moving."

"As I understand, the Cluster is destroying star ships at will." McClintlock sipped his coffee. "The Confederation needs vessels to find this thing and destroy it. Unifying this world and bringing it into the Earth Alliance is the best way to make sure the Confederation gets the erdonium it needs."

"I've seen the Cluster." The commander's voice took on a razor-sharp edge. "Believe me when I say stopping it is my highest priority." He sipped the coffee. "However, I still want to understand why these terrorist strikes are happening."

Hill sighed. "We don't fully understand it either. All we know is that these are immigrants from New Granada hired into the mines. They're unhappy and the Rd'dyggians are supplying them."

"So, it's essentially a strike." Ellis gave a firm nod.

"If it were, I wish the strikers would tell me the terms." Hill shook his head.

Ellis sighed. "All right, tell me specifically what you want me to do."

McClintlock held his hands out to the side. "If you want

production to continue, you can start by chasing the Rd'dyggian ship away."

"Chase away an allied ship ... a big allied ship, I might add ... with a destroyer?" Ellis coughed, suppressing a laugh.

Hill leaned forward. "If you can't do that, call in a bigger ship. In the meantime, we need you to support our claim." His ears flushed red, betraying his annoyance. "We intend to make our intentions known to the leaders in New Des Moines within the week. Your support should help us quell ... disagreement at this difficult time."

Commander Ellis heaved a deep sigh. "Allow me to talk to the Rd'dyggians and the New Granadans. I'll see what I can do to stop these attacks on your facilities. If needed, I'm authorized to call in more force."

"Now that's what we like to hear." Hill tapped his index finger on the desk. "However, I fear talking to the New Granadans will just waste time. Once our land claim is approved, it would be more helpful if you persuaded the Confederation to send ships to help us enforce our claim." The governor shrugged. "In the meantime, stop the sabotage."

"I'll do everything I can." Ellis stood and straightened his jacket. "Good day, gentlemen." He turned on his heel and marched out of the office.

Hill chuckled to himself. "I think that went quite well."

McClintlock shook his head. "I don't see how. Ellis is on his way to meet with people in New Granada. What do you think will happen once he gets their side of the story?"

Hill shrugged. "It doesn't matter. Ellis gave us exactly what we needed."

☠

A slight gee-force pulled Ellis into his seat as the launch lifted off from the Tejo City space port. Ellis opened a channel to the *Firebrandt* and the communicator answered. "Check records. Who is New Granada's governor?"

The communicator's holographic image faded for a moment as he moved away from the transmitter, then sharpened again. "According to our records, New Granada is a collection of city states with no single governor or president. Our government has never recognized any of those states, although New Des Moines seems to be the largest and most influential of the city states."

Ellis frowned. He had set a course for the ship and had considered opening an official channel as he had with Tejo's governor. He realized he had a better way to learn what was happening on the continent Tejo wished to annex. "I'm changing course," said Ellis. "I'm going straight to New Granada."

"But, sir," protested the communicator. "We don't know whether or not they're hostile."

"They won't be hostile to me," Ellis snapped, then regretted it a moment later. The communicator had expressed just the right concern. "My new course is for the city of Succor along the Nuevo Rio Grande. If I don't contact the ship within twenty-four hours, leave orbit and report to Titan."

"Aye aye, sir," responded the communicator.

Ellis turned off the teleholo unit and entered the new coordinates into the computer. It had been years since he had spoken to Firebrandt. As a child, Ellis found Firebrandt an intense, uncomfortable presence. Growing older, he attributed those feelings to Firebrandt's questionable past. Somehow it seemed like the old pirate's sins had tainted him.

The commander checked the relative time. It was late afternoon in Tejo City. Given travel time, he should arrive in New Granada in the early morning. Ellis placed the launch on autopilot and leaned his seat back. The bucket seat proved almost more comfortable than his bunk and he dozed despite the coffee he'd consumed in Hill's office.

The proximity alarm woke him. Readings indicated the launch had reached a point less than a hundred miles from Succor. He'd flown around the planet's night side and the sun now rose in the east, illuminating the lush countryside below, much greener than the almost-barren Tejo. Tall trees covered the ground. A flock of bird-like animals lifted off from their branches. Ellis searched his memory. His mom had called them fledermice. Soon the little town came into view. The clumps of trees and brush gave way to orderly squares where crops grew in neat rows. Nearby flowed a wide river. He could well understand why space travelers who had been left to the galaxy's wiles had called the place Succor.

Ellis scanned the town and the adjoining fields. Soon, he found a large house on a broad rise overlooking the river. The scanners indicated that erdonium comprised over forty percent of the house's structure. Since New Granada had no erdonium in its rocks, that meant a spaceship. He soon spotted the house. An enormous field surrounded the homestead. A landing pad had been built nearby. He set the launch down and contacted the ship to let them know he'd arrived at his destination and instructed them to wait another twenty-four hours before taking action.

As Ellis stood and straightened his uniform jacket, he considered the military's use of the twenty-four-hour day. Sufiro had a twenty-six-hour day and other worlds were even farther out of sync with Earth's clock. He stepped through the launch's airlock and strode toward the house.

Ellis knocked, then placed his hands behind his back. Roberts answered the door, sitting in an old, brown hover chair's black-cushioned seat. "This is a surprise, especially after watching this morning's news from Tejo."

The commander's brow furrowed. "News from Tejo? I don't understand."

"I think you better come in." Roberts drifted back from the door.

Ellis entered and closed the door behind him.

Roberts led Ellis to a large sitting room where Ellison Firebrandt and Fire Ellis watched a teleholo dais. Light flooding in from the morning sun made it difficult for Ellis to see what they watched. Roberts cleared his throat. Fire turned and jumped to her feet. "Mark!" She stepped forward and took his hands. "Mark, is it true what they're saying on the news?"

"I don't know." Ellis shook his head. "What are they saying?"

Ellison Firebrandt stood. Ellis's chest tightened and he wanted to flee, but held his ground. The old pirate's hair had turned white and crow's feet puckered the skin near his eyes. Ellis fell back a step. "It's good to see you, Mark, but I do wish the circumstances were different. You'd better come and see this and maybe you can explain what's going on."

Ellis stepped forward. His grandfather made no move to embrace his grandson or shake his hand, but he indicated a chair and had him sit.

Firebrandt tapped some controls next to the teleholo dais and a news report played. A reporter announced Tejo's plans to annex New Granada. Rocky Hill's head replaced the reporter's. "We are assured that we have the Confederation's support in this matter."

Ellis blinked when his own head replaced Hill's. "It never made sense to me why this planet isn't unified under one government." Ellis remembered saying the words, but they had been ripped out of context. After a brief cutaway to reaction shots from Hill and McClintlock, Ellis's image continued speaking. "I am here for one reason, to get the erdonium moving. If unifying the planet will make that happen, I'll support it."

The reporter appeared again. She displayed a chart of Cluster sightings. "So far, the Confederation Space Fleet appears no closer to understanding the Cluster. Admiralty officials insist they need more ships to track down and stop the Cluster before it takes more civilian lives. In order to do that, they need erdonium from Tejo."

With that, the teleholo image cut back to Ellis. "I've seen the Cluster. Believe me when I say stopping it is my highest priority."

Firebrandt turned off the display.

Ellis shook his head. "It's true that I'm here on Sufiro to restore erdonium production. However, I planned to speak to the Rd'dyggian captain who has been aiding the people disrupting the mining operations before making a decision about whether or not to support the annexation of New Granada. I also told him I planned to meet with New Granada's leaders."

Firebrandt snorted. "Well, you've come to the wrong place. I'm just a farmer these days. I'm no longer a leader. You need to speak to Manuel Raton up in Nuevo Santa Fe."

Ellis narrowed his gaze. "That's actually some of the information I needed. I also wanted to get your take on what's happening." He glanced around to everyone in the room. "I'd like all of your opinions."

Firebrandt stood and pulled a pipe from his pocket. He walked over to the table, opened a jar, and filled it with tobacco. "Twenty years ago, Sam Stone bought out Espedie Raton. He then arranged his death to keep him silent. A year later, Stone along with Mary Hill—she was Rocky's mother—hatched a scheme to make the mines more profitable. They invoked some wartime conscription act as an excuse to kidnap people from New Granada and force them to the mines for no pay."

Ellis frowned. "This has been going on all that time?"

"Not exactly," chimed in Roberts. "Manuel Raton stopped them and for a while things were fine."

Fire nodded and picked up the story. "Until this business with the Cluster started. At that point Sam Stone ordered the abductions to resume and now it seems the Tejans have decided to annex New Granada to solidify their legal standing."

Firebrandt lit his pipe. "What's more, it looks like they're using you to justify their actions. Not just to the people in Tejo, but the people in New Granada."

Ellis slumped forward. "Great way to start my first command." He looked up. "So how do the Rd'dyggians fit into all this?"

"If we help the captive New Granadans, we're committing an act of war. If the Rd'dyggians do it..." Firebrandt shrugged. "It's their planet, they can do whatever they want."

"At least until it's a unified planet," said Roberts. "At which point, Earth can negotiate transfer of its jurisdiction from the Rd'dyggians."

Ellis sighed. "I have to admit, it begins to make sense now. I just wish I had a clear path forward."

"What?" Fire blinked at her son.

"I'm sorry, mom. It's an internal matter. The Confederation has limited jurisdiction over the planet's internal matters." Ellis shrugged. "If New Granada had joined the Gaean Alliance, I might be able to do more. As it stands, I can't stop Tejo from proceeding with their annexation plans and I'm under orders to find a way to stop the sabotage of mining operations."

Fire's face reddened. "What the hell do you mean? After learning all this, you're still going to help those people hurting the New Granadans?" She jumped to her feet and loomed over her son.

Firebrandt strode over and put his hands on his daughter's shoulders. "Easy, Little One. He's right. The Confederation's only interest is erdonium production." He looked down at Ellis. "You can't solve that problem without addressing the abductions or the annexation issue."

Ellis blinked. "What do you mean?"

Firebrandt guided Fire back to her seat and then settled into a throne-like easy chair. He smoked the pipe for a moment. "This is no mere fact-finding mission. You're here to get the shipments to resume, correct?"

Ellis nodded. "If the terrorism stops, the shipments return to normal."

"If the terrorism stops, Tejo will round up the dissidents and force them to mine erdonium." Fire sat down next to her son. "They will continue to abduct people from around the planet to work for them."

"If Sufiro joins the Earth Alliance and the Confederation, the whole abduction issue can be resolved through legal channels." Ellis's words held a hopeful note.

Roberts shook his head. "It could take years, maybe even decades for that to work. Long before then, there's a good chance the current actions will escalate into a full-scale war. It would be better to resolve this situation now than later."

Ellis sighed. "So, why didn't New Granada seek Alliance recognition?"

"Didn't see enough advantage to press the issue." Firebrandt spoke the words around the pipe stem.

Roberts nodded. "Joining the Alliance would have meant assuming national responsibilities. We're on the frontier, a continent good for individual farms and not much else. I think the last thing anyone in this room wants to see is New Granada become a suburb for anyone, much less Tejo."

Ellis stood and pointed upward. "There's a war going on out there."

"A war? Really?" Firebrandt snorted. "You've never seen

who pilots those Cluster ships. You have no idea what their motives are."

Ellis steeled his nerves and strode over to face his grandfather. "I may not have met them in person, but I've seen what they've done to human life. How dare you suggest this isn't war? These are the beings who killed my father."

The old pirate captain nodded. "I know about the Cluster. We don't know why they've destroyed the ships they have. I also know about Tejo. They take human lives for pure profit. I agree the Cluster must be stopped. All I'm trying to say is that Tejo must be as well or else the war in space isn't one worth fighting. We must know we're on the side of right."

Ellis closed his eyes. He needed air and some time to think. "Excuse me." He stepped toward the front door.

"Mark..." Fire jumped up and started after him.

Firebrandt stood and grabbed her shoulder. "Don't."

As Ellis stepped through the door, he noticed tears on his mother's cheeks. He didn't want to leave, but he needed some time to process all the information he'd been given. Hill and McClintlock had betrayed his trust and used his words to imply his tacit agreement with their plans. That noted, preventing Tejo from claiming New Granada was outside his mission's scope. He had one mission, get erdonium production to resume, but how would he accomplish the task?

Ellis walked down the hill, away from Firebrandt's house. He found a cigar in his jacket and lit it, then clasped his hands behind his back. Even though Ellis found his pirate grandfather a formidable presence, the commander respected him more than the two petty administrators who had tricked him into sounding like he agreed with them.

He looked around and found himself in the middle of the town called Succor. He hadn't paid attention to the buildings he passed while brooding on the problem he faced. Now, he looked around and took in the scene. Tin Quonset huts, adobe structures, and wooden buildings surrounded him. He even spotted an old building with weathered shingles and white trim on the windows. He walked up to it and touched it.

The door opened and a little blond-haired girl skipped out.

She stared at Ellis with wide eyes and smiled. Ellis returned her smile.

"Whatcha doing?" she asked.

"This house reminds me of one I lived in when I was your age." Ellis's problems seemed to melt away.

"It's my house!" The girl clapped her small hands together. She inclined her head and studied him. "You look like Mr. Firebrandt on the hill, only your hair's kinda red brown."

"I'm Mr. Firebrandt's grandson," he admitted.

"I like Mr. Firebrandt. He's a nice man." She smiled and waved then skipped away, singing. Ellis walked to the river. He sat down on the sandy bank, watching whitecaps form over a cluster of rocks. The river gave life to the little town behind him. An old wooden water wheel groaned nearby as it turned. The water reminded him of stories about how the ocean once gave life to his home. He considered the little girl and the tiny town. He considered Tejo's industrial complex. He sighed as he reached a decision. A tear trickled down his cheek as he realized it could end his career, but he wiped it away because he knew his career mattered little compared to the lives of New Granada's people.

Ellis returned to Firebrandt's house around noon. Without prelude, Firebrandt led Ellis toward the dining room. With his arm around his grandson, the captain whispered, "You've come to a decision?"

Ellis nodded. He started to speak.

Firebrandt put the index finger of his free hand to his lips. "If you've made up your mind, I'm proud of you."

Ellis stopped, turned and looked at his grandfather. "You don't know what I've decided."

"You're not deferring a decision to the Admiralty on Titan?"

"I could never do that." Ellis held up his hands. "The Admiralty would never confirm my posting. I'd remain a lieutenant forever."

"Then as I said, I'm proud of you." Firebrandt flashed a winning smile that Ellis believed would inspire a spaceship crew. "Your mother wants us to have a lunch as a family—no arguments, no politics. I happen to think that would be good for all of us."

Ellis nodded, beginning to understand his grandfather's charisma. He also liked the idea of lunch with his mother. His stomach growled, as though emphasizing the point. Firebrandt led his grandson into the dining room.

They sat and talked through the meal. Firebrandt wanted to hear about Ellis's career to date. Ellis told of life aboard the cruiser *Astrolus* and how it differed from his new life aboard a small destroyer. In return, Firebrandt and Roberts told stories of their days as privateers aboard the *Legacy*.

Firebrandt laughed as Roberts retrieved an apple pie for dessert. "And to think. It all ended because my mother exiled me to this planet."

Ellis narrowed his gaze. "What?"

Firebrandt grinned at him. "You've never heard the story?"

Ellis shook his head.

Firebrandt chided his daughter. "You've been negligent in your duties. You didn't tell him enough bed time stories."

Fire grinned as she sampled the apple pie. "There's no reason you couldn't have told him the story."

The captain looked back to Ellis. "My mother, Barbara Firebrandt, captured my ship and left us with just enough fuel to reach Sufiro."

Ellis's jaw fell open. "Barbara Firebrandt was your mother?" Ellis covered his mouth with his hand. "Why, that means she's my great grandmother," he whispered, half-afraid someone at the table would hear. A newfound sense of pride in his family welled up within him.

Firebrandt told the story of *Legacy's* capture. He told of the years that he resented his mother for ending his career. Despite that, he now thanked her. His years on Sufiro, he said, had been the best of his life. "As long as the Tejans don't ruin it."

Fire glared at him.

Ellis held up his hand. "It's okay. I've decided the only way erdonium will move again is to fix the problem on Sufiro. If Tejo marches over New Granada, the slavery will continue. Even if the Rd'dyggians leave, the revolt won't end. That's the flaw in their logic. One problem remains, though. If Tejo releases the slaves and no one's there to replace them, the erdonium still won't move. The fix is simple, but it requires Rocky Hill's fair consideration. Would the present miners work in Tejo for fair wages and good homes?"

"It would be a reasonable proposition. Keep in mind, though, I don't speak for the planet," said Firebrandt. "There is one possible flaw in your logic."

Ellis nodded. "The Tejans may be so profit hungry they won't agree to a reasonable offer."

"You've read your history." Roberts winked.

"The bottom line is that slavery and expansionism are a disease that will destroy this planet. If the Tejan leaders are too profit-oriented to listen to reason, I will remove them, appoint reasonable people and get the erdonium moving that way." Ellis realized his hand trembled.

Firebrandt grinned. "Now you're talking like a pirate."

"Perhaps I needed to meet a pirate to find the answer." Ellis stood. "I should get back to the ship."

"You can call the ship." Firebrandt stood and placed his hand on his grandson's shoulder. "Please, stay with us this afternoon and tonight."

Fire nodded, a tear in her eye.

"All right, I'll stay."

Fire joined her father and son. Three generations embraced, uncertain of the future.

Chapter Seventeen

CAMLAN PASS

John Mark Ellis entered Governor Rocky Hill's office in Tejo. He wore a standard duty uniform and stubble speckled his cheeks and chin.

Hill narrowed his gaze. "Well, the Confederation commander returns at last. Clyde McClintlock tells me we still have a Rd'dyggian ship in orbit and work has not resumed at our mines. Have you accomplished anything since your arrival?"

Ellis shrugged and dropped into a chair across from the governor's desk. "I've done far more legal research than I ever thought a ship's commanding officer would be required to do." Ellis leaned forward. "Among other things, I've confirmed that holographic manipulation is a crime within the Confederation."

Hill snorted. "Holographic manipulation is defined as the generation of *simulated* footage based on existing footage. Our news channels broadcast nothing you didn't say."

"There is legal precedent to challenge the use of material that misrepresents the speaker's intent." Ellis struggled to keep his voice even. Rocky Hill and Clyde McClintlock had misrepresented his mission and it angered him, but it wasn't his main reason for visiting the governor. "I also researched the legal definition of slavery and I would contend the 'conscription' of New Granadans qualifies."

Hill sighed. "Commander, there are many lawyers who would take up both those contentions and tie us up in court for many weeks, if not months. In the meantime, there is an alien called the Cluster destroying ships out in the galaxy. Your masters want it corralled and stopped as soon as possible. What action do you propose to take?"

Ellis folded his hands, hoping the simple solution would

271

work. "Earth's admiralty has authorized me to agree to a pay increase for Sufiro's erdonium. At a higher rate, we can go to the New Granadans and propose they work for fair salaries..."

The governor held up his hand, cutting off the commander. "Do you really think that will work? We already give them food and shelter. They're already riled up. I have no problem in principal with giving them a salary, but I don't think money's enough to convince them to return to work."

"Taking them away from their homes and families will tend to disincentivize people." Ellis rubbed his stubble-covered chin. "We would need to assure them that the situation is temporary and for the war effort. Once the Cluster is contained, they would, of course, be free to go home."

Hill stood and put his hands behind his back. "You seem to have made up your mind that our actions are all about profit. You see, Clyde McClintlock and I grew up in New Granada. We know how backward it is. Tejo can bring the entire planet up to a high, uniform standard of education and well being."

"Europeans said much the same things about the Africans they captured to work in their homes and fields. They repeated their story when they grabbed land from Native Americans and Australians." Ellis stood and placed his hands on the desk.

The governor shrugged, then began to pace. "Chase the Rd'dyggians away and get the New Granadans back to work first. If you do that, I will agree to open up negotiations for better pay."

Ellis shook his head. "I can't do that unless you agree to pay people up front. The Rd'dyggians have every right to be here. Unless you help me out, there's nothing I can offer the New Granadans to encourage them to go back to work. The only other choice would be to bring in workers from off planet."

"Do you have any idea how long that will take?" Hill stopped and turned around to face Ellis. "Why are you so opposed to us conscripting New Granadans? They're nothing but farmers. They contribute almost nothing to the galaxy as a whole. We can improve conditions on this planet if you will help us talk sense into them."

The commander's shoulders slumped. Rocky Hill just talked in circles. Ellis took a deep breath and composed himself.

"You miss the reason for the Confederation's existence. We live in a loose knit structure so people can choose to live how they wish. True, most people seem to flock to vast metropolitan areas like Tejo City, but not everyone wants to live that way. Different people have different needs."

Hill opened his arms wide. "Then we agree to disagree." The governor sat down and folded his hands, resembling a schoolteacher trying to be patient with a petulant student. "Now, it's obvious to me this simple erdonium problem is too much for you. I think it would be best if you went back to your ship, flew back to Titan, and had a real captain come out and handle this situation."

Ellis stood straight and looked down at Hill. "You can be certain I will send a full report of my observations to my superiors and it will contain every legally questionable thing you've done. If they agree, it will be my pleasure to escort you from this office and take over as military governor." Ellis turned on his heel and stormed from the office.

He almost regretted his final words to the governor. He may have overplayed his hand, but the officious little prick wore on his nerves and he hoped the admiralty would back his threat.

Manuel Raton and Edmund Swan stood on a hill near Raton's house. Below them marched the New Granadan volunteers in almost perfect unison. They had been practicing with the weapons Arepno provided and learning to use the built-in computer interfaces to improve their accuracy. Raton and Swan nodded to each other, pleased with the discipline the force exhibited.

Edmund Swan's handcomp beeped. He acknowledged a message from Arepno. The handcomp translated the Rd'dyggian's words. "We have trouble, brothers."

"We're ready for trouble." Swan gave a curt nod.

"Trouble is my middle name." Raton folded his arms.

Arepno didn't answer for a moment and Swan wondered if the translation algorithm had difficulty with Raton's idiom.

"It's a good thing you are ready, Manuel Trouble Raton." It sounded like Arepno attempted a joke, but the tone was serious.

"What's going on, old friend?" asked Swan.

"Perhaps it would be best if I could show you rather than tell you," said Arepno. "Can you go to your teleholo unit?"

"We'll be there in less than five minutes." Raton nodded to Swan and the two climbed into Raton's hover and drove back to his house. Inside, Raton activated the teleholo. The scene around Raton and Swan changed. It appeared they had been transported to the Rd'dyggian ship's command center.

Arepno sat, strapped into a round, concave chair, surrounded by a warm mist, consistent with his home world's humid air. Swan had heard tales about Rd'dyggia and appreciated that teleholos did not transmit odors. Rd'dyggian ships did not have graviton generators, making Swan grateful that he and Manuel were only holographic projections.

A Rd'dyggian battle ship's command center did not resemble a human star cruiser's bridge. Arepno sat in one corner of the six-sided room. Instead of sharp corners, the room's walls rolled into one another as well as the ceiling and floor. Five officers occupied the other corners. Each officer sat behind a pedestal with a control terminal. At the command deck's center stood a narrow column supporting a broad dais.

Arepno nodded, acknowledging Swan and Raton, then reached forward to his control terminal. As he activated the terminal, Sufiro's three-dimensional image filled the dais in the room's center. Rd'dyggians had been in space much longer than humans and possessed sophisticated imaging technology.

The Rd'dyggian computer labeled all known satellites and ships in orbit around the planet. Swan shrugged. "All looks normal to me." Then again, he didn't think the Tejans would be foolish enough to attack from orbit. The Rd'dyggian cruiser and Confederation destroyer could easily dispatch any small Tejan vessel.

"Do not be deceived into thinking nothing is wrong." Arepno touched the control surface. "Humans know no end of treachery." He zoomed in on the high coastal mountains near Manuel's home outside Nuevo Santa Fe.

Snow already covered many peaks. Only a few narrow

roads traversed the mountain range. Three habitations were marked and names hovered over them. Swan nudged Raton. "Who are those people?"

Raton shrugged. "Hermits for all intents and purposes. I know them. They come into Nuevo Santa Fe for food and supplies, but otherwise they keep to themselves."

Arepno continued to zoom in and three shimmering airship-sized bubbles appeared. Swan realized they must be airships covered in stealth fabric like some mercenaries and tactical units used. Cloaking bodies that size was difficult, but airships moved slow enough for the cloth to be somewhat effective. Underneath the airships, they could just make out a sizable encampment of soldiers. "Now here is an older image." In the older image, the airship-sized bubbles and troops sat on the coast. Arepno overlaid a grid, which gave them the image scale. He zoomed in closer and estimated the encampment contained as many soldiers as the entire population of Nuevo Santa Fe. Soldiers milled about among tents while the stealth airships hovered overhead.

"When I first saw this, I thought the Tejans engaged in folly coming over such rugged terrain on foot, supported by such primitive craft." Arepno swayed from side to side.

"Highly magnetized rocks and dust in the pass and valley keep scanners from functioning making high speed assault vehicles impractical," remarked Swan.

"The winds will make getting airships through the mountains a challenge." Raton narrowed his gaze. "Even so, covering them in that stealth fabric is brilliant."

Arepno looked at Raton. "We would have missed the airships if we had not detected the distortion from such large bodies. The airships will get good lift in the current cold conditions and there is minimal turbulence this time of year. Coming through the pass will put them right on top of your troops. They could decimate your defense force and raise their flag over New Granada. The Tejans acted with stealth, intelligence, and forethought." Arepno looked from Swan to Raton. "This invasion plan must have been established quite some time in the past. Since then, they purchased the gear they needed to cross the mountains." The warrior's mustache wiggled for a moment. "My people do not believe in slavery. Now that I see the time and expense wasted on this enterprise, I am further convinced of its foolhardiness."

The Rd'dyggian captain sent all relevant tactical information to Swan's handcomp. Without warning, he terminated the holographic call. Swan and Raton stood in the teleholo room.

"Our best strategy is to place our people at Camlan Pass." Raton stepped outside. "We should be able to pick the Tejans off as they come through."

"It's a large force." Swan followed Raton. "We'll whittle down their numbers but they could still overpower us."

A dust cloud approached. It proved to be a hover with two occupants. One had long, flowing white hair and a beard. A woman with black hair sat next to him. They parked and climbed from the vehicle. Swan wondered what brought Ellison Firebrandt and his daughter to their doorstep.

"Arepno messaged me just a little while ago," said the one-time pirate captain. "I got here as soon as I could."

"While driving up from Succor, we got word from John Mark." Fire pushed a strand of black hair over her shoulder. "He's returning to his ship. He sounded pretty upset. He had just met with Governor Hill and figured something might be happening."

Swan looked from Fire to the captain. "Manuel suggests we move the troops to the foot of Camlan Pass."

Fire's brow furrowed. "How do you know they'll come out there?"

Firebrandt smiled at his daughter. "There are many routes out of those mountains, true, but there's just one pass large enough to accommodate an army that size and airships."

"Seems like old times." Raton grinned, then looked to Swan. "How long before the Tejans make it to the pass?"

Swan checked the tactical information on the handcomp, then performed some calculations. "We have just about twenty hours at their current rate of progress."

Raton glanced over to the nearby pass. "Lots of time to get our troops into position." He entered the house, retrieved an amplifier, and secured it around his throat. He ran to the hill's summit and waved his hands so the troops could see him.

They stopped their exercises. Squad leaders formed up ranks. Meanwhile, Firebrandt, Fire, and Swan joined Raton on the hillside.

Once Raton had the attention of the forces below, he walked down the hill a short distance, giving the impression that he brought the people into his confidence. "Those Tejans are up to their old tricks. They think they can fool old Manuel by coming through Camlan Pass." Scattered laughter sounded from the assembled troops. "We need to get over there tonight and find positions to ambush them. I want everyone to take their weapons and get to their hovers. Drive to the meadow immediately below the pass. I want the platoon leaders to reform your groups there. We'll camp out tonight and wait for them to poke their heads out tomorrow."

The crowd cheered. As with most armies engaged in training exercises, Swan knew they were bored and appreciated the prospect of action. They broke ranks and ran to their hovers, shouting and singing.

"Hardly an efficient, organized fighting force," grumbled Swan under his breath.

Raton turned off the amplifier. "You can keep your efficient, organized fighting force. That's what the Tejans are sending. Our people are defending their homes. Whether our people are efficient or not, it will be almost impossible for enough Tejans to get through Camlan Pass tomorrow."

Swan nodded. "Then we'd better get over there ourselves."

"Absolutely, my friend."

Firebrandt looked at the two men. "Perhaps Fire and I should stand by here. If the Tejans do break through the line, we can warn others down the valley. Also, I can get data to my grandson in the destroyer overhead. There may be something he can do to lend a hand."

Swan punched commands in his handcomp. A moment later, Firebrandt's beeped. "I've just sent you the tactical data Arepno gave me. Forward the data to Ellis's ship. He'll need the data to find the troops and cloaked airships in amongst the mountains."

Fire narrowed her gaze. "If Mark knows the Tejans are in the mountains, wouldn't he be able to find them without the data?"

"Maybe." Firebrandt shrugged. "I'm sure Arepno would remind us that Rd'dyggian technology is superior to human tech. Besides, Mark can use all the help he can get. Those airships aren't that easy to spot unless you know what you're looking for."

"Let's go!" Swan clapped his hands together. With that, the ragtag defense force collapsed their camp and moved it to the base of Camlan Pass. The troops checked their weapons and prepared themselves for the coming battle.

Swan walked through the camp and spoke to numerous soldiers. One couple from New Des Moines offered to let him share their rations. Swan tried to refuse, but they insisted. He took a small portion. "What brought you to New Granada?" he asked.

"We were undersea farmers on Earth," said a woman named Elsa. "We lived in a small one-room apartment. Even the bathroom was in the same room as the bedroom."

Elsa's partner, Soo Lin, nodded. "We earned two weeks of vacation every year, but never enough money to go anywhere. We felt like prisoners on our own planet. When we heard about New Granada, we saved up enough money for a one-way ticket."

"The Tejans abducted one of our neighbors to work in the mines." Elsa shook her head. "To me, that sounds just like conditions in the undersea dome back on Earth. I'd die rather than go back there. I want our neighbor to have his freedom back."

Soo Lin pulled Elsa close. Swan excused himself and spoke to other defense force volunteers and listened to many similar tales. Some invited him to sing songs with them. A platoon opened a bottle of liquor they'd distilled from corn they imported from Earth. Swan took one drink, then left them to their revelry.

Manuel set up a tent with two cots inside. Swan climbed onto his and tried to go to sleep, but the faces of the New Granadans ready to defend their homes came unbidden to his mind. He hoped he would be able to send them all home after the battle and wouldn't have to bury any of them. He knew such a wish was a vain one.

☠

John Mark Ellis spent a fitful night aboard the *Firebrandt*. His alarm woke him before dawn at Camlan Pass and he padded into the head across from his bunk. He studied himself in the mirror and considered removing the stubble, but decided to wait another day. Instead, he splashed a little water on his face and padded back to his bunk. The commander activated the forcefield, got dressed, then stepped out to the bridge.

"Commander on deck!" Rubin made the announcement as he arrived. Ellis retrieved a cup of coffee from the beverage dispenser at the command deck's stern, then plunked down in his chair. He cursed as coffee splashed his knee. "Status, Mr. Rubin?" grumbled the commander.

"We're still monitoring the Tejan ground forces. They moved through the night and seem to have come to a stop some ten miles from Camlan Pass, sir," reported Rubin.

Ellis sipped the coffee, trying to wake up. "Let me know if they move." He brought charts and maps up on his display, considering how best to support the New Granadan forces.

"Message from the planet, sir," reported the communicator.

"Go ahead, Mr. Weiss." Ellis continued to nurse the coffee and didn't lift his eyes from the maps.

"The New Granadan forces have engaged the Tejans at Camlan Pass, sir."

Ellis sat up, now wide-awake. "Mr. Rubin, have your sensors shown any movement?"

"None, sir." Rubin shrugged.

Ellis swallowed the remainder of his coffee and tossed the cup in the recycler. "Mr. Rubin, what specifically have you been monitoring?"

Rubin's eyes darted from his display to Ellis. "I've been monitoring their airships' movements. Even though they're covered in stealth fabric, they're large and easy for us to lock onto. To get the troops themselves, I'd have to scan in the IR, looking for the heat signatures from the people, but it's tricky given the interference in the mountains."

Ellis nodded. "That's okay, B-Com. Scan the IR. I know local dawn will make it even more difficult, but let's try to find out where those troops are."

"Aye aye, sir." Rubin typed several commands into his

console. An image of the pass appeared in the command deck's holographic viewer. He highlighted the airships, their bubble-like outlines difficult to see compared to the surrounding rocks. He activated another control highlighting a mass of people in red out in front of the airships.

Ellis considered the display. "The airships seem undefended."

Rubin nodded. "I don't read any ground defense, but my sensor readings are dubious at best."

The commander rubbed his chin and grinned. "There are no records of military airships in Tejo. I suspect those are the merchant craft they use to haul goods from city to city, conscripted for this exercise and covered in stealth fabric." He pointed to Weiss. "Have the ground crew prepare my launch. Then see if you can raise those airships. Warn their crews to abandon ship." He pointed to the gunner. "Adkins, come with me."

"Aye aye, sir." The gunner jumped to her feet. According to her record, she had no ground combat experience. She followed Ellis to the launch bay and stepped through the airlock into the landing craft.

"Mr. Rubin reports launch is prepared and ready to cast-off," said Weiss through the intercom.

"Thank you, Mr. Weiss." Ellis and Adkins ran through the pre-flight checklist. Satisfied, they nodded to each other.

"Disengaging," announced the commander. The airlock doors closed and the clamps that held the vehicle in its pocket on the ship's flank released. Ellis fired a gentle thruster burst and the launch moved away from the ship. He stared out over the panorama of space, Sufiro extending beneath him. Vast, white clouds played over the surface, the water sparkled blue with a green tinge.

Ellis nodded to Adkins. "Run a weapons diagnostic. I don't want any misfires when we get down near the surface."

"Aye aye, sir." She pulled up the checklist on her console and ticked off items. At last, she grabbed the handles that maneuvered the hepler turret mounted atop the launch and fired several bursts. "Weapons functional and ready, sir."

"Then here we go." Ellis located Camlan Pass on the scanner

and entered the course. The ship shot down. He put Sufiro's sun behind him so their entry into the atmosphere wouldn't be seen. As the ship hit the atmosphere, automatic shields popped on and flames shot around the craft as it bounced and tumbled through the atmosphere. "Reentry, the old-fashioned way!" declared Ellis.

Adkins gripped her armrests, eyes shut. "This is worse than an EQ, jump, sir. At least with a jump, you're not usually conscious!"

Ellis laughed. "This is exhilarating!" Twenty miles from the surface, thrusters kicked in controlling the launch's descent and they raced toward the mountains.

"Sir, we need to be careful." Adkins's voice trembled.

"Mind your guns. I'll mind the boat." Ellis swiveled the joystick to the right. "Hang tight! We're going to get even closer to those mountains."

"That's what I'm afraid of!" She reached over and activated the targeting scanners.

Ellis struggled against an updraft, but continued the dive. "Scanners won't work. You'll have to target visually." The peaks rose up around them.

"Visually?" Adkins belched and looked a little green. She grabbed the turret controls. As they approached the airships, her focus improved.

The craft lurched to one side as Ellis swerved to miss a higher peak than the map indicated. When he corrected their course, he spotted the shimmering telltale where the airships hovered over the ground. They would have to get close for Adkins to hit the virtually invisible craft in the mountains. Ellis accelerated. A hepler beam burst against the launch's forward shields. The commander couldn't tell whether it came from an airship or the ground. Adkins returned fire. She blew a hole in the first airship's bag. The transparent ship rippled as it wafted to the ground like a leaf from a tree in autumn. She fired another burst. It must have hit an engine's fuel cell. The second airship blossomed into a fireball. Ellis pulled the joystick back and gained altitude as fast as he could.

Adkins looked over to Ellis. "Did we get them?"

"We got two of the three. That destroys most of their

supplies and should put a dent in the Tejans' morale." The commander eased up on the assent and put the craft into a gentle upward spiral. "You did good, Adkins."

A column of fire and smoke erupted just before an earth-shattering shock wave knocked the ground troops off their feet. Edmund Swan rose bloody and bruised from the ground and watched the black smoke cloud rise into the sky. He examined the destruction with his cybernetic eye and tried to estimate the explosion's strength based on what appeared in his field of view. "Damn," he whispered. He guessed Ellis must have located and destroyed the stealth airships carrying the Tejan supplies.

Raton called out to the troops using the voice amplifier. "They're cut off. After them! After them now!" The New Granadans charged toward the Tejans. The Tejans tried to fall back into the mountain pass, but found themselves bottlenecked. The New Granadans picked them off, allowing the anger and frustration of the last few months and years to come to the forefront.

At last, another voice amplifier activated. "This is McClintlock. We surrender! Give us a chance to pull our troops out and tend to our wounded."

Raton called a halt to the advance. Swan examined the bodies on the ground. He estimated the New Granadans slaughtered over half the Tejan force. A decisive victory. His eyes panned over the corpses on the ground. Young Tejan soldiers sprawled across the brown grass. Some had lost heads. Others had holes in their guts. A few still lived, but had lost legs or arms. If they received care in time, they might survive. Swan didn't know whether New Granada had the medical resources to deal with so many injured.

His stomach could no longer take the carnage. He lurched over to a gully and vomited.

Raton found him a few minutes later. "You're a mess, my friend."

"We need to get doctors on the scene."

"Firebrandt's already on it. They're on their way." Raton held out his hand and helped Swan stand again.

"We should get the men organized into a burial detail."

Raton nodded. "Let me take care of the details on the field. Why don't you go check with Firebrandt, see if you can learn any more about what happened to the Tejan airships."

Swan wanted to pull himself together and help more in the battle's aftermath, but he knew Manuel was right. He should go check in with Firebrandt. They may have to regroup and take the battle somewhere else. He trudged over to Manuel's hover and drove back to the house.

He found Ellison Firebrandt and Fire standing outside, looking toward the pass.

"Is the battle over?" asked Fire when Swan stepped from the hover.

"We heard McClintlock surrender. We should check with the Rd'dyggians and make sure the Tejans continue their retreat."

Fire nodded. "Do you think the Tejans would try a second attack?"

"Manuel and our defense force gave them a sound beating. I think the war is over," said Swan.

"This isn't war." Firebrandt spat on the ground. "This was an act of greed and power by people who wanted to dominate the planet at all costs. These people don't care about the real conflict happening in space. God knows what the Cluster is or what it wants. Now that this has happened, I have no idea how John Mark is going to get the Tejans to mine erdonium so more ships can be built."

Swan led Firebrandt and Fire back in the house. He dropped into a chair. "At least New Granada won this conflict."

"No one wins in this kind of conflict." Firebrandt looked into his daughter's face. The old pirate captain, brushed a strand of hair from her eyes and for just a moment, he flashed a bittersweet smile. He looked away. "That explosion could only have been a Tejan airship. I can't imagine they have enough people or resources to keep pushing this conflict. At the very least, we may be able to negotiate with them now."

Fire reached out and squeezed her father's hand. "I'll go call Arepno and see what they're observing from orbit." She walked back toward the room where Raton kept the teleholo.

When the launch returned to its bay aboard the *Firebrandt*, the technicians remarked on the vessel's scorched nose. Whatever had been fired at the launch had been a nasty weapon. John Mark Ellis went to his quarters and retrieved a bottle of wine from his space chest. Champagne might be more appropriate for a celebration, but the commander hadn't been that prepared.

He strode forward to the command deck. Adkins reported the Tejan National Guard's retreat back into the mountains. The commander passed glasses around and poured wine. Ellis poured the final glass for himself, then raised his glass in toast. "Here's to Chief Petty Officer Adkins."

Cries of "Here here" rose from around the bridge. Ellis touched his glass to Adkins'. He then sat down in the command chair to consider his next course of action.

An alarm light flashed on Weiss's terminal. The communicator sat upright and inclined his head, as though listening to a voice only he could hear. "Something's just jumped into the Sufiro system and it's approaching the planet." He displayed an image on the holographic viewer. Ellis squinted at the tiny object.

"Magnify and enhance," ordered Ellis. The holographic image grew larger. Although it remained fuzzy, Ellis recognized the Cluster.

The commander's head cleared. "All hands at alert status!"

The Cluster sped toward Sufiro, then whipped around the planet and settled into a circular orbit.

Sweat dripped down Ellis's side. "Bring us alongside."

"Aye aye, sir," said Rubin.

Ellis turned to Weiss. "Communicator?"

"I'm on it, sir. No response from the Cluster."

"Damn it." Ellis sat in the command chair, helpless.

No death rays or signals came from the monstrous ship. It just orbited, as though watching and waiting for what would happen next.

Part IV: The Cluster

The Year 2973 Earth Standard Calendar

"When I first saw the Cluster in the sky, I was in awe. The sunlight reflected hypnotically from all those mysterious orbs. Somehow, I think we all knew the end was at hand."
—Suki Firebrandt Ellis from *Sufiro, A History*

Chapter Eighteen

A NEW PERSPECTIVE

John Mark Ellis leaned forward in the command chair and studied the Cluster's image in the holo viewer. The orbs reflected space and the planet below so well they seemed almost transparent, like the airships he'd just attacked. He reminded himself of Richard's advice, to understand the art, to understand what the Cluster viewed as life's essence. An unexpected serenity settled over him as he stared at the mysterious vessel. He shook his head and reminded himself of the destruction he'd seen. He forced himself to remember the *Courageous*, ripped open and dead, and tried to understand that in the context of the feelings he experienced. Despite reminding himself of the destroyed ship and his father's loss, he sensed more curiosity than malevolence. The earlier attacks may not have been a mistake, but somehow, he didn't think they had been malicious.

Ellis closed his eyes and forced himself to concentrate. Where were these ideas coming from? Was his imagination acting up? He turned his thoughts to the routine. "Position report, Mr. Rubin." His voice sounded distant to his own ears.

"Holding position five kilometers astern of the Cluster. We're over Sufiro's Great Ocean. Our orbit will carry us over New Granada in five minutes." The tension in the B-Com's voice seemed misplaced to Ellis.

The commander reached into his coat pocket and retrieved a cigar. He used it to point to the holo viewer. "Give me a tactical display. Show me where the Rd'dyggians are relative to us." The holographic image shrunk. Glowing dots indicated the Cluster and the *Firebrandt*. Arepno's ship maintained a higher orbit. "Contact Arepno. Ask him to hold position relative to us.

I hope that will help avoid an attack."

"Aye, sir." The communicator touched his forehead and for a moment looked as though he'd entered a blissful state. He blinked and faced the commander. "The Rd'dyggians acknowledge the request."

Ellis nodded. "Contact Manuel Raton in New Granada and Rocky Hill in Tejo. Give them an update on the situation and suggest they move their people to shelters as soon as possible."

Rubin narrowed his gaze. "How will people take shelter against the Cluster?"

The commander considered that for a moment. "I recommend underground shelters where possible, caves, mines, cellars, bombardment shelters … that sort of thing."

"Yes, sir." Weiss touched his forehead and began mouthing words.

Ellis placed the cigar in his mouth. Even without lighting it, the cigar helped him focus.

"Planetary leaders have been informed," reported Weiss. "They will do their best to get people to safety."

The commander checked the tactical display. The Cluster continued its steady orbit with the *Firebrandt* tailing them. "Advise the admiralty of our current situation and ask whether they've learned anything about the Cluster since we've been here."

Again, Weiss touched his forehead. His mouth dropped open and his eyes widened. "My God."

Ellis stood and put his hand on the communicator's shoulder. "What's the matter?"

"I'm getting no response, sir." Weiss shook his head. His eyes shimmered with unshed tears. "It's as though nobody's out there."

Ellis noted Rubin and Adkins sitting upright and exchanging glances. Ellis thrust the cigar in his mouth and considered what the report could mean. "Could the Cluster be jamming our EQ signal?"

The first mate shook his head. "I didn't think signals sent through EQ space could be blocked."

Weiss narrowed his gaze. "That's not quite true. The Alpha Centaurans have created some theoretical models, but they haven't been able to make it work in practice."

"Excellent." Ellis patted Weiss on the back. He needed critical thinking from his officers. "Can you find the closest EQ communications relay and bounce a message from there to the Rd'dyggians. We know they're okay."

Weiss gave a curt nod. "On it, sir. It'll take a couple of minutes."

The commander returned to his chair. "Take all the time you need. If you get no reply, contact the Rd'dyggians via standard intrasystem protocol and determine whether or not they received the message."

While Weiss attempted to contact the Rd'dyggian ship, Ellis considered the Cluster anew. Up until this point, every attack had involved cutting ships open, almost as though the Cluster dissected them. Did the Cluster see other ships as life forms? Did it not understand that the ships contained living organisms? Maybe it tried to understand the ships. Is science the art? Somehow that didn't seem right. If so, the Cluster would investigate more than ships.

Weiss interrupted the commander's thoughts. "No response over EQ frequencies. Radio does seem unaffected. The Cluster must be able to jam signals sent through EQ space."

Ellis rubbed the stubble on his chin and grunted. They'd found a new piece of the Cluster puzzle. Now he just needed his ship to survive long enough to get that information back to the admiralty. "Looks like we're going to have to go it alone then. Use radio to send a status update to headquarters."

"The message will take centuries to get to headquarters via radio," protested the communicator.

Ellis nodded. "At least history will know what happened to us if things go wrong. Besides, someone may intercept the message along the way." The commander stood. "I'll be in my cabin. If the Cluster does anything at all, call me."

The commander entered his small cabin, activated the forcefield, and lit the cigar. He sat down at the desk, opened a document and began jotting down notes to organize his thoughts. The Cluster had been searching for something by dissecting ships. Something about Sufiro attracted the Cluster. The Cluster could make jumps like star cruisers and it could manipulate EQ space—what most sailors called 'the Beyond'—in ways that even the galaxy's more advanced races had not yet mastered.

Could the Cluster be interested in Sufiro's erdonium? That would make some sense given the race's apparent ease manipulating the Beyond. Then Ellis considered the *Courageous* and his father's ship, both discarded after their respective attacks. If the Cluster really wanted erdonium, why not salvage the ships it destroyed?

He considered the problem from another angle. The Cluster seemed to attack ships after they showed some sign of intelligence, either scanning, attacking, or running away. The Cluster then cut into the ship to see what it contained. Humans killed whales because they saw whales as commodities and as creatures placed on Earth by a divine being for their consumption. What if a creature from within a ship went to the Cluster before it attacked? He tapped the desk. It might doom his ship or even the planet if he made a bad guess.

He extinguished the cigar and lowered the forcefield. Ellis returned to the command deck and pointed to Weiss. "Open a channel to Manuel Raton."

As soon as they received Weiss's signal about the Cluster, Raton returned to the battlefield. He affixed the amplifier to his throat. "My friends, you have shown yourselves to be calm under fire today and you saved New Granada. Now, I need you to return to your homes and see to the safety of your families." He pointed overhead. "I am told the Cluster, the very reason the Tejans started abducting us, has entered orbit. The best thing you can do is get back home and get your families into shelters. If you have a storm cellar or a root cellar, go there. If there are caves near your towns, go there. Get to the strongest buildings you have and get under cover."

The men and the women on the field, interrupted from their rescue, burial and cleanup details, looked up at Raton in shocked silence. After a moment, most gathered their tools and helped fellow wounded soldiers into transports before leaving for home.

Two dozen people huddled together in the field. They talked among themselves, then two women strode toward Raton. He met them halfway. He recognized Soo Lin Zhao and her partner, Elsa Novak, undersea farmers from Nouveau Baton Rouge. "There are still wounded out here on the field," said Soo Lin as she pointed back to the other people who had gathered. "We're volunteering to stay and help where we can."

Raton nodded. "You're right. I'll help too." He took a moment to key a message to Swan into his handcomp, telling him where he was. He then joined the group working on the field.

He helped Soo Lin load a woman with a broken leg onto a stretcher and took her to a hover. He turned around and found himself facing Fire Ellis. She held a first aid kit. "Where do you need me?" she asked.

"Fogacita!" He blinked. "I need you someplace safe. Take your father and get back to his homestead."

"I will, as soon as we have all the wounded attended to."

"All right, the more of us dealing with this, the faster it will go." Raton smiled at her. "I wish the circumstances were different, but it's good to have you back on Sufiro."

She squeezed his shoulder, then turned around to look for the next person to help. Raton followed suit. The first person he found had already bled out on the ground. He frowned, sorry that person wouldn't return home. Elsa Novak approached. "We're taking all the people who didn't make it over there." She pointed to a row of corpses awaiting a better time for burial.

Raton sniffed, then helped Elsa carry the body over to the others.

When they finished the job, his handcomp chimed. He had a message from Swan. John Mark Ellis had called with an urgent matter. He looked around. The people in the field seemed to have things well in hand. He hiked back to his hover, then returned to the house.

He found Ellison Firebrandt sitting outside. "Mark is on the teleholo with Edmund."

Raton entered the teleholo room where Swan faced the

young commander, both wearing determined scowls. Ellis sat on his ship's bridge. Swan turned. "Manuel, see if you can talk some sense into the commander here."

Raton's brow creased. "What do you mean?" He sat down next to Swan.

"I've been thinking about all the Cluster attacks." Ellis leaned forward. "In each case, the Cluster observed signs of intelligent behavior, either a scan, an attack, or a retreat. The Cluster then tore into the ship looking for something. When it failed to find it, it went away."

Raton pursed his lips. "That makes sense. Go on."

"Something attracted the Cluster to Sufiro. I don't think it'll take long before it starts searching for whatever it wants here and that may result in the destruction of my ship, the Rd'dyggian ship, or even Sufiro itself." Ellis sat back and folded his arms. "I think the best way to prevent that would be to show the Cluster what beings inhabit Sufiro and who occupies these ships. I'll suit up, take a thruster pack, and go over to the Cluster myself."

Raton looked from Ellis to Swan and back again. "You're right that all other attempts to deal with the Cluster have failed and your suggestion of something to try sounds as sensible as any other I can think of." The sheriff heaved a deep sigh. "Does it have to be you?"

"I can't ask anyone else to try this." Ellis folded his arms, mind apparently made up.

Swan leapt to his feet. "So, what happens if this plan fails and the Cluster attacks us anyway?"

"I don't intend to be rash," said the commander. "I want to wait until I know everyone on the planet is as safe as they can be. I also want to make sure the Rd'dyggians agree with this plan."

Swan frowned. "Why not just wait and see what the Cluster does?"

Ellis shook his head. "I think that could be dangerous. The Cluster may decide to search for whatever attracted it. Their search methods are always destructive."

Raton held up his hands. "I would give it at least a day to make sure everyone is sheltered as well as possible." He pointed to the commander. "That gives you a chance to sleep on this plan and decide if it really is the best one."

Ellis turned to face Swan. "Can you think of a better plan?"

The former lawman growled low in his throat. "I can't, but that's not the point." He returned to his chair and blew out a breath. "We don't know what will happen when you go to the Cluster."

The commander lifted his chin. "You're right, but even if things go wrong, we'll learn more about the Cluster. I don't think this plan jeopardizes anyone who isn't already in danger."

Raton nodded. "Let's talk again tomorrow morning. We'll think about it here as well and see if we can come up with some other suggestions."

"Sounds good to me and thanks." Ellis nodded to his communicator. "*Firebrandt* signing out." With that, his hologram faded.

Swan jumped to his feet again. "I can't believe you're encouraging him to try this."

Raton shrugged. "Do you really think I can stop him?" He stood and strode from the teleholo room. They found Fire had returned from the battlefield.

"The wounded have been transported to hospitals." Fire brushed a strand of hair behind her shoulder. "The dead are all awaiting an appropriate time for burial."

"Thank you, Fogacita." Raton looked back at Swan, then turned and led Fire to the kitchen. He told her what Ellis proposed to do.

She frowned and looked down at the ground. "So far all Cluster attacks have been deadly. I don't want Mark to try this, but I know why he doesn't feel he can ask anyone else. I'll talk to dad and see if he has any other ideas. If we can think of any other suggestions, we'll let you know."

Raton couldn't help but admire Suki Ellis's strength. He wanted to pull her into his arms, but knew this wasn't the time. She needed to consider the ways she could save her son.

"I think dad and I better get back down to Succor and make sure everyone there is safe." Fire flashed a weary grin, then leaned forward and kissed Manuel on the cheek. She turned and left the room.

Raton and Swan followed her out. They watched as she and her father departed. Raton turned his gaze skyward. It was just after noon, but he thought he caught a glint in the sky. Was it the Cluster? What would it do next?

Clyde McClintlock had ridden back to New Granada's northern coast in a carryhover. There, he had boarded a shuttle which carried him along with a contingent of troops back to Tejo City. They arrived at the Mount Matthews Military Compound long after midnight. The next day, he would have to face Rocky Hill and explain what happened. He went to his office. He didn't bother to turn on any lights. The soft glow from the computer displays was sufficient to light a path to his desk.

He thought about continuing through to the back room where a cot waited. Exhausted as he was, he knew sleep wouldn't come. He dropped into the chair behind his desk and put his head down on his arms.

Clyde remembered the excitement he and his sister had shared when they traveled from Earth to Sufiro almost forty years before. He remembered when his father had assembled the prefabricated house on the empty plot of land the adults around him called New Des Moines. He remembered the hard work, but most of all, he remembered the joy of those times.

Now, Clyde sat alone. Major Ellwood had fallen at Camlan Pass. The image of her body lying on the ground covered in blood returned time and again, haunting the colonel. He thought of bodies missing legs, arms and heads. Despite all the training the Alliance Navy had given him, he could never have pictured sights so awful as the ones he had seen that morning.

After speaking with Manuel Raton and Edmund Swan, fatigue washed over Ellis. Between attacking the airships, the adrenaline rush triggered by the Cluster's appearance, and then deciding on an action to take, Ellis had been taxed to his limit. He excused himself to go to his cabin. A moment later, Adkins looked in on him. "Shall I have the cook send you some dinner, sir?"

Ellis nodded, then ate when dinner arrived. He contemplated a second cigar and thought better of it. He removed his coat and hung it up. Without bothering to activate the forcefield, he sat down on the bunk, pulled off his boots, then crawled between the snug sheets. For just a moment, he thought someone lay in the bed next to him. Something warm and soft seemed to press against his back. He thought, perhaps, the wall somehow radiated heat. He turned over and touched the wall. The metal was ice cold. As Ellis rolled back over and adjusted the blankets, he couldn't shake the sense that something accompanied him in the bunk.

The commander had been something of an introvert his entire life. He often found the company of whales preferable to that of humans. The presence seemed strangely comforting and he began to think his feelings were an afterglow from the day's adrenaline, wine, and cigar. Vivid images formed in his mind. The images were like strong memories of things the commander had never seen. He "remembered" New Granadans in dark mine shafts being threatened with disciplinarians, as though he had been there. He felt the agony of being kicked and hit while in the mud. The commander could imagine a hepler thrust in his back as soldiers led him to a carryhover, all the while worrying about his family's safety.

He shook his head hard enough to make himself woozy. Despite that, he couldn't stop the "memories." He imagined himself on a battlefield with mighty mountains on either side. A thunderous roar sounded just as a violent wind knocked him off his feet. Screams of horror and utter terror surrounded him. Vast, frightening emotions filled his soul.

Ellis looked up as someone cleared their throat. "Are you okay, sir?" B-Com Rubin wore a worried frown. "I heard you scream."

The commander blinked a few times. "Must have been a nightmare," he said.

"Aye aye, sir." Rubin stepped away. Ellis listened as his echoing footsteps receded down the corridor.

Clyde McClintlock screamed. He jumped back from the desk, then dusted himself off. He blinked at the computer displays' glow, then returned to his seat. The colonel stared open-mouthed. He could have sworn he had returned to the battlefield at Camlan Pass. Instead, he had fallen asleep at his desk.

Wild, conflicting thoughts ran through the colonel's mind. He missed the simple pastoral days of his youth. He remembered his father bemoaning the sinner, Firebrandt, yet he remembered no gross immorality in New Granada's people. The more he dug through the layers of memory, the more he found that he missed the simple life in New Granada. The older he grew, the more embroiled he became in Tejan politics, the more complicated life became. McClintlock remembered how much his father regretted leaving New Granada. Yet, when he tried to return to New Granada with a mission of making life better for them, they slaughtered his troops to repay him. Tears flowed as he thought how Major Ellwood would never again stand at his door, tapping her foot or clearing her throat, trying to get his attention.

Now the Cluster orbited Sufiro, putting everyone in grave danger and stripping him of any semblance of power that might have remained after his defeat. He reached up and turned on a small lamp on his desk. "Computer, call Anne McClintlock." It beeped to acknowledge his whispered command.

Once again, a warm pressure nestled against the commander's back. "That's why you came, wasn't it?" Ellis kept his voice low, but speaking helped him focus his thoughts. "The conflict's strong emotion drew you here." The presence seemed to leave and a sense of peace and contentment washed over the commander. He drifted into a pleasant sleep.

The image of McClintlock's sister appeared on the teleholo dais next to his desk. She wrung her hands and looked at her brother. "Hi Clyde. You look awful."

He hadn't bathed since the battle and guessed grime still covered his face. "Hi sis." He forced a grin, then scratched an itch and grimaced at his gritty and oily hair. "I just got scuffed up a bit during the battle with the grenades."

"Don't use that word," she snapped. "We were both raised in New Granada. Those are our people as much as the Tejans are." She raised her finger at her younger brother. "How could you have gone over there and attacked them?"

"Tejan interests were at stake." He spoke the words, but for the first time, it seemed like nothing more than a justification.

"The only thing at stake was Rocky Hill's bank account!" She closed her eyes and took a deep breath.

"We're the ones who lost." His voice caught. "Now, we've got the Cluster to deal with." He tried to discern her location from the background. It didn't look like her normal teleholo room. "Are you safe?"

"I'm in a shelter Rocky Hill's marshals rigged up. I don't know if I'm safe or not." She narrowed her gaze. "Clyde, I want you to consider what happened in New Granada. I want you to think about our dad and how much he loved this planet."

"That's almost all I've done for the past several hours," he said. "I've been trying to rationalize what we did in New Granada. Right now, it doesn't seem right."

"It never seemed right to me."

Clyde put his head down on his arms again.

"Clyde."

He heard her, but didn't look up.

"Clyde, if the Cluster ever leaves, promise me one thing."

"What's that?"

"Make things right." He looked up in time to see her reach over and terminate the call. Clyde turned out the desk lamp and trudged back to his cot where he fell into a fitful slumber.

The next morning, he showered and dressed. He scanned the monitors as he grabbed a cup of coffee. The tactical displays still showed the Cluster, the Rd'dyggian ship, and the *Firebrandt* in orbit. A report flagged for his attention revealed they'd lost all communication with the Alliance and the Confederation.

He sipped coffee and enhanced the Cluster's image. Something seemed to "click" in the back of his mind. Somehow, he knew Rocky Hill would be there soon and he knew what he would do when he arrived.

As expected, Rocky Hill stormed into Clyde McClintlock's office.

"Well?" Hill planted his fists on his hips. "What are you planning to do?"

"Do?" McClintlock looked up from the display. "About what?"

"About the Cluster! About the New Granadans!" Hill dropped into a chair opposite McClintlock. "We need to get rid of the Cluster and once they're gone, the New Granadan situation will be even more critical. This encounter buys us the Confederation's sympathy. We can unify the planet, but we need to be ready to strike as soon as the Cluster is gone."

"You want to attack again?" McClintlock set his mug on the table with a thud, sloshing out some of the coffee. "They destroyed two airships. Most of the National Guard is dead." The colonel's voice hitched, but an eerie calm came over him. "The only way I could go forward at this time would be to conscript our own people."

Hill's used-hover salesman grin appeared. "Why not?"

McClintlock looked into Hill's eyes and he questioned their friendship. He stood. "Mr. Hill, the sole reason for pursuing this war is your own greed." McClintlock walked around the desk and leaned against it, facing Hill. "I had no problem with our initial invasion because I agreed that it would be the best way to quell the uprisings. Now I see the uprisings were justified. Unifying the planet is just an excuse to enslave New Granadans so we can have cheap labor."

Hill clenched his teeth. "This is not about me. Every Tejan has profited from New Granadan workers. Tejo would not have been built nor grown as it did without money. Sam Stone may have used migrant labor, but look where it's brought us. You wouldn't be in this office if not for the New Granadan workers."

"Yes." McClintlock held out his hands. "Look where it's brought us. Do the ends ever justify the means? My father was mayor of New Des Moines before moving here."

"He left, because he knew how much greater the Tejan dream could be."

McClintlock straightened and clasped his hands behind his back. "Mr. Hill, I'm placing you under arrest before you destroy both Tejo and New Granada."

Hill reached into his coat. McClintlock tensed. As the governor drew a hepler, the colonel leapt, knocking Hill from the chair. The hepler skittered across the metal floor. The governor gasped for breath. The colonel turned a somersault and made a grab for the fallen hepler. Flailing with his hands, Hill caught McClintlock by the ankle. The colonel tried to shake him loose. When that failed, he twisted and screamed as he turned his ankle in the governor's strong grip.

Hill regained his breath, crouched, and lunged for the hepler. He missed, but sent the pistol clattering further into the corner. McClintlock gritted his teeth, forcing himself to stand. He grabbed the governor's collar and yanked him to his feet.

"The madness ends now," growled McClintlock.

The governor tried to scramble out of the colonel's grip. "Let go!" Hill wrenched himself around and reared back to knee McClintlock. The colonel released his hold. Hill lost balance and fell to the ground. Again, he scrambled for the fallen pistol.

McClintlock drew his own pistol. "Stop!"

Hill grabbed the hepler and began to turn.

"Drop the pistol," ordered the colonel.

Hill's eyes blazed with fury.

The colonel aimed and fired. The pulsed beam sliced the governor's hand. Hill screamed as his hepler dropped to the floor. McClintlock stormed over to the governor and lifted the little man by the back of the collar and the seat of the pants.

"Computer," called McClintlock. "Open channels to medical and security."

"Communication channels open," reported the computer.

"This is Colonel McClintlock, medics to my office right away. Security, send an armed escort."

Moments later, medics swarmed into the colonel's office

with an anti-gravity stretcher and strapped Hill down. The security guards stormed in just as they finished. McClintlock ordered the guards to place the governor under arrest.

"What charge?" asked the senior security guard, dumbfounded.

"Treason," said McClintlock. "He's plotting Tejo's downfall."

Tears streamed down his childhood friend's face as the medics carried him to the base infirmary followed by the security contingent.

Alone again, the colonel sat at his desk, shocked to realize that he had just started a military coup. He realized he needed to finish the job.

McClintlock opened a channel to his security forces. He declared martial law and ordered them to take control of Tejo City's government building. He then looked up the Mao Corporation's records and contacted the local manager in Camp Jones, Caroline Chung.

When he called and explained what he'd done, her mouth opened and closed as she struggled to find words. "How dare you impose martial law at a time like this! What will happen with the Cluster?"

McClintlock considered that and shrugged. He sensed nothing but contentment from the Cluster. "I don't think it will pose a problem for much longer."

Chung's brow furrowed. "Really? How is this all going to affect Mao Corporation interests?"

"For the better, I dare say." McClintlock tapped his fingers on the metal desk. "It's time for the madness to end."

Chapter Nineteen

AN END TO HOSTILITIES

John Mark Ellis awoke early the next morning. He stared at his cabin's ceiling as he replayed the images and emotions which had swirled through his mind the night before. As he considered the images, he became more convinced the Cluster didn't want to harm him. He threw back the blankets and walked across the way for a brief shower of recycled water. After the shower, he washed his face in fresh, warm water and contemplated the beard again, which seemed to be growing in well. He wasn't convinced he liked it, but decided to let it grow a while longer.

He returned to his bunk, dressed, then walked back to the mess.

Adkins smiled at him. "Good morning, sir. You look well rested."

Ellis nodded. "I slept well, thanks." He grabbed a tray and the cook served him breakfast.

He sat down just as Rubin arrived. "Weiss has been monitoring communications. It seems as though word has been spreading that people need to get under cover. The Tejan marshals have been getting people into mines and shelters. In New Granada, things are less structured, but people are doing their best to find safe havens."

Ellis sipped his coffee. "That's good to hear."

Rubin narrowed his gaze. "Are you still planning to space walk to the Cluster today?"

Ellis nodded and took a bite of oatmeal.

"Mr. Weiss and I have discussed it and we volunteer to go in your place."

Ellis met Rubin's gaze and shook his head. "I appreciate

your sentiment, but I won't risk anyone but myself."

Rubin leaned forward and kept his voice low. "With all due respect, I checked your record. I've logged more hours with a thruster pack than you have. Weiss is an experienced communications specialist."

Ellis sighed and lowered his spoon. "Francis, this isn't about skills or about attempting to make contact. It's about one person appearing to the Cluster as naked and harmless as possible. It may zap me. It may do nothing. Maybe it will talk. If it will, I want Weiss here in the ship to record it. I won't risk anyone else getting hurt."

"It's Frank, sir."

"I do try to be frank with my officers." Ellis narrowed his gaze.

"No, I mean if you're going to address me by my first name, please call me Frank."

The commander snorted a laugh. "Oh. Sorry." He sat back and folded his arms. "My orders stand, though."

Rubin folded his arms. "I won't try to be insubordinate and push that, but I wanted to let you know we're ready to help."

"You can help by being ready to get me if something unexpected happens." Ellis took another sip of coffee.

Rubin nodded, somewhat mollified. The commander finished breakfast, then accompanied Rubin and Adkins to the command deck. Weiss already occupied his station. The Cluster dominated the holo display. Again, peaceful, calm emotions settled around Ellis like a warm blanket. He had an overwhelming urge to stay in the seat and not attempt the space walk.

"Contact Manuel Raton," ordered the commander.

Weiss acknowledged. As soon as Nuevo Santa Fe's sheriff replaced the Cluster's image in the holo viewer, the sense of peace and contentment vanished.

Ellis leaned forward. "So, are people finding shelter?"

Raton lifted a handcomp. "I've heard from the mayors of all the major cities in New Granada. They've gotten the word out. We can't guarantee everyone has listened, but everyone's been warned and people are getting to the best shelters they can."

Edmund Swan joined Manuel. "Tell me again, Commander, why you think going over to the Cluster is the next best thing to try."

Ellis took a deep breath, then sat back. "So far, people have tried scanning the Cluster, running from the Cluster, and shooting at the Cluster. People have held still and blacked out communications. All of those things have resulted in destroyed ships. It's like watching Ahab pursue Moby-Dick with an attitude of fear and anger. I think sitting here and waiting reinforces those emotions. Going there may not be better, but I don't know what else to try. I hope it'll show the Cluster that small, intelligent organisms inhabit the planet and the ships and we're willing to face it as an equal. Maybe it'll convince the Cluster it won't need to destroy a ship or decimate the planet to learn that."

Swan gritted his teeth. "I don't like it, but I agree. I don't see a better option."

"Then you agree that I should try this plan?" Ellis folded his arms.

Swan held up a finger. "I can't stop you, Commander. All I ask is that you call your mother and grandfather. Discuss this with them. If they agree, then by all means see what happens."

Raton looked from Swan to Ellis. "I agree. You should speak with your family."

Ellis nodded, then turned to Weiss. "You heard the men, please contact Ellison Firebrandt at his homestead."

When Weiss terminated the call, the Cluster's image returned.

"Please keep the display on tactical while you connect the call," ordered the commander.

Weiss complied and a chart of the Cluster's position relative to the *Firebrandt* and Arepno's ship appeared. Despite that, Ellis still sensed something soothing his emotions, trying to make him feel content. As he waited for Weiss to establish contact, he noticed the emotional levels wavered. One moment, he became so content his eyes fluttered closed. The next moment, the contentment vanished to the background and he grew edgy. If he had to characterize the sensation, he thought it reminded him of someone tuning an old-fashioned dial.

"Contact established." The communicator's words broke through the commander's thoughts.

Ellis looked up to see his mother and grandfather facing him from the holo viewer. He detailed his plans to space walk to the Cluster and why he thought it was the next best thing to try. "The problem is, I'm beginning to have second thoughts."

"Because of us?" Fire lifted her eyebrows. "Mark, if you're worried about us, don't be. As you've said, if the Cluster is going to attack the planet, I don't think your actions will change that."

Ellis grabbed the sides of his head. "No, it's more like feelings I've been receiving."

Firebrandt's thick eyebrows came together. "Feelings?"

"It's as though my emotions have turned against the whole idea of going to the Cluster." Ellis rubbed his hands together. "Every time I look at the Cluster on the ship's holo, I feel as though I'm being manipulated. Even now as I'm sitting here … I know this may sound crazy, but I think they've been trying to contact me through my emotions."

Ellis looked down at his hands, then back up to his grandfather and mother. "Last night, I had an experience. I'm not sure whether to call it a dream or a vision or what." The commander focused his thoughts, then told his mother and grandfather about the terrifying images he had received the previous night. "It's as though they tried to tell me the reason why they came here. It's almost like they communicate through emotions."

"Combined with some form of visual imagery." Firebrandt's brow furrowed.

"Are you sure they were trying to communicate with you?" asked Fire. "From what you describe, is it possible you intercepted some kind of emotional signals to their home base? Maybe their language does involve some kind of emotional modulation. Maybe you're just sensitive to that."

The commander frowned. "I suppose…" He considered it for a moment, then smacked his knee. "No, it can't be happenstance. The presence, the warmth, it just felt too personal. Maybe I am sensitive to their way of communication, but I think this 'signal' was directed to me—or at least the people here."

"All right," said Firebrandt. "Do what you must, but I want you to let us know when you're back."

"Yes, sir." Ellis forced a brave smile. He then turned to Rubin. "All right, let's get this over with."

"Airlock crew has been notified," said the B-Com. "Your suit is standing by. Mine's also ready."

Ellis stood. "I thought I made it clear I would do this alone."

Rubin shrugged. "You were also clear that you wanted me ready to get you if something went wrong."

The commander strode back to the airlock with Rubin on his heels. Two petty officers stood beside a space suit. They helped Ellis remove his jacket and boots, then helped him put on the space suit over the simple jumpsuit all human military personnel wore. The simple garments made getting in and out of environment suits much easier than the old days when one had to strip down to underwear or less. The senior petty officer attached the commander's helmet to the suit while the junior petty officer attached his gauntlets. Rubin hefted the thruster pack from the rack and placed it over the commander's shoulders. Ellis belted it in place. They ran through the suit's checklist.

Ellis nodded to the petty officers. They opened the airlock's inner door. The commander entered. As it closed, he noticed Rubin began to don his own space suit. The gauge on the wall indicated the air was being evacuated from the lock. Once the dial reached zero, the outer door cycled. Ellis stepped out into the nothingness beyond the ship. Free of the ship's graviton generators, he had to take several deep breaths as he reminded himself he wasn't falling toward the planet below.

He oriented himself and faced the Cluster. For just a moment, the sense of comfort returned. Then, like someone flipped a switch, fear replaced the comfort. Ellis wanted to hit the thrusters and get as far away as possible. Did the Cluster do that or were those his own emotions? He swallowed and steeled his nerves. He reminded himself to be open to the Cluster, like he was open to his friend, Richard.

He tapped the thrusters and shot toward the Cluster.

Which wasn't there anymore.

"Commander! Reverse thrust." Weiss's voice came through the helmet intercom. "The Cluster has just jumped."

Ellis forced himself to comply. He reversed thrusters and held position, just a little ahead of *Firebrandt's* bow. Was that where the sense of fear came from just before he moved forward? Had it tried to warn him off so he wouldn't be caught in the jump's EQ wake.

"Commander, are you okay?" Weiss's voice rose in timbre.

"I'm fine, Mr. Weiss." He fired thrusters, turning around. "I'm returning to the ship."

He reached the airlock and pulled himself in. He closed the outer door, then waited for the airlock to cycle. Through the window, he noticed Rubin already removing his suit. Ellis activated the suit radio. "Mr. Weiss, please check whether or not interstellar communications have been restored."

"I have contact with Titan, sir," reported the communicator.

"Inform them of the past two days' events. Tell them I'll file a full report once we've wrapped up the erdonium situation."

Weiss acknowledged.

The ship's inner door opened and Ellis stepped through as Rubin donned his jacket. Ellis removed his helmet.

"How are you doing, sir?" Rubin took the commander's helmet and set it on the rack.

"I feel like a rat who's been run through a maze." He unbuckled the thruster pack. "What do rats in mazes think of their human captors? How do they perceive the maze?"

Rubin lifted off the commander's thruster pack. "Why would anyone put rats in mazes?"

Ellis smiled. "You must not have taken the history of science course at the academy. Experimental psychologists used to test theories on laboratory animals, such as rats. A common cognitive test was to run a rat through a maze. It helped to gauge learning behaviors."

"Animal cruelty laws would prevent that now."

"I'm not sure if the act of running through a maze is the cruel part." The petty officers helped the commander take off the environment suit. "Euthanizing the rats at the experiment's conclusion could be considered cruel. That's often what happened to rats who outlived their usefulness." Ellis sat down and put on his boots.

"So, does this mean we passed whatever test the Cluster

had for us?" Rubin handed Ellis his uniform coat.

The commander stood, took the coat, and strode forward to the bridge. "I don't know if we passed or not. I think I may have ignored a warning."

"Maybe that was part of the test."

Rubin's words caused a chill to shoot down the commander's spine. Once they reached the bridge, Commander Ellis dropped into the command chair and gazed at the holo of empty space. With the Cluster gone, an emptiness opened in his gut. It took him a moment to identify the feeling as loneliness. He shook his head and tried to bring his thoughts back to the erdonium problem.

Weiss sat back as though stunned. He turned to face Ellis. "New developments in Tejo, sir. You'll never believe it."

Ellis leaned forward. "Not much will surprise me after today. Try me."

"Clyde McClintlock has taken over the government. He's declared martial law in Tejo." Weiss shook his head.

"You're right." The commander's eyes widened. "I don't believe it." Ellis opened his mouth to speak again, but Weiss cut him off.

"Sir, Colonel McClintlock is signaling. He wants to meet with you in his office at the Mount Matthews Military Compound."

Ellis turned to Rubin. "Please have the landing crew prepare the launch."

"You're not considering going down into the heart of a military coup, are you?" Rubin rubbed his hands together.

Ellis pointed to Weiss. "Tell McClintlock I'll be there." He stood and straightened his jacket, then turned to face Rubin. "Are you coming? If we're going down into a coup's heart, I should have an armed escort."

Rubin leapt to his feet and followed the commander back to the launch bay. As they stepped into the bay, Rubin retrieved a hepler from the weapon's rack and handed one to his commander. Ellis nodded approval. They entered the launch and the airlock hissed shut. Ellis settled into the pilot's chair and Rubin sat next to him. They ran through the preflight checklist, then Ellis detached the launch.

Rubin turned to face the commander. "Are you sure about this? We're going down to meet with a man who just betrayed his own government. We could find ourselves prisoners of that government."

"I know, but I have a feeling I'm not the only rat who's been running mazes."

Rubin narrowed his gaze. "You think the Cluster is responsible for this?"

"If not directly, then I think it may have scared McClintlock into taking action." Ellis shrugged. "I just hope it's action that will benefit us."

As they approached the surface, Ellis noticed a Rd'dyggian launch on the ground. He set the launch down next to Arepno's craft.

When Ellis and Rubin stepped from the launch, two armed guards in gray uniforms with faces like stone met them. Rubin's shoulders slumped as though his worst fears were coming to pass. The guards led them into an elevator, then through labyrinthine tunnels to the colonel's office.

Colonel McClintlock and Captain Arepno sat facing each other.

The colonel stood. "I'm glad you could come." Dark circles outlined McClintlock's bloodshot eyes.

"The Gaean Alliance won't appreciate a National Guard colonel declaring himself leader of one of their member continents." Ellis sat opposite McClintlock.

The colonel dismissed the armed guards with a wave, then sighed. "No, they won't. Believe me, I never wanted to be Tejo's governor. It's a situation I hope to remedy in the near future."

Arepno's purple mustache wriggled. "You did not call us here to complain of your problems as a leader."

McClintlock shook his head. "No, I called you here because I wanted to formally acknowledge my country's defeat. We tried to invade New Granada for reasons I now see to have been unsound."

Ellis snorted. "We could have saved a lot of trouble if you'd realized that sooner."

"I'm sure you can appreciate my position. I was a military

officer following orders." McClintlock tapped his fingers on the desk.

"I do not understand," said Arepno. "It goes against Rd'dyggian military philosophy to follow orders without question."

McClintlock nodded. "Perhaps, I should have had a course in Rd'dyggian military philosophy." He looked from Arepno to Ellis to Rubin. "Gentlemen, I acknowledge defeat and I am prepared to make any military reparations required."

Arepno slammed his fist on McClintlock's desktop. "End slavery!" The translator unit's words were just audible over Arepno's shout in his own language.

McClintlock jumped back. "I plan to." His voice trembled.

Ellis sat forward. "If you end slavery, what will you do to get erdonium production back on track?"

The colonel stood up and moved over to the wooden liquor cabinet. He retrieved a bottle and offered it to those gathered. Arepno complained that alcohol was toxic to Rd'dyggians, but wanted a drink. Ellis declined. McClintlock ordered a glass of water brought in for Arepno. The colonel poured himself a glass of scotch, downed it and poured another as a gray-uniformed soldier brought water for Arepno. The colonel returned to his seat.

Ellis tapped the desk. "Erdonium production."

"Yes," sighed McClintlock. "At this moment, the Mao Corporation is negotiating a buy-out of all erdonium mines in Tejo."

"Is it really so simple? You'll still have a worker shortage once the New Granadans go home."

Arepno sipped the water and eyed Ellis. "Commander, the slavery must end."

"I know, but the erdonium must move so the Confederation can continue its hunt for the Cluster. We've learned new things from our encounter. It may help us in the future."

Both McClintlock and Arepno stared at Ellis. He knew they wanted more information, but this wasn't the time.

When Ellis refused to say more, McClintlock continued. "Caroline Chung will take advantage of the Confederation's offer to provide more funding for workers. Also, the martial law remains in effect until the erdonium production resumes." The colonel shrank from Arepno's gaze. "The solution will include an end to the slavery."

Ellis nodded, satisfied. "Then I believe I'll have a drink, Colonel." The colonel poured a scotch for the commander. Three glasses came together saluting the new peace.

☠

Ellison Firebrandt opened the door for his grandson and invited him inside. Ellis's first officer, Mr. Rubin followed. The former privateer captain had difficulty reading the emotions that played across his grandson's face. They sat down at the long table in the main room. Fire and Roberts joined them a moment later. Ellis filled them in on the events of the last two days.

"The worker deficit will slow production, but erdonium mining will resume." Ellis flashed a self-satisfied grin.

"I suppose that means you'll be on your way back to Titan?" Firebrandt looked from Ellis to his daughter.

"Soon," said Ellis. "As soon as I know the conscripted New Granadans are free to do what they want."

Fire reached out and took her son's hand. "What's next for you?"

"I want to talk to the admiralty about what happened here. Maybe I can convince them to assign the *Firebrandt* to a special mission. I'd like to try talking to the Cluster. I think there's some hope."

Firebrandt noted a longing in his grandson's words.

Fire met her son's gaze. "You almost sound like you lost a friend." She brushed long, black hair behind her shoulder. "Remember these are the bastards who took your father from us."

"I know." Ellis looked down at the table, deep in thought. After a moment, he looked up again. "Mom, please understand. I'm not convinced the Cluster is out to do us harm. I think they're studying us. As I said earlier, I think they may even be trying to communicate with us through our emotions. It's like all those years ago when you asked Richard what he wanted in exchange for an oral history of the whales from their perspective. You need to know how to listen in order to have a conversation."

Rubin cleared his throat. "You've been saying that all along, but I haven't felt anything and I've heard nothing from the rest of the crew. Is this just intuition, or do you have actual evidence that the Cluster is reaching out to us?" Rubin glanced around the table as though trying to ascertain whether everyone else understood something he'd missed.

Firebrandt winked at the young man. "Always remember, Mr. Rubin, a ship commander must be careful to whom he reveals what information." The captain turned his attention back to Ellis. "By the same token, a commander must learn to trust his first officer and pass along all he's come to understand."

Ellis nodded and reviewed all the incidents he experienced. Some repeated information he'd already revealed in earlier meetings. Then he relayed what happened during the space walk and the sudden emotional shift from comfort and warmth to fear and dread. "Maybe it's just me." Ellis shrugged.

"I wonder why you're the only one who picked up those feelings." Rubin snapped his fingers. "As we left the ship, you said you thought maybe the Cluster influenced McClintlock."

Ellis rubbed his beard as he considered Rubin's words. "I thought the timing seemed convenient, but he indicated the battle itself changed his mind. That makes as much sense as the Cluster influencing him."

Firebrandt stood and retrieved a pipe from the fireplace mantel. "But who are they, what do they want? What is the Cluster?"

Ellis shrugged. "I don't know. My best guess is that whoever pilots the Cluster has evolved far beyond humanity. To them, we're like a one-celled animal under the microscope."

"Or a rat in a maze, sir?" Rubin grinned.

Ellis nodded.

Roberts cleared his throat. "You think they communicated with you. If so, that would seem to imply they know you're intelligent."

Ellis's eyebrows came together and he looked at Fire. "You're the one who suggested I could have been eavesdropping on communications not meant for me. Or, perhaps they're using emotions as a way to communicate because they don't regard us as intelligent."

"Somehow, we have to convince them." Fire stood and walked behind her son, rubbing the tension from his shoulders. "If it is a misunderstanding, it's cost thousands of people their lives. Not to mention your father's life."

The commander's eyes glimmered with unshed tears. He cleared his throat.

"Communication with the Cluster doesn't sound trivial." Firebrandt shook his head.

Ellis leaned back in the chair as his mother returned to her seat. "I still feel the communication was deliberate. Now that we have a clue it's happening on an emotional level, we have to try again."

"I don't know about anyone else, but what I feel is hunger," complained Roberts.

Firebrandt nodded. The adrenaline rush that had been present for the past two days while the Cluster had been in orbit faded and everyone's energy levels waned.

Roberts cooked dinner and the five ate. The Cluster crisis dissolved almost as quickly as it arrived. Conversation moved to more routine matters.

Ellis looked at his mother. "When do you think you'll return to Earth?"

"I haven't decided, but I've been thinking about writing a history of Sufiro. I may stick around for a little while and conduct some interviews." She lifted a forkful of mashed tubers to her mouth.

Ellis and Rubin finished their meals. The commander stood and nodded to Rubin. They went out to the launch to return to the ship. Fire, Roberts, and Firebrandt followed them outside. The commander hugged his mother. The two officers stepped aboard the craft. The airlock doors closed with a hiss. With a thunderous roar, the launch's engines fired, propelling the craft back to its home in the stars.

☠

Manuel Raton punched the air when he and Edmund Swan heard the Cluster had left Sufiro's orbit. He was less pleased about returning to the grizzly work of burying the dead in a battlefield near his home. He sent word around Sufiro for help. Religious leaders came and consecrated the ground. Undertakers prepared the bodies and New Granada's mayors arranged for a solemn ceremony.

Two weeks after the battle, the first New Granadans came home. Some did agree to stay and work for the Mao Corporation in exchange for fair wages. Raton learned Nuevo Santa Fe's mayor planned a big celebration. There would be many drunks and surly people with hangovers the next day. After checking messages, the sheriff walked back into the living room and found Swan seated on the old battered sofa. "It'll be a busy day tomorrow, amigo," said Raton. "So, are you going to be a slacker, or can I deputize you?"

Swan grinned. "Well, I was a deputy sheriff before. I can be one again."

"Good!" Raton patted his friend on the shoulder. "I was hoping you'd get a real job. Now you can afford to get your own place."

Swan glared at Raton.

The sheriff shrugged. "It's been good to have the company, but without a crisis, we'll drive each other crazy." Raton turned his attention to Espedie and Carmen Raton's picture hanging on the opposite wall. His thoughts drifted off to the war. "I thought I put the Tejans in their place twenty years ago only to have them try to control the planet again. Do you think this new peace will last?"

"Time will tell." Swan shrugged. "Maybe it's time for you to unify New Granada like you'd planned to twenty years ago. Join the Confederation. People know who you are. They'll vote for you."

Raton snorted. "That's not a half bad idea. Besides, if New Des Moines served as the capital, it would give me an excuse to move away from this graveyard."

Swan released a bitter laugh. "At least the neighbors are quiet."

Raton frowned. "Sometimes, I think about the life my

parents left behind. Earth has been at peace for hundreds of years. But the people had no freedom. My dad came here because he craved freedom. Still, freedom devolved into war. I wonder, was coming here any better?"

"Is freedom the price of peace?" Swan sighed. "God, I hope not." The former marshal followed Raton's gaze to the picture. He knew about Espedie and Carmen raising their children on the farm. He had heard the story of how they met their end. Swan considered the violent deaths he had seen in Tucson as a deputy sheriff. "It may not be much consolation, but at least your parents died standing up for their values."

Raton looked away from the picture. "For one brief shining childhood, this planet was beautiful."

"This planet is still beautiful." Swan stood and walked to the window. "Ellison Firebrandt wants to keep it that way."

"Ellison Firebrandt won't be here forever."

"Are you so sure?" Swan leaned on the windowsill. "Even if he does die, and I'm not so certain he will, his dream will live on with us."

Ellison Firebrandt received a call from his grandson. "It looks like all the business here is wrapped up. I've been ordered back to Titan," said Ellis.

"I'm sorry to say your mother isn't here right now. She's up in New Des Moines conducting interviews for the book she's considering."

"I look forward to reading it." Ellis sighed. "I hope to be in touch soon. I'm glad I got to know you better."

Firebrandt smiled. "Likewise, and Godspeed."

Before the pirate captain stood, Arepno signaled. "Time for me to depart, old friend. I'll be glad to get back to the vines and trees of my homeland."

"I'm glad you shepherded us through this difficult time. Safe travels, old friend." The captain had grown tired of good-byes. He stood and strolled through the house, feeling old. He walked through the front door and looked out at the swift, flowing river and Succor's green fields. Roberts came up behind him.

"You look like you're feeling sorry for yourself." Roberts folded his arms.

"I wonder where all the time has gone. It seems only yesterday we raided ships for Earth, but we've been here almost forty years now. Do I even serve a purpose anymore?" Firebrandt pushed his hands deep into his pockets.

"Fire will be home soon. I'll make a picnic, like the ones we shared when we first landed." Roberts turned and went inside the house.

An hour later, Fire returned. Good to his word, Roberts prepared a picnic. They set out a blanket and enjoyed the warm, balmy evening. Insects buzzed along the river. A fledermouse cried out.

Fire took in the landscape. "While in New Des Moines, I heard the sale of the Stone mines to the Mao Corporation was finalized today. Clyde McClintlock announced elections for a new governor will be held next week. I think I'll stick around and see what happens. I think it would make a good ending for my book."

"I wish Suki could be here," Firebrandt sighed.

"She would have liked this night." Roberts reached out and took his friend's hand.

"It's been years since I've enjoyed a quiet night like this." Fire smiled.

"I'm happy to hear that." Firebrandt thought back to the early days, remembering the exile. "When I realized I couldn't escape Sufiro, I decided I had to make a go of taming this world. Maybe we've finally succeeded." He looked around at Roberts and Fire. He wondered what his mother would think if she'd seen what happened on this world. For the first time, Firebrandt wanted to thank her for what she had done.

Roberts sat back in the hover chair. "If taming this world had been easy, would you have survived this long?"

Firebrandt pondered that. He'd feared his reputation as a pirate interfered with building an ideal world, but it allowed him to bring Arepno back to help. He may have given his grandson some good advice based on his experience. He encouraged Swan to lead New Granada's defense. What was a pirate, but a person who didn't play by anyone's rules and sought a better life for himself and his crew? Maybe he was still a decent pirate after all. "Are you suggesting it's time for me to move on?"

Fire laughed. "If you died, this planet would fall apart. Mother's dream would die along with your victory."

"Then I'd better not die," said Firebrandt. "I'll be a pirate forever!"

Afterword

I wrote *The Pirates of Sufiro* in 1994 while employed at Kitt Peak National Observatory outside Tucson, Arizona. It sprang from my love of space opera and anime, along with the stories my granduncles and grandaunts told about homesteading in Texas and New Mexico. I envisioned the story of how a frontier planet would be settled and the conflicts that would arise as people moved there.

In early 1995, I recorded several of my coworkers and me reading the book. I edited the recording together with some music and sound effects and released it through my company Hadrosaur Productions as a series of cassette tapes that I sold at science fiction conventions in Arizona and New Mexico. That was the very first edition of the novel. Soon after the audio tapes were released it was picked up for print publication.

The book remained in print more-or-less continuously from 1996 until 2017. During that time, I recorded a second audio edition for the website Podiobooks.com which went live in 2006. In 2017, I reacquired the publishing rights. Twenty-two years is a lot of time to get feedback.

I've been listening to that feedback and I have grown as a writer. Since *Pirates* was initially released, I've published eleven other novels plus about eighty short stories. I knew I had not told Captain Firebrandt's story as effectively as I could have, so when I got the rights back, I endeavored to make it stronger and flesh out details better. My only guideline was that I could not change any plot point that would impact the sequels.

I hope you've enjoyed this visit to the planet Sufiro and this opportunity to get to know its residents. Please do take a moment to share a review at the retailer where you purchased the novel. I continue to listen and learn.

David Lee Summers
Las Cruces, New Mexico

317

About the Author

David Lee Summers lives in Southern New Mexico at the cusp of the western and final frontiers. He's written novels about space pirates, vampire mercenaries, mad scientists in the old west, and astronomer ghosts. He's edited thrilling anthologies of space adventure that imagine what worlds discovered by NASA's Kepler mission might be like. When he's not writing or editing, David explores the universe for real at Kitt Peak National Observatory. To learn more about David or his books visit his website at http://www.davidleesummers.com